Craig Marriner was born in New Zealand in 1974. He was raised and schooled in Rotorua. In the days since, he has mined gold in the Aussie outback, worked security at English soccer stadiums, wintered on an angry Ruapehu, MCed at an Amsterdam comedy club, haggled in the markets of Istanbul, and slept in more train stations than he cares to remember. His ambition is to hitchhike from Cape Town to Copenhagen, his favourite drink is a stiff bloody Mary, and he's known to be less than pleasant company when the All Blacks are losing. *Stonedogs* is his first novel.

stonedogs

craig marriner

VINTAGE

A VINTAGE BOOK
published by
Random House New Zealand
18 Poland Road, Glenfield, Auckland, New Zealand
www.randomhouse.co.nz

First published 2001, reprinted 2002

ISBN 1 86941 4764

Design: Elin Termannsen
Cover photograph, artwork and design: Esther Bunning
Printed in Australia by Griffin Press

To Denis and Mum: for shelving the 'get a real job' speech.

To Debbie: for planting the seed with story.

To Shaq', Monique and Caleb: love ya's to pieces.

To Mike and Helena Z, who I owe much more than they know.

To Shereen: for 'giving me peace'.

To Auntie Lona, who lives on in our hearts.

To Sab, best friend of thirteen years, all four legs of him.

To Nana (though she's to read no further!).

And to Granddad (though he'd of hated 'every bloody word of it').

Many thanks to Michael Gifkins and Harriet Allan.

They're at it again. Flexing muscle, that is. Hardly surprising really: the sun's been down for hours. Hardly disappointing either: it's what we've been waiting for.

Two of them: big; Maori; smooth. 'Doormen' they call themselves.

Though after his curt eviction from the doors of their fief — the shove in the back almost toppling the kid — I doubt *he's* of a mind for such euphemism. No, as he collects himself and turns back to face them, I'd have to guess he has other names in mind.

Bastards? Pricks? Tyrants? All of the above?

He's not saying it aloud, though . . . he's not *that* drunk. His face isn't saying it either, nothing but wronged innocence there, a desperate snatch at drowning pride.

But he'd do better to swallow it — swallow it dry — for he can still escape if he's quick enough; quiet enough. The window's shrinking rapidly, though. He's the first of the night, you see — the first to be marked — and the locals are looking restless.

The forecourt of Deuces, our fine city's premier ARC (adult recreation centre), is no stranger to these scenes. Neither are we. We know the rules.

7

It's safe enough out here, though. In the car park. Behind smeared glass. I've got a brother at my side, and though he's no fighter, the dude can drive like Senna himself. We may not get full audio, but the view from here is bitchin'. Ring-side seats. BYO refreshments: sweet Mary Jane and a box of Red Lions.

Yes, as sad as it sounds, this is hardly our first evening passed in such fashion. Of paramount importance its work may be, but even the Brotherhood needs diverting of a weekend.

In front of the club, the kid's still protesting, and Mick reads the score as I do. Spellbound: 'Unless he cuts his losses riiiiight about now, that guy's night is quickly gonna shift from piss-poor to shit-house.'

Oh, yes, we know the rules all right, my amigo and I.

Me, eyes stapled to Act One unfolding before us: 'How long do you give him?'

Mick muses on this a while. Finally: 'About a minute, I reckon. The apes won't do it themselves, though; no glory in a kill so small . . . and they can't be *that* bored yet. But one of their lackeys'll soon be up for it.'

Me: 'You're not wrong. And even if you are, some cunt in the queue'll take the points.' The 'doormen' and co may be the elite right now, but when the jungle juice flows, the Fiendish Beast lacks no minions. Not in these parts.

And that push in the back may as well have been a bull's eye.

'I'm picking two minutes, though.'

'. . .You're on. What are the stakes?'

'Joint rolling duties for a fortnight?'

'Done. Time starts . . . now.'

But I may've spoken too soon, as from the foyer of the club comes our first volunteer.

Fat; mean; native. Linked to the 'doormen' like the jackal to the lion.

His hooded eyes assess centre-stage quickly, learn that the titbit has stayed within reach — a mere slither or two — and then he relaxes, sups on the post-glow, trades banter with his betters.

But their stock of apt platitudes will expire very shortly.

Me, half drool, half cringe: 'What do you think his crime was, anyway?'

Mick, distracted: 'He either jostled a member of the ruling body and associates, spilled piss on one of them, managed to get served in the drinks queue ahead of them, or . . .'

But I beat him to it, announcing the crime that in these parts is capital: '. . . or he spoke with a bitch the said clique had its eye upon.'

HOW FUCKING DARE HE! BIND HIM TO THE YOKE! STAKE HIM IN THE SUN; WINDFALL FOR BUZZARDS AND MAGGOTS!

Outside, around the forecourt, the gallery waits eagerly. Breaking from their activities — queuing to get in, shooting the shit, burning Mary Jane — many eyes are on the hunter, and he resists temptation for no longer than I augured.

He swaggers toward the kid, and I can see his lips wiggling, the ritual accusations inflating him fully. Every tingling gaze locks on him — 'better than TV, ladies and gents' — and attention cloaks our hero in a sensual shroud.

It tugs at his lips, a gloating leer, dark with promise.

And finally, at this unveiling of his nemesis, our pissed entertainment grows aware of his status. Too late though. *Way* too late. As the stalk is completed, a futile denial, perhaps a plea, is seen to be mouthed.

Only 'stalk' it is hardly, for caution plays no part. And why should it? Why *should* our bloated carrion show prudence? Even if his prey were *not* white, semi-paralytic and half the hunter's size, respect of any nature need not be awarded.

Our protaganist is *connected*, you see.

And his quarry quite alone.

The kill is seasoned thuggery: a heavy left shoulder, three driving paces, and the drunk boy with a mum waiting up is on the back foot, fumbling for balance . . .

. . . window enough for a cudgel of a fist to pound jaw unopposed, probably unseen.

Like a hungry dyke, the patsy goes down, head bouncing on cold concrete . . .

. . . his conqueror looming above, wallowing in the moment, holy ire blunting his gaze as it wolfs down the homage on offer around him.

Me, thickly, hunched forward in my seat: 'Oh, man, I felt that from here.'

Mick, a delicious wince: 'I doubt that kid felt a fucking *thing*. He will tomorrow though.'

And the tomorrow after that. Perhaps a lifetime of tomorrows if he's eating through a straw for the next three months.

But the twist of guilt is weaker tonight — many thanks, Lion Breweries — and I know I'll be back again. Why fight it? I'm human, you see, a cog of the Juggernaut. And me and my race, with our thumbs and our wheels, need regular doses of the good Lady Drama.

'We watch, therefore we are.'

Yes, even as the scavenger's eyes drop once more to his kill, even as the fat, dirty prick clearly weighs the merits of 'lengthening sentence', even as the stakes are upped viciously and a real chill sweeps the audience — blows poison bubbles through my spleen — looking away is beyond me.

But in the temple of my mind a mantra is heard. I've no need to glance at my comrade; Mick's expression surely mirrors my own — hypnotised abhorrence, kittens before the mamba — and I know his inner chant is at least as loud as mine, of a strain very similar . . .

Don't do it, you fucking arsehole cunt. Don't do it, you fucking arsehole cunt. Don't do it . . .

Running beneath this, though, in a shadowed recess of my conscious — like a streak of corruption through damp wood — a part of me, thankfully a tiny part — a part I seldom have the courage to acknowledge, let alone confront — *wants to see it happen*.

Wants to watch a kid, barely old enough to shave, have his ribs made like Humpty's.

Though I know it would leave me emotionally mauled, a part of me wants to see our leading man's rendition of the Taihape Tap-dance.

Why?

Because I'm human. Like most, my soul offers anchorage to the Fiendish Beast.

But a few seconds later, the predator spares us, sneers a dismissal, withdraws to the door, to camaraderie, bumping shoulders with bourgeoisie.

Mick's the first of us to speak, sighing post-orgasmically: 'Thank fuck for that.' Then, checking his watch, pleased with himself: 'And I hope your fingers are in good shape, McPike: one minute and twenty-seven seconds makes you a raw loser.'

Soon, with the cast between acts, Mick takes a Zippo from the dashboard, conjures flame with a flourish and resurrects the roach he clasps, forgotten for minutes now. His thin lips pucker as he tokes, and in the car's dark interior the ember lights his long face like a jack-o-lantern, reflects from the lenses of his Lennonesque specs. His dainty fingers shy from the heat, deftly gripping the very end of the stained paper.

At last he breaks off, smoke held deep, where it'll stay for the mandatory twenty-count named in *Habitual Drug-Users Monthly*, that fine publication of which my associate and I would own a quarter share, were our world only fair.

Unconsciously, Mick rasps a hand across the bristles of his head. His red locks were consigned to history just days ago and Mick's struggling to adapt. He's copped a lot of shit for the move from us longhairs, but, though I've yet to concede as much, it don't look half bad. Mick's is a head well shaped for baldness, a state one can never be certain of until the plunge is taken. Many, like Mick, seem somehow cooler for a lack of hair. Others, even the fair of face — a claim Mick's *mother* wouldn't make of him — come away from a shears job looking like something Sigourney Weaver would consign to hard vacuum.

In addition, to those who don't know him, the look certainly adds to Mick's staunch points — and when you're as runty as he is, this is nothing to shake a stick at.

His roach goes out , too small to smoulder, but Mick is clearly unwilling to surrender yet.

Oh, yeah, as I've always maintained: to spot life's stonedogs just observe how far down someone tokes their doobies; the persistence with which he/she extracts optimum THC levels.

Swigging on hollow aluminium, I learn that my beer can's barren. Only cracked it as Jabba the Gutt waddled into contention for the feather-weight title. At least I think I did . . .

Shrugging it off. Crushing the can, as is my way. Pitching it in the back with the others. The lid from another is hastily lifted, a third of its contents successfully seen to.

Mick, hoarse from his toking, eyeing the roach like a bird might a worm: 'Seen that safety-pin, man? I'm pretty keen to pinball this bastard: it's the last of it.' Then, courageously, he lights the Zippo and hoists it — lantern-like — and begins a forage of the debris near his feet, the flotsam piled across *The 'Dan*'s floor in drifts.

Not an enviable task considering *The 'Dan* was last cleaned around the time Cobain took up mural art.

I choose to ignore Mick's question; ease back and watch him search for a while, amusing my eyes, impressed as always by his methodicalness.

Because in this situation — and I'm speaking from experience — your average druggie rummages willy nilly through the trash for a minute, declares the task hopeless, then puts his/her faculties toward filling the void with a surrogate implement. Mick, however, is not your average druggie.

Were the safety-pin located in the proverbial haystack, Mick would find it. It might take him years, but he'd find it. Trust me on this.

After calculating the minimum distance he need walk in order to build a stack independent of the original, Mick'd begin a minute inspection of the hay, depositing that declared 'free of pins' upon his new pile. It's just the way he is: Mr Methodical, Mr Logic — when I'm in a good mood.

A bad mood: Mr Pedantic.

Either way, his proclivities leave him an asset highly cherished by the Brotherhood . . .

. . . the sacred order to which we swear blood oath.

Mick, bent to the floor: 'For fuck's sake, there's enough organic matter down here to keep the Coromandel in compost for the next coupla planting seasons.'

But he hunts on grimly, a serf to instinct, covering the floor by search pattern.

Though both of us are greatly responsible for her present state of adulteration, neither Mick nor I can claim sole ownership of the black-primered behemoth in which we currently linger: the Sherman tank replica known throughout Vegas as *The 'Dan*. Tricky Dicky was 'retiring' around the time *The 'Dan* was birthed in the Big Red Land, and she's since seen registry beneath a plethora of shepherds. Her upkeep at the moment, however, is maintained by the coffers of the Brotherhood, the car featuring prominently on our shadowy list of assets.

We kind of inherited *The 'Dan* from an older mate of ours who got banged up a year or so ago. In happier times Luke used to do a half-decent 'Good Ol' Boy', hence the title ('Well, if Ah were you, bouy, Ah'd be fixin' to *buyrn* that Jap'nese piece'a sheit an' bah mah'self a *Hol*-dan!').

We all agreed to pass a few hundred bucks on to Luke's missus and baby as soon as we could.

It remains one of those 'do it next month' things.

Mick, shuddering, diligent eyes brave inches from the contaminant: 'This car is some fucked-up loathsome shit, dude. We really should clean up one of these days.'

Me, apathetic: 'Yeah. Tomorrow.' I've a vague recollection of glimpsing the pin near my feet — somewhere between an empty oil pack and one of Lefty's used rubbers — but I choose not to share this: stoning's the last diversion on my mind right now and I fear the floor too greatly to risk being roped into assistance.

Ordinarily, though, on a drink-free night, I'd bend for a K Road she-male before I'd watch Mick blow the last of the gunja solo. But for me Fris and Sats are given to the worship of Mr

Brownstone. You see — as with most punters — weed for me is an introspective lodger, best hosted in confined company.

Certainly not when hopeful of tracking down a warm, wet cavity in which to park Mr Jonathan Thomas.

Because, let's face it, for all but a gifted elite, chatting up chicks when stoned is like trying to eat when not hungry.

Not that the chances of laying paws on a piece of snatch from the passenger seat of *The 'Dan* could sincerely be described as strong.

Weak? Yes.

Effectively non-existent? Bingo.

Strong? *Nein. Non. Nyet.*

So if pussy patrol be your objective, one might ask, *why do you languish out here, in the carpark — boogie clothes awasted — while the club's interior surely drips with tight, succulent growler?*

The answer is simple: *Fear yet grips me.*

I have my moments with the birds, make no mistake. Six feet of height — albeit a narrow six, vegetarianism not being conducive to robust muscle growth — a head of longish brown hair and eyes once described as 'jade-chunks in ivory' (so what if the bloke bit pillows?) at times compensate for a face implacably gripped by mediocrity. At least it is now, once again, twenty-hood having recently extracted it from Acneville, Hades.

However, I must confess to an affliction bestowed upon me by either upbringing or genetics (I'm yet to pass verdict on which; let it be said that when I do, sentencing shall hold no clemency).

Shyness.

Yes, that instinct toward philandering, present in me no less than in any male of the red-blooded persuasion — my hankering to number among the monogamously challenged — has been given an enormous hurdle; some would say shackle.

Timidity; modesty; all the caddishness of Bashful Dwarf.

As such my dormant womanising instincts — my fragile sense of rejection — require the fuel of at least three more

14

rapidly downed brewskis before a pulse of any cogency can begin to throb.

A sarcastic jeer from the cheap seats: *And the bar of this club enforces a policy of teetotalism?*

Oh, no, reply I. *They sell piss, all right. A wide diversity, and at thrice the price of the stuff I currently drop.*

At last Mick locates the warped and blackened safety pin. Muttering: 'Eureka.'

Settling back, he takes his roach, impales it on the pin and puts flame to the thing. It catches alight; is allowed to burn, in time extinguished with a measured puff and a veteran's timing. Mick then waves the smoking pin beneath his proboscis, welcoming fumes through an ample nostril.

Burn, baby, burn.

As I sip, a disturbance ripples the congregation near the club's door. A passage hastily develops and, within seconds, another punter strides into the night.

Though this one decamps in a fashion distinctly more dignified than the last.

Lean and tall — inches more than myself, all of them in full use — black hair to his arse almost, the newcomer's leather jacket hangs from him as I imagine one does from the Pres of the Hell's Angels California chapter. Some who try for this look, attire themselves so — leather, jeans, cowboy boots — do little but expose themselves to mockery or worse.

This dude just looks cool.

And mean.

No doubt his carriage has much to do with both: he holds himself as though god were running low on spines when his turn rolled round; handed him a broad sword instead.

On top of this the guy's good looking. So much so that if it weren't for the dark goatee he sports, one might almost have had to label him Pretty Boy.

The fashion with which he exits, with which the gallery still to regard him, leaves it apparent that, inside the club, he has recently been involved in some breed of incident. But unlike the previous lead in this limelight, this big dude might as well be alone for all he lets it affect his expression.

Style to burn.

Breaking from his indulgence, Mick looks up, absorbing the sudden shift in centre-stage status quo. Passing hoarse judgement: 'Uh-oh.'

The newcomer scouts about for a second and locates the fall-guy lying in the courtyard, only now beginning to stir. He moves in for a closer inspection. Stiffens.

I hear what he says from here, disgust in words like scum. 'You absolute *fucking* wankers.'

He turns back, faces the party nearest the door: Jabba with peers and superiors all eyes, perhaps five of them in all.

Without thought I initiate a play. Thought — or at least reasoning — is outlawed for the moment, bravery being a liability I possess but a pittance of. Mind you, even *I* own more of it than wee Mick, Mr Analytical — he stays put as I throw open my door, leap from the womb to bleak asphalt, beer can clutched like a standard.

And, as though a platoon of *Spetsnaz* stand at his back, AKs locked and loaded, the leather-wearer confronts those present of the ruling clique, narrowing the distance by five assured paces, aggrieved hands bunching.

Jarringly casual in the sudden silence: 'Who did it?'

No reply.

Tick followed tock, followed tick . . .

'Simple question, fellas. Which one of ya's fucked the kid over?'

With as much alacrity as propriety permits, I power-walk toward the scene. Even as all other spectators are at pains to remain just that, I enter from stage right, strutting through my dread, swigging at my can like a man on a mission who just doesn't give a fuck.

And at this point a strange occurrence takes place. Though they hold the high ground, though numbers, colour and weight are stacked firmly in their corner, though they surely stand to lose great face in the eyes of the gallery — and many more beside, once the rumour-mill starts turning — the governing body, with its virtual impunity, its proclivity for draconian sentencing, suddenly appears at a loss.

It seems they've recognised what it is before them: this prehistoric force of boundless unpredictability. They've realised that a habitual response to *this* challenge could well breach the seals of a box once owned by a lady named Pandora.

Prudence must now play a role in their rejoinder, for the insurrectionist is not alone, as cursory appearance implied.

In his head, they can see, insanity rides shotgun.

Demands met only by silence, with half-hearted sneers, Justice takes its inquisition further. Addressing the gallery, voice carrying effortlessly: 'Heaps of you's musta seen it. One of ya's show some nuts and tell me who the arsehole is. C'mon, don't be pansies *all* ya fucking lives.'

And as is often the case with bruised herds — with flocks shepherded harshly — one shedded fleece has others quickly learning that bleating's not for them after all.

Some stocky character in cargo-pants, piping up to the surprise of most: 'It was him: the fat one with the red turtle-neck.'

As if he's been fingered to the might and paranoia of the NKVD, Jabba glares a quick promise at the second mutineer . . .

. . . as smiling blue eyes harpoon him. 'Well, aren't *you* just the baddest fucking hardman in the whole of Maoridom!'

I'm almost there. Might even make it with time for my play. Things will precipitate rapidly from here, though. I know the rules.

Jabba's back goes up in a show of strength, yet he can't resist a sidelong glance, assessing the mood of his autocratic associates.

The rebellion builds mordant momentum. 'What a *tough* cunt you must be, bro. Not only is that joker bleeding on the ground over there *half* your weight, but he's been up at the bar

17

slamming straight shots of Beam all fucking night — that's why he spewed on that bloke's shoes like he did. But you still found the balls to *waste* him, eh? *Man*, I'm so im*pressed* with you I'd like to take the time right now to invite you back to my place: we'll blow a few joints, toss back some of the old man's cognac, and when you're good and ready you can stroll upstairs and *fuck* my little sister!'

I clap the crazy bastard on the shoulder, seemingly unaware of the looks groping me as all and sundry rework the equation. A counterfeit gleam lights my eyes, but I will myself to project the notion that it has *nothing* to do with the uprising, that such trivialities are way beneath me. '*Here* you are, Barry, ya prick!' My voice is an eager babble, and by his face I see that Barry is snared by it; he seems to shelve the chaos he's surely seeking. 'You've gotta come *quick*, man!'

Though it's something in which I take no pride — well, not often anyway — a teenagehood on the edge of the rails has equipped me with a certain 'feel for falsehood' when pressured. And sometimes when not. Fully aware of this, when springing to my comrade's rescue I didn't bother premeditating anything, confident my 'instinct for disinformation' would step into the breach admirably, as it so often seems to.

Without prompt, at 8000 R.andell P.atrick M.cMurphys, it goes on line. To Barry, as if we're alone: 'Sonya Kennedy's down at McDicks. Me and Mick've been chatting her up for about an hour.'

The said person happens to be a luscious female of the hot, blonde and amply chested variety. Indeed, it is often argued that Sonya has played the lead in more masturbation fantasies than any other girl from our town and generation.

Like myself and multitudes, Barry has the horn for her big time. Only his horn is bigger on the grounds that, given the right circumstances, he's of the type to actually stand a chance of shafting the dirty slut.

The masque continues. 'She's fucking *trashed* too, man. Been drinking vodka all night. She's *well* up for it and all she can ask us is where the fuck *you* are, ya jammy prick! She spilled her guts, reckons she's had damp undies for you for years. You gotta come, bro, and *fast*: Jason Phelps and them are on their way to pick her up.'

The big tweaked puppet leaves the blocks like Ben fucking Johnson, practically hurdling the catalyst of the episode without so much as a glance, beating me to *The 'Dan* by a good two metres, where Mick, having fired her up earlier — as any good pilot should — spirits the Brotherhood clean away.

One rescue officially consummated, thank you very much.

And make no mistake, a deliverance it was. Barry's a tough prick; he's got balls the size of watermelons, too. He may even be as crazy as those bouncers suspected (particularly when pissed). But when all was told, the bastards would've been left no choice but to bite the bullet and jump him en masse.

Barry may be a scrapper; Jake the Muss he assuredly is not.

{ ARCHIVES: The Flawed Cog

— *Gator McPike? Hi, how are you? If you'd like to come through? My name's Raquel Boucher. Nice to meet you.*

— *Wahay! You've certainly got the Dead Fish handshake down pat there, Raq. That's an attempt to put me at ease, yeah? A subliminal prompt toward intestinal spillage?*

— *Ha ha. That's a good one. If you'd like to close the door and take a seat? As you may be aware, I'm the school's new Guidance Counsellor.*

— *Bravery or just plain masochism?*

— *Ha ha. That's a good one. No, nothing of the kind, I'm afraid. OK. I'm curious: how did you come to be called Gator?*

— *Long story.*

— *. . . Which you've no wish to share. Fine. No problem. OK, then . . . I wonder if you've any idea why you're here, Gator?*

— *Because the Law of Natural Selection is yet to fault my design.*

— *Hmmm. No, I meant in a more immediate sense.*

— Because progressive society programmes its clones in cloistered environments?

— . . . No, I'm really trying to find out if you've any guess as to why you've been referred for counselling. And, forgive my frankness, but maybe we can do it without the sarcasm?

— Whatever you fancy, Raq. Sarcasm, after all, is the cheapest brand of wit. Am I right?

— Possibly.

— That's good enough for me. OK, I've a fair idea why this 'union of minds' thing we've got going here came to pass, but, to be frank, I'm a little fucked off about being catalogued behind my back as one 'in need of help'. For that reason I'm gonna make you spell it out. Why am I here, Raq?

— Perhaps we can do it without the profanity also?

— Like my Grandad was wont to say, Raq, 'Swearing is deplorable . . . unless done well.' And, thanks in part to the great man's tutelage, I happen to be one of the art's more accomplished practitioners.

— Well, your Seventh Form dean, Mr McKillop, thought a chat between the two of us might prove . . . conducive to the standard of education you're presently receiving.

— Euphemisms aside . . . ?

— OK. In the past year and a half, since School Certificate, you've reportedly become a markedly different student. Back then you were being touted for an A Bursary. Since, your attendance has slipped quite drastically, as have your grades. Several of your teachers are reporting a . . . belligerent shift in attitude. You've been seen in the company of expelled students. You're a well-known smoker around school; indeed, there are rumours of your involvement in cannabis . . . and worse. Your personal grooming has taken a shift for the worse: haircuts seem to be a thing of the past for you, shaving a monthly chore. Your contributions to school sport and culture have all but ceased. Your name has become a daily feature on the detention lists, and, most worryingly of all, you've been involved in several incidents of violence about the school yard.

— And to top it all off, my dietary intake seldom features all five food groups?

— *Will you talk to me, Gator?*

— *. . . I wouldn't know where to begin.*

— *Let's start with what your goals are.*

— *Hahaha. You don't even* wanna *know.*

— *Let's start with what you're goals were, then. Teachers around campus tell me that until Sixth Form you were an aspiring and industrious young man. In those days where did you see yourself in, say, ten years' time?*

— *Ha. I wanted to be a doctor.*

— *And you now find that contemptible?*

— *Despicable.*

— *Why?*

— *Because the single most tangible factor in the Earth's broadening destruction — this defecation of our own nest — is the burgeoning of human populations. This given, what kind of a twisted, blind, gormless motherfucker gives his entire existence to the rescue and preservation of human-bloody-kind?*

— *. . . Do you like animals?*

— *Well, I boycott utterly the practice of rearing them for slaughter. Does this qualify as like?*

— *You tell me. Does it?*

— *Emphatically.*

— *In view of this, then, if you've an interest in healing, have you perhaps contemplated a career in veterinary medicine?*

— *Problem here, Raq, is that for every animal lover in the world there are a thousand arseholes out there happy to, in the name of a buck or three, subject the 'lower' creatures to all manner of degradation and atrocity. A vet no doubt feels this carry-on rammed down his throat day in and day out. On top of this, university attendance raises moral issues for me. Today, though, I shan't bother with either of these arguments as there's a more pragmatic reason why I've no interest in studying. Namely, the prospect of fettering myself in chains made of tens of thousands of dollars excluding compound interest. I'm the type who stresses over owing a mate a twenty-buck bet on the footy, Raq. Do you know what I'm saying?*

— *You're saying you'd find tertiary study prohibitive thanks to the student loans scheme?*

— *Someone fetch this woman a fifty-dollar meat-pack.*

— *Where there's a will there's a way, though, surely. You could work for a few years and then study.*

— *And where would you have me working without experience or tertiary comfort-ticket, Raq? Shall I become a chattel of progressive society; of the careering Juggernaut? A worker bee stunting itself at tasks that disgust me? Or shall I take occupation and do what we of the West are encouraged to from birth: 'Aim for the Top', 'Surpass the Mediocre', phrases effectively meaning: shamelessly flatter your superiors — people one would seldom bother speaking to were it otherwise — kiss arse until your lips bleed and render one's nose thoroughly brown; place on hold encumbrances like self-respect, honour, trustworthiness to one's peers; show conscientiousness and work ethics to gulag standard and resort to all manner of shenanigan in order that this come to the notice of Those Who Matter; stab one's workmates — i.e. the competition — in the back with any misdemeanour the ruling class might conceivably find fault with; polish boots and chase brownie points and sniff, sniff, sniff. I'm afraid that's just not me, Raq.*

— *What you're telling me is that . . . is that your outlook on the future — both cultural and environmental — has grown so pessimistic you really don't see much point in trying any more?*

— *A simplification, but a not wholly invalid one.*

As we pull from the ARC, Barry waves a finger at the 'doormen' on reflex alone, and at this point someone who hadn't been friends with the dude for years might find themselves wondering how it was I so easily sidetracked him from the wrong he witnessed; was so visibly incensed by. How can a person work up a head of indignation to the point where personal safety ceases to be an issue, and then — through nothing more than a whiff of prime pussy — abandon the quest for justice so utterly and instantly?

Well, hypothetical party, the answer's double pronged.

22

Firstly, more so than anyone I'm yet to come across — Christ let it remain so — Barry lives in the moment. He does what takes his fancy from minute to minute, hour to hour, without observable thought for the morrow. Barry decided some years ago that his chosen lifestyle couldn't accommodate concepts like 'aftermath' and 'consequence' and 'accountability'. He thus liquidated these puritans from the realm of his mind so comprehensively that at times I have to wonder if he even remembers what they look like. I've seen this guy commit more acts of extreme bravado than Evel Knievil, and the number of occasions on which he's landed me fair and square in the shit do not bear reflection.

One icy July when we were fifteen and loaded on an uncle's home-brew whisky, Barry drove us in a mate's car — an RX3 death machine — into the forecourt of a busy Shell station and proceeded to lay a standing burnout. ('Vive Nigeria, ya fucking capitalist *wank*ers!') This was nothing unusual. What was, was that after a few minutes of smoke, mechanical bedlam and the clamour of forecourt attendants, the burnout showed no sign of abating. Indeed, even when Barry's record of four minutes twenty-eight seconds had been well and truly smashed, his feet continued to work their magic on brake, throttle and clutch.

At first I found it all outrageously funny. By the time the oinkers appeared, I'd have cheerfully had Scotty beam me to the streets of sunny Knoxville in my 'Uncle Sam Swallows' T-shirt.

At that point Barry killed the engine, leapt from the driver's seat and legged it across the park, down to the lakefront, the fascists in hot pursuit. I took the opportunity to slip from the scene, but not before witnessing Barry make good his escape. Not even checking that the chase was looming — it was — Barry pelted to the end of a jetty and entered the drink in a technically flawless swan-dive.

Did the oinkers' commitment to peace, liberty and justice for all extend to pursuits through near-zero waters? Did it fuck. Barry swam about a click due west, made shore, then phoned for a pick-up unmolested.

Once word of the episode filtered through our extended circles, Barry's rep underwent a meteoric ascension — from legend to demi-god in one easy drenching. Of course my role — I contacted the owner of the car and had him report it stolen — went largely unsung, leaving me to milk what I could from the roles of Eye-witness and Chief Mouthpiece.

Another time, New Year's morning, the Mount, five of us were sleeping off our debauches in *The 'Dan* when a blue squealer tapped on the window, enquiring if we were OK.

'Immeasurably,' I replied.

Satisfied, the fascist moved to depart, at which point Barry awoke. Seeing blue, he clambered across two inert bodies, threw open a door, uttered an oft-quoted phrase — 'Fucking pig cunt!' — and punched the man flush in the face.

More pork materialised, enlivening an otherwise dull morning with a game of Let's Fuck Over the Big Psychotic Kid.

All things considered I couldn't really blame them. Still, the dude's a brother: I was left no choice. Pleading, I jumped around the fracas like a bitch, dodging blows, making a general obstacle of myself, persuading them to stop eventually amid threats of oinker brutality charges.

So yeah, I guess there's no real overlooking the fact: any headshrinker worth their salt would surely take a keen interest in Barry.

In teenage social networks terms like 'mad', 'crazy', 'nutcase' are bandied about frequently — have come to connote little more than extroversion. Barry receives such compliments regularly. The complimenters, however, seldom realise just how apposite their words in fact are. Little do they know that for Barry a spell in the Laughing Academy probably wouldn't go astray. At the worst, the world would be a safer place for a while.

It's bizarre, though. When he decided to exterminate his sense of reason, before he'd throttled the life from it completely, it apparently found the will to issue one last directive. To occupy the vacuum it insisted Barry appoint some manner of successor.

And it — or he — chose me.

Accordingly I, of all the human race, have the ability to control the guy.

Sometimes.

Oh, and the second part of my double-pronged answer?

Though no friend of Barry's could ever want for a truer ally, he doesn't always fight for reasons of philanthropy. Indeed, some suspect his spine has a streak of black running *right* through it.

I know tough guys who rumble for love of the sport, to assert dominance, to show off, guys who seldom go beyond uncle.

Barry's not always one of them.

At times the thug in him refuses to be contained. A Hyde-like creature dependent on the raw purity of damage infliction.

When this craving arises Barry usually looks for bad guys.

Sometimes he can't find any.

I fear his soul offers calmer harbour to the Fiendish Beast than many.

Right from the onset of tonight's near brawl, then, I was able to assume that Barry's heart was not immovably fixed on retribution for the martyr's cause. You see, under different circumstances — say if the guy had chundered on, or around, *Barry*'s shoes — it could just as easily have been him doing the hunting.

And, unlike Jabba, Barry might not've stopped.

He's a bright dude, though, our Bazza: big reader, good student in his day, demon on the chessboard. I'm not sure why he turned out the way he did. It certainly wasn't through domestic turmoil: his folks advocated 'family meetings' over smacking.

They're also filthy rich.

Perhaps, then, Barry's pubescent metamorphosis was more extreme than most as an unconscious backlash against *this*, a perceived 'Little Lord Fauntleroy' stigma.

Or was he just born bad?

Then again, having watched him evolve — competed alongside him in the crucible of teen culture — I sometimes have to wonder if Barry didn't simply *select* viciousness as a character flaw.

Psychosis, after all, has a mystique entirely of its own.

{ ARCHIVES: The Flawed Cog

— *Have you perhaps given thought to devoting time toward making a difference on this score, then? Some pro-environment career, perhaps? Gaining a measure of direction through action, so to speak.*

— *Nails and heads, Raq.*

— *You* have *given this thought?*

— *Correctomundo.*

— *And you've resolved to . . . ?*

— *That's classified. I could tell you . . . but then I'd have to top you.*

— *Ha ha. You feel you can't bring me into the fold, so to speak?*

— *To do so would constitute a breach of loyalty.*

— *Against whom?*

— *I'm not at liberty to answer that.*

— *But surely . . .*

— *Don't go there, girlfriend.*

— *. . . You're serious, aren't you?*

— *Terminally.*

— *. . . Fine. That's your prerogative. Where were we, then? Ahhhh, yes. Well, this world view of yours is certainly a large impediment to the development of a young man. Together we can work through this, but we'll need more than the half hour I've scheduled you for. For now, let's . . .*

— *By god, Raq, you must be vastly more talented than looks suggest! Fancy that: an extra hour or two in your company and the looming finale to decades of idiocy is magically made to look rosy!*

— *. . . For now, Gator, let's focus on the more immediate issues. I hope you'll forgive a little candour. I want to remind you that anything discussed in this room goes no further without your express permission. . . This cannabis use of yours: how often do you smoke?*

— *Well, recently I've made efforts to cut back, Raq. I'm down now to one, two . . . four sessions daily.*

— *Really? And that's good, is it?*

— *All things are relative, Raq. Jim Morrison would've viewed my habit as a healthy one.*

— *Jim who?*

— *Never mind.*

— *Well, what about these rumours of harder drugs? For your sake, I sincerely hope they're unfounded. Does, in fact, your . . . 'recreation' ever digress so far?*

— *Your fears are squandered, Raq. I imbibe heinous chemicals only when I can lay paws on them. As a non-Aucklander devoid of legal income, this isn't often.*

— *It's true then? The rumours are true?*

— *The truth is a virus, Raq.*

— *. . . I . . . I find it quite shocking that a kid with your ability . . .*

— *The ozone layer once had ability.*

— *. . . and intelligence should become involved with drugs and remain so . . . so unalarmed by it! I'm sure you're bright enough to see where a life like this might lead. I can perhaps fathom a little experimentation, but why would you let it protract?*

— *Because when I'm toasted, Armageddon actually seems worth sticking round for. Arch-drama, you see?*

— *What about these fracas you've been involved in recently? Does it worry you that violence also seems to be evolving into a staple of your existence?*

— *You can't be fucking serious! I help smack over a few homie goons — members of a caste that's turned gang-bashing into a divisional sport — and all of a sudden word in the staffroom has me as some kind of crack-crazed street-tough? Jesus Christ, if you Establishment clowns had handed discipline and justice out to the right people in the* first *fucking place, guys like me wouldn't* have *to fight fire with petrol just so we can leave the house of a weekend with our heads high! It's too late now! Several years ago the homies were allowed to bring to the streets a watered-down version of nigga gang culture and it's following exactly the same trends as Seppoland, minus the shooters — those come later, when they've graduated, when they're all patched up!*

— Please calm down, Gator. You obviously have strong feelings about these issues, but there are better methods of channelling one's angst.

— . . . I apologise. I don't know why I'm spitting the dummy at you about it, anyway. It was inevitable; written in the bones. We Westerners thought we'd 'outcivilised' the Fiendish Beast. We were wrong. It's as patient as the ocean, Raq. Just as fucking ruthless and just as unstable. It's in cahoots with the Juggernaut, and they've eased the gates of history back open again. It's slithering through as we speak, Raq . . . and this time it's staying.

Right till The End. }

2

Me, bringing Mick up to speed from the back seat: 'Eh, man, Sonya Kennedy's out the front of McDick's. She's off her tree and been asking for Baz all night.'

'Ahhhh, yeah.'

'We've gotta rush, though, eh? Remember, she said those geeks were on their way to pick her up?'

Mick's not slow. Never has been. 'Yeah. What time was she expecting them? 'Bout 12.30, wasn't it?'

''Bout then, yeah. How we looking now?'

'12.25.'

Barry, drooling: 'Hope she's still there. Cheers for coming to grabus, eh lads.'

Me: 'Honour among thieves, bro.'

'What's she wearing anyway?'

'There's no way in the *world* I'm describing to you what that horny cunt's done itself up in tonight, 'cause if I were to do such a thing you'd cough your filthy yoghurt all *over* the shop . . . and I've still got brewskis on the floor up there.'

'Wise precaution. Mind if I grab one?'

'Climb into the bastards. Send one back too, will ya?'

Phhsst.

Phhsst.

The city streets quiet, we slide through the neon disease. The Chilis groove from a speaker near my ear. Mick and Barry blaze up a gasper each, easing windows down. I ran out earlier; find I'm too embarrassed to bludge another. *Can't be that pissed yet.* I needn't have worried: like the gentleman he often is, Barry hands one back unprompted.

Down Renton Street, traffic near non-existent. Mick nonetheless remains inside the speed limit and we've all donned seatbelts unthinkingly. An act that probably appears anomalous, Model Citizens not being a category in which one would readily group us. Inversely, it's this very fact that prompts our estimable example: when the law's a line one crosses habitually, it's a fun-lovin' criminal of minuscule intelligence — or rigorous principles — who invites upon himself inessential porcine attention.

We three don't spend as much time together as we once did. Barry shifted to the Smoke a while back, lured by the Jism. He returns a couple of times a month, though: our commitments to the Brotherhood demand regular rallying.

We're all aware of our roles within the fraternity; are each hamstrung without the other.

I guess you could call me the brains trust, the CPU, the chief cabalist.

Mick's aversion to booze, his 'pacifism', his Jewishness, his inherent pragmatism, qualify him to act as our driver, treasurer and editor. His freckled little fist maintains an iron grip on our war-chest, and few of my plans are actualised without Mick's approval and fine-tuning.

And Barry? Barry's our actions-man. The Minister of Offence.

McDick's is a little busier than the rest of town. About the carpark scattered knots of night-children gravitate upon the open doors and stereos of muscle-cars. And some not-so-brawny-cars. Most of these cats are a year or two behind us on the learning curve; too young to gain access to pubs and clubs on any recurrent basis. Party-chasers. Parties of those you know, and of those you don't. Somewhere to drink, toke, sleaze, scrap. Places like McDick's suffice when the party scene runs dry of a weekend.

My confederates and I are of an age to enjoy the best of both worlds.

At least we pretend we are.

There's even a few slices of skirt on display here, some of it thoroughly mouth-watering. But sobriety is a state from which I'm not far enough removed to yet suggest a pit-stop. Besides, if we *were* to go sniffing, chances are some prick would inform Barry that they had been here all night and Sonya Kennedy — not to mention *The 'Dan* and her occupants — most certainly had not.

Me: 'Ah, fuck. It looks like she's gone already.'

Barry, wetly: 'I'll get out and ask some of these clowns.'

Mick, executing a quick circuit: 'No point, dude. She said she had to wait for Phelps and 'em under the minaret, and that if she weren't there when we rocked back then she'd bailed already.'

Barry, ardent: '*Cunt*! Any idea where they were taking her?'

Me, fallaciously gutted: '*Naaa*, man. Didn't think to ask, eh.'

Mick, commiserating: 'Oh, well, bro. At least ya know her ham-castanets are greased for ya. Next time ya see her just slide straight on in.'

Within a few seconds Barry sighs: 'Yeah, I guess that'll have to do. Fuck it, I might even give her a call. I think Lefty's got her number.'

Me: 'On that I'd be willing to stake a lot of money.'

Though it's at the forefront of our minds, none of us bothers voicing the lamentable statistic that Lefty's actually shafted Sonya more times than any of us have even tossed to her.

Barry: 'Cheers for trying to sort us anyway, lads.'

Tandem: 'No probs.'

Barry: 'Where to now, then? I don't wanna hang with these toddlers.'

Mick: 'Speaking of the weevil, I s'pose we should head to Junky Moe's and collect Lefty.'

Me, knowing the answer: 'Must we?'

Mick: 'Should really. Running pretty low on juice and he promised to throw in a tenner.'

Like I said, Mick's a kike. Were there a market for dandruff, he'd carry a tomahawk.

Barry: 'Yeah, and his uncle's s'posed to take us out fishing Sunday avo. Can't see that happening if we let him walk home.'

And so we depart, in search of our missing fragment, the fourth musketeer.

Lefty, though, is yet to be initiated into the Brotherhood. Or, for that matter, to learn of its existence — no brother can be found to second his recruitment nomination. Come to think of it, no brother can be found to *first* the fucking thing.

But this isn't a barrier to Lefty performing services for us. Obliviously.

Arch-treasonists can brook few scruples.

Barry's soon proffering the packet again. 'You dudes want another fag?'

Mick's an instant starter, and after an inner struggle (of at least three milliseconds) I opt to take one as well.

Not that I need the damn thing. I've been meaning to quit for years. Hardly the healthiest habit for an asthmatic. Still, I don't regret the decision to start smoking. And that's exactly what it was for me: a decision. Not some gradual slide into dependency begun by stray, daredevil puffing. No, one Fourth Form evening I simply sat up in bed, took a good long look at my life, and decided to start inhaling the white stuff.

Hours later saw me the proud owner of a pack of Camel 25s.

Best move I ever made, really. You see, at the time my social life was enduring something of a recession. Awkward age anyway, socially. Stuck between two realms: the first, a place where hours of amusement are no further from hand than an ancient tennis ball; the second, a vast, forbidden shadow-world beginning to embody Arcadia itself. On one side, go-home-stay-home and backyard cricket; on the other, budding breasts and DB six-packs.

And here they were, at break times, with their earrings and attitudes, gathering in backwaters colonised by forebears forgotten, the torch handed on, year after year. While their schoolmates played touch rugby and handball, these cats smoked cigarettes. With style. Drenched in the glamour of the rebel.

Rumour spread of their deeds; claimed smoking was but a prelude, an initiation. The real hedonism lay within. *Alcohol!* it was whispered. *Marijuana!*

Chicks who go all the way!

Because, naturally, the type of girl who took up with the Smokers had morals distinctly less puritanical than those of her peers. Thus, while a little spit-swapping and arse-groping was beginning to come the way of us mortals, scuttlebutt suggested that many of the Smokers were *actually getting their pricks wet!*

One pimply lunchtime then, having furtively nailed some Ventolin sustenance, I sauntered across main field to an infamous tree on its far border, swapped nods with a classmate recently converted, then sat down and lit up like I'd been doing it since Dunkirk.

And yeah, perhaps I *did* doom myself to a life of ragged respiration. Of perennial unfitness. A premature and harrowing death.

But I also lost my cherry three days out from the big one five.

Priorities, people.

Five minutes and another beer later — I can feel it now; I even lean from the window and yell 'Howzit?' to some honeys; the wave one of them returns leaves me giddy, gagging for the fray — we locate Lefty out front of a bar named Junky Moe's.

He's locked in a tight set of tonsil-tennis with a slice of prime crumpet. Lefty spends a lot of time at this sort of thing.

Mick coasts in alongside, sits on the horn, quashing the tender moment.

Lefty, surfacing, peeved but relieved: '*Oh*, you bastards aren't actually *here*, are you? I thought we said 11.30?'

Lefty's the type guys love to despise. Ludicrously handsome;

33

fat lips default set on 'toothy smirk'. Shaggy blond hair seeming always to fall in a rakish arrangement, even first thing in the morning. He's of only medium height, a touch overweight too, but in a tight T-shirt and jeans he contrives to make it look brawn.

Lefty tangoed through puberty without a single zit, has body hair only where it's wanted, and the TAB have closed all wagers on the bet that he'll hit sixty with a full head of locks.

There's one in every crowd.

Out here in the gloom, babe in his arms, the nearest street-lamp seems to wash over Lefty as if he's subject to the wiles of a Broadway lighting man.

Me, out the window: 'Half eleven o' the clock was indeed our agreement, fine sir. Sadly, pressing matters arose.'

Mick, too low to carry: 'Yeah, I had to duck home and tape *Coro Street* for the old girl.'

Only then do we identify the piece moulded to Lefty's body: the babe in the tiny black skirt. Brunette and gorgeous. Tallish. Slim. Perky tits. Tight snatch — according to Lefty she has anyway.

Unlike a lot of high-class fanny, though — which intimidates me witless — Becky's is the kind of fragile beauty that emboldens as it captivates. And she's an absolute darling. Caring to a fault, Becky even knocks guys *back* with a smile. Rejection from her is a near sensual experience.

Trust me.

Trust Barry also.

Given her love most males would launch a life-long campaign to preserve and cherish it.

Lefty just pisses on it.

Barry, surprised and pleased: 'Becky! Howyadoen, baby? I didn't know you were back!'

Becky, a voice that has your pulse catching: 'Hi, Baz. Hi, Gator.' There's a melancholic chord in her tone, though. There often is these days. 'I got back last Thursday. Nice to see you guys.'

34

Me: 'I hope you're gonna hang around this time, Becks. Vegas ain't the same without ya.'

She grins and blushes at that, god bless her. 'I hope so too. I might have a job working at . . . '

Lefty, brusque: 'We gotta make a move anyway, Beck.' He prises her off him and opens the door. I slide over for him grudgingly.

Becky, to Lefty, the rest of us forgotten: 'Are you *sure* you have to go?'

'I told ya, darling, I'm working early tomorrow.' Lefty doesn't actually have a job. In fact, excepting a yearning to number among the nation's finest cunnilinguists, Lefty's got about as much drive as a hippie on an elephant cull. 'I'll phone ya next week some time.'

A slither of desperation: 'Do you promise?'

'Yep.'

Shutting the door — sidelong eyes making sure we're all watching — Lefty pulls her to him through the open window, snogging her deeply, holding the kiss. Her arms seek him, and Lefty's hand snakes up almost absently, a finger rubbing her nipple erect.

He would've reached out and stroked her beaver, I'm fucking sure of it, except that only Barry would have noticed.

And the worst part is, Becky would have let him.

Gladly.

She's panting when at last he lets her go.

Lefty, smirking: 'You be good now, won't ya?'

Her eyes hold a manic sparkle. 'I love you.'

Mick's seen enough and pulls away, but not before Lefty can look her dead centre.

'I love you too, baby.'

The lying cunt.

Appalled silence holds for a block or three.

Mick, over his shoulder, caustic: 'You haven't done *her* in a while, Lefty. How come you didn't bring her along?'

Lefty, peeved: 'Oh, I was planning on doing *exactly* that . . . then I discovered the useless bitch's up on blocks.'

Mick: 'Whadaya mean?'

Lefty: 'You know. Got the painters in?'

Me: 'You're a total arsehole, man.'

Lefty, snapping: 'Oh, fuck you, Gator.'

Barry: 'I second the allegation.'

There's just enough wrongedness in Lefty's tone to leave him safe, in a place resembling the moral high ground. 'Fuck you *too*, then.'

You see, it isn't just Lefty's looks that ensure he pulls more pussy than Hef ever did. The dude seems to have an inner meter with which he can measure a person's mood. Lefty being Lefty, if normally he dared address Barry — or even me — in such a fashion, we'd be only too pleased to threaten him with a busted gob, make him back-down in humiliation, savouring every inch of it. Ordinarily, the guy's obsequious to the point of nausea. The sexual envy he inspires in males — tacitly cultivates and thrives upon — ensures that he need constantly patronise in order to remain within a social circle. He worms his way into the affections of guys with as much shamelessness as he does the ladies, and when he decides the time is right to win a degree of respect by sticking up for himself, his gift for human intuition tells him exactly how far he can push his luck.

Mick, incredulous: 'Are you actually denying that your conduct toward that chick is big-time shabby?'

Lefty, whining aggrievement: 'Yeah, I *am* gonna deny that! So the bitch digs me and I don't have feelings as strong for her? I can't help that.'

Barry: 'You sure can help the way you keep her hanging on, though, cuz.'

Lefty: 'Why should I? She's a big girl: she can decide when she's had enough. I'm only bloody human, man. Why should I turn down a nice root when it comes my way?'

Because you could be up some other piece, even one just as tidy, at the drop of a fucking hat.

But I don't say this. None of us does. Our jealousy maintains an embargo on the words.

And so this recurring dispute resolves itself in the fashion with which it does always: with Lefty steering it around to us having to either vocalise this emasculating truth, or back away.

That solitary sentence would demonstrate his guilt conclusively: push him into a corner from which there could be no extraction. And, as usual, we don't have the spine to utter it. To nakedly acknowledge his colossal superiority over us in the arena that to males means so fucking much.

We all know it, all four of us, but Lefty never goes beyond alluding to it.

Insidiously.

He knows that were he to take it further, the small amount of goodwill he holds with us would vanish faster than a hooker's hymen.

This time he makes a mistake, though. Into the sick hush he foolishly looses a shot that begs for a punishing counter-volley.

'Why the fuck would I ever wanna get a full-time thing going with a schizo like *her*, anyway?'

Me, springing from cover with a war-cry, beating the others by inches: 'Perhaps because you're the only cunt who could help her through it; try and mend some of the damage you've done! She was fine before *you* sleazed into her life.'

His riposte is too quick, too loud. 'That's a *fucking* crock of shit!'

'Oh, no it isn't.'

She and Lefty used to be an item. Until Becky caught him cheating one time too many. By dumping him she hoped to teach him a lesson, have him come running with declarations of fidelity. He didn't bother. Even when she weepingly crawled back to *him*, Lefty wasn't interested. And why would he have been? He was sick of having her around, and he knew he could bang her any time he liked regardless.

Something he chose to do from time to time over the next nine months, sometimes even managing to keep the fact from his current girlfriend, chicks he had no qualms about flaunting in front of Becky whenever they were present at the same gatherings. Which — considering Becky tracked him with the diligence of Inspector Morse — was often.

Becky went downhill steadily, visibly, but we were all surprised when she opted to have Mr Gillette adorn her wrists with some inkless tattooing.

It's hard to say whether she was counting on being found or not, but that's what happened. In any case, if it *were* simply a cry she were making, Lefty didn't seem to hear it. If he did, it certainly didn't annul her attractiveness to him. Sadly, nor did it enlarge it. Things progressed as they had for another three months.

Becky then drove her dad's Subaru through the front window of Farmers and found herself sentenced to a spell in the Laughing Academy.

She's been in and out twice since, and based on tonight's evidence I'd have to guess that Lefty views the hat-trick as a unique challenge to his age-old talents.

We're stopped at a deserted red light as I debate whether or not to tear into the cunt. Again.

But I'm a happy drunk — if a little rowdy — and when pissed I take pains not to dwell on the negative. When I do I find the euphoria difficult to recapture.

It seems as if Barry and Mick are going to let it rest, and I'm still of two minds when a car jammed with more snatch pulls up alongside our passenger door.

Lefty and Barry have their windows down in microseconds.

Lefty, peering into the Honda's depths, wheedling: 'Is that *you* in there, Stephanie?'

Barry knows the driver from somewhere. 'Howyadoen, Amanda? Long time no see.'

Though several divisions from Lefty's league, he's a bit of a babe-killer in his own right is our Bazza. When he can be arsed, that is. Because among other things, Barry tends to prioritise mates ahead of getting laid. I've seen the dude turn his back on

38

dead-cert roots just to be in the car with the boys when they forsook a party, off to trawl for trouble, or to rip up some field, whatever.

This attitude is something I find enormously refreshing — all the more because I certainly don't share it, and neither does any other cunt I've ever known — and I guess it contributes substantially to the reasons I maintain my hazardous association with the mad bastard.

Amanda sounds pleased to see him. Girls usually are. 'Barry! What are *you* up to?'

Barry lives with a bird up in the Smoke, been steady with her for a couple of months. But he's not one to let this hinder him should something else win his attention. Like every other male ever to draw breath, Barry holds faith with the truism 'what she doesn't know . . . '.

I find it a tragic indictment on the female gender, though, that a guy with Barry's rep — he's someone many blokes cross the street to avoid — seems to tickle temptation in the lasses; to stimulate some incorrigible impulse toward peril, in a fashion not at all dissimilar to the way they get pumped over motorbikes.

Of course, as a hardman, to engender this reaction it helps to have some looks to go with it.

Lefty seems to be getting a nibble as well. From the centre of the back seat Stephanie's practically squashing her companion in a bid to present him her attention. 'Where have you guys been tonight?'

Lefty: 'Oh, we started out round at Barry's place, had a few beers and watched a movie, *Predator 7*. You've just *gotta* see it, eh! Fan-*fucking*-tastic! Anyway, from there we shot round to this chick Sandy's crib to pick up a tinny — good pot, too: she gets most of her gear through the Black Power and you know what sort of dope *those* dudes grow! *Ahahahaaa*. Yeah, so we skinned up and shot out the lake for a blow; ended up bumping into Zane Jackson an' em out there . . . '

Lefty's on a roll. In fact, when it comes to talking he's always on a roll. The dude's got a mouth like a busted sandshoe.

Of course, that he manages to spout a near constant flow of chat eighteen odd hours a day is due largely to his armour-plated sense of rejection. Because, like most big talkers, ninety per cent of what Lefty says can best be described as a load of old bollocks. Something he seems to trouble over in no way, shape or form. Even when the fact is bluntly pointed out to him . . . which, in our company, is frequently.

It seems clear to me, then, that this is the single most vital factor behind exercising a 'gift of the gab'. Namely, the will to toss out an idea, question, anecdote, and not feel stung when the reaction it elicits is unfavourable. The audacity to leap straight back to the floor directly after being told, 'I've got absolutely no idea what the fuck you're going on about, pal,' seems to me a gift of priceless dimensions. Because, by the simple law of averages, the greater the flow of dialogue springing from one's mouth, the higher the odds of saying some-thing opportune. And one fitting remark seems to invalidate five preposterous ones.

Yes, in the Global Citizen's perennial struggle to Win Friends and Influence People, a thick skin is without doubt the most baleful weapon with which one can be armed.

So while most of us hacks are left contesting the Love Grand Prix in beat-up Holdens, Jap imports, the odd sports car, god not only saw fit to equip Lefty with a Formula One Ferrari, he was also kind enough to mount a heavy machinegun on the fucking bonnet.

And even as I watch, spellbound, Lefty's titanium plating insulates him through yet another stupefying act. 'What are you guys up to now?'

Stephanie: 'Oh, we're gonna drop Cindy home and then head to Deuces.'

Lefty, grimacing: 'Bad move, eh. That place is totally blacked out tonight. We've just come from there. You'd be better off some-where else. I tell ya what, there's a cool party up at Bison Hall.'

The said carousal is no doubt fictitious. This is a favoured ploy of Lefty's. Upon arriving at the 'location' he'll utter the classic: 'Shit, the oinkers must've broken it up already.' Or the timeless: 'Oh, *no*, Rachael's gone and given me the wrong address again.' By this stage a bond exists between the two crews and Lefty can often milk this to arrange an alternative rendezvous. 'If you guys've got nothing better to do either, we're heading up the mountain for a session.' Or, failing that, talk his way into their car — 'Which way are ya's heading? . . . Hey wow, I need to get near there! Ya couldn't drop me off at all, could ya?' — and sniff for a fresh kill in the back seat.

Stephanie: 'Really? We've sorta gotta meet some friends at Deuces, though.'

Strike one.

Lefty, 'solicitous': 'I promise ya, you'll *really* regret it if you go there. It sucks to the *max* tonight. Why don't ya's follow us? We were at this party earlier and its going *off.*'

Stephanie, rueful: 'Can't. Sorry. We promised to catch up with these guys. They'll *kill* us if we pull a no-show.'

Strike two.

Boldly, Lefty steps up to the plate again. 'They can come too. Let's cruise to Deuces, round them up, and then head out.'

'Na, I think they were pretty keen to rage at Deuces till the earlies.'

Strike three.

Undeterred, Lefty swings *again*. 'What about you? We've got room in here if ya wanna jump in?'

Stephanie: 'Oh . . . na. Maybe some other time. I'd better stick with the girls tonight.'

Unbe-*fucking*-lievable! The guy just let himself be shot down *four* times in front of *eight* peers!

Given that I'm pissed, I'd've been willing to let that happen once. Perhaps even twice might I've contrived a jestful means for the second swipe. But *four*? And every attempt unsubtle?

I know men who would do murder for a hide that tough.

I happen to head the queue.

When it comes to Lefty and womanising, though, good looks aside — because, at the end of the day, unless one bears a

41

striking resemblance to Quasimodo or Pitt, personality is the more telling element — there's one certainty that breaks my heart: though Lefty has assuredly parted more mutton-curtains than the rest of us combined, that he has also received many more *rejections* is a statistic of equal incontestability.

The Law of Averages, man.

That and thick skin.

History's most lecherous alliance.

By my book, Lefty at this point should be experiencing humiliation, shame, self-doubt. But, as he sits back in his seat, sparks up a coffin-nail, he doesn't appear in the least put out. Indeed, he seems almost *pleased* with himself!

It hits me like a tackle: *Has this cunt actually calculated his rejection/scoring ratio? Is he saying to himself right now, 'That's three. Should be saddled up next time round, the time after at the worst.'?*

And, of course, the more knockbacks he accumulates, the more refined his technique grows.

The more lethal the strike rate.

Up front Barry seems to be happening upon a more mortal angle.

Amanda: 'What was that acid like you'd just dropped when I last saw you?'

Barry: 'When was that?'

'You know. We were in The Freezer?'

'. . . *Oh*, yeah. You were with Alan and 'em, right?'

'Yeah.'

'Ammm, yeah, it wasn't *too* bad. Pretty rough comedown, but that's par for the course with that stuff. It pays to get pissed before it wears off.'

Amanda, tentative: 'Is there any chance of you getting us any?'

Barry, musing: 'Not too sure.'

At times I think Barry sees himself as some breed of New Age narco-Shaman. Charged with the holy duty of escorting heathens and the faithful alike through the Doors of Perception.

Who makes it back he doesn't give so much of a shit about.

Offending the guy by asking him to score for you is a near unrealisable task. Were he in the process of assaulting you, and for some reason you blurted your position on the market for a banned substance, Barry would likely stop, help you up, and determine your exact requirements. Unless we're running dry, he hardly ever taxes either.

Barry, pondering: 'Those that we had that night in The Freezer were Snowflakes, but I know for a fact there's none of them in town at the moment. There might be a few Cobras around, though. Mick? Trudy got any Cobs right now?'

'Na.'

'How 'bout Pete, Gator?'

'Na, man, he's got fuck all of anything.'

Barry, to Amanda: 'Are ya's after anything in particular?'

'Not really. We're just sick of booze and blow.'

Smiling: 'Amen to *that*.'

Lefty, suddenly: 'Ah, *shit*! Guess what? I can get on to Fat Freddies at the moment!'

Along with Bart Simpsons and Spinning Tops, the said items constitute the current Holy Trinity of the ever-shifting LSD scene: my faith in Lefty's claim is therefore minimal.

Amanda, animated: 'I've heard those are really good!'

Barry, ruminating expertly: '*Welllll*, yeah. They're not too bad. Not too bad at all.' He turns to face Lefty, voice dropping to a confidential — and menacing — mutter. 'Are you for real?'

Lefty, emphatic: '*Yeah*. They're forty each, I know they're holding, and I guarantee someone'll be home.'

'"Guarantee"?'

'*Guarantee*, man.'

'This'd better not be a come-on strategy.'

There aren't a lot of areas in which Barry'll tolerate being made to look 'all talk'. You show him up over *drugs* . . .

Lefty, leaning forward, whispering: 'It *is* a come-on, because once we've sorted them for acid, once their brains are in fucking Disneyland, they're ours for the taking. But *no*, it's not a bullshit line to string them along.'

'How can you know someone'll be home?'

''Cause the dude who knocks them out reckons there's *always* someone home, and he's dependable.'

Barry, staring hard: 'Last chance to level with me.'

Lefty, affronted: 'I'm straight *up*, man.'

Barry, turning back to the girls: 'Yeah, that's sweet as. They're forty each.'

An excited buzz breaks out in the wench-wagon.

Amanda: 'How many each will we need?'

Barry, straight-faced: 'That depends. Are ya's all virgins?'

Giggle, giggle.

Amanda, coy: 'In this domain we are.'

Lefty, turning to me, whispering in a hiss: 'Hear *that*? *Acid*-virgins! We'll all chip in for a bottle of hot stuff, slip 'em a few drinks on top of the headfood, and they'll be putty! Fucking *putty*, man!'

Sick prick.

But, beer having gnawed holes in my civic mask, I can't repulse a rush of blood at the notion.

Barry, lecturing to the girls: 'Well, these Fred's are the dog's bollocks, so you'll only wanna start with a quarter-trip each. Give it an hour, see how you're feeling, then take another quarter if you're up for it. It's my shout for the lads, so I'll be getting four — one trip each — but you guys'll only need about three between ya's.'

This is the first I've heard of any 'shout for the lads'. Barry's good like that. However, the sickly stirrings of excitement/nervousness that generally preface an acid trip don't yet kick in for me: pulling while tripping is an even harder task than nailing it stoned, so I'll be standing aloof from this pilgrimage until I've loosed a salvo or two on the carnal front.

Amanda: 'One twenty, then.'

The birds conduct a prolonged whip-round.

Amanda, at last: 'Yeah, we've got enough on us now. How do ya cut them up, though?'

44

Me, on daring impulse: 'A sharp instrument's often an ideal starting point.'

And earn a collective giggle; relief sliding like warm treacle.

Barry: 'Well, how about we deal with the practicalities when the score's been made?'

Amanda: 'No probs.'

'Follow us then, ladies.'

Mick steps on it.

Mick: 'Where to, Lefty?'

'Head up to . . . don't *call* me that!'

Mick, 'puzzled': 'Why not?'

'Because it's not my *name*!'

Barry, contradictory: 'No, no. The correct phrase would be, "Because its not my *given* name".'

Lefty, whining: 'It's not my *any* fucking name!'

Me: 'Then why does half of Vegas call you Lefty?'

'They *don't*!'

The three of us in delighted unison: '*Oh,* yes they do!' We've actually rehearsed this; the 'Lefty' thing is another of our recurring squabbles.

Lefty, sulking: 'Fucking forget it, then.'

Mick: 'Where to, Lefty?'

Silence.

Barry: 'Where *to*, Lefty?

A sullen grumble: 'Head toward the ghetto.'

Me, disgusted: 'Ahh, for *fuck's* sake! It's after *midnight*, man!'

We score from the ghetto often. As does many a white face. Every second house in there shelters a seller . . . if your credentials are in order. Even then, though, for our ilk, entering the ghetto at night is a fool's game.

Lefty, defensive: 'Don't worry, I'll go in.'

Mick: 'Considering this is your score, that goes without saying.'

'I know, I know.'

We're soon passing the multiplex, outside of which a pack of fifteen-odd homeboys are lurking, queuing for strife when the late sessions spill out.

At the sight of them a charge of fire — and revulsion, I'll not deny it — goes off inside me: the primal reaction of the hound scenting foxes.

Or perhaps vice versa.

And at a stroke, all the shadowy fissures dividing our quartet are filled in and bitumised. They say a need to piss fades real fast when you're under the crosshairs.

I hear Barry's knuckles crackle, fists clenching reflexively.

Lefty, muttering: 'You little arsehole motherfuckers.'

And I have to check myself from reaching for his shoulder.

Even Mick, the avowed 'pacifist' of our band, offers a belligerent sneer.

Put crudely, we despise these pieces of shit.

Abominate them.

They're the SS to our Partisans; the Roundheads to our Cavaliers; Saladin's hordes to the Lionheart's Crusaders.

Take heed, folk of Gotham: the menace might be fingered before it's upon thee. Sooties to a number, the age spread runs between ten and eighteen. They sport the uniform of the coca-colonised — baseball caps, NFL tops, plundered designer trainers, anything with a Seppo reference — topped in fake gold chains, chunky finger and earrings, often bandannas (red and white, green and white, blue and white) indicating for which of the 'real' gangs they'd one day like to prospect.

But it's not just the clothes that finger them as poison. It's the numbers. These cunts behave so atrociously, have earned so many enemies, they'll seldom show their faces in town in squads of fewer than twelve.

And it's the body language. They might as well have FUCKHEAD stencilled on them in fluoro. The walk is stauncher than Tyson: kicking at signs; drenching shop-fronts in spit and urine; constantly shadow-boxing, shouldering and sparring with one another; sneering at and staring down near anyone who approaches; cracking what to their pea-brains pass as jokes, buffeting the streets with jeering laughter; whistling and ogling at women of all ages, scaring them shitless and loving it.

Nobody's likely to hand any Nobel prizes to the people I call mates, but as wild as we may at times act, for near all of us there are certain lines that shall never be crossed.

For these homie arseholes crossing those lines is a fucking bonding exercise. Morality to them is an encumbrance others choose to carry, an Achilles heel to be targeted.

When the suit is right, many of this country's darkies are wont to pluck the trump card from their ethnic minority hand: levelling allegations of racism. And, on occasion, I'm sure the play constitutes more than an unassailable cop-out. But I'm here to announce first hand that this legion of Lawless Brown Youth plaguing our urban streets of a weekend night is without doubt its most tangibly racist fragment.

You see, it's a safe bet to say that if I, or any other white male between the ages of thirteen and twenty-five, were to encounter this group — or one of the multitudes similar — beyond the public eye, and sometimes within it, we would be attacked en masse. Extraordinary circumstance aside, it's as simple as that. That's not to say that the plus-twenty age group is safe — far from it. I'm simply passing on the secure wager.

But it's not that these guys have vendettas against Pakeha — most of them couldn't even *spell* Waitangi. They're just so full of violence and group bravado they zero in on anyone with a manifest difference.

Something easily articulated.

Something like skin colour.

('Let's *waaaste* the white cunts. They bigger'n us, but there's *only* two of 'em. Fuckin' bawl'eads are all shet, anyway.')

I've lost count of the number of times I've been set upon by homies. Without provocation. And never in a fair contest.

Oh, no.

Their favoured pastime, when running with a good-sized squad, is to surround one or two dudes — sometimes three, on a brave day — a few years above them in social standing — the choicer scalps, guys they wouldn't look at twice were the odds even — and goad themselves into fighting mood with a barrage of insults. No matter how much diplomacy, patronising, *abjection*, one employs in an effort to defuse the encounter, the inevitable outcome is a 360-degree fist and boot beleaguerment.

And brother, let me tell you, you do *not* want to go down.

Alone, a lot of them are reasonable people. I know this for fact. But once a group exists, a burning expectation develops for an individual to demonstrate his *staunchness*. And as soon as one of them makes a move, the others are sure as shit going to rise to it.

This isn't to say that they don't war among themselves. It isn't difficult for the various factions to identify contrasts enough to get healthy feuds up and running.

(— "Is bruva's wif the Rats. Look at those green scarfs. Show those round '*ere*, wool yu?'

— 'Fuckin' Boys' 'Igh faggots. Heights College all the *way*, beau.'

— "Member that arsehole from rugby? 'E was playing faw Waikitie when I got sent orf that time.')

But should there be a white target market present, these fluctuating blocs are ever amenable to impromptu alliance.

Often, outside concerts, battles of the bands, talent quests, after-balls, the bigger parties, where revellers spill out and congregate, groups of homies will enter the scene quietly, always on foot, drawn by the scent of plunder. In small, inoffensive knots they orbit the fringes like hyenas at a lion kill, practically ignored, gathering strength as word spreads, more and more trickling in. Groups who may have brawled tooth and nail just a week before relax in the solidarity of a common enemy.

At last the jokes and taunts grow louder, directed at party-goers. Cigarettes, beers, are cadged with growing belligerence. Advance parties subtly move in, and the gathering at last perceives a foreboding ambience. Behaviour stiffens, and though few are prideless enough to vocalise the shifting balance of power, certain crews begin to disperse, making their excuses with face-saving damage control.

The enemy running scared, reducing the odds further, the carrion are galvanised.

Finally, punches are thrown and it's suddenly on for fair and for foul.

And if behaviour of this ilk weren't lamentable enough, of recent years these 'kids' have begun demonstrating tendencies even more sinister.

The axiomatic 'respect for one's elders' has never been a tradition rigidly observed by the X Generation. The homie element, though, has taken this irreverence a step or ten further.

Age means *nothing* to them. Utterly nothing. Like creatures of the Serengeti, the single commodity that might win their deference is strength.

According to the local rag, three old-timers were exiting the RSA last Friday, at about 10.30, while a squad of homie vermin happened to be passing. One of the vets was knocked down, ostensibly by accident. A second of the elderly trio had the effrontery to declare, 'You lads ought to show a bit more courtesy on the pavements.'

One of the homies backtracked, approached the protester, and spat directly in his face.

His friends found this staggeringly funny, and, inspired by the reaction, the homie shoved the vet backwards. "U the *fuck* do yu think *yaw* lek-sha-ring, yu old *cunt*?"

In token protest, the old digger raised his walking stick . . . and was smashed squarely in the nose for his troubles. Down he went, his former comrades-in-arms soon joining him, all three attacked and kicked for long seconds.

Amid breathless giggles, the homies then fled the scene.

Without even lifting a wallet.

It would seem that the Fiendish Beast has dug a large, warm lair in many of their hearts.

Barry, through his teeth: 'There's Dusty. Let's just jump out and *hos*pitalise the little fuck.'

49

Said individual is fifteen years and five and a half feet of squeaky voice and malice. A lot of them are bigger, some older also, but perhaps because of his animal cunning, his total ruthlessness — a slant toward acts of violence appalling from a kid his age — Dusty seems to command the obedience of almost all Vegas's homies. This given, he can quite safely be named the city's unofficial public enemy *numero uno*.

Any one of us — and about 200 of our peers — would part with a lot of cash for the chance of encountering this little hoodlum with a squad of fewer than nine at his back.

Because it just doesn't happen.

Mick, the voice of reason: 'No one's getting outta this car unless one of ya's has a Smith & Wesson down his waistband.'

I've no wish to confront the enemy under these terms anyway. Neither does Lefty. But we're both happy to have Mick — a man with none of our pretensions — do the backing out for us.

Barry, however, can't let the opportunity pass without some manner of engagement, and as we slide past the theatre, all eyes fixed on us — they know the car well — he hangs his head from the window, singing like an Alabama banshee, Luke-style: 'An' if dem cotton playnts get rotten . . . '

I scramble across Lefty, thrusting my head into the slip-stream in nice time to pick up the second line: 'Den we doan pick very much cotton . . . '

Tandem: 'In dem auuuuuld cotton feelds back home!'

A fifteen-finger ovation and we're past, the muff-mobile hard on our arse.

Barry, passing me a fag: 'Well, Ah'd jus' lark t' congraj'late ya on sum marty farne sangin' dere, pardner.'

Me: 'Dat's narce a y' t' poynt ayeett, friend. An' let me 'ssure yuu, wun dese days we goan' lynch dat lil' asshole.'

Within five minutes we're deep in the suburbs. Mick indicates a left turn, nearing the ghetto.

Mick: 'Shit.' He pulls to a halt beside the kerb.

Me: 'What's up, dude?'

'The chicks high-beamed me. Must wanna say something.'

They pull up along our driver's side. Some redhead in the back seat *(ain't no stunner, but I'd sure as hell fuck it for practice)* addressing me with a smile: 'What'd you guys say to Dusty and 'em?'

Nicely fortified, I grin back at her: 'We said that fine things come to those who wait. What's *your* name, anyway?'

'Alice.'

'Don't worry, I'll spare you the song.'

Smiling wider: 'Thanks.' Businesslike: 'We stopped ya's to find out why we're heading for the ghetto.' With a finger, she admonishes me impishly. 'Didn't your mummy teach you that it's dangerous in there?'

Strangely enough, when I was a kid attending the primary school whose catchment encompasses the ghetto, my mummy used to give me permission to ride my bike down here and play at the houses of my best friends until all hours.

I decline saying this, though: I fear being painted collaborator.

'Well, what we didn't realise when we said we'd score for ya's was that Lefty here was planning on using a house in the ghetto.'

Stephanie: 'Who's "Lefty"?'

'The guy beside me.'

Lefty: 'Don't *call* me that!'

Alice, baffled: 'Why do ya's call him Lefty?'

Lefty, frantic: 'If you fucking tell them, I'll tell them why you're called Gator!'

Alice, to me: 'Gator, eh? What's your last name?'

'McPike.'

Three of them in harmony: '*You're* Gator McPike?

Me, eventually: '. . . Ahhhhhh, yeah. Why?'

Of a sudden Stephanie can't take her eyes from me either. 'Don't worry, it's nothing bad. We've just heard the stories.'

Her revelation tears my tongue from its roots. *Chicks I've never met are telling stories about me . . . and no cunt saw fit to inform me of this?*

I feel Lefty squinting at me; can't quite read the look.

Alice: 'Some say you're the Chosen One.'

Some blonde in the passenger seat, chuckling: 'Others say you're the Antichrist.'

Stephanie: 'Why *do* they call you Gator?' And the flooding rapture of her interest in the source of my nickname over Lefty's almost has me urinating.

Speech is still beyond me, but Barry, god bless him, kicks in with pristine timing. 'Cos when it combs t'drinkin' and luvin', he gat the app'tite of a bayou ala-gayda.'

The whole car laughs, and then Amanda speaks up from the driver's seat. 'So who gave you the name originally?'

Lefty can't take a second more of this. Blurting: 'He got the name when he was seven and it wasn't through any "drinking" or "loving".' His eagerness to subvert my spell in the spotlight, however, coaxes an enormous oversight. Namely, in the origins of *my* nickname, there isn't an awful lot to take shame in; in the origins of *his* there most certainly is. 'On a primary school farm trip he was playing rugby in a field, wasn't looking where he was going, and sprinted end-on into an open gate. Knocked himself out cold. Ended up in hospital. *Ahahaaa!*'

They laugh, but in a 'with you' sense.

Alice: 'Geez, at least you walked away with a phat nickname.'

Mick, positioning the stake: '*Wellll*, seeing as you unwarrant-edly carried out your threat to reveal the origins of *Gator's* name, *Lefty*, I think it only right that someone enlighten the ladies as to yours.'

Lefty gulps audibly. Stuttering: 'N–, n–, no *way*, man! That's not *fair*.'

Stephanie: 'Oh, come on, you guys *have* to tell us now!'

Barry, clearing his throat, ceremonious: 'If you'll allow me the honours, gents.' Louder: 'Yeah, it's like this, girls: a coupla years back . . .'

Lefty, reasoning with a toddler: '*Don't* do this, Barry. *Please*.'

Barry ignores him. 'A couple of years back me and . . . '

Lefty, desperate: 'If you tell them, I'm not going in to score the headfood.'

Barry turns to him, real slow. 'Pardon?'

Lefty, hesitant: 'Y–, you heard.'

Calm as a pike-pond: 'What was that word you gave me before, when I expressed doubt in you? It began with a "g", I believe.'

Lefty, fumbling for the aggrievement that occasionally allows him to swim these waters: 'Yeah, but not with you guys . . . '

Barry, open smile: 'Oh, I'm sorry. I can't have been listening when you worked that particular clause into your *guarantee*.'

Lefty drops his eye, blushing already.

Barry: 'Yeah, like I was saying, ladies . . . '

Jason's family used to live close to our high school. He slept in a bach tacked onto the garage. A good distance from the house as well: a dude could come and go, smoke, toke, drink, without parental obstruction. Sweet crib, too, man: TV, video, sound-system, double bed, carpet, couches, naked bimbos all over the walls.

I remember my first visit to the joint: Fourth Form, I guess it was. Gator took me round for a coupla ciggies. Only started at the school a week before; hadn't actually met Jason yet. Inside the room someone had taken a vivid and made a list on the ceiling of a couple of dozen 'activities':

Missionary*************
Doggy********
blow-job******
pearl necklace**
cunnilingus*******
tit-suck****************
finger-fuck**********************
sandwich
cross-over
standing*****
standing doggy****
shower-fuck***
analingus***
threesome*

orgy
fist-up
DVDA
double bassing********
DKFT*****
anal doggy**
anal missionary*
tit-fuck******
lateral*******
chick on top facing**********
chick on top away******
69er********
hand-job***********
toe-job***
chick on top anal
golden shower*

'Who the fuck lives out here, Gator? Long Dong Silver himself?'

'More to the point, what do you reckon DVDA is?'

'It's the ultimate in hard-core porn acts, man — double-vaginal double-anal.'

'You're not serious?'

'I fucking well am. I read about it in Penthouse once. It's a position requiring four male contortionists and one very talented lady.'

'I s'pose you know what DKFT is as well, then?'

'I should bloody know: I pioneered the drop-knee-full-teapot.'

Over the next year or so Jason's pad evolved into a kind of social club. Any one of about a dozen of us were liable to show up there at all hours of the day or night. Had some times round there, I tell ya.

Anyway, about a year after I arrived on the scene, one summer avo', me and Gator wagged last period and shot round Jas's for a bong or four. He'd wagged the whole day on account of having some bitch over in the morning. When we arrived, his old lady's car door was open, like she was just heading out or something, so we snuck round the back, jumped the fence, then crept through the long grass towards the crib, quiet as thieves.

The door was ajar — it was rooted and tended to creep open if ya didn't slam it hard — and from inside came the sounds of some slut getting shafted. The noise was tinny, though, from a distance like, and she seemed to be moaning in tongues. A spasmodic slapping sound was almost drowning her out as well, its rhythms way out of sync with hers.

Gator whispered to me, 'What the fuck's he gone and pulled now, the prick?'

'Dunno, bro. But I'm sure as hell gonna take a Jack Nohi.'

So we eased the door open and crawled in, knowing the arse-end of a couch would hide us. But once safely behind it, we saw that the bed was empty, and, standing slowly, learned that the doxie getting dicked was none other than Humungus Helga, that darling of the Kraut porn scene.

And there sat Jason, sprawled on the sofa, not three feet below us, eyes riveted to the TV screen, pants positioned for maximum ankle warmth . . .

Playing Han Solo on the pink Darth Vader.

Caught purple-handed.

Though we were directly behind him, so close were we to the guy it's a wonder his sense of smell didn't alert him. But it didn't, and Jason stayed ignorant of our presence for the next few minutes, enjoying a whale of a time, too. Left hand pounding. Easing back from the gravy-stroke . . . hard at it again.

Build 'er up . . . ease 'er back down . . .

With a remarkable display of professionalism, me and Gator actually managed to keep silent throughout.

Finally, Jason brought himself to a teeth-grinding orgasm, bucking like a landed marlin, coating his bare stomach in several wads of baby-batter.

Through a process of sign language, Gator graciously assigned me the honours. I thanked him with a nod, before casually enquiring, 'So how was that for you, anyway?'

Well, the wanker flew across the room as if a hornet had crawled up his Jap's eye. At least he would've flown across the room, had his feet not snagged in his trousers and brought him tumbling to the *deck, spoof going everywhere.*

Only then did we laugh and, oh, Christ, I tell ya, oxygen debt and stomach cramps very nearly killed the pair of us.

Several minutes later Lefty tearfully swore us both to secrecy, an oath we took with mentally crossed fingers, thirty-odd punters learning of the incident before night-fall.

As if one of them has loosed a lager-bomb, a moan of collective distaste goes up from the ladies.

Someone, muttering: 'You dirty bastard.'

Face set, Lefty stares out his window, sucking on a durrie like a man intent on emphysema before the week's out.

Times like this I almost feel sorry for him.

Almost.

I guess it seems strange, the three of us hanging with the dude when we so obviously loathe him. But I'm sure he's not the first person in the world to remain part of a group that they weren't really wanted in. That Mick and myself have kicked around with Lefty since Form One — a few years before Lefty reached the conclusion that when god filched one of Adam's ribs, his goal was in fact the creation of Lefty's personal harem — no doubt has much to do with it. As well as that, as I've said, the guy's mastered the art of parasitism to the extent that, should ever need arise, I'd back him on worming his way into the affections of Beelzebub.

And yes, let's have a moment of candour: we also keep Lefty on for crumb-feeding reasons: the old 'trickle-down effect'.

Mick, to the ladies: 'Anyway, we'd better go and do the deed.'

Amanda: 'Yeah, cool. We're a bit dodgy about driving in the ghetto at night, so we might just meetcha's back here.'

Mick: 'Sorted. Seeya's soon.'

Alice, passing me a wad of cash, which I hand on to Barry for counting: 'Later, Gator.'

From my newly realised 'legend' status, as we pull away I find the nerve to drop her a suggestive wink.

Lefty, whining: 'What'd ya *do* that for, Barry?

Baz: '*Ah*, ya fucking deserved it, man. Old Gator had them on their knees and you greened out and tried to steal his thunder.'

Lefty, hollow: 'That's a lie.'

Mick: 'Whatever ya reckon, Lefty. I don't know what you're worried about, anyway: every cunt in town already knows ya got snapped having a onesome.'

'*They* didn't!'

Me: 'They do *now*.'

Tandem minus one: '*Hahahahaha*!'

Untenably left out, at this point Lefty actually cracks a half-smile himself. 'I guess it is pretty funny.'

Mick: 'Good onya, Lefty. That's what being a man's all about, mate: making mistakes and not caring.'

We turn into the ghetto proper, uttering the usual rites.

Baz: 'Fuck me, someone's left the gates unlocked after curfew.'

Me: 'Ya might wanna edge her up a few clicks, Mick: at this speed they'll have the wheels off before you've even seen 'em.'

Lefty, grave, betrayal apparently forgotten: 'We are entering a zone of rampant uncleanness. Passengers are advised to secure all windows and doors.'

Functioning streetlights are few and far between in this part of town — too tempting a target for kids with no hopes — and darkness cloaks the ghetto. Some nights you could almost mistake it for just another suburb.

Until you pass a house where an after-pub party is in full swing, spilling out the front doors. Groups clustered about guitarists, singing for all they're worth — *jingjajing ajingjajinga-jinging* — inhibitions banished by Mr Brownstone, united for once, thrilling with the only real solidarity they ever seem to capture, one that lives no longer than the strings on the gat. Toughs eyeing one another off; toughs embracing with the tearful remorse of the very drunk. Painted women squealing and cackling, nursing broken faces, pathetic creatures beaten to this wheel since time forgotten. Shattered bottles glinting on the road. Grubby kids sitting or sleeping on the footpath, waiting on parents who won't surface until sun-up or later.

Just anuva Friday in the gheddo, bro. See yu fullas 'ere next Thursday. Oh, an' Satday, tu. Maybe even Sunday if we got any pingas left. Not Monday or Tuesday, though: be wading faw my dole. Just bread and budda faw the kids till Wensday. Then we orf again. Cherrrrr, bro!

Mick: 'Which way, Lefty?'

'Take the next left.'

'What number?'

'86.'

We see the vehicles well before the address, all of us hoping it's coincidence. No such luck. 86 is '*packt*'. Mick squeezes into a space within the row of cars, most of them suped Holdens, Falcoons, Valigrunts — *The 'Dan* fits in a treat.

A mini party is taking place on the front lawn, within the ring of cars parked on it, making it difficult to size up individuals. It seems, though, that both sides of the divided state house are equally full: all the lights are on behind taped and cardboarded windows, both doorsteps jammed.

Barry: 'We sure picked a *top* night to visit this place.'

Mick's the first to perceive the gathering's true colours — green and white. Dismayed: '*Oh*, for *fuck*'s sake!'

Lefty: 'What's the matter?'

'See that gorilla on the lawn, the one between the ute and the EA Commodore?'

We all pick him out.

'Wait till he turns round, then read the back of his leather.'

As it happens a chill grips my bowels. On the rear of the jacket is a picture. An emblem.

A *patch*.

The head of a rat, its snout too long — obscenely long — stubbled, toothy, smirking. It wears an infantry helmet, cocked at a rakish angle, and in the background, behind the creature, a dappled smear suggests an army at its back, tearing to gleeful battle.

We've all seen the patch before — on TV and closer — this

nationwide symbol of fear and violent crime. The words encircling this specimen are thus wasted on me, but I read them anyway, glutton that I am. THE RABBLE — VEGAS CHAPTER.

Given the vital clue, our eyes of a sudden identify Rabble paraphernalia everywhere: more patches scattered about, green bandannas, jerseys, beanies, cut-off gloves, a Rat flag replacing a broken window.

Me, quietly: 'Lefty, my boy, thanks to you, somewhere in this world a village is without its idiot.'

His reply is equally hushed, as though we fear drawing attention — as indeed we do. 'How was I to know the cunt lived in a fucking Rabble house?'

Barry: 'How well do you know him?' Dude could be at the flicks for all the consternation he betrays.

Lefty: 'He roots my cousin Melissa sometimes. We've toked together a bit, round at her crib, and he said whenever I needed Freds just to cruise round here. He said they weren't his, but that the fulla he lived with, the one shifting them, was desperate for the bucks and keen to up his clientele. I could tell he was a tough cunt, but I'd *never*'ve suspected he was Rabble.'

Barry: 'He's not patched then?'

'If he is, I've never seen him wearing it . . . and Melissa's never said anything.'

'Must be a prospect. Wouldn't live in a Rabble house otherwise. How old is he?'

Lefty: 'Twenty-five-odd.'

Barry: 'Fits, I guess.'

Me, sighing: 'Ah, well, at least we won't die wondering.'

Barry: 'Meaning?'

'Well, the score's obviously off, isn't it?'

Barry: 'Like fuck. I practically gave my *word* to those chicks, and Lefty *did* give his to me. We can't let them down now: you know how suckful it is when you're all primed to do some A-class and the contact goes and bums out on ya.'

I'm left a little astounded by this. 'Well, yeah, subjecting someone to that's a pretty tough thing to have on ya conscience, but when ya wake up in an IC ward with a drip in ya arm and a tube up ya cock, I'm guessing it begins to seem a little like the lesser of a few evils.'

Barry, dismissive: '*Nah*, he'll be right. He's got a well-connected bro in there, and they're gagging for the business. He can close the deal and shoot straight out, no dramas.'

Me, dubious: 'You wouldn't seriously send him in there, would you?'

Barry, incredulous: 'Course I would! He *knows* one of the pricks! You know what these Rangis are like: in with one, in with 'em all.'

'Yeah, maybe in a room with about five of them strumming on a six-string. But this is a *gang party*, man. Assuming he can stay alive long enough to even *locate* his man, it only takes one person with a slightly badder rep to decide Lefty's trespassing, up and give him some lip, and ten of them are gonna play Let's Kick White Boy Till He's Shitting Organs just for a fucking *laugh*.'

Barry, scoffing: 'You're over-reacting.'

Lefty's pretending to be half asleep. He wants in there about as much as he wants to donate his pork sword to medical science, and he knows I've far more clout with Barry than he'll ever have.

I clap Mick on the shoulder. 'What, are you a silent partner in this?'

Mick, shrugging: '. . . I dunno. I'd love a Freddy, and if Lefty's got a good contact . . . '

Lefty: 'Well, I hardly know the guy, really. He might not . . . '

Barry, rounding on him suddenly: 'Shut the fuck up and get *in* there, Lefty! You gave me your word, and if you don't at least give it a shot, you're getting out of the car right here and walking home — you've got my "guarantee" on it.'

At this time of night Lefty's got about as much chance of escaping the ghetto on foot as . . . as he has of scoring A-class from a Rabble house.

Lefty may not feature highly on my Chrissie card list, but leaving him to *this* is out of the question. 'Fuck, you can be an unreasonable cunt, Barry. If he walks from here, I'm walking with him.'

Barry, to me, not far off a shout: 'Why do you always have to *pull* this shit? Who the fuck died and appointed you every cunt's guardian angel anyway?'

Before I can reply, Lefty, who it seems hasn't a huge degree of confidence in my ability to sail him from these straits, suddenly glimpses salvation. 'Fuck, there he *is*! I can *see* him! Give me the money *now*!'

Barry hands over the notes quick smart, and Lefty's gone.

At the edge of the overgrown lawn he hesitates, face to face with the plunge. He glances back at the car, once, and I can almost hear the gulp as he commits, stepping gingerly toward a knot of drinkers, feet embracing the grass as though it holds land-mines. I watch their backs go up as they grow aware of him, patented scowls quickly donned, and then he holds his hand out to one of them. It's shaken, but with tangible reluctance.

Drifting away, the pair talk for a couple of minutes, recipients of pointed stares.

I kill the remains of a beer can, crush it, crack open another, my last.

Lefty jogs back to us, head bowed to Mick's open window. He wears a shaky smile. 'It's sweet . . . but he wants us to go inside. He reckons the guy dealing them needs cash chronically and will wanna see all our faces so he can give us all the go-ahead to come back and score whenever. He's trying to build his customer base.'

Barry, voltage thrumming, 'What do ya's reckon?'

Mick, to Lefty: 'Can't ya just say we're in a rush and have him bring them out?'

'I tried, but no go. From what I can guess, this dealer's pretty high up. Joe wants to use us to earn some brownie points.'

A building sense of challenge — almost a slide into despair — shouts that any chance of staying out of this is eluding me rapidly.

Lefty, banging in more nails: 'He *guaranteed* we'd be sweet in there.'

With Barry staring at me, I can think of no pertinent artifice, and, with booze in my veins and Lefty painting so rosy a picture, straight chickening out has ceased to be an option. But I'm certain Mick's not up for this either. In the hopes of his ingenuity outweighing my own, I throw it over to him. 'What do you reckon, Mick?'

But, eventually, he draws a blank as well. '. . . I dunno.'

Barry, caustic: 'Ahhh, will you two stop pussyfooting! We've got an escort into the joint, the dealer's a big cheese and he's gagging for our custom! What could go wrong?'

My gut knew it was coming anyway: I'm mentally ready. Resigned. '. . . Let's do it, then.'

The gods of peer pressure chuckled.

On reflex, Barry slips out of his leather jacket, hiding it under the seat. We all do the same with our collars, dusting off the black T-shirts beneath. I drain my can in one hit, ditching the empty, wishing for once in my life that'd I'd bought Waikato.

As we lock doors Barry's practically bouncing. Mick and I exchange a long stare.

Start across the road.

Barry, level and pumped: 'No stress, dudes. In and out assignment. Christ knows we could all use a regular acid contact anyway.'

Joe meets us at the lawn, shakes all our hands. No taller than me, and just as skinny, he contrives to seem benign despite the ragged black clothes, the green Rat's scarf around his thigh, the beanie pulled down close. 'Yeah, yeah, yeah, yu fullas gotta meet Charlie, eh, then yu's can come back an' score whenever.' But his eyes hold a nervous twitch, and — brownie points or not — I have to wonder how much face Joe stands to lose by traipsing through the party with four 'ballheads' in tow.

Mick: 'Yu sure this is sweet, bro?' unconsciously, he's adopted the gutter Maori cadence one is well advised to use when trying for ingratiation with them.

Joe, a little too blasé: '*Yeah*, bro. Yu's wif *me* now. Just stay close.'

At least he's calling us 'bro'. When addressed by one of these guys, so long as he refers to you as 'bro', you can rest assured you're in his good books. On the other hand, if he starts calling you 'beau', initiate a salvage rapidly.

As he leads us toward the door, as the revellers grow aware of our presence, I don my practised 'An *ego*? *Me*? You've *gotta* be kidding' face — expression completely clear, eyes wide, a little overwhelmed, infinitely approachable.

Few patched members out here, numbers made up mostly by associates and prospects.

This is what becomes of those homies who graduate, those for whom the dream of gang life isn't tarnished by brushes with the law, by an overload of violence: a baptism of years terrorising streets, rumbling every weekend, hunted by untold enemies, running when the odds don't suit — sometimes not being fast enough — stealing and mugging, gaining personal recognition from oinkers. Years of this tend to sort the men from the boys, whittle chaff from the hardcore.

Darwinism in accelerated, perverted microcosm.

The guys surrounding us now — silent of a sudden, begging us to make eye contact — represent the distilled essence of the venom strutting our city streets of a weekend evening. Though no less vicious for it, these dudes have survived the life's first stages; had their doubts and fears eroded by incessant conflict. Unlike most of their adolescent apprentices, running amok even as I speak, these young men have found belief in their strength as individuals. They've fought outside the pack, forged their 'talents', their 'staunchness' in the crucible of victory and loss. If there are points involved, these cunts will *take* a beating almost as soon as dish one out.

This, of course, makes them *so* much more dangerous.

Thanks to their being accepted into this outer circle of gangsterism, thanks to their moving on to bigger and badder things — the initial perpetuation of a life of serious crime — these young tigers — guys who've grown too big and mean to find much thrill on the streets — move on, drift away from that segment of the circle which interlaps our own. Drugs aside, the realms of adult Maori crims are an ocean from ours, and as such they all but cease to exist for us. It's thus easy to forget that the thugs we've dealt with throughout our teenage lives don't all tire of the life and grow consciences.

Some just get harder.

And though at this stage the wars they wage with their own kind intensify to the point where there's no longer much occasion to target us ballheads, though they begin to look upon Pakeha as little more than a handy source of revenue — drugs, burglary, car conversion, 'guvmint benafits' — they haven't actually forgiven us for whatever it was that drew their antagonism in the early days.

A practical lesson I'm given now with hideous surreality.

Picking my way through their midst, an arctic python settles round my chest. Squeezes.

If I wasn't pissed instinct would be too loud: I'd abort, guaranteed, right here, right now. Sober as he is, I've no idea how Mick makes his legs push him steadily deeper.

And deeper.

Joe, to his peers: 'It's all right, yu fullas. Charlie wants t'see 'em.'

A few hackles go down, but not enough for comfort.

And then one of them steps from the pack, moves into our paths.

Though mean of face, he's better looking than most. About my age. Strong features, Asiatic eyes, six foot something and a hundred-odd kilos of loose-forward muscle. Neat dreadlocks frame his face, a few Rasta beads worked into one of them. He's got style, too. Unlike the ragged woollens and denim around him, he wears a nice white shirt, pressed blue jeans, tan shoes.

He's the type of Maori who leaves white women in need of fresh panties.

In our path, the force of the guy's presence brings our party to a halt.

Joe, repeating rather tentatively: 'They OK, bro.'

The warrior ignores him, brushes past cavalierly, and, as the distance closes, his scowl's directed at none but me.

Lefty and Mick step subtly away from me; I feel Barry tense his fist.

But the warrior's too quick for him. In a split-second he's onto me, throwing his arms around my neck in a feral bear-hug. A brilliant grin lights his face. 'What the *fuck* are *yu* doing 'ere, Gatey?'

I hug him back for all I'm worth, and not through relief, or to impress anyone around me. I hug him back for no other reason than that this guy was once my best friend in all the world and I haven't seen him in years.

'*Steve*, man!' Grinning like a split watermelon. 'Long time no *see*, cuz!'

Like sorcery, the enmity drowning us lifts, and, confused frowns aside, the prospects return to their conversations.

It's funny: I don't recall ever hugging any of my white mates. Sure, when pissed up we do the old arm and shoulder thing, but a full-on embrace? Forget about it. I'm not even sure when last I hugged any of my male *family* members. Yet whenever I'm out on the juice and run into the old Maori bros, the first instinct is to embrace. Handshakes come later.

Why the fuck is that?

Steve lets me go with one arm, holding me close with the other. 'This is the *last* place I thought I'd ever see *yu*!'

Me, beaming: 'Where *you* been hiding, bro?'

'Oh, here and there, Gatey. Was working in the bush down Wairarapa way faw 'bout a year or so. Then I went back t'tha island wif Mum faw a few months. Now I'm out at Tok', working in the sawmill.'

We fall into giggles, trading mock punches.

On my first day at the programming plant, Steve was already ensconced as a playground legend. A five-year-old hit-man, a figure none of the older kids even seemed to fuck with. Rugby and bullrush at lunchtimes consisted of Steve versus all those mad enough to go against him.

A shy little pale-face among eighty per cent Maori, for months I stood in awe of Steve, maintained a prudent distance. Until one day, walking by a building, he'd happened to come barrelling round the corner at full speed, sending me tumbling like a doll before a freight train.

Hurt like *fuck*.

Now in those days — even more so than these — I was no Captain Courageous, but a good dose of inflicted pain serves to subvert fear and deference like nothing else. So with Steve looming over me, I'd bounced back up, tears mingling with blood from a graze.

Steve, imperious: 'Watch where yaw going next time, honky.'

I married a couple of phrases I'd overheard from someone, thought sounded pretty cool.

'Get fucked, you black cunt.'

I watched Steve reel with shock . . . and then his eyes had narrowed perilously. We stared off for a good ten seconds — it was a bright day and I remember studying my reflection in his eyes — and as the immediate pain faded I found myself in large regret of those words, whatever they meant.

I didn't let it show, though. And neither did I look away. Not once. Had I, and things would have gone differently, of that I'm convinced.

A small crowd developed around us, and some of the advice on offer helped steel me.

'*Waste* 'im, Steve!'

'Yeah, give 'im the bash, Steve. Honkies can't fight!'

Then a teacher happened along — as they do — mercifully taking me to have my wounds dressed.

The next day, though, as the lunch-bell rang and I left my classroom alone — as usual — Steve was waiting for me. He threw me his rugby ball — which I somehow caught — demanding: 'Played much rugby, honky?'

Lying through my teeth: 'Yep.'

'Let's go, then. There's a big match on today and yaw on my team.'

66

That was that. Brothers through the lean and the fat.

Countless sagas on the playing fields; photo-finish at athletics day; school camps and day trips; carnal stirrings; Steve delivering me from older boy rancour, time and again; a team of Maoris and me scooping the regional cricket comp, to the silent disgust of rich district pussies; weekends and evenings at one another's houses; endless adventures; on together to intermediate and high school; first *real* girlfriends; sharing the wondrous decadence of a cigarette; parties and drinking; adjacent seats at exams, passing him answers when rep footy kept him from study. Other mates coming and going, but Steve always there, like bedrock.

And then one day his dad was killed in a forestry accident and Steve just disappeared.

Through the grapevine I found out later that the death had shaken him badly, that he had started running with dodgy older cousins, hitting the bottle like tomorrow wasn't coming, busting too many heads.

Because though he was hard as nails when the need arose, Steve was like most Maoris raised on love: he had a heart of fucking gold. In school Steve had just as much time for the ugliest, wimpiest, shiest kid in class as he did for the hottest babe. He coaxed the best from those around him, jesting and laughing all day, and by Standard One, Steve was loved by all. So long as he emerged intact from teenagehood, Steve was fated to live a good life, with good jobs, raise a good family.

But the need to prove themselves — perhaps a siren song from that warrior tradition — leaves a lot of Maoris like Steve vulnerable to derailment by delinquent peers. The shock of losing his dad evidently made Steve an even juicier target because by all reports he lost the plot big time.

Maybe shame was the reason he never contacted me. Or maybe he blamed Pakeha forestry big-wigs for skimping on the safety budget.

In any case, I heard that his mum made a salvage, dragging him off to live near his father's marae on Matakana Island, straightening him out with doses of culture and ruralness.

But now I find him at a Rabble house.

Dropping my voice: 'Are you prospecting, man?'

His look fills me with deja vu — *Puh-leeease*. '*Naaa*, man. Just in town t'see tha old lady. Got back from the clubs and I wanted some dak, so I shot round 'ere. Cousin's patched up and 'e's *always* got blows.'

I introduce him to the crew. Steve knows Mick and Lefty pretty well anyway: we all did a year's programming together in Form Two. Barry he immediately picks as a scrapper and the handshake is icy.

Steve, mystified: 'Why are yu's here, anyway?'

Me: 'Scoring some acid. The dude selling it wants to see all our faces so any of us can come back alone.'

Startled: 'Yaw going *inside*?'

'Ahhhhh, think so.'

Joe's been waiting patiently. 'She's sweet, bro. They wif me.'

Steve throws him a frown — *and your point is . . .?*

Joe, reassuring: '*Naaaa*, bro. No one'll give a fuck. I was *ordered* t' spread the word and bring new scorers in.'

Weighing it for seconds, Steve eventually shrugs. 'Might as well do it, then.' He beckons us in close, muttering: 'Yu guys noe the drill, but amp it up a few knots — piss these guys orf in their own pad and they'll swallow yu's whole, guaranteed. Don't look any of 'em in tha eye, or say *any*thing to *any* cunt, unless yu shaw they speaking t'yu first. Then yu say whatever's gonna make 'em happy. If it ain't workin', wait faw me or Joe t'rescue yu.'

With Steve's presence, I'm able to press on with a semblance of aplomb. He's the single person on this Earth behind whom I'd walk to hell and further.

So I do.

Through the front door. The smell hits me before anything else — body odour, stale beer and urine, weed and ciggie smoke, dog-hair . . .

Marley wailing.

Yeah, Bob, whatever ya reckon.

With sledgehammers and tools equally subtle, the divided dwelling has been united, a huge arch smashed in the wall, leaving the 'living room' the size of a small hall. The carpet may once have been blue but is stained and burnt beyond recognition. Curtains mere army-issue blankets nailed to walls. In place of wallpaper, banners of martial arts stars and boxers, enormous dope symbols, centrefold sluts — even the odd black one. On the ceiling a Rat banner takes pride of place.

The light is reddish and low; smoky haze thins it further.

Embracing the smog like a nurse through mustard gas.

And within their palace the mighty hold court. Lounging on decrepit furniture, slouching against walls. Super-predators basking at the peak of a vile food-chain. This is what remains when the final crumbs of softness and virtue are pounded and baked from the ranks of the prospects.

Concentrated machismo.

It's warm in here, but patched leather abounds; Jesus, the depravities endured to earn it, they probably shower and *fuck* with the things on. Like lions over productive prides, the patch is their mane, the fat theirs by right, sloth an instinct.

Bullying pure survival.

If intimidation has a face, I'm in its presence. Wild afros, filthy dreads, shaven heads. Facial tattooing amplifying the image: skulls, axes, profanity — nothing tribal here.

Oh, no.

Their lifestyles spit in the face of their heritage; tradition and history reject them utterly. The one force that may have reversed their upbringings, offered redemption, they chose to shit on gleefully.

Associates and molls wait on their betters, fawning, laughing when proper, massaging egos with hard-learned strokes.

Incredulous, one of the larger individuals stands, points us out, hollering for everyone: 'What the *fuck*'ve we got '*ere*?'

Mossies in a redback burrow.

Joe, all but tugging a forelock: 'It's OK, Tapeka. Charlie wants t' see 'em.'

Theatrically dubious: '*Oh*, 'e *does*, does 'e? Charlie told yu t' bring a buncha *bawl'eads* fru 'ere while we 'aving us a rage?'

Joe, cringing: 'Well, 'e said this to me 'bout two weeks ago, an' I've bought a few fullas fru t'meet 'im since, sum of 'em bawl'eads tu.'

Another patch joins Tapeka, this one smoother and shorter. Black hair slicked back, compact as a kauri stump. Under a patched vest his arms are lumped in muscle enough to punch a man's head clean off; hands tattooed in chain-mail gauntlets.

Even among this hierarchy he shines as something of a leader: the authority of the proven headcase guards his personal space like a moat. Aloof: 'Yu and these clowns beda 'ope yaw fuckin' right, Joe.' Unlike the prospects, none of these fully fledged Rats bother scowling any more; with the aura they've cultivated, a sneer is more artfully ominous, *Il Duce* style. 'Else there's gonna be sum 'eads kicked in *real* soon.'

An expectant sigh caresses the gathering.

For me one of the most frightening aspects of these people is their very roguishness. When hearing or reading of them, it's comforting to picture a pack of shambling Neanderthals with the intelligence quotient of dung beetles; drug- and booze-addled troglodytes whom one might outwit or outrun with ease. But this is the case only rarely. Some of them are attractive to look at. Some have wit and flair; charm, you would have to say. Some have what approximates to intelligence.

And they all possess an animal cunning more developed by far than many of society's 'success' stories: an artfulness to see you ambushed and fed upon should you make the mistake of overlooking it.

Add to this the depth of the foundations the Fiendish Beast has sunk into their souls, and you've raw material Heinrich Himmler may have found fleeting use for.

Steve speaks up, deferring by virtue of turf only: 'Ne'mine these fullas, Hemi. I've known 'em faw years. They sweet as. They got no love'a the pigs.' His eyes pick out a few of the lesser beasts. 'Anyone noe where Charlie is?'

Hemi, placated by a whisker: "E's upstairs rootin' sum pig. Go up an' tell 'im what's hap'neen, Joe.' The prospect scrambles to obey. 'In the meantime, yu's wait ova there, and doan touch nufing . . . or else.' His eyes indicate an empty corner, which we obligingly occupy.

Every foot further from the door twists my dread dial viciously.

We effect ignorance of the eyes canvassing us, engage in some halting small-talk, cosy as nuns in a knock-shop. Steve saunters across to a crate of Waikato big bottles, helping himself, uncapping it with his teeth. No one seems to mind, some patch waylaying him with a joint and a question of the well-being of some cousin or other.

The party stutters back into life and, to my surprise, nothing dreadful takes place for a whole hour (all five minutes of it).

And then Hemi swaggers across to us.

Barry alone stands tall in the teeth of the gangster's force-field.

Singling him out — no doubt because of this — brandishing a joint the size of a cudgel, Hemi smirks a challenge. 'Shotie, beau.' It's not a question.

Barry: 'Cher.'

Hemi, to his audience: '*Ouuuuu*, this fulla might *look* like a bawl'ead, but 'e's got a Maori *tongue*.'

Chorus, on loud cue: '*Huhuhuhuhuhu!*'

Disguising the act, Barry draws a deep steadying breath, bracing his insides for a battering as Hemi reverses the mammoth doobie, maw spread wide, thrusting the joint into his mouth, ember first, sealing it with his lips.

There's something implicitly sensual about shoties. Ordinarily, even men who are close will seldom in their lives find reason or wish to occupy each's facial space — unless, of course, they happen to be shirt-lifters. Yet the default solidarity shared between stoners often sees even the most macho of *strangers* trading their very breath without an eyelid batted.

Hemi begins blowing, Barry stooping to catch the smoke.

And unless the blower's of clement disposition, taking shotguns from *standard* joints is rigorous enough. Accepting one off a doobie *this* size, from some arsehole hoping to embarrass you . . .

But Barry works it skilfully, inhaling a little faster than maximum stoneage dictates, half air, half smoke, yet not so blatant as to cop out: there's not an eye in the room unglued to the scene.

Hitting the high-air mark, Barry backs off, nodding gratitude to Hemi quite convincingly.

Then, for the barest second, as he moves down the line, Hemi's eyebrows raise in grudging respect.

Though he clearly struggles for the will to remain still — avoiding Hemi's stare as though it's Medusa's — Mick takes his shotie like a man also, unable to stave off a snorted cough or two towards the finish, but swallowing the fit that wants to savage him.

Lefty, however, decides to make a point, pacing his intake to suck pure smoke . . .

. . . and starts to splutter at the halfway line, jerking away as if stung.

Silently, I implore him: *Hold it down, ya useless prick!*

But, as if to spite me, Lefty erupts, loosing a broadside of coughing that mauls him for a good five seconds.

Half the room cackle their delight at his failure. The patches, though, are way too cool for that shit, content with sneering grins.

All *we* can do is leer our own contempt of the cunt, but I feel Barry seething like static.

My number comes up, and by his disdainful smirk Hemi expects a quick wicket. As the distance between us narrows to inches, he stares through me blankly, as if at a witness behind the line-up screen: it's like sharing a wardrobe with a peckish anaconda.

But I know what I've got to do: my precursor dismissed for a duck, I have to put quick runs on the board, smash the bowler from the attack, take the match with an over to spare. Even though, with the amount of piss I've consumed tonight, weed's the *last* thing my system needs.

Ironic how almost any doper will gladly deliver a sermon on the evils of toking when shit-faced: a sure recipe for a four-hour stint at the wheel of the porcelain bus. Once juiced, though — the immortality factor well and truly in residence — most tend to disregard lessons learned with a bit of the old 'She'll be right'.

I've every belief that the gear in this abomination is primo — one shotie from it enough to blow my lights for hours — but I resolve to face that music when the maestro arrives.

What choice have I anyway?

Hemi aims the thick stream at my face and I begin nice and easy, inhaling only hard enough to capture all the smoke, confident — for an asthmatic smoker, you see, I've a set of lungs like a Micronesian pearl-diver. Half full, I drop my *nose* to the stream, blocking a nostril, inhaling smoke through the other. Then I swap nostrils. Then swap again. And again.

I feel the bowler angering, throwing it out harder, narrowing his cheeks in an effort to concentrate the output, a ploy referred to as a 'step-up', an ambush a seasoned campaigner like myself should never fall victim to. I don't, proceeding with calm ease, switching back to standard inhalation with a triumphant last suck that fills me to capacity.

Closing my eyes, I stand erect, chest puffed like a bantam rooster. I feel the room hanging on the sight of me, imploring the white boy to cough (*I doan even noe if I cood do that!*) and satisfaction bleeds across my face. I count slowly to five and, very deliberately, unleash a cloud to make an oil-fire wince, sending no fewer than three perfect smoke-rings wafting toward the ceiling.

I nod thanks to the bowler, a show that fools no one but must always be maintained.

He struts away, ostensibly apathetic.

And the hostility around us eases some. (*Faw a bawl'ead this fulla can smoke, bro! No way on earf that cunt's a nark.*) The

73

music seems to get louder, conversation takes off, laughter erupts of which we are clearly no font.

It seems the snow wolf has won for his pack a degree of rodent acceptance.

Barry, sidling in close to me, grin kept casual, barely: 'Did I ever tell you that you're nothing less than the Messiah reborn?'

I drop him a wink. 'Habitually.'

Across the room Steve slips me a subtle thumbs up, and, waiting for Joe to reappear, we settle in almost comfortably.

Me: 'Wish I had a fucking beer.'

Barry: 'Seconded.'

Lefty: 'Why don't I go out the car and get a couple?'

Mick: 'Because you won't come back.'

Lefty, wronged: '*Yeah*, I will! Why do ya say I won't?'

Mick launches a prosecution of his argument, recapping some of the many instances when Lefty has indeed gone AWOL from dubious settings, but at this point my attention is snagged by the sight of a girl entering the room from an area that may occasionally pose as a kitchen. In black jeans, a tight red T-shirt that highlights her firm tits well, her prettyish face — even behind garish layers of make-up — seems familiar. Short and slim, she's quite pale for a Maori, and when her eyes meet mine I place her instantly.

Me, mouthing: *Vicki.*

Vicki, stunned: *Gator?*

She looks around sharply, as if expecting somehow to find herself in the wrong house. *Gangsters, arse-lickers, molls. No,* I'm *in the right place. Can't say the same for* you, *though.*

Again she looks the room over, this time in more pragmatic fashion, and seems to arrive at a decision, walking slowly across to me. She's weaving a little, but, as pissed as she might be, when she arrives Vicki's careful not to stand too close, arms folded across her chest like a barrier.

As she speaks, even her face and voice are mindful of showing none but the most cursory interest. 'What are *yu* doing 'ere?'

74

'Scoring. Long time no see.'

'I *reckon*.' A grin tries to grab her, but she throttles it. ''Ow long's it been?'

Quickly calculating: 'Six years, I guess.'

I can feel noxious attention spreading to me again, and I know I'm treading thin ice. But what can I do? I can't just send her away. Besides, I don't want to: we were good friends once, Vicki and I. Even so, my body language, like hers, becomes an epitome of non-flirtation. 'Do you come here much?'

Vicki, nodding: 'I starded going out wif Hemi a coupla years back, 'anging out wif all these fullas and that. When we split up I . . . I saw a coupla tha others faw a while. Now they're my family, really.' She smiles at this, but its heart seems vacant, her eyes duller than I remember.

I'm guessing the Fiend's been visiting my Vicki. How can I doubt it if she's running with these mongrels?

Not that god had cut her much slack from the outset.

We'd become friends early in primary school, the roots of our bond in intellectualism. Just two bright kids working together on special projects, something to 'stretch your minds beyond the curriculum'. That's all it takes: specious chalk and cheese given alibi for bridging rifts, discovering that, essentially, there is no more shallow a yardstick than palpable distinction — hue, sexual equipment, parental bank balance. Fuck, it happens with kids often, happens any place in the world where contrary elements are merged without bias.

And then we gain 'maturity', inherit the toils of our forebears.

We used to discuss all manner of things, share each other's dreams. Vicki had an older sister who used to read to her, take her to the library. Sometimes I'd go along with them, walking the six k's gladly, the three of us laughing all the way.

But Vicki had a mother she scarcely knew: a mother who drank all night, slept all day.

She also had a father whose idea of discipline was a clenched fist.

She wanted to be a biologist, had the brains and the will for it too.

75

Yet by Form Two the spark had been murdered, the black eyes occurring so often that Vicki lost the will to face school; slipped into the murk.

'So what are *yu* doing wif yawself these days?'

'I'm in the Craft of Arch-Treason.'

She *does* laugh at that, and for an instant I see the woman she should have grown into. 'Same old Gator. 'Ave yu seen Steve?'

'Yeah. Surprised me as much as seeing you.'

He comes over and for a while we all shoot the shit, reliving the high times, the days when what really matters is who you are beneath it.

The shotgun I nailed takes hold in earnest, mingling with the booze, swiss-cheesing my brain. My voice soon sounds miles distant, the volume of the room ebbing and sighing. The reflectiveness of dope, overconfidence and distortion of alcohol, clash violently, conjuring absurd thoughts, visions which nevertheless at times hold lurid insights. My body begins to tingle and buzz in time with the room's throbbing ambience, my companions evoking in me a nostalgia of excruciating sweetness.

The conglomerate effect is stunning, something more akin to an A-class substance than a bit of pot and liquid from the corner wholesaler's. On the rare occasions I'm silly enough to mix the two these days, this early stage of the buzz is fucking fantastic, a kosh-like trip not wholly dissimilar to the rougher strands of acid.

And the intensity of it just builds.

And builds.

Until, within an hour, the sensation reaches the point where, eyes open or closed, the world can no longer be kept from performing its dreaded merry-go-round enactment.

Then comes laughter of the liquid variety.

And not a good solid up-chuck either, to leave you feeling miraculously better. We're talking gut-cramping retches for bile and dribble and less. Choking, hawking, spluttering on hydrochloric acid, wishing for death and swearing all manner of priestly resolution, often until morning.

But for the moment 'she'll be right'.

It seems that Hemi's been cooking. He works the room, flourishing a huge iron frying-pan filled with mussels, boiled just enough to open the shells. The smell alone floods my mouth with juices, though in this condition I'm less capable of eating than I am of captaining an aircraft carrier. Theatrically magnanimous, Hemi shares his treasures among the exalted few, pointedly ignoring the rejecteds' wet lips.

Charlie eventually materialises. He commits our faces to memory, giving each of us a nod: a key to psychedelia.

Charlie, to Barry: ''Ow many yu's want, then?'

'Seven.'

'*Seven*?'

'Yeah. We're sorting out a few friends as well.'

'Bring 'em round next time. So long as they sweet. Doan want no soft-cocks, fullas 'u might squeal if they get busted.' Even without the sudden eyes, the threat is plain.

Barry, casually counting out cash: 'Na, these ones are chicks. I don't know too many chicks I'd give dealer contacts to.'

Charlie, handing over seven small objects, as innocuous in appearance as scaled-down postage stamps: 'Yeah? Good. Mine dew, wooden mine sum *white* pussy faw a change.' His gapped grin could repulse a sex offender. 'Bring 'em round anyway. We'll put 'em on the block. Yu can go larst.'

'*Huhuhuhuhuu.*'

Tapeka, eyes lighting: 'Speaking'a that, u's turn is it tonide, anyway?'

Hemi: 'I doan 'member, bro.' Chin high, he casts a lordly gaze about the room, and I feel a strange tingle grip it. Some seem suddenly aroused, others wary.

Making a show of things, relishing every second, Hemi's gaze falls finally on Vicki beside me. 'It's *yaw* turn, innit?'

A flash of dismay twists her face, and she shoots me a look I interpret as a plea for help, or a wish I were miles away. Her eyes then beg the gangster. '*No* it *ain't*! I went *last* Friday, '*member*?'

Deliberation purses Hemi's fat lips for a good few seconds, the gallery hanging on his response. At last, implacable: 'Na, doan 'member that. And even if I did, if I say it's yaw turn, then it's *yaw — fuckin' — turn*.'

To myself I try to deny what's been set in motion. But the relish on the faces of the patches, the sympathy and relief — even some jealousy — on the faces of the molls, sniggers at the attempt. I've heard about these gang 'blockings', and as I watch the strength leave Vicki's posture, the realisation of what is soon to happen to her hits me like an upper-cut.

They're gonna strip her naked, spread her wide, and take turns fucking her. My Vicki, the quiet, smiling whizzkid, who should have worked with animals, is about to be violated by upwards of twenty thuggish villains, many of whose dirty black cocks no doubt retain forensic traces of her from the Friday before.

A single tear snakes down Vicki's cheek, and then, with a grimacing spasm, head bowing, a dull acceptance seems to claim her.

Steve catches my attention, nods toward the door, and, the deal done, I feel my compadres' equal eagerness for departure.

Still holding the frying pan — now filled with empty shells — Hemi informs the room: 'Same old story, boys: I'm first. Arfda that, yu's can do what the fuck yu's like. Let's go, bitch.' As animated haggling breaks out around us, Hemi saunters toward the kitchen . . . and its long undressed table.

Shuffling, Vicki moves to trail him.

Me, pitching it low: 'You don't have to do this, Vicki.'

She stops, turning to me, and I watch a flare of hope and trust go off in her eyes.

Then Hemi looks back, frying-pan in one hand, notices her lagging, notices the direction of her eyes. He strides over and, with a rough hand, spins her about, demanding: 'Whadid 'e sayda yu?'

Vicki, shrinking: 'Nothing. Let's go.'

She attempts to lead him away, but he grips her by the throat, hard, glaring over his nose. Mordantly surprised: 'I guess

yu didin' *'ear* me prop'ly! I wanna noe what this bawl'ead *said*.
Now if yu doan tell me whadit was, I'm gonna fuck you up yaw
arse . . . and make *alllll* the boys do the same. That's a promise,
bitch.'

True terror flays Vicki's eyes, and she instantly wheezes: ''E
said I didin' 'af t' do this!'

Forgetting her, Hemi fronts me with a look of mad relish that
turns my legs to foam. My disgusted horror for Vicki — my
awareness of her existence — evaporates in an icy deluge.

Steve, brusque: 'It's time I got these fullas outta 'ere anyway.
C'mon, Gator.'

A buoy in a heaving sea, I whirl towards him . . .

. . . as a grenade goes off near my ear, the floor rushing for me,
vision fading in rapid increments.

The last thing I perceive is an empty Rothmans packet, half
crushed and discarded, inflated to ten times its usual size.

PREGNANT WOMEN: SMOKING HARMS YOUR BABY

Though he spoke low, Mick heard what Gator told the girl —
'You don't have to do this, Vicki.' — and almost swooned with
surprise and dread.

Jesus fucking Christ, don't let her hear!

But the late JC wasn't listening: Vicki turned to Gator as if
Redemption were tattooed on his chest. Hemi turned a second
or two later, and the gist of what had happened seemed clear to
him.

Sense of ruin building, Mick looked to his fellows, barely
hearing Hemi accosting the moll. Lefty was a hair's breadth from
bolting; Barry watched developments with what might have
been fascination.

Mick, slapping Barry's shoulder: 'Let's get the fuck outta
here, *now*.'

And then things really turned to shit.

A snarling beam cleaving his face, Hemi swung the pan two-
handed, like Chris Cairns playing the pull shot, attempted to
smash Gator's head into row twelve of the southern stand.

Heart catching, Mick looses a squeal, something masked by Gator's almighty grunt, and time seems to slow: mussel shells wafting like leaves; the *dong* of iron on skull, lingering like church bells; canned fanfare sweeping the studio audience; Vicki's face frozen in stark dismay; Lefty strolling for the exit, knees pumping. Only Gator remains in real-time, collapsing like a scarecrow with its feet jerked away, blood welling from his skull with all the poise of a tiny spring Mick once encountered on a bush walk.

Survival kicking in, Mick spins for the door . . . to find it choked by wild-eyed prospects, charging in for investigation.

A stranger inside him speaks, for a second ignoring the appalling circumstances. *At least I won't have to shrink in shame whenever I look back on this.*

But this sense of helplessness in the face of savagery features high on Mick's list of primal dreads.

In a stroke, horror has him immobilised in its flawless suit of ice. Sound comes in waves, vision swimming at the edges. This is all the fear from Mick's every nightmare delivered in one berserk charge, the dope in his head making it all so *sensually* surreal.

In his life as a teenage party-goer, Mick has seen violence, some of it ugly. To his consternation, he's even been forced to fight once or twice. But, despite the fantasies he and Gator verbally enact, this current hand holds cards Mick has all his life prayed never to arrive.

This is capture by Gestapo, awaiting interrogation.

This is a runaway cotton nigger, bloodhounds yapping in background.

And Mick is brought face to face with the filthy creature at his core. A stinking pariah who would sprint on a path of newborns were it the only route from an inferno.

A wretch he hopes lives in everybody.

From *this* inferno, though, no such trail exists, and as the room fills around him, Mick feels his dick shrivel to a peanut, his jaw quivering like a Parkinson's sufferer's.

Steve, furious but in control: '*Fuck*, yaw an arsehole, Hemi!'

He kneels to Gator, but Hemi shoves him away. 'I ain't fuckin' done wif 'em yet, cuz. Not by a *longgggg* stretch. *Maoris* noe beda than t'mess in Rabble affairs; wait till yu see what 'appens when *bawl'eads* do it.' The gangster shrugs out of his vest, businesslike, handing it to an eager associate, a look of focus about him, a barber preparing a haircut.

Vicki, grabbing him, tears streaming, hysterical: 'It weren't 'is *fault*, Hemi! *Doan . . .* !'

Hemi, to a nagging blowfly: '*Fuck* off, bitch.' Almost absently, he sends her reeling with a short hook across the jaw.

A quick look passes between Steve and Barry.

Steve then throws an arm around Hemi, taking advantage of the manner with which Vicki has spun him from Gator, pulling him further around, voice wheedling but loud enough to snag attention. 'There's something you gotta *know* 'bout 'im, Hemi . . . !'

Smooth as spilled oil, Barry hoists Gator by the armpits and starts for the door, only then noticing how congested it is. Face declaring he seeks a toilet down which to flush his burden, he manages to cuff Mick across the ear, hard, denting his trance.

Barry, hissing: 'Find a way outta this fucking hovel!'

Instinctive logic takes over, leaving the answer suddenly simple. Very deliberately, Mick leads the way through the hole in the wall that links the split house . . . and there it is, just as his subconscious had told him.

The dwelling's mirror-image doorway, wide open and blissfully empty.

Shouts rise from behind.

Hemi: 'Bring 'im the *fuck* back 'ere! I'm not *done* wif . . . !'

Steve: '*Lissen* t' me, bro! 'Is old man's a *cop*: heada the Vegas drug squad! 'E'll be round 'ere *every day* if yu doan let it go! 'E's a . . . !'

Hemi, roaring: '*I* doan give a fuck if 'is old man's heada the whole bawl'ead *guvmint*! You fuckin' get outta my way *now*, Steve, or, cuzin or not, yu just as fuckin' dead as 'e is!'

Mick floats down the steps, Barry and a dragged Gator following hard. Fresh air tastes of distilled salvation; is too rich and sudden — Mick spews across the grass, barely breaking stride.

They've reached the middle of the lawn when a shout is relayed to the handful of prospects who remain outside. '*Stop the white cunts!*'

Mick runs. Finds himself hurled to ground effortlessly. Clutching Gator like a prize, Barry attempts to fight his way clear, one-handed, but, fists flying, two of them soon have him held.

Punters pour from the house, a ring encircling the thwarted escapees with horrifying rapidness.

Steve, muscling his way through, yelling into Barry's face: '*Fuck orf*, bawl'ead!' He shoves him violently toward the road, his manner confusing Barry's captors, who let him back away. Steve then rips Mick to his feet, holding him near.

Gator, though, beginning to mumble and clutch at his head, remains at black boots like an offering.

Steve to Mick, whispering: 'Wake yaw mate up an' tell 'im if 'e can't run in less than a minnit 'e's fucked.'

On autopilot, Mick kneels to Gator, just as Hemi arrives. '*Cher*! Now yaw *mine*, cunt!'

With a steel-capped toe, he kicks Gator's midsection with everything he's got.

Once . . .

. . . *twice*.

Agony mutilates Gator's face, vile gargling echoing like dodgy plumbing.

An unconscious moan crawls from Mick's lips. A cornered bird, his eyes dart from face to face unseeingly.

Steve restrains Hemi, rescuing Gator from a third kick, Steve's own anger patently near overload. 'That's *enuf*, man!'

Hemi, snarl almost gone now, eyes glazed by violence done and foreseen — a kid at a *Star Wars* film — 'Enuf? *Huhuhuhu*! Yu should know me beda than *that*, cuz! I ain't even *starded* on 'im!' And then he pulls Steve close, whispering for his ears only, but Mick, silent at their feet, catches every word: 'Ain't noe *way* I can back orf from this in fron'a all my boys, Steve. *Yu* noe tha pro-do-coal. So take the uva bawl'ead and fuck orf, no 'ard feelings. What yu doan see woan 'urt yu.'

Steve, intense near to tears, but just as low: 'This kid's as good as a bruva t' me, Hemi.' Nose to nose with his cousin. 'Yu got no i*dea* the things me an 'im've bin through. If I leave 'im to this I'm *nothing*. Fuckin' *nothing*, man. I'll *die* befaw I live wif that.' Teeth clicking closed: 'So let me promise yu *this*: yu 'urt 'im once maw and, befaw the week's out, I'll be back 'ere for yu wif a fuckin' shotgun . . . And yu noe *me* well enuf t'noe I ain't bluffing.'

For long seconds they stare off, passion shuddering Steve in pulses.

Until eventually, with a scoff like a hiss, Hemi pushes his cousin away. '*Tsssssss*. 'U said I wan-ed t'urt 'im sum maw, anyway?' His eyes sweep the gallery, daring dissension. 'We all noe 'ow soft bawl'eads are: giv'im any maw an' I'll be up faw fuckin' murder.' He forces a grin across his lips. 'I'd beda finish my lesson, though. Can't let 'im leave wifout 'is medsin.'

And in seconds Hemi's freed himself, standing over Gator, dick in hand.

Hoots of pure glee light the congregation.

Steve grimaces disgust, averts his head, but is plainly willing to accept the compromise.

Rescued then betrayed by developments, Mick, half anticipating an act of molestation, jumps in surprise and alarm when Hemi takes deliberate aim, sends a jet of urine spouting at Gator's half-conscious head.

Around him, Hemi's flock cheer like a crowd with a match-clinching try.

Flopping like an epileptic, dribbling vomit, Gator turns his face away, arms lifting weakly, and Mick can see that he hasn't a clue what's happening to him.

Thank fuck.

Two chuckling gangsters move forward, taking Gator's arms and standing on them, pinning him in position as Hemi's full bladder picks off its targets.

Mick has to turn away.

But by the time Hemi dribbles his last a queue has formed behind him.

And it's five wet minutes before Steve and Mick can drag Gator clear. Soaked, they bundle him murmuring and twitching into *The 'Dan*'s back seat, head lolling as if from a snapped spine.

With Barry at the wheel, they drive through town in black silence, and, minutes later, help Gator fully dressed into the hot natural baths of Ruikau Park.

```
{
  Archives: Surfing the J-Curve
  Report # 88395728.
```

(Compiled from data amassed by Informant O.C. 57846.)

The said informant observed apprentice cogs S.V. 568645 and S.V. 567791 beyond permissible orbits. Specifically, they were sighted on a gentle, grassed hillside fronting a wooded lake (non-productive overhead preserved and endured for the recreational bribery of Overseer Caste). Side by side, in programming-plant uniform, they lay upon the bonnet of that vehicular anachronism inside of which they have previously been scrutinised. (A single unit to last decades? What were our forebears thinking? A sleeker, less longevous model is what these two need, the payments on which would do so much towards discouraging this bothersome unortho-doxy.)

Worryingly, closer inspection by the diligent informant exposed the RED- and BROWN-haired pair as guilty of more than mere Desertion of Post and

Trespass. It was revealed that the insubordinate twosome were engaged in consumption of the dreaded Sloth&Dream Weed, and a routine eavesdropping of their emissions suggests their heads house direly defective programming.

BROWN: Are you gonna marry that fucking thing?

RED: Oh, sorry, bro. Here ya go. I was miles away. [He hands BROWN the noxious creation. Wistful] Fuck, I'd love to be out on one of those boats.

BROWN [*harsh with smoke and mutiny*]: Yeah, and I'd love an extra inch or five of beef-blunderbuss.

RED: Ain't *that* the truth.

BROWN [*feigning anger — the pair seem fond of thespian camouflage*]: What are you trying to say?

RED [*feigning severity*]: That you're hung like a castrated fruit-fly.

BROWN [*'angering' further*]: That's a goddamn *lie*! You know full well that the donning of my trousers is a three-leg operation.

RED [*'contrite'*]: Oh, yeah, that's right. My mistake.

BROWN [*'appeased by an inch'*]: See that it doesn't happen again.

[*For a time the flawed cogs are silent, the incendiarism of the Sloth&Dream Weed sullen in eyes drooling over betters at play*]

RED [*without warning*]: So, man.

BROWN: So what, man?

RED: So why don't you do what you've been promising to for weeks now?

BROWN: Namely?

RED: Quantify the incitements and objectives of this Brotherhood of yours. The one for which you've apparently had me performing 'outer-circle duties' for some time. I'm sick of nebulous notions. Nail this shit down for me.

BROWN: [*'sceptical'*]: Do you seriously consider yourself

ready to have your security clearance upgraded? [*'Bleakly grave'*] You're aware that the only way out from this point is victory or death?

RED: Dude, I'm about as serious as a heart attack.

BROWN: That's pretty fucking serious. [*Draws some 'pensive' breaths, in time reaching an 'onerous' decision*] OK. You asked for it. Henceforth, you're to view yourself an inner-circle member. Prepare for your indoctrination.

RED: How many inner-circle members are there?

BROWN: Rule number one: until proven in the field, new members shall learn the names of no other members. Because of the Brotherhood's momentary shortage of cyanide capsules — and a dentist to install them in fillings — should you be captured, subjected to torture, and find yourself nearing breaking point, the Brotherhood needs to know you'll preserve its integrity by biting through your own tongue and bleeding to death. We're not yet prepared to do this.

RED [*'haughtily dismissive'*]: Oh, na, you can trust me, man. My only fear in life is self-betrayal. I'd happily suicide if it meant keeping faith with fellow revolutionaries. The Other Side holds no fear for me; in fact I'm eager to learn what it looks like.

BROWN: That's good enough for me, then. [*Ceremonious pause*] The Brotherhood's inner-circle is currently composed of two members.

RED: You mean two members apart from us?

BROWN: I mean two members.

RED: Cool.

[*Forsaking his seat, Brown spends a moment rummaging through the vehicle's interior. He returns with pen and paper, resuming his lounging atop the 'car', back supported by the windscreen.*]

BROWN [*as he draws*]: Lesson number two: are you familiar with the concept of the J-curve?

RED: The biological concept?

BROWN: Affirmative.

RED: I think so. [*He speaks slowly, assembling the threads as he goes*] Is it when the population of a species in a given area . . . enjoys unprecedentedly positive preconditions for life . . . and increases at an exponential rate?

BROWN: Correctamundo. [*Finished, he offers* RED *the piece of paper*] Behold: a factual J-curve, constructed from data seared onto my consciousness.

RED [*holding the sheet before him*]: That's a pretty fucking steep J-curve, man. What's the species? Some strain of swamp amoeba?

BROWN: You work it out; lateral thinking is highly prized among the Brotherhood. A clue: the X axis denotes years.

RED [*musing*]: Years . . . ? That'd mean the zero signifies 0 BC then, and everything to the right of it is Anno Domini . . . Soooo, that given . . . [*As if it has winked at him,* RED *suddenly reels from the graph, sitting up smartly. He glares at his accomplice, back at the paper. He looks up at last and all traces of irony have been blasted from his voice. Dismayed*] It's *us*, isn't it? It's mankind!

BROWN [*remaining, by contrast, eerily phlegmatic*]: Bing-go.

RED [*groping for mitigation*]: It can't be! Are you *sure*? The stats, I mean! Are you positive they're correct?

BROWN [*nodding once, coldly*]: The data are indisputable. The fact is, it took our venerable species millions of years of evolution and development to reach the figure of three billion members . . . and then we doubled in five decades.

[*Dazed,* RED *scans the forest around them, as if seeing it for the first — or last — occasion*]

RED [*almost a wail*]: But this is fucking *hideous*!

BROWN [*yawning*]: Am I to take it that, according to natural law, you're aware of the pitfalls faced by a population locked on a J-curve?

[*For an instant* RED *appears braced to shout, or maybe run. Instead he snatches the pen from* BROWN's *hand and, like an act of outrage, scores the graph with a finishing touch.*

BROWN *gives* RED's *work a quick appraisal. His tone then is almost gentle.*]

BROWN: What does that line mean to you?

RED [*frost in his throat*]: Apocalypse, man. Human Armageddon. }

3

I remain in my room for four days straight. Dealings with the world are beyond me. Lingering concussion cobwebs keep the hours hazy, an effect assisted by liberal doses of pot and Panadol. My old lady used to be a nurse: she checked me over and reached the diagnosis of no broken ribs. Pissed blood for a while, though. Couldn't tell her *that*: she'd have had me down the A&E in two minutes flat. Thankfully, it sorted itself out.

Haven't even ventured as far as the corner shop yet. I slipped Mum my ATM card, gave her an open mandate on shopping and cooking.

Mothers, eh? Where'd we be without them?

As teenagehood and its boundless selfishness fades, I'm beginning to realise I'm lucky to have a mother who even gives me the time of day. *Christ*, I was a prick! I'm hardly alone in that, but now that I can look back with open eyes this doesn't make my actions any easier to stomach.

Filching money from her purse. Convincing her that lending me the car (her hard-earned and maintained conveyance) was in fact a *good* idea; driving it in all manner of pissed and drugged-up states; laying down squealies and handbrake slides;

89

never once coughing up for wear and tear — hell, never once even *washing* the fucking thing; transforming it into a mobile dope-den; shafting the missus in the back seat, once on the bonnet, an act to leave a sizeable dent, of which I disavowed all knowledge. Throwing parties and piss-ups as soon as Mum departed for an overnighter. Thrusting spotting knives — filched from her good dinner set — into stove-top, heater or fireplace, as soon as she departed for . . . for *anywhere*. Smoke burns in the carpet . . . while she paid for my inhalers. Urine patches all over a lawn I outright refused to mow. Booze bottles at a quarter their manufactured proof thanks to siphoning and water or tea refills. Endless verbal abuse.

Man, I knew *every* fucking thing.

It got to the stage where she just let go, stopped censuring, or even advising, me, disapproval coming only in grimaces, in sighs.

At the time this was heaven.

Recalling these expressions *now* flays my insides.

Only when I started working — months after burning my final bridges with the programming plant — paying regular board, acting with a semblance of maturity, did things mellow between us. Though she wished more for me, Mum saw my job as the beginnings of a salvage operation.

So yeah, she wasn't exactly brimming with enthusiasm when I pulled the pin and opted to have Wellington foot the bill for a spell.

I've made tentative advances toward apprenticing her into the Craft of Arch-Treason. ('Don't you see? Capitalist society is destroying its natural habitat, damage to ultimately result in Man's *own* annihilation. Should folk *not* draw the dole, then, what would that money be spent on? Building a new road? Damming another river? Funding a GE experiment? Thus by claiming the dole and prolonging the life of the natural world, at the same time we're doing our *fellows* a favour by extending protection to the grassroots on which they've forgotten their survival depends!')

But these efforts have so far been deflected. Though the Juggernaut has used her callously, I fear my mother remains a reactionary.

There's nothing like a wee crisis to nullify family acrimony, though. When I staggered in the other morning, Mum even accepted my manifestly phoney account of events without question (shock had sapped my instinct for disinformation).

Though I believe she'll soon query my Listerine consumption — two bottles a day must seem a little obsessive.

And my mouth still tastes of piss.

Yet, excepting this deathless flavouring, I'm not as traumatised as one might expect a victim of facial urination to be. Thank fuck I was barely conscious throughout the incident: put to such use, urine must burn like acid, leave itching scars.

But what frees me most from inner torment is the fact that by being slashed upon, I surely dodged a bullet far worse.

It seems I've been run to ground by the Fiendish Beast . . . and all it really did was relieve itself on me.

Yes, as the pain in my side fades, I'm beginning to expend all excuse for staying bedroom bound. Beginning to question — if not through shame at my ordeal — why I feel the need to hide in here.

And finally, with a heaving sigh, I face up to the fact I've been quietly ducking. It *is* shame . . . but not with the world in general.

With my friends.

Since they left me at the hot pools — I made them explain what exactly took place; convinced them I needed time alone — I've not heard from them. And I can't say their silence is puzzling: who'd want to hang with a dude who's been pissed on by upwards of ten crusty black cocks?

Though perhaps they're more ashamed of themselves than me. After all, technically, they allowed it to happen.

I ardently pray for this to be the case. To have to begin recruitment afresh will set my agenda back months, if not years. And for a fraternity of one, the telling perpetration of Arch-Treason is a virtual impossibility — when winter's blizzards rage, the lone wolf succumbs while the pack hunts on.

Not to mention the security hazard posed by allowing inner-circle members beyond my sphere of influence.

And yeah, losing my three best mates would suck as well.

I take a moment to give solemn thanks for Lefty's innate cowardice. Had he remained to bear witness to my fate, plans for my relocation would already be under way — Newfoundland might have been ideal — for not only would Lefty have found subtle means of refreshing my memory of the experience every ten minutes for the remainder of my life (*'Busting for a slash, guys.'* *'Well, I damn near pissed myself laughing.'*) he would also have extracted excruciating revenge by effectively broadcasting a detailed description of the episode on Radio Vegas.

The clock hits one; I decide it's high time to begin my day, time to motor-vate. Rolling from bed, I briefly consider break-fast . . . discard the notion. Toy with the idea of washing and brushing . . . decide it can wait. Get stoned and read for half an hour? By god, the lad's a genius!

(A part of me knows that half an hour will stretch out to two or three — cannabis being procrastination's mistress — but overlooking this beforehand is a simple task.)

Opening the top drawer of my dresser I'm confronted by enough drug paraphernalia to see me jailed for several lifetimes should I strike an inclement beak with the power of non-concurrent sentencing.

True to routine, I grimace at the sight, even as my hands enter the drawer, sifting through the felonious debris.

Blackened tinfoil — smeared with cannabis oil, lit from beneath and inhaled — to tally to square metres should one ever unscrew and assemble the stuff.

Spotting knives — upon which, once heated to redness, oil and weed might be burned. Straws and funnels — manufactured from pen-shells and bottles — through which smoke from spotting might be breathed. Sewing needles for the allocation of oil; for 'pinball'. Metal cone-pieces used in conjunction with water and bucket bongs, some purchased — ornamentally legal prior to deflowering — some hacked from aluminium cans.

Simple bongs made from such cans. ('First cut a hole on top. Not too big or your weed'll fall through. Yep, that'll do ya. Now poke another hole the same size underneath. That's ya carburettor; some people prefer not to use one; you'll have to decide for yourself. Then all you do is put a little gear on top, light 'er up, and suck like hell through the mouthpiece. Hold that baby *deeeeep*.')

A reeking plastic bottle which served time as a water-bong, before wear compromised its airtightness. ('Fill 'er up and leave it in the fridge ovanight. I tell yu, bro, yu ain't neva smoked nufing so smoove in yaw *whole* fuckin' life.')

Standard pipes bought, borrowed and made — including one ingenious device manufactured from the plastic case of an asthma inhaler, tinfoil fixed across its empty head.

Scissors for the mulling of buds, for the halving and quartering of strong acid.

Plastic capsules that once housed cannabis oil. ('Forty bucks a hit, dude. Tastes like shit, though. Not sure what kind of crap they mix it with, but it'll get you wrecked a few times a day for a week or so. Oh, yeah, *much* better value than a tinny.')

A razor blade for the powdering of lumpy speed.

Packets of blue and yellow ZigZag, old and new, many hopelessly glued by moisture, strewn through the drawer like leprechaun bog-roll.

Evil-green hash-oil stains clinging to everything. Lighters in all manner of condition. Empty and near empty matchboxes, some so aged the writing's faded to illegibility. The stubs of candles, used when running low on incendiary products . . .

For perhaps the hundredth occasion in three years I resolve to dispose of this evidence of fun-lovin' criminality . . . tomorrow.

Skulking toward the side of the drawer a Sportsman packet yields its treasure: a small lump of seedless bud, rock-like in its solidity, layered in purplish filament. An insignificant amount of blow to the uninitiated, perhaps, but to such as myself this represents three return trips to Stonesville. More, were I to bong or pipe the stuff. Recent tribulations in mind, though, I've been a trifle decadent of late, savouring the inefficient luxury of small solo joints.

Locating a functioning packet of skins I settle back against the pillows and, with scissors, reduce my ration to a manageable consistency, mixing in a little tobacco. Tearing a strip of cardboard from the ZigZag packet, I roll it into a slim roach, placing it, and the dope, into a paper.

A minute later and she's ready to burn. I cross to the window to blow it: I'm yet to get around to confessing my habits to the old girl; she plays the role of ignorance well.

Before I can ease the curtain back, however, a hard tapping on the glass damn near precipitates a hygiene incident.

Who the fuck could that *be?*

A voice, furtive: 'Gatey? Yu there, bro?'

Only one person in this world calls me 'Gatey'.

'Steve?' Drawn curtains reveal the man himself, crouching between the roses of Mum's back garden. I open my window — a big swing-out job — and Steve vaults himself up and in.

Frowning sheepishly, in jeans and tanktop, he's looking as robust as ever. He's had his shoulder tattooed since I last saw it — a yin-yang bordered by a loop of razor wire — and it don't look too foul. In fact, when one considers the hideousness of the body 'art' kids in gang circles often acquire, it must be said that Steve's walked away happy as a broke bastard on Dad's Day.

'Cher, bro.' I realise I'm wearing little but daks and a smile; shrug quickly into a pair of dirty trackies.

We shake hands and sit on the edge of my hurriedly made bed.

My deeper anxieties of earlier suddenly banished.

Because, in addition to the mortification I expected to feel when reunited with the lads, I never really got used to having a friend as cool as Steve: the mere anticipation of the guy's presence often stirred in me feelings of inadequacy. This despite the manner with which his bonhomie unfailingly dispelled such fickleness whenever we met.

As it does now. On both counts.

Me, grinning: 'What's wrong with the door, bro?'

'I was a bit worried yaw old lady might be 'ome and blame what 'appened on me.' He frowns deep concern: 'How are yu, man?'

His anxiety gives me a warm fuzzy, a sensation that never fails to embarrass me, even when alone. Shrugging: 'Not too bad. My head didn't really need stitches. Mum wanted to whip a couple in anyway, but she would've had to cut my hair, so I said 'fuck that'. She just cleaned it right up, and it's healing OK. I was a bit woozy for a while there, but' — I drop him a blow-arse wink — 'back on form now, bro, just as sharp as ever.'

Chuckling: 'Yeah, sharp as a bag'a wet hair. What 'bout yaw ribs? That cunt kicked yu fuckin' *hard*.'

I play it down, like I always played down hurts when Steve was there. 'Bit sore for a day, but nothing damaged.' Hemi's boot marks still flare in me whenever I twist at the trunk.

Steve seems set to question my health further, but I see the resolve flee his eyes; he looks at the walls instead.

Can't say I blame him. I'm not sure how *I* would tactfully phrase the question: *So, how are you dealing with the stigma of being drenched crown down in a gallon or five of recycled Waikato Draught?*

But I'm not about to leave it lying between us. 'Look, man, what you did for me was fucking unreal. I mean, I haven't seen you in years and you go and risk your life to get me out of something my own mouth started. So I ended up getting pissed on? Who *gives* a fuck? I was asleep through it all, and the other alternative was for Hemi to kick me to intensive care or further. I know which option I'd take any day of the year. I consider myself one lucky motherfucker.'

Disturbed: 'But doan yu feel like . . . like . . . I dunno, *dirty* or something? *Violated*? If it was me I doan think I could live wif it.'

'That's 'cause you're a tough cunt. Given a choice, you'd

probably have opted for the *beating*. Me, I just pretend to be tough for other people's sake.' I soften the disclosure with a snigger. 'Pride's baggage cowards like me ain't got the room for, bro. Like I used to say to you, them Old Testament bible bangers didn't view pride as a sin for no reason.'

Steve seems to relax a bit, although, paradoxically, he also appears a little disappointed. 'I'm fuckin' glad then, bro. I thought yu might've been scrubbing yawself wif sandpaper the larst few days or something. I thought I made the wrong decision, might've given yu a ticket t' the Laughing Academy.'

I decline mentioning the mouthwash. '*Fuck* no, man. You made the best of a shithouse job, that's all.'

'Thanks, bro. I was kinda hoping yu'd say that.' He reaches across and musses my messy hair. 'And yu ain't no coward either, honky. Now, yu gonna light that joint or fondle it all day?'

For a while we sit back and shoot the shit, sharing the doobie between us.

Me: 'So how come you never got in touch after you left school?'

Penitent: ''Ard to say, bro. I'm fuckin' sorry, anyway. It weren't fuck all to do wif yu. I took a bad turn, starded down the same road cuzin Hemi's at tha end of. I was pissing it up *hard*. Running wif the prospects an' 'em. Crashing at people's 'ouse's I didin' even noe. 'Aving smashes, fucking dudes up wifout even 'membering, getting fucked myself sometimes. Week after week. When I was straight I'd always decide that enuf was enuf: it was time to look yu up. But I guess I didin' want yu t'see me like that. I thought yu might've bin 'earing 'bout me, bin . . . bin disappointed and shit, and I knew yu were in classes wif just the brainy fullas by then. I thought yu'd be embarrassed by a hood like me.'

'How'd ya snap out of it?'

'Was tha old lady, yu noe.' Chuckles: 'Her and tha acid. I went to some rage in the gheddo one night. Pissed it up faw *hours*. Same old story: gats; Marley; two or three big scraps. Some chick got bottled by 'er old man, ended up in tha ambulance . . .

and we just *kept* drinking. 'Bout two I dropped some tabs and started trippin' pretty hard. Everyone else crashed, but I coodin sleep. Was a cool trip faw a while, but yu noe what it's like when yaw comin' down, and yu still see things differently, but all the euphoria's faded, and yu sometimes end up looking at things a bit too long?'

'*Tell* me about it.'

'Well, that was me. Sittin' on the couch wif all these *wasted* Maoris crashed out ova the floor, among the spilled piss, and the blood, and the glass, and the tipped ashtrays. And I got t'noticing and thinking 'bout 'ow *old* some of these cats were, and *none* of 'em working, same shit every weekend — every weekend a "long" one — mope till dole day, start it all again, week after week, year after year.

'And then this *kid* come down the stairs, can't of bin three, snot and tears all ova 'is face, pants wet and full. 'E walked through the room *shaking*, like it was fulla sleeping lions, and I 'membered the noise of the rumbling from earlier, the screaming and yelling. Must have taken 'im *ages* to work up the courage t' walk through. 'E never even noticed me sittin' there, wide awake. 'E went into the kitchen, opened the fridge and pulls out these faw beer bottles — wif the acid in me they looked almost bigger than 'e was — placing 'em on the floor, jumping wheneva 'e made a noise, cryin' real soft all the time. Finally 'e cleared enuf space t' drag out a plastic bag from the back a the fridge. 'E digs inside it and pulls out an old raw carrot . . . starts eatin' the fuckin' thing skin and all. Poor little bugger was *starving*. Hadn't bin fed in fuck knows 'ow long.

'And then the front door opens and my *old lady* walks in! Fucked if I noe 'ow she tracked me down. Thought I was hallucinating at first. Scared the *shit* outta me. I 'adn't spoken to 'er in months. She was dressed all tidy. You noe Mum: pretty short, fat and a bit ugly, but she'd really done 'er best to get tidy, and to me, *man*, surrounded by all that filth, she looked a million fuckin' dollars, an angel just faw me. And here's me, black jersey and jeans that 'ad bin washed about when I last had — 1969 it felt.

'I was expecting 'er to really fuckin' tear into me, but she just stood there and looked me over like . . . like she'd been called t' 'ospital t' ID me on a morgue slab. I coulda cried, man. Then she hands me a photo. Wifout a word. It's one'a me and Dad. He's squatting right down. I'm 'bout two, walking away from him, all wobbly, but wif this big expression like, "Hey world, look at *me*! I'm *mobile*, man. Yu cunts just try and stop me now." But Dad's got his arms ready to catch me, and even though 'e's smiling a bit, 'is eyes are *concerned*, bro, like 'e's not shaw I'm ready faw this.

'And sittin' in that room, the photo and tha acid made it all so *clear*, hit me like buckshot. Wherever Dad was, if 'e could see me then 'e was seeing me in the same light as I was seeing that scared liddle toddler out the kitchen: confused and starving, dirty in and out, not a hope in hell, ploughing steadily downhill.

'I *did* cry, then. Just blubbered away like a bitch. Not just tears — sobs as well, man. Couldn't help myself. But it weren't *me* I was crying faw. Not at *all*. It was faw Dad, 'cause after all 'e'd done to set me on the right path in life, all the concern and love 'e felt faw me, all tha 'opes 'e 'ad faw me to make something of myself, I'd repaid him like *this*? Worse, I'd used his death as an excuse to shit on 'is dreams faw me!

'And Mum says, "It's yaw father's unveiling tomorrow. I'm going to Matakana faw it. I want yu t' come wif me."

'So I did. Stayed on at the marae for six months afterwards, laid off the piss, got fit, sorted my head out again.'

For a time we just sit quietly, passing the joint, neither feeling the urge to speak, sharing a Mia Wallace 'comfortable silence'. The doob burns down and I kill it in the ashtray, both of us nicely toasted by now.

Steve: 'Mind if I score a drink, bro?'

My own mouth's as dry as a nun's nasty. 'Go for your life. Grab me one as well, eh?'

He returns with two mugs of water, and by his face I see that something big's fermenting in him.

His question is a little half-hearted. 'How 'bout you, anyway,

Gatey? Right from day one yu 'ad it in yu to go places. Yu should be in varsity by now.'

I want to ask him what's *really* on his mind . . . opt to go with the diversion. 'Don't really see the point.'

Frowning: ''Ow do yu mean?'

I get heavy on him, as I know I can. 'I believe if too many more of us thought crims chicken out and take the Juggernaut's bribe — swallow the "if you can't beat 'em join 'em" slogan — within a decade or four our good Earth's gonna be little more than a fucking slag heap.'

Steve, staring hard through dope-red eyes: 'Yu really believe this?'

Me, adamant: 'Yeah, I really *do*. And I'm not the only one.'

He nods. 'I noe. I've met a lot of ova-brainy cunts 'u think that. But I've met a lot *maw* who're just happy decidin' 'ow best t' join in on the gang-bang. The rest of us dummies toe the line wifout much thought, looking out faw number one . . . Why doan yu go t'varsity and get skilled up in something that'll help yu make a difference?'

Me, shrugging: 'Dunno what, bro. Science was never my strong point, and anyway, for every ecologically conscious scientist these days there are five who sell their souls to the capitalists. Once upon a time the title "scientist" automatically implied integrity. Not any more.'

I take his silence as permission to go deeper. 'A lot of idealistic students take up law, aiming to become environmental lawyers, but a year or three down the track, with a debt running into tens of thousands and first-hand knowledge of where the money *really* is, when it comes to the crunch most of these faggots pussy out as well.'

As I'm speaking, Steve takes out a pack of Dunhill and lights up a couple, handing one to me.

'Sure, there're plenty of "professional" careers to study for that don't seem vampirish at face value, and *yeah*, maybe these types *are* less carcinogenic than the corporate class. But at the end of the day they all owe their positions of privilege to the masses forced to live as non-entities, in a world where technology should've made the need for a working class obsolete. And almost all "professional" types are at least indirectly culpable for helping preserve this fatal status quo of ours: their gratifying lives are oiled by the Juggernaut's blood money; they're the layers of its bureaucracy.'

I really need a hit on my inhaler before I'm going to get much enjoyment from this cigarette . . . but I'd take part in a Ugandan orgy through condom sanctions before parading this fragility for Steve.

Me, a little wheezy: 'I suppose there *are* students who graduate with worthwhile degrees and ethics, but these are just a drop in the ocean, grunts to rush the *spandau*s.'

Steve: 'What 'bout yaw writing, man? All through school yaw pen was lethal.'

I sneer off the compliment, inwardly chuffed. 'I ain't written fuck all since an essay on metaphors from *The Crucible* Seventh Form English. Never made it back to class to collect my mark, either.'

My mark topped the form, according to the English teacher who phoned in a bid to keep me studying. He was a fine teacher and a fine dude: he even sympathised with the Brotherhood's ideals. Damn shame he lacked audacity, striking no bigger blow in life than occupation in a programming plant, and at the polishing stage of the production line, an area of near impotence for even the committed saboteur.

For this I despise the man.

Me, continuing: 'You're right, though. In this war a good writer's the equivalent of a well-armed fifth column: serious destabilisation. But it's a matter of identifying a gainful medium, and so far that's proving beyond me. If I'm to fight I've gotta recognise a means of direct action.'

Steve just shrugs unconcern. 'Yu got the brains and the 'nads faw it, bro. Yu always did. If there's a way *yu*'ll find it.'

His faith in me occasions an absurd spurt of confidence.

Steve, reflective: 'Kids, man. Yu've always got on all right wif kids, and the younger the mind, tha easier t' shape. I reckon that's worth 'membering.'

Half-hearted: 'Yeah, I've thought about that myself. The Net could hold answers. Everyone's a publisher on the Web. Or a storyteller. I've thought of going deep cover: masquarading as a Samaritan. "Kids need to learn a love of reading. Story alone can achieve this." Stories from abroad and from closer: stolen, home-spun, combinations of both, tailored to different age brackets.'

'And . . . ?'

'. . . And under the bullshit I'll be spreading the dread: mining young minds, conscription through fiction.'

Steve, distracted: 'Sounds good. Give it a crack.'

Shrugging: 'Yeah. Sure.'

This time the silence is tense. Whatever's troubling him wants airing.

Me: 'You gonna spit it out, bro, or what?'

A lopsided grin: 'Yu stool read me like a book.'

'Yeah, a speaking book on compact disc.'

Eventually: 'I just can't stop thinking 'bout tha ova night.'

Me, grimacing: 'Let it go, Steve. I'm the one who got slashed on, and I'm over it already.'

'. . . It's not just that. It's the way those cunts wreck lives like it's a game. Prospects, molls, family members, crime victims. Yu wouldn't *believe* tha amount'a people that chapter alone 'as screwed over. The day after that . . . that shit went down wif yu, I 'eard . . .' He trails off; shies away.

'You heard what?'

He stares at the floor. 'Vicki.'

A chill grips me. 'What about her?'

Steve, sighing, shaking his head: 'Hemi bashed her up bad after we left. Broke her jaw, smashed a heapa teeth.'

Loathing attacks like skinworm. '*Ahhhhh*, fuck. All because of me.'

Steve, snapping: '*Get* fuckin' real, man. That's what those guys *do*. If they ain't rapin' chicks, then they bashing or blockin'' 'em. Yu were just an excuse. He woulda found anuva reason ovawise.'

I nod, desperate to believe this. 'Is she in hospital?'

'Yeah, but . . . but before he'd let anyone take 'er up, 'e made 'er go on the block.' With deep reluctance: 'They did 'er in tha arse too.'

This time I'm seized by utter revulsion. Snatched in its jaws and shaken. Nothing but raw glimpses of the Fiend fill me with this . . . this *vileness*. I'm yet to experience a worse emotion: it's like having your soul groped by festering claws.

The spasm eventually passes, leavening anger, and queasiness, and the deathless, clichéd, ancient *Why?* 'That fucking prick! Ah, god, the complete *cunt*! Fuck, I hope someone gets him one day!'

Suddenly Steve's eyes are shining at me ferally. 'Why leave it t' fate? Fuck "someone". Fuck "one day".'

I reel in the face of this, Vicki all but forgotten. 'You're not serious?'

'Wanna bet?'

Caustic: 'Steve, it's *the Rabble*. You jerk around with these guys, you wind up in a wooden box — mathematical law.'

Showing teeth: 'Not if yu do it well.'

'What are you talking about?'

'Can yu honestly tell me that after what they did t' yu, after what they did t' Vicki, after what they almost did t' me, if yu 'ad the chance t' get even wif these arseholes, at no risk to yawself, yu'd turn it down?'

Gobsmacked: 'Wake *up*, bro! The phrases, "revenge against the Rabble" and "without risk" are mutually exclusive. They do *not* belong in the same sentence. They don't belong in the same fucking *volume*!'

Steve, angering a little: 'Hear me out, wool yu?'

I sigh futility, but offer him a 'whatever' shrug.

His explanation lasts a full five minutes; includes a visual aid, produced from a pocket.

Afterwards I shake my head, appalled by the presentation.

'You've lost your fucking *mind*, man. You simply aren't hooked up right any more.' But, to my enormous dismay, a kernel of deep excitement has begun transmitting from the base of my spine . . .

Steve hears it; grins like a buccaneer. 'Go get in the shower, Gatey — you stink. Then I'm taking yu out faw lunch — chicken enchiladas faw me, yu can 'ave the guacamole nachos. After that it'll be time faw yu t' make a phone call faw me, confirm something I suspect. By *that* time yu'll've straightened up and the paranoia'll be gone. *Then*, my friend, yu and I are in business.'

Me, searching for clean clothes and sanity: 'I'm not fucking hearing this.'

'Oh, yes yu are. Yaw two mates are gonna hear it as well: we need allies.'

Archives: Dead Race Walking

[*As shadows lengthen around the lake the eyes of our budding mutineers unseeingly follow the boats cavorting below them. The happy whizzing of engines, the faint whoops of the skiers, flutter up their hill . . . them seem to freeze as they strike the dread enshrouding BROWN'S new recruit.*]

BROWN [*quoting his cohort*]: 'Armageddon'. Yes, I couldn't have phrased it better.

RED [*shock yielding stubbornly to alarm*]: There's simply no way to sustain that kind of growth. It's like building a tower higher and higher and higher . . . Jesus Christ! What are they *doing* about it?

BROWN [*eyeing him sharply*]: If by 'they' you refer to 'the powers that preside', what they're *doing* about it is avoiding eye contact with mirrors and overdosing on the new opiates of the people — consumption and asset amassment.

[RED *moves to speak; is overridden*]

BROWN [*loud*]: Your question would be better phrased as, 'What are *we* doing about it?'

[*With a visible effort,* RED *seeks to match* BROWN*'s dissembling irony. Even so, when he speaks he's helpless to disguise a tremor.*]

RED: What *are* we gonna do about it? Pioneer some waterborne contraceptive and sterilise a generation or two?

BROWN: Lesson number two — or is it three? Who cares? Next lesson: exponential population growth isn't the problem itself . . . it is simply one of its most dangerous reverberations. In the Third World especially, population explosion is an *effect* of poverty, not a cause.

RED: D–do go on.

BROWN [*strident*]: In its quest to save Mother Earth and humankind from humankind, the Brotherhood will face three enemies: the Fiendish Beast, the Quenchless Core and the Careering Juggernaut.

[*Intrigue gradually reprieves* RED *from frigid thoughts.*]

RED: They sound fearsome and worthy adversaries.

BROWN [*'indignant'*]: 'Worthy'? Oh, they are worthy, make no mistake. Worthy of sodomised ejaculation from ICBM warheads.

RED [*ironic mask now re-donned firmly*]: One takes it these forces feature not on your Christmas card list. Elucidate.

BROWN [*grimly businesslike*]: Right. The Quenchless Core is ancient, though not universal among us. The Quenchless Core resides in the breasts of most, a singularity demanding regular meals of assets and possessions, 'achievements' and 'distinctions'. The satisfaction of these it absorbs without trace. Then nothing else will do but that it feed once more.

RED: You're speaking of greed?

BROWN [*snapping*]: By *god*, man, I speak of the Quenchless Core and none *other*! Greed is a euphemism behind which the Core's black evil might shelter.

RED: You say it's not universal?

BROWN: I say it *wasn't* universal. The Quenchless Core finds homes in only one animal, and even then, over the centuries, many of *our* societies were free of it also. On the few occasions it attempted infiltration into these, they were wise enough to recognise its true face; they dealt with it summarily.

RED: Societies like the Australian Aborigines? The Kalahari Bushmen?

BROWN: Precisely. And many others besides, some remembered by history, some remembered by none, for the past was penned by those who annihilated real men.

RED [*postulating*]: And now, like an uncontained super-virus, the Quenchless Core has colonised all?

BROWN [*impressed*]: Nice choice of words. You're a quick learner. You could go far within the Brotherhood.

RED [*extrapolating further*]: The Quenchless Core found loam in the hearts of Europeans. And, of course, the modern world became Europe's child.

BROWN: And grows more so by the day.

RED: What else? I think I'm getting a feel for this. What of our second enemy? Speak of the Juggernaut.

BROWN: The Careering Juggernaut is what became of Humanity when its Quenchless Core was converted to nitrous oxide, fitted with a supercharger, and appointed Lord High Sovereign.

RED: Again in English?

BROWN: From the tyranny and avarice of feudalism sprang the tyranny and avarice of capitalism. Then, as now, the fundament of capitalism was that it must grow or die, spreading through new markets, harvesting more and more resources, weathering financial fluctuations through diversification and expansion. From this need sprang the European drive toward imperialism, and, with 'God' as vindication, the New World was colonised, its people 'delivered', its resources and labour 'made available for the economic good'. Through biblical sentiments of human pre-eminence over nature, the capitalists inscribed her looting onto society's DNA.

Later, as the sway — and justifications — of Christianity wavered, capitalism even deified a new absolution: the Church of Economics. After World War 2, western governments with their neo-colonial foreign policies — anything from economic blackmail to the backing of proxy rulers to outright invasion — ensured that the world's fledgling nations remained 'free and open' for market exploitation.

Over these times then, across the globe, capitalism, with its laws of production for production's sake, undermined all local cultures, becoming more and more inexorable as its proceeds and power concentrated.

Brick by brick, mind by mind, the Juggernaut was begun . . . driven by many . . . steered by none.

RED: And now?

BROWN: Now, backed by its puppet, the state, capitalism's teachings reign unhindered; are the basis of virtually every national society. Ignoring its fundamental incompatibility with life — the fact that without the perpetual acceleration of growth, consumption and population rates, a capitalist economy implodes — capitalism has humanity inhabiting a glittering house of cards. Economics plasters the walls in jargon we believe we'll die without, as though GDPs and FTSEs are what we truly owe existence to, their equations and needs the very fabric of life. Profit maximisation has become a code of practice absorbed at the breast, buzz words in whose name abominations are perpetrated hourly, legally, *morally*. The entire planet, and all upon it, has become fuel for the utopia of growth.

Yes, according to Economics, Consumption is the new Salvation, for without it there can be no Growth . . . and without Growth and 'Progress', humans must be 'mere' animals after all.

And the Juggernaut crashes on.

RED [*dry*]: 'Growth': interesting term. But what is it they wish us to grow *into*?

BROWN [*sneering contempt*]: They have no idea. It's just the done thing: economics demands it. And when a species reaches plague proportions — as ours has, living by codes *necessitating* expansion — it can be said that its environment — its larder, well and nest — becomes increasingly finite. Not good news for those with the courage to look beyond balance books.

RED [*nodding*]: And even those masses capitalism exploits most adopt its maxim of mindless acquisition, whole lives given to the race to become the wealthiest headstone in the compost heap.

BROWN: And capitalism's PR man — economics — has become so slick, whenever in the world left-wing leaders attempt to slow the Juggernaut's charge by placing life ahead of figures, a few graphs flashed at news time, a little 'business disconfidence' and the constituency bays for Red blood.

RED: With timing and timbre to rival trained seals.

BROWN: And the 'free' market proliferates; is pitched as a concept as essential as oxygen. And as, through globalisation, growth and consumption leap more and more firebreaks, the Juggernaut accelerates, building heedless inertia, preaching as it obliterates its own preconditions for life.

RED [*struck by sudden insight*]: But no sane society would *do* this; would consume and expand for no reason than that a rich few assure it it must; to the point where its existence is threatened by its deeds. Fair enough, that we've gone too far is a relatively new realisation, but *everyone* knows the truth now. Yet we're not stopping! We're devouring *faster*! Fuck me, you and I are living in a world ruled and maintained by principles that are *actually* insane! The human race as we know it is driven by the mentality of cancer!

BROWN [*drawling*]: And the Establishment brands us delinquent?

[*Neither of them speaks for some time. They gaze into space,
betrayal in their eyes, disgust in their smoking.*]

RED [*pensive*]: The sad part is that even as we speak, you and
I are aboard this Juggernaut, aren't we? Sharing the ride.
Whenever we chuck some juice in *The 'Dan* here; every
time we pick up some beer; chance food poisoning at
McDick's, the Juggernaut crashes on. Though we're only
schoolkids — and barely that anymore — we're cogs of this
fucking thing

BROWN [*shrugging*]: Don't let that bother you. Our parents
left us no other means of survival . . . for now. Besides,
you're overlooking one of the Brotherhood's mottoes: 'If
you can't beat 'em, join 'em . . . then poison the fuckers
from the inside.'

RED: What do we target, then?

BROWN [*lips skinning from teeth unconsciously*]: Big business
(and its state lackeys), the multinats, the corporate 'elite'.
Few realise it, and even fewer admit it, but all of us dipshit
consumers are dancing to the tune of these executive arseholes.

Just look at the stats: ninety per cent of the world's
wealth is owned by the richest ten per cent of the population. Last year in the US, one-third of the country's
earnings went to the top *one per cent*! In whose fucking
interest is it to maintain the status quo?

You see, because the bigger corporations can compete
more effectively, capital has a tendency to concentrate. It
also needs to diversify. So throughout its modern life-span
not only has capitalism made sure its tentacles spread into
all facets of life, and all regions of the planet, it's also
ensured that these tentacles became increasingly
powerful, and originate from fewer and fewer nerve
centres.

RED: Of course. And money equals power. And for what do

these outfits exist solely? To make more money. Therefore their enormous power bases are brought to bear on nothing but the hunt for greater profit.

BROWN: Absolutely. Under globalisation, corporations are now free to give their 'investment' to the lowest-bidding government, thus attracting better tax incentives, reduced worker rights legislation, lower environmental controls, etc. This effectively means that a nation wishing to join the global village and 'prosper' must lower the living standards of most its constituents, and sacrifice more and more of its ecological well-being.

RED: And to 'compete' other nations must undercut *these* nations.

BROWN: Correct. [*Darkening further*] But we're now witnessing the shadowy development of strategies even more menacing. As capital centralisation continues, power moves into the hands of fewer and fewer, the enormous clout the capitalists wield is symbiotically banded into organisations like business roundtables, chambers of commerce, trade organisations . . . And because capital is the life-blood of the world's grow-or-die economies, these groups have more sway over the conditions of people's lives, and the treatment of the Earth, than arguably *any* elected body. And for what do they use this power exclusively?

RED [*not bothering to answer*]: But what are they thinking? [*His agitation grows with each sentence*] These people already have an . . . an obscene amount of wealth. More than they could spend in lifetimes. And they must see where it's all leading! In their heart of hearts they *must*! I bet if you pumped them full of truth serum, they wouldn't be able to envision a world in which their grandkids aren't screaming, 'What have you blind bastards done to us?' And yet the plunder goes on! Our good Earth, our miraculous mother, is on her last legs . . . and the rape continues. Unchecked! What are they *thinking*?

BROWN: When one strives to fix a numerical value to all things, one loses the ability to analyse as anything but a calculator. [*A disgusted scoff*] Besides, their propaganda apparatus is so slick, the capitalists are claiming the moral high ground. [*A pompous falsetto*] 'Perhaps the system *does* have flaws — show me one that doesn't? — but the solution is to forge ahead. Man's only salvation is progress.' [*Back to bleak levelness*] They neglect to mention that they've monopolised progress and can see no further than quarterlies.

RED [*a while later, low*]: This Juggernaut's gonna kill us. It's gonna kill *everything*. You realise that, don't you? Someone has to make it see reason.

BROWN [*dismissive*]: It won't listen. It *can't* listen. It knows only consuming, *nothing* of living. To urge that it revise its consume-or-die values is to ask it to question its organs and flesh.

RED [*in time, flat*]: Then it must be slain.

BROWN: Quickly and utterly. ⎫
⎬
⎭

4

Wednesday, 8 March, 8.17pm

We find them in the garage of the house Mick shares with his older sister and a couple of her friends. The hood's up on *The 'Dan*, but both seem more interested in pool than mechanics. Between jobs up in the Smoke, it seems Barry's been staying with Mick these past few days.

Barry, chagrined: 'Sorry we ain't been over all week, Gator. We were a bit worried you might be gutted with us, and . . .'

Me, clipping the back of his head: '*Fuck* you, man. You should know me better than that. You three saved my arse, plain and simple.'

I spend the next minute assuring them that being urinated upon hasn't reduced me to a quivering pile of doubt.

Mick: 'Sweet as.' He seems genuinely relieved. 'We were a bit worried the Fiend had knocked the fight from our chief cabalist.'

'In your fucking dreams, pal.'

Barry: 'I feel a celebration's in order. Scored some nice skunk yesterday. Anyone fancy a bong or five?'

Me: 'You might just wanna hold off on the blows a tick, Baz. Me and Steve've got a proposition we need to outline for ya's.'

Something in my tone hooks their full attention.

111

'We're listening.'

I tell them of Vicki's fate following our departure from the Rabble house the other night. 'This tilts the scales for Steve and me: we're keen to stitch these cunts up. What we . . .'

Mick, incisive: '*Hang* on, hang on, hang on!' Alarm seems almost to have jolted the glasses from his nose; he takes a second to resettle them. 'I'm sorry for that chick. Honestly. And what they did to you, Gator, that was *well* out of order. But let's call a spade a shovel here. This has knocked your noses so far out of joint, you cats are *actually* proposing to wreak vengeance on *the Rabble*? Am I right?'

Steve: 'Yep.'

As though we're plague-carriers, Mick shrinks from us unconsciously. Head shaking: 'Sorry, guys, but if you need help with *this*, you've come to the wrong . . . '

Barry: 'Ease up there a touch, Mick.' A stillness has claimed him. 'I don't know Steve too well, but after the other night I wouldn't be surprised to learn that he's got more balls than brains. Our Gator, though, he's a different proposition. This boy's no prick's fool. If he's up for this I'm all ears.'

I'm a little uncertain how to take this . . . shrug it off inwardly. 'Mick, I know on the face of it there's not enough in this for you to risk getting on these guys' shit list. I'll tell you what, though, the risk is minimal, and, if successful, we'll each walk away with more than just the sweet taste of ice-cold revenge.'

Mick: 'Namely?'

Steve: ''Ow does a quarter share of 200 gs sound?'

Silence.

Long, loaded silence.

Barry breaks it at last. 'That sounds better than a ripe bint with hands so small they make my cock look thirteen inches.'

Mick, restrained: 'I think one of you's'd better start talking turkey.'

Steve takes his cue. 'I doan 'af t'tell yu's not a word said in 'ere tonight goes beyond these walls.' His eyes tell us that anyway as he slips off his jean jacket, arranging a stool so that

112

his back's against *The 'Dan*, feet on an upturned bucket. 'All right. Now yu all noe enuf 'bout tha Rabble t' undastand what I mean by chapters? Good.' He takes the time to spark up a fag. Draws a couple of puffs. 'Yeah, well, anyway, most chapters are named after tha area they based in, right? Except faw one of 'em. Nefarious, it's called. Even though it's got its headquarters in Wellington, it's composed of 'ard nuts from all ova the country. They're led by a fulla named Donk. As the pres' of Nefarious, this effectively makes 'im the head honcho of the whole gang — the chief cheese, the big man on campus. Anyway, Donk's deputy recently got banged up faw a twelve-year lag, which means the "position became vacant". That cousin'a mine 'u made such a lasting impression the ova night, Hemi, well 'e once did time wif Donk, and at a convention in Taupo a few months ago Hemi licked Donk's arse so well Donk put 'is name on a shortlist faw the number two spot. But Hemi 'as t' earn it . . . of course.'

He pulls an empty paint tin to him, flicking ash inside it. 'Now, these Nefarious boys are into some heavy shit. *Real* gangster stuff. Gambling rackets, protection, drug smuggling, prostitution, chop-shops, fences: yu name it. They're raking up *big* capital. And they're federal — they stomp where they please, regardless of turf. Faw a patched Rabbler this is where it's *at*. If Hemi was t' go in there as *number two*, whatever pinga 'e's used t' scraping up round Vegas'll suddenly seem like M'noply money.

'Obviously, t' land this job 'e's willing to take risks. And 'e 'as. At the convention Donk told Hemi a story, a story 'bout a Nefarious member sent to Amsterdam round June last year, loaded wif Rabble cash. This cat was unda orders to score a coupla 'undred of *the* most primo outdoor skunk seeds money can buy. All legal, of course: yu can buy 'em over the counter there if yu got enuf ping. And because it's legal those dope crazy Dutch motherfuckers've refined growing to a *science*. They got *institutes* devoted to it. If cultivated well, not only will one'a these seeds turn into some'a the most lethal blow in history, but it'll give yu a yield of three or four *pounds*.'

113

Mick: 'That's leaf as well, though, right?'

Barry, eyes glowing: 'Like fuck. I've read about the seeds they produce in the 'Dam, man. Those Dutch cunts wouldn't use leaf to wipe their arses. When they forecast a yield, they're talking bud and bud alone.'

Steve: 'Fuckin' oath. So this gangster walks through Auckland customs wif a heap o' these seeds on 'em; up his arse, in his guts. 'E heads down Welly and 'ands 'em orf t'Donk. Only Donk's not a 'undred per cent sure 'ow best t' grow 'em — 'e don't wanna leave fuck all to chance. And by the time 'e thinks 'bout maybe keeping things a little 'ush 'ush, the whole chapter's 'eard about it and wants the job. Donk doan noe 'u t' turn to — loyalty doan count faw tu much when yu got plants in the bush worth what these are. Every cunt's gonna be gossiping, and it'll take at least a few guys t' set up the plantation, and even wif threats flying word of its whereabouts might spread . . .

'Then Donk chats t' Hemi in Taupo. Hemi knows this bawl'ead from the joint who studied Dutch growing techniques on 'is OE in Europe, one of those mad hippie cunts wif too much brains faw 'is own good, degree in 'orticulture, the works. Grew a shitload 'imself up Norfland before getting busted and banged up. Got busted through a *deal*, mind: the pigs never got near any of 'is sites; 'e reckons they were watertight. And Hemi says to Donk, "'Old off faw a week, bro."

'Hemi then tracks this grower cat down, but the dude doan want nufin' t' do wif such a quantity. So Hemi roughs 'im up a liddle, puts the squeeze on 'im, threatens his missus and rug-rat, and all of a sudden Woodstock's 'is nigga.

'Next, Hemi contacts Donk, tells 'im 'bout Woodstock, puts forward a proposal: trust 'im wif the job, and Hemi'll do it wif just 'imself, Woodstock, and some prospect — a kid 'e can scare senseless, a kid 'u doan 'ave the contacts t' unload big amounts of pot, a kid 'e can send up there camping when the plants start t'flower, wif a shooter, t' guard the crop night and day, just in case. Then, when 'arvest rolls round, Hemi'll 'ead up there 'imself and supervise proceedings. 'E can then take the gear sumwhere and bury it; give Donk directions t' the grave; the big man takes over from there.

'Donk thinks this over, does his maths, phones Hemi back: "I want a 'undred pounds of seedless buds. You wanna skim some, that's your business, but if I give yu my seeds and, in six month's time, yu hand me back less than a hundred pounds of mind-fucking ganja, yu and me's got a beef that ain't goin' away. Pull it off and yaw my new number two. And I want directions t' the site in case I decide t' check up on yaw liddle venture."'

Barry, breathless: 'What'd Hemi say?'

'He said, "I'm yaw nigga."'

It's early March: planting time was months ago.

Barry: 'So he *did* it, then?'

'Yep.'

Mick, ever the cynic: 'How do *you* come to know all this?'

'I went round tha pad 'bout four weeks ago, looking t' get sum grass. Run into sum decent fullas there, 'ad nufin' t' do, so I stuck round faw a few. I scored this chick and fucked 'er in Hemi's room. When I woke up she was gone, and Hemi and anuva patch, Johnson, were whisperin' away in the corner, sharing a joint. I sleep pretty rough, so 'e musta ruled me out as an eavesdropper. I could tell right away they were on 'bout something confidential; I didn't wanna get up and walk out in case they started to wonder 'ow long I actually *had* bin asleep. So I played possum faw safety, listened in to amuse myself. 'Eard pretty much the whole story. Hemi was 'olding sumthing in 'is 'and. 'E flashed it to Johnson once or twice as they were yakking, then 'e kicked 'im out, gave me a good long look, rolled it tight and stuffed it in a hole in the top corner of the room, behind a poster. 'E left, and when I went back t'the party a while later, I 'elped him get well smashed wif a few voddies in 'is beer while 'e weren't looking. When 'e'd crashed, snorin' 'is head orf, I checked 'is stash. It was a map — good one, tu. I got some shit together and made a copy, snuck tha original back and pissed orf. I didin' really plan on doing fuck all wif it, but it seemed like tu good a card t'let pass, just in case.'

Barry, mesmerised: 'So you know where this crop *is*?'

Flat: 'I could drive us there in about eight hours.'

Mick, whispering: 'Jesus fucking Christ.'

I'd been too stunned to iron out all the finer points with Steve earlier; think of one now. 'Why was he letting this Johnson cunt in on the secret?'

'Johnson's Hemi's hit-man. He's a pitbull: just as loyal, just as dumb, just as mental. Wif all that's at stake, Hemi's getting a little paranoid; 'e wants sum extra muscle when 'e goes up faw 'arvesting. I guess 'e's worried one'a Donk's boys might've found out what's going down, put together a double-cross.'

Barry, salivating: 'Let's fucking *do* it. Let's bail tomorr–'

Mick, sharpish: 'Calm *down*, Baz, for fuck's sake!'

'But . . . '

Loud: 'But if Steve had told us the shit was on planet Krypton, and we'd need to battle mutant pterodactyls to get at it, you'd still be keen as mustard . . . just for the hell of it. How about letting us rational folk thrash this thing out properly? After all, if we decide to have a crack at this and it turns to shit, there's three outcomes to choose from: one, we return empty-handed — possible, but not likely; two, some or all of us end up with eyes that don't blink any more and dirt in our mouths; three, the fucking fascists nab us with enough blow to make Fred West's sentence look like PD.'

At times Mick's innate scepticism is a source of huge frustration to me. Right now, it's just what the surgeon stipulated.

Barry: 'OK, OK.' Hands up, he makes a show of composing himself . . . but rapture haunts his gaze like flame.

Mick: 'All right, Steve, first things first. So you can locate the plantation. You're positive of that?'

'Yeah.'

'What if the map was coded or something?'

Me: 'He knows his cousin, man. Trust him on this.' Without the map there's a Plan B anyhow, but I don't want this can opened just yet: Mick must be allowed to cross-examine without bias. Not for no reason is he the Brotherhood's editor.

Mick, reluctantly: 'All right. We'll take that for granted. Now you're *certain* you know when the harvesting gonna go down? It couldn't happen early, could it?'

Steve: 'No chance.'

Marijuana's a sun crop. To thrive it needs warmth and long summer days. The astute horticulturist therefore plants his seedlings around early November, or as soon as he's certain winter frosts are *finito* for another year. With luck, the plants lap up the sun for a good few months and in time produce flowers — buds — the only section of the plant that counts for narcotic purposes. These should be allowed to develop for as long as possible, but must *not* be in the open when the weather turns to shit again. Therefore, climatic anomalies aside, harvest generally takes place around April.

Steve: 'Hemi's gone to a *lot'a* trouble, and anything above a hundred pounds is 'is t' tax. Yu really think 'e's gonna 'arvest early and cost 'imself several grand, just t' be on the safe side?'

Is he fuck. This guy's Quenchless Core clearly sucks faster than many.

After some steady seconds of contemplation, Mick also nods agreement. 'Here's the double jeopardy question, then: can you be sure when exactly he's gonna send his goon up there to stand guard duty? Unless you can pinpoint that *exactly*, the risks are untenable.'

Steve: 'Oh, I noe exactly, all right.'

Mick: 'When?'

''E's there already.'

At this disclosure even Barry appears a little put out. 'So we're gonna be blundering through strange bush, with a tooled-up prospect hidden somewhere, on land he knows like his foreskin, awaiting all comers?'

Me: 'Like fuck. We've got a deep-cover spook on the payroll.'

Mick, agitated: 'What are you talking about?'

Steve: 'On Hemi's map there was a phone number. A *cell*-phone number.'

Mick stares from Steve's face to mine. Back again. A flare goes off.

Reverent whisper: 'Woodstock?'

Me: 'Someone hand this man a big fat cigar.'

Barry, dubious: 'Have you turned him *already*?'

Steve: 'We phoned 'im 'bout two hours ago.'

Mick, almost sneering: 'And what? He said, "Yeah, you're right, fuck Hemi", and threw his lot in with you?'

''E took a liddle more persuasion than that. I got Gatey t' speak first: we decided a fellow honky should bowl the first over. 'E opened the door faw me. Then I told Woodstock I knew of 'is predicament and 'ad a safe way out of it faw 'im — "All I ask is that yu hear me out," I said. 'E agreed. Not only did Hemi black-mail 'im into this, 'e's also 'ad 'im sittin' up there night and day since the crop went in, tending it daily, adjusting the chemical balance of the soil, extra waterings 'ere and there, keeping possums in check, trimming the plants, blah blah blah. I knew all this befaw 'and. The first thing I pointed out t' Woodstock was that Hemi obviously got 'im t' let a couple of the plants go t' seed early on. Woodstock confirmed that. Now Hemi 'as these primo seeds coming out 'is arse. I asked Woodstock 'ow difficult it is t' grow 'em just perfect, and 'e said it weren't easy, that they needed constant attention from sumone wif the right skills. I then asked 'im 'ow 'e felt 'bout spending every summer camped up there faw the rest of 'is life. 'E said Hemi gave 'is word it was just this once. I asked 'im, faw the sake of a few 'undred grand, 'ow much 'e thought the word of a Rabbler was worth. Woodstock went real quiet for a while. 'E then confessed that, wif all the time 'e'd spent bored shitless up there, 'is thoughts 'ad been straying along these lines maw and maw. Then I pitched 'im the plan me and Gator cooked up this aftanoon . . . and offered 'im as much grass as 'e could stuff into three rubbish bags.'

Steve pauses. The sun has disappeared, unnoticed. Red tips of fag ends are almost all that light the garage, reflecting from wired faces. Steve's gaze travels us all; he milks the tension like an ice-age storyteller.

Mick's the first to break: 'And?'

'. . . And he said he's my nigga.'

It's me who finally speaks, shifts the counsel forward. To Steve, as I dawdle across to the light switch: 'I think you'd better give 'em the details of the plan, bro.'

Steve does, and by the time he's done my pulse is racing like a sprinter's. 'What do ya think, Mick?'

For the first time today, I spot heat in Mick's eyes. His voice has the lead of resolve in it. 'Can we trust this Woodstock?'

The 'we' tolls like a gong to me. *Oh, fuck. He's up for it. At least he will be, given a little more time to convince himself.*

My balls shrink a little further; a fresh charge of excitement — *fear* — rushing through me.

Steve: '*I* reckon we can trust 'im. What I told 'im 'bout Hemi weren't no bluff. Anyone who noes 'im'll tell yu that extorting sum bawl'ead out of 'is summer every year is something Hemi'd do faw a *laugh*, let alone faw a few 'undred large. Deep down Woodstock 'ad known this too. I just reinforced it, chased away 'is denial. Until I gave 'im a lifeline, the only option 'e 'ad faw gettin' 'is life back was t' disappear wif 'is family, something 'e's shit-scared of. This way 'e gets the Rabble orf 'is back, and returns to 'is old life no worries. We can trust 'im all right, 'cause this is tha only chance 'e's got. Even if 'e called Hemi and warned 'im 'bout me, wif *this* type of money at stake, Hemi'd never let 'im orf as a thank you; Woodstock admitted this 'imself.'

Mick's reasoning seems to follow a similar route. After a while he nods gently. 'Yeah. Yeah, that's how I'd feel in his shoes. And so long as Woodstock's sweet, it sounds like the solid base of a good plan.'

Barry, muttering like a kid on Playstation: 'Ah, man, this is gonna be fucking *huge*.'

Mick, the squandered question for Steve, the look for me: 'What'll Donk do to Hemi?'

Barry, grin dripping: 'Take a wild guess.'

Steve, soft: 'Donk'll 'ave 'im whacked, no questions asked.'

Me, to Mick: 'Can you live with that?'

Steve: 'If yu can't then yaw a fuckin' bleedin'-'earted fool.

Nefarious may be the hard core, but Vegas Chapter ain't exactly saints . . . and Hemi's the big cheese. Wif 'is own 'ands — and this is only what *I* know of — 'e's put at least twenty people in 'ospital, most of those guilty of fuck all maw than wrong place, wrong time. 'E's raped at least five chicks in 'is time — that's *actual* rape, snatched orf the streets, fucked by guys in masks — and yu'd need a fucking *calculator* to work out the amount of molls 'e's pressured onto the block. When 'e's in the Joint he fucks guys — always white ones — 'cause control turns 'im on. Who *noes* 'ow many futures 'e's ruined by gettin' kids mixed up in the gang culture: "bringing through the new blood" 'e calls it. Nearly all prospects 'af t' do lags before 'e'll patch 'em. 'E gives 'em assignments t' test loyalty and meanness: "Bring me a 4WD before midnight; seek out this fulla, in this pub, and fuck 'im up good; break into this 'ouse, fuck the women and do any guys who give yu trouble." And I noe faw a fact that 'e's ordered hits on at least two dudes, both of 'em carried out by 'is boys.'

Mick rolls his eyes. 'My name ain't Gandhi, man. Let's do the world a favour.'

Piss on me, will you?

{ Archives: Duty and the Beast

[*While the breathless boatees pack up, tail-lights gay in the gloom, RED eases down from the bonnet. Crossing to nearby trees, urinating on them, he casts malevolent eyes across the line of 4WDs towing their toys back to town.*]

RED [*over his shoulder*]: With these *Armani*ed pipers schmoozing us all up the gallows, it's no wonder crime's on the increase.

BROWN: Which brings us neatly to our third target.

RED [*almost solemn, zipping up, resuming his position on the bonnet*]: The Fiendish Beast. What *is* it, man?

BROWN: Given the right conditions, it's a force that can find a home in us all; in some more easily than others. [*Expounding*] The Beast is as ancient as survival itself; still rules those tracts mankind is yet to corrupt. The *Fiendish* Beast, however, is what became of the Beast when evolution swelled the human thought-machine to its present ludicrous dimensions. Because we then had the 'intelligence' to invent applications for the Beast beyond its natural role.

RED: I see. For us intelligence might have made the Beast all but obsolete? Yet intelligence and wisdom failed to evolve in tandem?

BROWN: Exactly. And so for thousands of years mankind inflicted itself with horrors from which the most savage of the 'lesser' animals fled in terror and confusion.

Yet there came a time when humans were able to believe they had moved beyond this ubiquitous brutality; gained prudence and enlightenment, compassion and tolerance. Not just for one's own, but for one's species as a whole. They named this The Age of Reason, and folk drank to peace and love.

[*Grim*] But the Fiendish Beast was far from dead. A macabre metamorphosis had taken place. Under edification, it could no longer swagger unmasked at all times, but it remained in many hearts just the same. Skulking. Sniggering. And, as if inactivity had bred in it unknown levels of yearning, when it now found occasion to lunge from hiding — often to the call of god, free enterprise, statehood — its gluttony was more appalling than ever.

It was the Fiendish Beast who guaranteed Hitler would find millions all too willing to believe his victims were Satan in disguise. It was the Fiendish Beast pulling triggers when the US Cavalry brought genocide to the 'savage' Native Americans.

RED [*catching the drift*]: It was the Fiendish Beast who insisted that if they didn't take the initiative, the Serbs of Bosnia would soon be raped in their homes by people they'd learned to live alongside.

BROWN: And it's the Fiendish Beast who ensures that even

humans of blemishless pasts are hypnotically attracted to all manner of ugliness.

RED: There are those crying that, in the West at least, the Fiendish Beast is all but beaten.

BROWN [*frustrated*]: And in the West we *might* have beaten it! By 1945, so revolted were we by its recent . . . *orgies*, committed social change may have seen it all but banished.

But to the powers that presided, the pursuit of capital took priority. And as it built speed, the 'social Darwinism' so lauded by the capitalists — the 'freedom' to trade without safeguards, to 'compete' without regulation — consolidated the privilege of the elite at the expense of the many.

RED: Most of whom are sentenced to a life of wage-slavery in dehumanised, autocratic workplaces.

BROWN: Damn right. *Now*, with this wealth polarisation reaching *hateful* levels, the fabric of our societies begins to unravel. The working class is left without hope of a fulfilling existence; with feelings of envy, of disenfranchise-ment. Categorised by the 'free' market as commodities — expendable ones at that — they lose all sense of self-worth; come to view themselves and others as less than human. The Fiendish Beast finds these vanquished souls worthy mediums.

RED: What about in the wider world? To what can we attribute the rising tide of ethnic violence?

BROWN: Even at a glance, the 'free' market must claim much blame. Unhampered capitalism means the monied will naturally defeat less wealthy competition. In a multicul-tural society, then, as capital concentrates, one ethnic group will come to dominate the others. Those left impov-erished grow resentful. Setting flame to these powderkegs is child's play for nationalist firebrands with personal agendas.

But on top of this, deeper probing suggests more insidious

roots. Because capitalism has never shirked at unleashing the Fiendish Beast in the interests of 'cost effectiveness'. Just look at the amount of right-wing despotism the West has pushed into power throughout the 'developing' world, arming handpicked tyrants, providing them with 'advisers', polishing their monsters in training camps, all in the name of keeping new markets and cheap labour pools 'open and free'. Now we have local 'elites' with everything to lose playing lower-class factions against the other, laughing as the competition butchers itself. And, of course, when manipulation flounders, western plutocracy — safeguarding its investments — is only too happy to assist more directly in the 'pacification' of 'evil elements'.

Contemplate this: the depths to which the capitalists will stoop in the name of profit is well documented . . . and the most lucrative market in the world today is the arms trade.

RED [*repelled*]: Of course. Patrician mafias see to that; western old-boy networks; the incestuous trinity: politicians, 'defence' chiefs, and the 'captains of industry'.

BROWN: Those who saw off the Kennedy upstart.

RED: Those who trained the El Salvadorian death squads.

BROWN [*bitter as bile*]: 'Peace in our time'? In your fucking dreams. Where's the profit in it?

RED: But in the West itself? In the endless quest for profit, though they've the power to employ all manner of shenanigan, surely the capitalists would never subject *us* to barbarity? They must draw the line at loosing the Fiendish One here.

BROWN: Don't you see? Like all bullies, these people seek to justify their victimisation. They do this through theories of 'Social Darwinism': that under the 'free' market the more worthy of society will rise to its peak and, through their 'brilliance', keep countless others in work, and thus alive — the 'talent-driven society'. That most of them 'earned' their 'talent' through inheritance, they're able to overlook neatly, as they overlook the fact that most of the work they generate is tantamount to latter-day enslavement. Nevertheless, the Establishment 'elite' sees itself as superior to, and essential to, your average citizen. Therefore anything that boosts their holdings must ultimately be 'progressive'.

RED [alarmed]: They'll stop at nothing, then?

BROWN: Example: the western war on drugs. This war was declared by politicians with as much genuine knowledge of drug use and its ramifications as you and I have of quantum physics. They declared drugs satanic, opting for strategies of total repression over social awareness and rehab. Years on, drug use has actually increased, while the prisons fill to flashpoint, many of these inmates guilty of crimes no more heinous than pacific escapism: people with their minds now destroyed by the brutality of incarceration. And the war continues.

Odd, though, how this campaign clears working-class society — the capitalists' vital labour pool — of so many of its less sheep-like elements. Odd also how prison construction's become a recurring sharemarket stalwart, a real 'growth industry'.

Mind you, given that business and politics have always been siblings — often quite literally — perhaps it isn't so odd after all.

Barry: 'I've got a question. Where the fuck are we gonna find some cunt with the laros to take *bales* of primo seedless off our hands?'

Steve: 'I was kinda 'oping *yu* dudes might 'ave sum solutions there. If I'd got the pot from elsewhere, I could prob'ly've moved it, but it'd all've been through dudes wif Rabble affiliation. Obviously that's not an option.'

Me: 'There's only one dude I know who might have the kind of contacts we're talking.'

Mick: 'Me too.'

Barry: 'Ditto.'

Unison: 'Bum.'

Steve, frowning: 'Who's Bum?'

Barry, ringingly: 'The high priest of Narcoism. He's about three years older than us. Vegas boy. Lives in the Smoke now.'

Me: 'We used to score off him a lot. Him and his mates were the dudes who could get anything. Tough cunts too; mad as hatters; death-metal freaks. But Bum never flexed muscle until he had to. He's a good guy.'

Mick: 'Loose unit, though. He's the type of dude who goes through people's medicine cabinets. He once swiped a bottle of pills from his Gran's rest-home, couldn't make out the label, dropped a few for the hell of it and shat arse-acid every ten minutes for the next week and a half. He thought it was a great joke.'

Barry: 'Then there was the time they landed some datura off a dude who wasn't sure how strong it was. On a dare, Bum nailed three glasses of it blind . . . he was still peaking the next day when his court date came up. He made it to court, but halfway into the morning he had to crawl under the defendant's gallery and whack a gram of smack up his arm, just so he could stop laughing at the judge's lazy eye.'

Steve: ''E sounds a liddle . . . *eccentric*.'

Me: '"Eccentric"? He once tried to enter the record books as the first man to reach the South Pole in T-shirt and jandals.'

'How far'd'e get?'

'Opotiki.'

Barry: 'At age thirteen, after examining all options thoroughly, Bum left school and took up dealing. He does all right out of it, too — when he remembers not to use everything he's got for sale. His shift to the Smoke was a career move.'

Steve: 'We'll be passin' through the Smoke. Yu's reckon 'e could be our man?'

Me: 'I'll tell you what, with what Bum used to manage to grow and rip from around Vegas every summer, he was sometimes doing deals with up to twenty gs changing hands. That's not bad for a city this size. He's been in the Smoke now for a year and a bit . . . and he had his foot in the door before he left.'

Mick, conviction growing: 'Yeah, I'm certain he could unload at least a lot of it in one hit, then bury the remainder somewhere and knock it out as he can. He likes us — trusts us. We can trust him too, guaranteed.'

Me: 'Even if not for his contacts, we've gotta go see him anyway.'

Mick: 'Why?'

'We've got a perfect murder to share with him.'

From Mick and Barry this earns a breathless giggle. 'Fucking A, dude.'

Some people do crosswords to stretch their minds, pass the time. Bum obsesses upon the perfect murder. Strictly as an intellectual challenge, of course.

And perhaps because his vocation might one day necessitate it.

Steve: ''Ow'd yu guys get t' noe this cat?'

None of us rushes to answer.

Steve: ''Ello?'

Barry eventually bites the bullet. 'He's Lefty's brother.'

Steve, sneering: 'Yaw not fuckin' serious?'

Me, sighing: 'Deplorably.'

Barry: 'Don't worry, man. He's nothing at all like Lefty.'

Mick: 'Yeah, this brother's actually *got* some balls and principles.'

Steve, shrugging half-heartedly: 'If yu's say so.'

Barry, sudden: 'Ah fuck.'

His tone snags us. 'What?'

'I just thought of something: Bum shifted about two months ago, and I've lost his new address. Any of you dudes got it?'

Me: 'Na, I was meaning to get it off you.'

Mick: 'Same.'

Me, to Barry: 'Don't ya know any of his mates up there?'

'Since I shifted up, I've only seen Bum a couple of times, just to score, really. I've met a few people round at his crib, but I never got any numbers.'

Steve: 'Can't we just get 'is new address orf Lefty?'

Silence is a stern reply.

Steve: '*Speak* t' me, boys.'

Me: 'Lefty's a devious fuck.'

Barry: 'He'll be curious. He knows the only time we contact Bum is when there's drugs in the offing. He'll want in; after all, he considers himself a part of the crew.'

Steve, flat: 'Fuck 'im.'

Mick: 'He'll drag his feet like no cunt's business.'

Steve: 'Just spin 'im a yarn. Say there's a mate of a mate u's passin' through the Smoke, needs t' score sum blow somewhere.'

Me: 'Lefty's a devious fuck.'

Mick, expounding: 'With anything concerning his mates and Bum, Lefty insists on acting the middleman, swinging a cut from things.'

Barry, scoffing: 'Yeah, even though Bum wouldn't piss on Lefty if he was on fire.'

Me: 'What about Stiff and the boys, the usual suspects? They should know where Bum is.'

Barry: 'Stiff's in the Joint. Grant and Mutt fucked off down the South Island a while back.'

Steve: 'Would Lefty's old lady give it t' yu?'

Me: 'No *way*. She goes spastic at the mention of our names.'

Mick, to me: 'Can't say I blame her. You pissing in her steam-iron that time was a *little* out of order.'

Me: 'Oh, and trying to dry her wee Felix off in the microwave wasn't?'

'I denied all knowledge of that.'

'Quite convincingly, too.'

Barry: 'We're digressing here, lads. How do we track Bum down? Gator? You're the ideas man.'

I draw a temporary blank.

'Let's sort it out later. Something'll turn up. Even if we have to *beat* it outta Lefty. We'd only have to hit him once and he'll find out for us how many craps Bum's taken in the last fort-night.'

Barry: 'We should start working out what we're gonna need, then. That's if it's a done deal . . . ?' His eyes pick me out. 'Are we up for this?'

I pussy out, passing it on to our editor. Knowing the answer: 'The last word's yours, Mick.'

He stares into space for a good twenty seconds, and I can hear his brain probing the plan, *flaying* the fucking thing, desperate for a flaw.

A large part of me hopes he finds one.

Mick, at last: 'I'm game.'

I release a breath I hadn't been aware of holding, the ratchet in my gut cranking a few notches tighter.

It's good stress, though. Stimulating.

For the moment.

It's the stress of the Tri-Nations decider, the Blacks hot on attack, four points down, two minutes on the clock. It's the stress of a chick eyeing you over, crossing the party to speak to her.

I offer a prayer to the gods that at no point does it become the stress of waiting for a quack to tell you if the tumour's benign or malignant.

The stress of knowing your name's on a Rabble shit list.

Me, from a distance: 'All right. We're going then. What's there to sort out?'

Steve, low: 'First things first: we need a shooter.'

Barry: 'That's not a problem.'

'Whose is it?

'Mine.'

Steve, doubtful: 'Yu licensed?'

'Na, but that don't matter. A High Court *judge* wouldn't get a licence for this baby.'

The mere thought of the weapon sends a shudder through me.

When he's not setting the world alight, Barry's old man's a big deer hunter. A few months before the fallen heir was evicted for the final time, while his parents were away on holiday, Barry stayed out all night and left a back door wide open. He'd earlier lamented the house's poor security to a mate with a penchant for burglary. All Barry wanted was fifty per cent of the fence, and the rifle — his father's prized 30-06.

Later, deeming it cumbersome, Barry modified the hand-cannon: cut the barrel down, fashioned the stock into a pistol grip. A 'responsible' peer of ours supplies Barry with all the shells he needs.

He hopes to put his creation to its intended purpose some day, of that I'm convinced. You see, Barry applies a scientific stance toward such matters; he's big on experimentation.

He wants to learn what it feels like.

Mind you, in all honesty, who the fuck doesn't?

Steve, shrugging: 'If it's good enuf faw yu cats, it's good enuf faw me. What else? Two of us'll be making the actual "confisca-tion" — that'll be me and yu, Barry: yu meet the physical requirements beda than these two — so we'll need t' throw together some disguises. Just a sackcloth'll do faw me, but unless yaw gonna wear gloves — and that'll look tu sus this time of year — yaw hands might give yu away.'

Me, remembering something: 'Mick, you still got that Uncle Rangi kit cached?'

Mick ponders a moment. Pleased: '*Yeah*, I *have*, actually!'

A year or so ago, incited by an ugly ambush near the centre of town, the Brotherhood implemented a ruthless counter-strike against the homie faction concerned. It was executed late one Friday, near Vegas central, and involved the use of outer-circle members, two cars, prepaid mobiles, an hour or so of scouting, and a Jacks bottle filled with a 50/50 mix of bourbon and bovine laxative (whole days were lost convincing Barry of the non-viability of rat-poison). Mick, true to job description, insisted on fine-tuning the action with the precision of a military operation, one aspect of which included his sister, a drama student, supplying us with an 'Uncle Rangi kit': a wig of dreadlocks, a neat stick-on beard — black, of course — and a pot of dark foundation.

The live run unfolded as an 'explosive' success, so much so that after they 'chanced' upon the bottle, both carloads of us contrived to trail the guzzling homies to the alley in which they were eventually caught short. Pants down in the headlights, the youngsters were in no mood for rumbling.

We were.

Me: 'We'll probably only need the make-up, but we'll take the whole kit anyway. We'll need to sort out some torches, and a heap of batteries, boy scouts' motto and shit.'

Barry: 'And some backpacks.'

Mick: 'And some gloves: can't be leaving fingerprints anywhere.'

Steve: 'What else?'

Mick: 'First, we've gotta make sure no one knows we leave town as a party. We should also jack up an alibi each, just in case. Me and Gator can tell everyone we're off to stay with Rick.'

Rick, an older mate of ours, lives in a caravan down the East Coast, surfing his life away. Mick and I have spent half the summer down there, fucking around in the bush, fishing and diving, smoking up a storm. It's a real piece of paradise and Rick's unlucky if he glimpses another soul in a fortnight.

Barry: 'Amy'll say anything I ask her to. It's just her and me in the flat at the moment, so she can just say we stayed in and watched the tube.'

Amy — Barry's woman in the Smoke — is good like this.

Mick: 'Steve?'

'Yeah, I'll sort somethin' out, sweet as.'

Me: 'What else?'

Steve: 'I reckon I'll stop in at the DOC office tomorrow and pick up a topo of tha area we'll be hittin'. The map I drew is rough as guts, so I'll transfer all tha info over t' the real deal.'

Mick: 'Yeah, make sure ya do that, Steve: the Brotherhood never moves till they've minimised all variables.'

Me: 'What else?'

Mick: 'No doubt we're overlooking all sorts of crap, but I'll draft out a precis of the mission tonight and compile a checklist. Gator, see if ya can come up with a few methods of substantiating our alibis.'

I've a couple in the database already — spot the reprobate. 'You and me, Mick, we just need to fill in a postcard each and send them down to Rick in an envelope, telling him to mail them to our olds. I'll phone him and sort the technicalities as soon as we know them. Barry, you'll wanna get Amy to go to a busy cinema on the right night and buy tickets to a film you've both seen.'

Barry: 'No worries.' He's fidgeting like a skint smack-head. 'That seems to be that, then, gentleman. A-fucking-men. When're we leaving?'

Steve: ''Arvest begins in a few weeks. The buds'll grow 'bout an eighth more between now and then.'

Me: 'In the context of the size of this crop, that's a fuck of a lot of money. In the context of the pot belonging to Hemi, the pitfalls of pushing the margin for error too far, I say fuck the extra dough: let's go *real* soon, keep the leeway as wide as poss.'

No one moves to fault this.

It suddenly occurs to me just how much fun I'm having. The cloak of conspiracy and fellowship draped about the four of us is nothing short of electrifying.

Steve: 'I ain't got a wagon at the moment. 'Ow do we travel?'

Barry, flourishing behind him: '*Da naaaa. The 'Dan*, man. Her preordained purpose is suddenly made clear. *The 'Dan* was *born* for the mission.'

Mick: 'And even if she wasn't — something I'm not questioning for a second — she's all we got.'

Steve, frowning: 'Will she make it that far?'

Barry, hands aloft: '*Heyheyheyhey*, bro! Not so loud. She'll get the shits with us. Treat her like a bitch you're desperate to screw and she'll swallow every time.'

Steve, grinning: 'I used t' own a Holden like that.'

Mick, abruptly: 'I hate to tell you guys this, but I'm skint till dole day next week.'

I seriously doubt this. Mick's a Yid: he hoards cash like a squirrel does acorns. But that's just Mick; I gave up resenting it years ago.

Barry: 'I'm broke too. I finished up at the building site last Wednesday, but my severance won't clear till next week.'

Steve: 'I've got about twenty bucks.'

Me, grinning at the irony: 'I'm in Mick's boat: screwed till the Beehive next shits.'

Lefty: 'I've got enough to cover everyone.'

The four of us jump like niggers unhooded at a Clan convention.

He stands by the door in the garage's far corner, 'butter wouldn't melt' mask firmly donned.

Mick finds voice first; not a tickled one. 'Where the *hell* did *you* come from?

Lefty, persecuted: 'Well so-*rry*. Isn't a guy allowed to visit his mates any more?'

Mick, almost shouting: 'Yeah, but it's traditional to fucking *announce yourself*!'

Barry's across the floor in six strides and a heartbeat; by Lefty's face I see he comes close to bailing.

Barry, silk on steel: 'How long ya been out there, Lefty?'

'Well, I . . . I went to knock and heard you's talking about something that . . . '

'How *fucking* long!'

A dog expecting a belting: '. . . *that sounded important*, so I was gonna leave, but listened a bit longer just to be sure, and then decided ya's might need my help.'

'Last chance . . . and that's a promise. How long?'

'The first I heard was you saying "A-fucking-men".'

Four brains do a rapid backtrack. Four faces frown and snarl; curse hushed vehemence.

Me, broken: 'Get out, Lefty.'

'Ah, come on, Gator! I won't . . . '

'*Get the fuck out*! Wait down the driveway, under the street-light where we can *see* your sneaky arse. And fucking *stay* there till you're called back!'

Tears apparently inches away, Lefty shuffles out like Dear John personified.

Barry, walking back slowly, growling: 'Of all the fucking luck!'

Steve, outwardly calm already: 'What now? Yu guys know 'im best. What 'e 'eard might not make 'im all *that* dangerous.'

Mick, disgusted: 'Unless we torture him, we'll never *know* how much he heard. The shifty prick might've been out there the whole time.'

Steve: 'What do we do, then?'

Me: 'Three choices: abort, kill him, take him with us.'

Barry, instantly: 'Let's ice the cunt.' I'm uncertain of his sincerity level. Seriously. 'Let's trick him into rounding up his cash, beat Bum's number out of him, phone the dude for a decent murder, then send Lefty to that big singles bar in the ground.'

Me: 'If only.'

Steve, dubious: ''E wouldn't go tell Hemi just 'cause 'e's sore 'bout being left out . . . *would* 'e?'

Me: 'Even if he did decide to fuck us over this, he wouldn't have the guts to go through with *that*.'

Mick: 'The guts to deal with the Rabble, *or* to shit on us so badly.'

Steve: 'What's the problem, then?'

Me: 'The guy's got a mouth like a kick-start vibrator.'

Barry: 'You wouldn't *believe* some of the things he lets fly once his tongue's done its warm-ups.'

Mick: 'Just to sound hard he'll tell some chick about these mates of his who ripped off the Rabble.'

Steve, terminal: 'That can*not* be allowed t' happen.'

Me: 'You're not fucking wrong. If we go *now* he's gotta come and be implicated. That way, when it's done, he'll be so terrified of exposure he won't even *think* about the event, let alone talk of it.'

Steve: 'Yu sure of that?'

Me: 'Absolutely.'

Barry: 'I still say we whack the slippery fuck.'

Again, I hand it off to Mick. 'What's the call?'

There's only two choices here. Given Lefty's stability, there's really just the one . . . and we both know it.

But I sense an upheaval taking place in Mick: the usurping of prudence, a potent tool of his arsenal. It fights with valour, defying the winds. Reason and fear offer stubborn anchor . . . but the tempest's ferocity is unknown to these climes.

Leaving ragged wounds where it clung, Mick's prudence is taken by the vortex.

Sucked into the Quenchless Core.

Mick, in a voice I don't recognise: 'Let's take him with us.'

I make the mistake of looking down. Viewed without a net, the hard earth seems to smirk at me.

But a rule's a rule, and this one has brought prosperity. Though a part of me shrieks protest — locked in a cell, thrashing like a drowner — I accept Mick's resolution, as I've trained myself to.

Fighting vertigo, I barely hear him trying to live with himself. 'We need his money, anyway, and we can leave him at Bum's, pick him up on the way back through.'

Steve: 'That ain't a half bad idea. So long as yu's're *positive* 'e'll keep 'is 'ole shut faweva afta.'

Barry: 'He won't say *shit*, mate. About the only time Lefty can be relied upon is when his arse's on the line . . . and then you'd bet your wedding tackle on him.'

Steve: 'Gatey? Yu up faw it?'

. . . Calm as the hurricane's eye: 'Let's get the prick in here and brief him.'

134

[*The daylight's almost gone now, and the lake is in repose. No more hulls disturb the water, just a warm rippling breeze. Stars sparkle in the lapping of the wavelets. The petrol fumes have cleared, and the only raised voices belong to insects and moreporks.*

Up on the hill, though, the tranquillity is but skin deep. Up on the hill, the insurgents plot on.]

RED [*lying full-length, staring at the sky*]: How can we possibly *fight* the Fiendish Beast? It's intrinsic in us all. In all *males*, at least. Just watch a group of young boys mucking around: unless they're playing sport, they're either wrestling, ninja-ing, or slaughtering one another with mock machine-guns. Look at *adults*, even: how many'll turn away when a scrap breaks out in a Super 12 match; change channels when the latest filmed police-beating hits Three News? I reckon the psychologists've got it wrong: the glorification of violence is an impossibility . . . violence is our most glorious force by default.

BROWN [*nodding*]: In this progressive environment it is. From the cradle we're brainwashed — 'aim for the top', 'if you're not fast you're last', 'excuses for losers', 'want it most or be found wanting', ad infinitum. Violence, of course, is competition's ultimate and most primal manifestation; small wonder we erect fantasies around it. But I sincerely believe that with social revolution, with the renouncement of progressive values — with the deification of living and subsistence in their place — one day we might unmask the Fiendish Beast, exile it for ever.

RED: But how does the Brotherhood counter the reactionary argument 'A vote against progress is a vote for barbarism'?

BROWN: There's no doubt the stability we enjoy as humans is owed almost fully to progress and the western ideals that drive it. But it's time to look at the wider picture. It's time to admit that, as a beneficial way of life, progress has

135

planed. In fact, we've already hit the downward curve. An arch irony is unfolding: the immense power and numbers technology has given our species, coupled with the Western mentality of 'bigger, better, faster, more', means we've reached a place where man has become his only real adversary . . . and his most dangerous to date. If progress could be regulated, or put in the hands of a finite, accountable number, perhaps it would be worth preserving. But capitalism makes a mad Pandora's box of progress.

RED: Fucking oath it does. Anyone with money has the right now to take knowledge gleaned by responsible pioneers, hire fine minds with less integrity, and work to unleash upon the world whatever technology might appeal to a market.

BROWN [*a scoff*]: And I don't need to tell you how concerned with long-term ramifications capitalism is.

RED: Thus 'breakthroughs', which *nobody* has had a chance to assess the impact of, are absorbed by society daily. Capitalism demands that man shut his eyes and *sprint* into the future.

BROWN [*nodding*]: But though we name progress an enemy, the Brotherhood doesn't seek a return to Dark Ages living and ethics. Far from it. What we're saying is this: under western values, progress has reached critical mass; it's become a tightening noose. But it's also improved our lives out of sight: given us the leeway to learn ways of life far better than 'might is right'. After we've liquidated capitalism, then, the Brotherhood will strive for a society based upon a marriage between the power of good that progress has brought us, and more indigenous-orientated, subsistence values.

RED [*enlivened*]: Oh, *yeah*! That's something worth striving for; worth *dying* for. How do we proceed? How to scatter the seeds of social revolution?

BROWN [*hard*]: We can't. Not openly. The Juggernaut would see us coming from miles off; would crush us unconditionally.

RED: What then? How do we fight?

BROWN: We of the Brotherhood are fortunate in that, to all practical intents, our three enemies inhabit the same vessel. The Careering Juggernaut is the Quenchless Core embodied and fitted with massive armaments. It's also become the Fiendish Beast's quartermaster. By warring upon the Juggernaut, then, we war upon all three, but such a behemoth can never be fought conventionally. Our weapons must be sabotage and ambush, duplicity and disinformation, arson and terrorism, chaos and assassination; our only shields audacity and total ruthlessness.

RED [*nodding, smile distant but bloody*]: I'm up for that. Bring it on, Mr J.

[*Both fumble in pockets for cigarettes. RED strikes a match, holding it for his accomplice; shaking it away absently*]

RED: You do realise just how stacked against us the odds are?

BROWN [*after a pause*]: Well, it'd certainly take a brave bookie to install us as favourites.

RED [*insistent*]: But look more closely at these enemies we've named. The Fiendish Beast might not yet be universal, but its acts are so contagious, those in whom it has little footing can be brought into the fold with ease.

BROWN: For sure. A million people from opposing sides might be suing for peace . . . it takes just one to plant a bomb among them. Folk collecting loved ones' limbs will brook no talk of the two F's.

RED: Now look at our remaining enemies: the Quenchless Core enslaved Europe, which enslaved the world, creating the Juggernaut, gifting the Quenchless Core a stronghold in the souls of nearly all. The American Dream became the Western Dream, which is now the Global Dream: all hail free enterprise and opportunity, i.e. the platform for anyone with a 'bright idea' to become filthy rich at any one time. Never mind that established gamblers have the table well rigged, the masses tacitly barred from playing, the dream utterly dependent on their poverty, overwork and nobody-hood. Who has time to lament this when the dream's spoils are waved beneath one's nose at every passing second? With each breath the dream whispers, 'Someday it could be you', ensuring collective tantrum at the mention of change.

And of the many who *do* recognise the fundamental flaws, few of these have the courage to advocate an alternative; we will find even apathists manning the walls.

BROWN: Ain't that the truth.

RED [*profound*]: By declaring this war, then, we've effectively become *traitors*.

BROWN [*sudden grin serrated*] Fucking oath. And it's not just *high* treason, betrayal of one's nation. That shit's for pansies.

RED [*energised*]: *Yeah*, we're seeking to betray our entire fucking *species*! Its ruling body and brainwashed electorate, at least. Thus, in judicial terms, we've just pioneered the ultimate crime: *Arch*-Treason!

BROWN [*shaking* RED'S *hand*]: How very well phrased! With you aboard, the Brotherhood's prospects grow rosier. From here on let our lives no longer be our own: let our vocation be our universe!

RED: I'll drink to that. Long live the Craft of Arch-Treason!

BROWN: Hear fucking hear!

[*The blaze in their eyes dulls slowly to a simmer*]

BROWN [*minutes later*]: Whose turn is it to roll up, anyway?

5

Though he lives in the Smoke and sees Bum intermittently, Barry's yet to visit the man's new abode, and the address Lefty produces is too brief. We waste an hour or so searching, and it's getting toward six when at last we locate the place.

The block of red-brick flats could be anywhere in working-class suburbia. About six cars cluster out the front, spilling across the kerb. From somewhere inside, the sacred strains of Black Sabbath soothe the neighbourhood.

As we park and lock *The 'Dan*, start up the communal driveway, a couple of skinheads emerge from a door, descend the steps, head straight for us. They're out of uniform but the 'haircut' might as well be a stiff right arm.

Pure poison, skinheads. Every last one of the fuckers. Few of them ply a trade in Vegas — too few rocks to hide beneath — but I've heard that their numbers up here are swelling.

At the sight of them my heart does an instinctive double-take . . . and then wallows in the muscle behind me; the sudden violence in the air like cordite. With my eyes I play a role for the skins — Man With Itchy Fists — as do Lefty and Mick alongside. Behind a gaunt veneer of coincidence, Barry and Steve fan out

139

across the cobbles, shoulders begging for a too-hard bump, forcing the cultural carrion to detour.

They know what's good for them: look down with time to spare, seem not even to consider a rearward glance.

Pumped by our victory . . . we lesser three, at least.

But god help us if we ever meet them in formation.

Our auras shift quickly, though, as we climb the concrete doorstep the skinheads just soiled, an acute reminder of the trade that flows through this place. It shows in our hunched shoulders, our bogus benign faces — as if body language alone can communicate to the neighbours our personal 'above-board' status.

Barry, for one, doesn't seem to give a shit. I reckon he'd stroll into an LA crack-house as if it were KFC, Vegas branch.

Without pause, he does the honours. *Bang. Bang. Bang.*

The music drops and a silhouette of ludicrous contours approaches the frosted glass of the front door. A relief I contain well warms my spine. Mick's sigh is loud to my ears.

Bum's home.

A swung door and the source of the clownish shadow is made luridly clear. I think the last time brothers as disparate as Bum and Lefty sprang from some poor bitch's womb was when Schwarzenegger played opposite Devito in *Twins*.

The man before me is a living cartoon, and at the sight of us a grin splits Bum's gaunt face from ear to ear, showcasing a couple of AWOL incisors he lost scrapping, has been threatening to have fixed for years.

Bum, from a height near Barry's: 'Ah see 'em starnding before mah, but Ah dinae bellleave it. Oan mah ern fucking doerstep, they be. Llong tame nae see, llads! Enterr an' be wellcum!'

Bum's about as Glaswegian as Bobby Mugabe. But as part of his job description the dude prides himself on a wide repertoire of accents; he's prone to impromptu practice. Bum's view is that if he moves all his pot as a Jock, his acid as a Kraut, his speed as a Cockney, his barbiturates as a Frog, his dried 'shrooms as an albino Currymuncher, should the blue squealers ever bust clients of his and sweat from them dealer IDs, they'll finish up hunting a gang of multinational phantoms.

That anyone who's ever laid eyes on Bum would select him from a line-up of 300,000 doesn't seem to trouble him unduly.

On an arm of rope-like girth and length, he thrusts a hand into my face, and, as always, I take it with something approximating gentleness. Built like a malnourished whippet — toast-rack chest painful through the fabric of his tight T-shirt — Bum looks as though he'd struggle to knock the top off an ice-cream sundae. But, as if he's on a constant noradrenaline fix, the man's strength is surprising.

'Gator! My favourite visionary! How the fuck are ya, bro?'

I beam back at him. 'Not too shabby, Bum! Not too shabby at all. Good to see ya, dude.'

Bum's eyes are a shade of blue so dark one might guess he was injected with Nazi dye in a master-race experiment. He's constantly accused of wearing contacts. But the animation inside them is even more noteworthy. When Bum stares at you it's as if the mountain of hallucinogens he's done in his life have rewired his brain in a manner that leaves him continually gleaning insights invisible to others.

His eyes *dance* with this second-sight.

'Mickey! Baz!' His hand continues the rounds. 'Nice a ya's t' awwive early f' once, innit? I weren't expecting ya's f'nuva 'arf 'our tops. You lot's gotta be 'avin' a facking larf.'

Bum also holds the dubious distinction of sporting the largest head of hair I've yet to encounter on a person. Tight blond curls erupt from his scalp at near right-angles, and only through a belligerently maintained middle part does he avoid the ignominy of 'the full afro'. Thus, more wide than high, the mighty mop hangs around shoulder level.

Lefty, engaging grin: 'Howzit going, Bum?'

Bum's face freezes over . . . and even the weakest of nods he eventually spares his brother is a patent effort.

I introduce Steve and Bum's all geniality again. 'Good to meetcha, man.'

Steve, a touch overawed, perhaps near laughter: 'Same 'ere, bro.'

We're ushered in.

Me, to Bum, smile dulling the accusatory note . . . just: 'You keeping truck with skinheads now, Bum?'

He's human enough to grimace. 'You know me, mate: if there was good gear on offer, I'd deal with the fucking Vatican.' Then, to cover his chagrin, waving an arm expansively: 'I vould like at zis time to pwovide you vif za gwand tour. To your wight, *ja*, ve are haffing za bedwoom slash livingwoom slash diningwoom slash kitchen. Frew zat door ve haf za toilet slash barfwoom. Gwand tour *kaput, ja*?'

Mick: 'Nice pile of bricks, Bum. A phat crib indeed. Very . . . vernacular.'

Despite the modesty of his dwelling, Bum's managed to load it with about ten or so punters, sprawled across the bed/couch, the dining table and chairs, the threadbare carpet. Like us, they're dressed for the heat in singlets and t-shirts. For most of them, though — also like us — it'd take a heatwave of Saharan dimensions to prise them from their black jeans. Long hair and tattoos hold sway, a shaven head or three, a couple of Maoris, and one tarted-up chick with red braids and a patch-work hippie dress.

Stonedogs, one and all.

The girl's a bit plump, but the cut of her dress hides this well; bares nice cleavage. Her vacant eyes look me over, her expression dreamy — a real 'take-me-to-bed' face — and when she stares a bit too long a hot flush momentarily clogs my throat.

When I'm pissed I can track these types from a mile off; *sniff* them down.

The room also contains a couple of anomalies. White dudes dressed more smartly than the others: collars and cargo-pants, short hair bryled back, gold chains and rings, designer stubble painstakingly sculpted.

Shore Boys. To them I instantly attribute the Porsche in the driveway — the one choked with stereo equipment worth roughly what the car is. Takapuna kids, backed by Daddy's capital, skimming an exciting sideline on the wrong side of the bridge.

It seems the Smoke relocation has allowed Bum's enterprise the luxury of diversification.

We're introduced, and though most of these dudes are older than us we're warmly received; Bum's a real 'any friend of his . . . ' type.

We do a round of handshakes, and, basking in my status as a favourite of Bum's, I even find the gumption to approach the chick. Grinning false assurance: 'Howyadoen? I'm Gator.'

She leans forward a little to take my hand and her cool touch gives me an instant rod-on. I'm stricken by a vision of her stubby fingers wrapped about my prick, squeezing . . .

She offers a dreamy half-smile. '"Gator", eh? I'm Sally. If I get too close will you eat me?'

Me, typically flummoxed: 'Only if you're in season.' And twig to the chance innuendo as soon as the words are gone. *For fuck's sake, man, what the hell was that? What kind of a pervert would say such a thing?*

I back away blushing, but she only chuckles softly, settling back again, and it's a good few seconds before I calm enough to realise that, given the company, my line was actually a sound, flirtatious reply. Had someone else come up with the exchange I'd have been in admiration.

Fuck, I'm a lame cunt sometimes.

Bum 'forgets' to present Lefty, but Lefty's more than used to penning his own intros. 'How y'all doing? I'm Bum's brother.'

Ten sets of eyes canvass him. It seems reputation precedes. 'So *you're* the infamous Lefty?'

Somewhat deflated: '*Ah* . . . well . . . yeah, I s'pose.'

In an instant, Sally's attention has zoomed and focused on him, her tongue flicking unconsciously.

Pickling me in the green stuff.

Sally, to Lefty, breathy: 'Bum's told me *alllll* about *you*.'

And with that his aplomb is restored. He seems to gain

143

several inches. Tossing his forelock rakishly, drawling through perfect teeth: 'Don't believe a *word* of it.'

The damp smile she offers him seems as reflexive as a poodle showing throat to the timber wolf.

A creature I would cheerfully have shot right now.

Instead I resolve to drop masturbation insinuations wherever possible.

She's way below his standard anyway — unless, of course, he cracked a fat and nothing tidier was at hand, or if he felt he stood to gain something deeper by dorking her, and as Bum lays on the hospitality ('Pull up a floor, chaps. What's your poison? Speights or Speights?') Lefty drops her hungry stare.

Settling to the carpet, I snatch a tossed can of piss from the air, careful not to shake it. Lift the lid.

Crossing to the table, Lefty seems not to notice as the whole house except him soon have cold beer at hand and Bum shuts the fridge. 'Just use ya blower for a tick, Bum.'

Bum, terse: 'Yeah? Well leave your spondolees on the table if you're gonna ring outta town, like last time.'

'Yeah, *course*.'

Bum, taking the seat across from Steve and myself, alongside the bimbo: 'Don't give me that "course" shit, pal. You never fucking have before.'

Mick and Baz settle into pleasantries with a couple of dudes, ritualised stuff. 'So what do you guys do?'

'On top of weed? Mostly acid and speed. Tried some Es the other night, but for what ya get — unless you're well into that dance shit — it's not worth the expense, eh. What brings you dudes to the Smoke, anyway?'

Mick: 'Vegas is sold outta the Paul Holmes CD. Thought we'd try our luck up here.'

Bum, to Steve: 'How was the trip up?'

Steve: 'Pretty decent, really. Mick noes 'ow t' get the most out of an old six: build up a head of steam and forget yu got a brake pedal. Fucks yu orf, though, when sum tool in a fuel-injected eight flies past yu on the straight then gets in the way cornering.

Mind yu, we'd still've bin 'ere a lot earlier if Gator 'adn't'a wanted t' stop and cut fence every few clicks.'

Rick, a goateed crew-cut: '"Cut fence"? What the fuck *for*?'

Bum, eyes swirling: 'He sees farm sabotage as his vegetarian duty.'

Rick, frowning: 'His *what*?'

'My vegetarian duty.'

Rick: 'How so?'

All eyes are on me . . . but there's no space for awkwardness on soapboxes. 'Well, my vegetarianism stems solely from my detestation of modern man's keeping of "livestock"; the way he strips animals of all natural autonomy, perverting their life-cycles, reducing a thinking entity to a number to be squeezed, subjected to whatever atrocity might turn a profit. Few farms can't easily be labelled torture centres, tributaries to extermination plants.'

One of the Shore Boys, bemused: 'So you cut Farmer Joe's fences?'

'That's right. Even minor spanners can postpone mechanised murder.'

Rick: 'So you believe it's wrong for man to eat meat?'

'Not at all. Natural selection intended man to be omnivore. What I object to is the way progress has created a system where man's predation takes place in a farm the predator never sees, a 'factory' to make the predator weep, a supermarket where *flesh* is equated with pasta and toothpaste. If one must rob another of life to survive, so be it. But he who uses faceless executioners forgets what killing is, thus trivialising the taking of life . . . and this is true evil.'

A grinning Bum: 'Don't listen to him, Rick. He'll have a rifle in ya hands in no time.'

Rick doesn't seem to hear him; stares into space with the mildly shocked expression I live to inflict on people. It's a look that says, *Don't speak to me for a while. This bastard's just thrown my accommodation with existence; I'd like a little time to reconcile.*

Sally, frowning: 'Well, if that's what cuts ya cake, good luck to ya, but I hope you don't go snipping fences anywhere near main roads.'

Me, nodding agreement: 'Yeah, given the current orthodoxy, almost any act of sedition must be perpetrated beyond the eyes of the great unwashed.'

Her frown deepens. 'That's not what I meant. I'm worried about your "freed livestock" wandering in front of cars.'

I give this a moment's thought. Can muster no concern. 'Ah, fuck that; there's too many cars in the world anyway.'

Sally, shrill: 'Screw the bloody *cars*! What about the people *inside* them?'

Pausing. Shrugging: 'Too many of *them*, too, really, isn't there?'

Barry: 'Fucking oath there is.'

Bum, still grinning: 'On that note, Gator, how's your "Final Solution" coming along?

This is enough to startle Rick back to the 'here'. Aghast: 'What Final fucking Solution?'

Me, muffled, embarrassed by this turn: 'Soul patrol.' Can't remember sharing this particular slice of Fantasia with Bum. Must have been during one of our many benders.

Barry, proud as punch: 'He's gonna go online and propagandise to the impressionable.'

Bum to Rick, winking: 'Yeah, so if the SIS smash the door down tonight, just go back to sleep . . . it won't concern us.'

(Lefty, wheedling in background: '*Hi*, Ang'. What are ya up to?')

Me, eager to change the subject: 'So, Bum, that scapel-like mind of yours conceived any decent murders lately?'

Fondly: 'As a matter of fact . . .'

(Lefty: 'Yeah, listen, honey, I won't be able to make it tonight . . . Na, it's nothing like that. Just have to be there for some friends of mine, sort of thing, ya know what I mean?')

Bum: '. . . me and Rick drafted one out the other night. Eh, Rick? Rick!'

Rick, snapping back to focus: 'What's that, chief?'

Bum: 'That hit we came up with?'

Rick: '*Oh,* yeah. The Lightning Tree. That's a fucking ripper.'

Bum, eyes giggling: 'If you'll pardon the pun.'

(Lefty: 'I *know.* The other night meant the world to me as well. I've seldom felt so . . . so *comfortable* with another person. I felt I could say *anything* to you; it was almost *eerie.*')

Mick: 'What's the drill with the hit?'

Bum, happily intent: 'There's a few variables involved. First, you've *gotta* have your own crib. Second, you've gotta wait for a decent lightning storm, at night, and then be able to get the subject to your place. You also need a park or field where you can be sure no cunt's gonna surprise you in the earlies.'

(Lefty: 'Yeah, babe, I miss you already too . . . I've gotta go now . . . I don't *want* to but I *have* to . . . OK . . . Yeah, I promise.' He looks at his watch, as if counting seconds; keeps an eye on it. 'Hang up the phone, hon . . . No, *you* hang up . . . I did it *last* time . . . OK, count of three: one, two, *three* . . . *Ahahahaaaa* . . . You didn't *either*! *Ahaha* . . . ')

Tony, a long haired Maori near the phone: 'This is making me fuckin' sick.'

(Eyes still counting, Lefty hangs up of a sudden, foolish smile dying with the connection.)

Rick: 'Yeah, then on the night of the storm you get the subject round to your crib somehow, immobilise them, tie and gag them, place them in a full bath-tub, amp up an old radio or something, hiff that in the drink with them, then wait till they stop hissing.'

(Lefty makes a note in a fat little book — his 'chicktionary'. Dials again.)

Bum: 'All you do *then* is transfer the subject to the boot of your car, drive to the said field — preferably somewhere near the subject's abode — dump subject beneath a tree, and fuck right off. Coroner's verdict: Death by lightning conduction.'

All who're paying attention: '*Hahahahahahaha.*'

(Lefty into the phone, deeply penitent. 'Hi, Tracy, it's me. Listen, baby, there's no easy way to say this, so I'll just get right to the point. With all that's going on at the moment I think we should have a break in our relationship . . . I want you to understand that this has got *nothing* to do with you . . . it's all about me. I'm just such a mixed-*up* cunt right now and I wanna spare you all the baggage . . . I guess what I really need is a little time, a little space . . . ' Abruptly, he jerks the phone from his ear. Whining: '*Shit*.'

Tony, gloating: 'She 'ang up on yu, beau?'

'Na, the fucking answer-machine ran outta tape.')

Some stocky dude labelled Andrew: 'I got a good murder.'

Me: 'Whadaya call it?'

'The Ice Arrow.'

Jackson, one of the Shore Boys: 'The *Ice* Arrow?'

'Yeah. The way I see it, most murderers're busted by way of the murder *weapon*, right?'

Bum: 'I'd have to say the body plays a larger role.'

Andrew: 'There's no need to be quoting from The Book of Hairspliticus, Bum.'

Smiling, nodding: 'Fair call.'

Andrew. 'OK, now you work out where your subject lives, then rent the house opposite. It's gotta be summer, though. Then you develop a mould for an arrow, fill it with water, and freeze it. Late one night then, you ring the subject from a prepaid mobile and convince him to step into his front yard. From the shadows of your own front yard you then take your arrow, fit it to a bow, wait for the subject to turn away, then spit the cunt from behind. By the time the feds get around to viewing the now deceased subject, the arrow's completely melted. Coroner's report: Murder by fuck knows what.'

'*Ahahahahaha!*'

Rick, at last, contradictory: 'Too many variables, boss. First, you've gotta be a shit-hot archer: could be a little embarrassing if ya feathered the joker through the calf. Second, you've gotta trust to luck no bastard witnesses the hit.'

Mick: 'You'd improve the odds a hell of a lot if you used a big, fuck-off crossbow.'

Sally: 'But just waiting for the house opposite to become available could take bloody years.'

Andrew: 'Well, maybe it needs a *little* fine-tuning, but aside from that it's the perfect murder, right?'

Barry: 'I don't know about that, mate, but I'll tell you dudes one thing: The Ice *Hammer*? Now, that's worth looking into.'

Sally: 'Anyway, all this perfect murder shit's a waste of time: none of ya's are ever gonna actually *use* one.'

Barry: 'What's the bet?'

He gains some endorsement on this, and Sally brands us all wankers.

Soon, Bum's throwing more beers around; appointing rolling duties to Sally, handing her a big bud.

Shore Boy One: 'I'm heading down the shop. Anyone want anything?'

Lefty: 'Yeah, dude, I do.'

'What are ya after?'

Me, interjecting loudly: 'He'll have a bottle of tequila, a copy of *Big Uns*, a box of Kleenex and a packet of Winnie Reds.'

'*Hahahahahahahahaha!*'

Later, a tap at the door and another chick is ushered in — some mousy little thing in tight shorts, looks barely fifteen, built like a hat-rack with nipples, hickies dotting her neck — and I feel room-wide suspense fall on her.

Sally: 'Vanessa! Did you do it?'

Vanessa milks the moment, her mock disappointment prompting a few grimaces. She soon grins, though, and the house sighs relief.

Rick: 'Fucking beauty!'

Tony, rubbing hands together: 'That's what I like t' see, Nessie, my girl.'

From a small backpack she takes out a plastic bag, removes from it several A4-sized sheets done up in glad-wrap, hands them to Bum.

His gaze thanks her profusely. 'Onya, baby.'

Me: 'What are they?'

'Snowflakes.'

It seems I'm abruptly in the presence of enough acid to put the fun back into fundamentalism.

Shore Boy Two, rubbing his hands together: 'Let the good — times — *roll*.'

Mindful of touching as little of the sheet's undersides as possible, Bum begins scissoring trips loose. 'Fucking A. But don't think you cunts can come round here and trip for free till the shit's gone, like last time. I've got buyers for almost *all* of this just waiting for the stuff.'

Barry, salivating: 'Good trips, Bum?'

Bum merely looks at him.

He then hands a chunk of at least twenty trips to Vanessa. 'Far yar foine sarvice, moi lass. Sell, loan or swaller, whatever playsus ya.'

Rick: 'How did my car go, Ness?'

Vanessa, stowing her wage: 'Like a bag full'a hairy dogs.'

Sally, lighting a joint: 'I *knew* you'd pulled it off. I just got that feeling that something sweet had gone down, ya know?'

Vanessa, conspiratorial: 'Yeah, I know. *I* knew it'd be cool before I even turned down the last street.'

Bum, eyes chuckling ambiguity: 'Of course you knew: you're a bitch.'

Sally, passing the joint: 'What's that s'posed to mean?'

Bum, to the wider audience, scissoring merrily: 'Have any of you's ever met a chick who didn't claim to some manner of affinity with the supernatural?'

I give this some real thought . . . and draw mostly blanks.

As do the others.

Mick: 'You're bang on there, Bum, my man. Almost every bird ya come across "believes" in something like: the Tarot, fate; astral travel . . . '

Andrew: 'Reincarnation, karma . . . '

Steve: ' 'Oroscopes, telepathy . . . '

Jackson: 'Hauntings, seances . . . '

Rick: 'Tea-leaf readings, ouija boards, palmistry . . . '

Barry can't help himself. 'Spontaneous human combustion.'

Neither can Lefty. 'Multiple male orgasm.'

Naturally, the girls are feeling a little victimised, but they're still smiling: the prospect of head-food keeps spirits artificially high.

Vanessa: 'It's just that you male arseholes are so obsessed with the physical world you've totally lost touch with the spiritual.'

Massing my nerve: 'I dunno 'bout that. What do ya reckon, lads? Those who believe in telekinesis, raise my right hand.'

'*Hahahahahaha!*'

Bum completes his task; caches most of the gear somewhere in a closet. Declares: 'All right, ladies and gents, queue here for the express to Lucy's Diamond Skies.'

General rejoicing.

Baz, to me quietly: 'What are we doing later?'

'Didn't we say we'd head out to a pub or something?'

'Yeah. We still on for it?'

'I'm well keen.'

'Sweet as. What's the time now?'

'Sevenish.'

Barry takes a quiet moment and I watch indecision mauling at him. Finally, his shoulders sag and he settles again, staring at Bum allotting acid with regret that seems almost anger.

When the whole house bar us are sucking on LSD — most merrily, though two or three are obvious slow starters, eyes a touch apprehensive; *What happens now?* expressions flashing — Bum asks us with a frown: 'You dudes sitting this round out?'

Mick: 'Yeah. We're gonna hit town in an hour or two.'

'So?' Bum's been dropping acid so long he could probably dock the Space Shuttle on the stuff.

Me: 'Wanna stay sharp as poss, bro.'

In a controlled environment — unless you're unlucky, and/or mentally unsound — LSD's a barrel of laughs. When you're well away from home turf, however, wonder and hilarity can easily become paranoia, disorientation, melancholy. Externals can become a hazard too, especially in a town like this. The fashion with which acid warps your thought processes through different dimensions can often leave you reading situations with almost sorcerous perception, but at the same time it can leave you blinkered to more immediate factors. And in a dark ARC heaving with a cocktail more dangerous by far — booze and testosterone — this vulnerability should not be borne lightly.

Bum: 'Fair enough. Just us dudes'll make another pilgrimage tomorrow, if ya's are keen.'

Baz: 'Amen to that.'

Me: 'Tell ya what, though, Bum, what are the chances of us scoring a little nose-candy off ya? For tonight?'

Even for the connected, down in Vegas good powder's only slightly less difficult to procure than tiger-penis soup. We're all well up for a toot or three.

Bum, regretful: 'Not strong, man. Not strong at all.'

Five flat sighs: 'Uh.'

Bum, winking at me: 'The chances of me *sorting* ya's for nose-candy, however, are significantly higher. Overwhelming, in fact. But the day you guys have to fucking *score* off me is the day I break faith with this honourable trade of mine.'

Mick, to Barry: 'Ya just gotta love this guy, yeah?'

Steve, uncertainly: 'What about our . . . our business 'ere?'

Without a word the onus descends on me. I accept it, as I know I must. 'Yeah, Bum, listen, man. Before your trip kicks off, have ya got somewhere we could talk a little shop?'

Bum just shrugs, but I can feel his ears pricking up. 'Let's step into the office.'

He leads me through to the shithouse/bathroom, a cubicle little bigger than a standard wardrobe, locking the door behind him. There's barely room enough in here for Bum and myself, let alone Bum, myself, and Bum's hair.

Bum, slamming the lid on the dunny: 'Be seated. Might I harve Miss Mills fetch corffee? She's recently retarned from hoeliday. *Darling* woman. Toetal peach.'

I lax back on the throne. 'Thenk yew, my good fellow, noe. I'm afraid I indulged *frightfully* oever brunch.'

Like a gothic marionette, Bum squeezes his tiny arse into a tiny basin, folding into what he contrives to make seem a comfortable position, one foot rested on a window-sill high in the room's far corner.

He doesn't procrastinate. 'What's the scene, jelly-bean?'

'We wondered if you'd wanna go in on a deal with us. You line up the buyer, we provide the wares.'

'What flavour we talking?'

'Blow. Outdoor. *Primo*. Durban Skunk. Seeds from the 'Dam.'

The waltz in his eyes quickens. 'This time of year there's fuck all outdoor anywhere. Up here, of course, we've got *indoor* skunk coming out our fucking arses, but most of that's got no body to it. Cunts get too greedy: churn out too many yields to keep good quality. Dudes get sick of smoking the shit. You know us meat and potatoes Kiwi druggies: give us prime outdoor *any* day of the week. But, as I'm sure you know, we're still a few weeks from harvest, so if you've got primo Durban Skunk, you could find a buyer for that at a National Party convention . . . with*out* my help. What's the catch?'

I'm careful not to break his gaze: this is more of a pact than a partnership — a murder/suicide pact (of sorts) — and, mate or no mate, Bum's the type you'll only cross once. 'We need you because we're expecting to be trying to move a shitload of the stuff.'

'As in . . . ?'

Breath deserts me; it comes out like a wheeze: 'About a hundred-odd pounds.'

Without transition, Bum's eyes are no longer dancing; they're marching.

Goose-stepping.

His voice drops, but where I sounded infirm, he just sounds predatory. 'Are you for fucking real?'

I can only nod.

Warm as hail: 'Now how the *hell* would five kids from Vegas lay mitts on a *hundred pounds* of Durban Skunk in *March*?'

Sickly: 'Do you really wanna know?'

His ponders this for a long while, my world fluxing around the axis of his eyes.

Bum, at last: 'Na.'

And with that I know he's mine.

Thank you and goodnight.

I'd had fleeting doubts, but at the end of the day Bum's a dealer: were he an ambulance chaser, this thing's a paralytic billionaire.

Bum, clarifying: 'At least I *do* wanna know, but only vaguely — enough to see them coming if it ever gets to that. And I need to know *now*, in case I end up trying to shift it to the same party you cats are . . . embezzling.'

My reply's as immediate as panic. 'It's the Rabble, man.'

He sighs long and low. Takes the time to light a gasper. Holding my eye: 'An amount like that — had to be one of the big players.' He lets me escape a moment later, and, staring into space, Bum's eyes begin to tango, oozing the spice. He savours his ciggie like it were cadged from the headsman. Distant: 'If it was anyone but you sitting here — or maybe Mick — I'd say "no fucking chance". But you guys are on to it. With you two involved I like the odds, and at the end of the day that's all this game boils down to: you keep your ear to the ground, minimise the risks, then dive in like a man with no doubts. I'll say nothing further on the matter, but just let me echo what I'm sure you know already: fuck this up in *any way* and you're dead, plain and simple. If the Rabble don't do you outside of prison, they'll sure as shit get you on the inside. You're a clever bastard, but don't take a *thing* for granted. Run through your plan *over* and *over*.' Eyes swivelling to impale me: 'And if there's the slightest heat on you after the job, you come the fuck near me ever again and I'll toss you to the wolves myself.'

Given the nature of our arrangement, Bum's within his rights saying this, but his harshness rams home the enormity of our venture by several brutal inches.

Someone throws an invisible switch; the stuffy bathroom loses five degrees.

Me, croaking: 'Shit, I need to get pissed.'

Quick as a punch — so quick I instinctively fear attack, nearly yelp and cringe — Bum's long arm raps me on the shoulder. 'If you've already decided you're up for this, what you need to do right now is chill the fuck out. What you *need* is to get a line of uncut Peruvian marching powder up your nostrils.' Seemingly disembodied, his face looms close to mine, and to my paranoia his sudden grin suggests any number of things. 'And it just so happens you're in the realm of the candy-man.'

{ Archives: To Shuffle With The Herd

> **Attention all workers:**
> **Bags and coats are NOT to be taken into the warehouse. They're to be left in the cloakroom provided.** Along with all pride, dignity and sense of self-worth.

True to tradition, the early shift have overrun the cubby-holes long ago. So, at an empty spot along the wall, Barry and I dump our belongings on the lino. A neat row of lockers face us from opposite, but staff got first dibs on these. Brown-nosers got second, leaving us standard robots with sweet fuck all.

True to tradition, Barry flips a finger at the miniaturised telescreen jutting from the wall above us. While he pockets his valuables, I begin work on the second sign.

Barry, for the first time today: 'Fucking wankers. What's the point having cameras in here if they can't stop dudes' bags being ripped off?'

Me, for the first time today: 'Read your contract, bro. "The company takes no responsibility for the welfare of employee property."'

Barry, huffing: 'Yeah, right. Where's the profit in paying the

155

insecurity staff to guard the belongings of expendable workers?'

Me: 'Only their reasoning is even more Machiavellian: this is a facet from Management Strategy, Section 78, Subsection 4C.'

'Which reads?'

'"A worker stripped of humanity is a component with fewer over-heads."'

Barry, noticing what I'm doing: 'You should watch it, dude: that one's in full view of the telescreen.'

Me, finishing: 'Who gives a fuck? It's D T Day.'

'Oh, that's right. I forgot all about it. Nice work, by the way.'

'Cheers.'

Queue here for signing in
and the surgical removal of another
eight hours of the prime of your life.

Barry rings the buzzer and, slouching against the wall, we await the leisure of an Apprentice Overseer (AO).

Barry, reflective: 'What's one pet hate every adult shares?'

'Pass.'

'Getting older. Am I right?'

Nodding: 'I'm guessing you'd struggle to find a western adult warmed by the ageing process.'

'And yet, had they the power, how many people in this very position — about to begin the day's work — wouldn't click their fingers and beam themselves instantaneously to the end of the day?'

'. . . I know I would. I'd do it the next day, too. And the day after.'

The AO arrives, rudely interrupting our profundities, clipboard brandished like a bull-whip.

Tutting: 'Trotter and McPike. Late again, gentlemen. What's the excuse this time?'

Me: 'Our flight from Sao Paolo encountered white-out conditions and flew smack into the Andes, killing most aboard. We were left the ordeal of traversing the ranges on foot . . . '

AO: 'Yeah, good one, McPike. You're about as funny as a fart in an elevator.'

Barry: 'Just sign us the fuck in, Gimp, or I'll ram that clipboard up your ringpiece. Sideways.'

The AO scoffs, but does as he's told. Barry's reputation ensures this. Still, I believe sniping alone would have seen Barry sacked by now, only even the real overseers can't be certain of escaping the shockwave.

Might is right is right.

At least it is when it's on my team.

The transaction complete, we don zombie masks and slot into our appointed roles.

Barry unloads trucks with a counter-balance fork-lift. I stand on the Goods In floor tallying the stock on incoming pallets. Office hacks match these quantities arriving to the quantities ordered, print location sheets. Guided by these, a crew of reach-fork-lift drivers transport the stock to its temporary home in the numbered shelves. More retrieve stock from these locations, taking it to sheep who scatter it through the pick-face at the warehouse's far reaches. Other sheep, pushing trolleys, shuffle up and down the pick-face, following computed directives, filling boxes with bits and pieces. A few more links down the chain, these boxes find themselves despatched to individual clients.

Over it all, telescreens take silent and thorough notation. AOs swagger, threatening 'loafers' into action. Overseers gather in corners, characterised by suits, cufflinks and smiles, locked in impromptu 'meetings' for just as long as they fucking well like, the steps of nearby sheep lent extra spring by calculating regard.

A mural of immense elegance.

To progressive eyes.

6

Lefty, from the front seat where he somehow ended up: 'I really need a feed before we hit the piss. Anyone else?'

Steve, Baz and I draw blanks. We're looking to get slaughtered tonight: at pub prices, to achieve such on a full stomach'd set us back at least forty bucks a head.

As usual, Mick's on driving duty. 'I wouldn't mind a bite myself. Pretty skint, though.'

I know for a fact that he's got sixty bucks in his pocket.

Lefty: 'This excursion's on me, remember? I don't mind throwing some chow down ya throat.'

'Sweet. What's your poison?'

'Burger Queen.'

'McDick's it is, then.'

There's no need to detour in search of the Juggernaut's vending machines: this is the Smoke; one encounters consumption centres every few kilometres. For the time being they retain the character of names — Epsom, Mt Eden, Newmarket — but for how much longer?

Logarithmically, names are so . . . *unwieldy*.

The spaces between — block after block, mile after mile —

158

are unrelenting nest and plant. Through it all we're gusted along by twin streams of units, purring, roaring, chugging improvements on a dying sunset as tainted as lust.

Soon a golden minaret summons the faithful, and spying a hole Mick eases *The 'Dan* down, swinging her across two lanes of traffic with reassuring insolence.

As he pulls into a park I suffer a change of heart, declare on impulse: 'Actually, grabus a coupla veggie burgers, will ya, fellas?'

They depart to offer homage; Steve has worship of a rival deity in mind. Producing a pre-rolled joint: 'Little bit'a gunja left from the drive up, boys. Not enuf t' wet all whistles present, but enuf t' get the three of *us* buzzing.'

Barry: 'Top man.'

Given that we'll soon be ensconced in a heaving ARC, I need a dose of Mary Jane about as badly as I need a three-way with the Topp Twins. But old habits die hard, and when you're straight forethoughts of being stoned are so easily overlooked. Besides, the male bonding to be supped from the three of us indulging in a sneaky session proves too tempting.

Against nasal denouncement, we resolve to decamp from *The 'Dan*.

Steve: 'Whada we say if we get back after they do, though? They'll noe we 'eld out on 'em strade away.'

Barry: 'Ahhhh, what's a good excuse? . . . Gator? You're the ideas man.'

The solution finds me in seconds. 'Let's get Uncle Rangi happening. We'll say we wanted to see if we could fool them.'

Barry, chuckling admiration: 'You're a fucking crooked bastard, McPike.'

He fetches the kit from the boot, jumps back in, the three of us giggling like kids in a pantomime.

Steve opts for the beard and mo — full, black, trim. 'Always wanted t'know 'ow I'd look wif one'a these.' He fixes it to his face, the sticky strips along its inside adhering easily. 'Never 'ad the patience t'grow one, though: too fuckin' itchy.' Barry straightens it for him, and Steve checks himself out in the rear-view mirror. 'Fuck! A few stone lighter an' I'd pass faw a dread-locked Billy Ocean!'

Me, trapping my own hair beneath Uncle Rangi's wig of dreads — longer than Steve's, but just as thin: 'A few stone *heavier* and you'd pass for Barry White, mate, the Walrus of Love himself.'

He turns to me, chortling: 'Fuck you, Medusa.'

'Fuck *you*, bro: you wear your hair like this by *choice*.'

Barry: 'I won't bother with the makeup. I think I'm scary enough as it is. Besides, I don't reckon I could handle looking *half* as foolish as you two do.'

Steve: 'Let's do it.'

Back at Bum's we each took the time to shit and shave, throw on collars, clean jeans, smellies, more personalised bitch-attrac-tant. Big-city nightshift is kicking in around us — the very air hums with it — and the Vegas boys are feeling the bizzo.

With wrong in mind we slip into the dark of back stage — among the effluent to the rear of McDick's. Judge it sufficiently barren for needs of nefarity.

The circle of idolatry forms; Steve lights up, tokes deep, hands it on, resumes talking. 'Yeah, yu's should'a *seen* this piece'a shit. Toby drives round my 'ouse in it, and I 'ear the fucker coughing and farting from 'bout a mile away.'

Barry, whispering lest he lose fumes prematurely: 'What was it again? A combi?'

Steve: 'Na, man, it was a Bedford bus. And I say t' the cunt, '"Yu aren't *seriously* gonna try and drive t' Whangamata in that thing?" He goes, "*Yeah*, man. It'll get us there, *sweet* as." So I thought, "Fuck it," grabbed my stash and jumped in faw a cruise.'

He breaks off to drag a second hit from the doobie, hands it on again.

Barry: 'Did he have a bus licence?'

Steve: ''E didin' even 'ave a fuckin' *car* licence!'

'*Hahaha*.'

Steve: 'And shit, I ain't neva sat inside a worse ride, eh. It was running on 'bout two and a half, I'd say. Uni joints damn near worn through. Can't of 'ad a warrant in four or five years. Plugs and points last changed in the sixties. Tyres so worn she almost skidded changin' lanes. Hissing constantly, man, as if she was set to blow 'er top. Temperature gauge read OK, but I'd've taken *Prebble* at 'is word before I took *that*. Graunching up a storm whenever yu changed gears, jumping outta fourth. But I tell yu what, it were peak 'oliday season and *no* cunt passed us all the way from Morrinsville t' Whangamata.'

Me, impressed: '*Yeah*? *That* fast?'

Steve: 'Na, na; tu much smoke. Went through 'bout . . . '

Baz, low and alert: 'Heads up, fellas. We got company.'

From the opposite direction a figure's approaching us. Too dark to make it out properly, but by its size it can only be male. The joint's with me, but I'm reluctant to toss or stub until there's real need.

Steve, muttering: 'It looks like Bacon.'

Even without the smell to condemn us, young guys seldom linger in urban backwashes to discuss the economic ills of Black Africa. A cold finger strokes my spine. This may be the last of the weed, but . . .

. . . Bum sorted us for nose-candy . . .

. . . and nestled among the wedding tackle we've each got a gram that abruptly gives off the heat of a supernova.

Steve's not wrong, but by the time this is verified the oinker's just a few feet away. The hand I hold behind my back shouts like clarion. I spy a nearby drain and take a shot, dart-like. It sails between two bars — *Legend!* — striking liquid with a hiss.

But the damage is done.

In the darkness, what I can make of the oinker's face beneath his peaked hat only goads my alarm. Some oinkers have hearts — seriously — are open to interpreting the law a little eccentrically when it's in the common good. But I intuit instantly that this fucker's not cut from that cloth.

Late thirties. Flat stare. Thick moustache. Mottled complexion. Spreading girth.

Oinker, delight barely in check: 'What have we *here,* then, fellas? Come to collect the trash, have you? Funny time of day for it.'

Barry, amiable: 'Na, mate, we're just getting a little air while our friends are inside having a meal.'

Translated from diplo-speak: *You know what we're doing here. You also know that hundreds of thousands of others around the country will, and have, been doing likewise tonight. We're consenting adults, we were at pains to be discreet, we're not making any trouble, and the longer it stays in our heads the less likely we are to get into trouble. You* know *this: you're a cop. How about letting it slide?*

But Holmes is having none of it. Scoffing: 'A little air my *arse*. You're out here smoking marijuana: you all *stink* of it! And I'm not blind: I saw the white Bob Marley here ditch the joint.' Leaves us hanging a while. 'I wanna know who you bought the reefer off.'

I can read this guy's history like a timeline: straight C student; second-rate sportsman; failed attempts to cultivate a 'hardman' image; lost cherry at age nineteen (to a twenty stone boiler); joined the Swineherd for the easy money and easier respect; first beer and 'parties' at oinker school; career at glass ceiling thanks to a lack of intelligence and charm; blames it on everyone but himself; seeking to amend things with 'sound' bust levels.

Steve: 'We ain't *got* no reefer, bro.'

Oinker, indignant: 'I'm not your "bro", Blackbeard . . . and don't insult my intelligence. At the very least I've got Dreads here on possession charges, and you two on suspicion. So if you dip-shits don't show me some convincing ID and then start naming names, the four of us are taking a little ride downtown.'

Barry shapes to speak but I cut him off — when dealing with obstinate oinkers, the dude tends to get conciliated-out pretty quickly. 'Look, sir, it was just a cigarette. We're up here visiting John's mum in the Middlemore Hospice, and . . . '

Oinker, finger ominous: 'Bullshit me *once* more — *any* of you — and you'll be in *serious* shit. It's already bad enough, but if you lot jerk me around I'll come down on ya's like a fuckin' ce*ment* mixer.'

I switch to 'I know I've wronged, God, but I'm just a misguided kid and look how remorseful I am' mode. 'Ok, Ok, it *was* a joint, but it was all we had! I promise. I can see how pointless lying to you is, so I'm straight up here!'

Oinker, imperious: 'Even if that *was* all you had, you've still broken the law and you're going to be punished accordingly.' Weighted pause. 'Unless you tell me . . . '

Steve, reasoning: 'C'mon, sir, if we weren't out 'ere 'avin' a quiet smoke, we could've been pissed by now like so many ova youngsters out an' about, mouthing orf, starting shit, firing up.'

Oinker: 'Until you break a *law*, sunshine, you can get as pissed as you like and you'll have no trouble from me. *Dope*, on the other hand, is *unlawful*. Can you comprehend that?'

Me: 'But as a civilisation, sir, where would we be if no one had ever resisted laws that grew outdated?'

He appears uncertain how to receive this.

And then Barry starts up in a tone that deceives me, has me letting him go on. 'You're damn right, though, officer. After all, booze *is* essential to the economy of this nation, right? Without it so many citizens'd be out of work.' He ticks the points off on his fingers. 'I mean, because of booze you've got dentists fixing busted teeth; panel-beaters repairing pranged cars; counsellors working on traumatised kids; undertakers burying gut and liver disease victims . . . But what the hell type of spending did *weed* ever generate for the economy? A few armchairs? A coupla thousand bags of Kettlefries? Big fucking deal, right?'

Shit.

Oinker, almost crowing: 'Nice one, my son. You've just pushed my patience as far as it goes.'

Me, pleading, no plays left but gambles: 'To prove we were smoking you'll have to fish around in that drain, and I promise you we have nothing else on us! Let us turn our pockets out for you and you'll see we're not worth your time.'

Oinker, smirking: 'No need. We're heading downtown, sonny. I'll send a rookie back here to collect the evidence. Meanwhile, at the station-house, I'll be legally detaining and strip-searching you shifty pricks. Let's go; back the way you came.'

Nobody moves.

I'm set to make a break for it, but I need to warn the others when the gun's gonna go.

Oinker, smirk hardening: 'I *said*, let's *go*.'

No effect.

With a theatrical sigh, Oinker's right hand reaches to his belt, takes out his big shiny truncheon. '*Don't* make me use this, lads. Turn around and walk back the way you came . . . *or else*.'

By now I'm frantic: almost ready to bolt by myself, let the others take their chances.

Perhaps pegging him as our trio's backbone, Oinker singles out Steve, pokes his ribs with the baton none too gently. 'Move out now, Blackbeard, or I'll jab you ten times harder than your old man ever did.'

Steve, level: 'Go on, then.'

Oinker's jaw compresses . . .

. . . but then he hesitates, perhaps pondering for the first time just how much shit he could be in if we've the balls to ignore his pretty uniform . . .

. . . ignore the muscle of a whole-*fucking*-state arrayed at his back.

Stepping forward, thrusting.

I don't even see Steve move. One instant he's standing there, tensing around the body-blow. The next his left fist's at full extension and the oinker's reeling as if electrocuted, hat flying clear.

The meaty *smock* — so much more disturbing (*enlivening*) than the Hollywood version — seems to arrive late.

Dashing past Steve's shoulder, snatching at the cue he lives for, Barry swings a big hay-maker.

Oinker's done this before, though; has enough presence to keep his feet and eyes on the job. He ducks the wild punch, bracing himself, positioning the baton to crack Barry back-handed . . .

But Steve's too fast for him again: skips in and traps the stick in both hands. Ripping it free. Gripping the handle. Up and down, quick as a piston . . .

. . . across the raised forearm with a *crack* like a splitting-axe on dry pine.

The copper squeals like a stuck sow, collapsing to his knees, all fight fleeing before this rush of pure agony.

By his thinning hair, Steve wrenches Oinker's face toward his. Bending, snarling into it: 'My old man never *'ad* t' hit me, yu fuckin' redneck *cunt!*'

Gifted a stationary target, Barry can't resist *or* miss: measures the guy's cheek, steps into the blow, full weight and strength behind a thick knee . . .

I look away, but the sound — rock on gravel — effects me like victory: I swallow mad whooping.

Beside the broken oinker, Steve drops the baton almost delicately and we flee the scene with steady purpose.

The 'Dan's near the building's corner; we're across no-man's-land in three heartbeats. Mick and Lefty are ready to go.

Thank fuck.

Only then do the tangibles pierce my false calm.

From the back seat, conversationally: 'Ya got a record, Steve?'

'Na.'

On impulse I go anyway, out the door, back toward the dark.

Fingerprints, man. All over the fucking stick.

But caution reveals voices; a sneaky peak, shadows shifting near the crime scene — McJob's slaves, roused by the oinking — and, stripped of choice, I'm soon back in the womb.

Its silent fellowship warms me near to tears.

'Don't ever get one.'

{ Archives: To Shuffle With The Herd

With a lull between incoming loads, Barry flicks his fork-lift in a rakish turn, coming to rest alongside me.

Barry, stretching gingerly: 'This shit's doing my head in, man.

These seats are fucking Dark Ages material. My back's gonna be filthy on me tonight.'

Me, resting against a high pallet: 'My feet'll be broadcasting a message all too similar.'

'Ya wanna swap jobs for a while? My feet'd love to shoulder a session.'

'As would my arse and back. Unfortunately, The Church of Cost-effectiveness views worker quests for balance as heretical.'

In the rafters I notice a swivelling telescreen pause in its arc, crosshairs centring on me. In a flashing tomb hidden nearby, I picture a smoking insecurity guard, pen in hand, beseeching betterment — Employee 25567, McPike, G. Paused from work beyond sanctioned break times at 11:53am. Resumed work at . . .

The fat fucker needn't have bothered: my dereliction is under the observation of a fat fucker vastly more baleful. Tonsured, bespecta-cled, middle-aged, in his magisterial drawl, Section Manager Andrew O'Conner had yesterday warned us to, 'Keep appearances right up tomorrow, lads. I'm going to be escorting a couple of staff from head office around site.'

In contrast to O'Conner, the said Inner Overseers are young and suave, smug and overbred.

Achievers, *the Juggernaut names them.* Go-getters.

Trading privileged information in monotones, the trio loiter not three metres from me, near the door of our Overseer's office, the man himself performing great feats of multi-tasking — attending his betters, while attempting to chide Barry and me back to work with the sheer force of his glare.

Barry, resting his feet on the dashboard of his machine, hands behind head: 'Why can't they let us all swap jobs a couple of times a day, or even a week, just to break the fucking monotony? I mean, you've got a fork-lift ticket, I can use a calculator and write, anyone can stick shit in boxes, it wouldn't take much to skill me up on the reach-truck, the office bums'd love to stretch their legs a bit, the reach-truck lads'd love a chance to get outside now and then on the counter-balance . . . '

As futile as it is, I'm seized by the urge to discard my cover for once;

to swing some overt blows. Me, voice raised to carry: 'Are you forgetting your indoctrination, Barry? I explained why it is that every
shit-kicker in this place is allowed to perform but one task. It's an
offering to our Lord Profit Maximisation. American Capitalists
pioneered the technique in the steel industry. The production process
is split into distinct, atomised functions and kept rigidly segregated.
This serves to de-skill the workers, maximising their expendability,
minimising their bargaining power, depriving them of pride in their
work and pride in themselves, leaving them more amenable to
exploitation. It also helps them quantify the exact worth of each 'unit',
and gives them a divide and rule tool: the fastest worker is rewarded,
the least is punished. And if one 'ambitious' little brown-nosing fuck
can maintain an exceptional output, "what the bloody hell are the rest
of you slackers playing at?"'

    Barry, in time: 'Yeah, well, I reckon that makes them a pack of
wankers.'

    We both effect ignorance as the pestilent stares boring through us
increase threefold. O'Conner is heard babbling to his overlords, trying
to steer them from this blemish in the tapestry.

    Me, loud and melancholy: 'It's hard not to pity them, though —
them and their god, Biggerbetterfastermore.'

    My confederate nods neutrally.

    'The poor sods shed tears, you see, on an hourly basis. Pining for
the heydays. Those heady times of the '30s and '40s when a work-
force could be had for the cost of thin broth, a coven of guards, and
the full metal jacket.'

    From sidelong, I watch O'Conner twitching like a man set to piss
himself. His superiors ignore his blurted chat-starters, dropping sleet
from their stratosphere, stabbing me with both eyes.

    Barry, a sarky compromise: 'Ah, well. They may strip us of names,
but they can never touch our Workingman's Pride.'

    Me, hearty: 'That's right. At least some things are sacred.'
Pronouncing: 'Workingman's Pride: up at dawn to give my days to
simple tasks — tasks as natural as nuclear waste; tasks I've come to
despise; tasks I could perform on twenty per cent brain function;
tasks whose compounded repetition leaves me in chronic pain. Got

fuck all to show for it. Might — if I'm careful — have a little to show for it when I get my life back at age sixty . . . and fucking well proud of it!'

Suddenly for O'Conner, the naked revelation to the brass that his aura alone isn't enough to keep the sheep in line becomes a lesser iniquity. Barking: 'What are the chances of getting some work out of you two today?'

Barry appears to weigh this. Articulates: 'Slim to non-existent.'

Me: 'Fear not, oh, great and corpulent one. My associate and I will redouble our efforts and redress these heinous misdemeanours . . . immediately after lunch. Let's go, Baz, before all the tables are taken.'

Even we, ordinarily, would not have dared go so far. But this day is no ordinary one: this is DT Day.

And so, at around half-past twelve, the first of the workers are herded to their appointments. Some go grudgingly, the resentment ingrained in their features more stark. Others depart willingly, affably, pleased for the break from routine.

It's these latter who've swallowed the dogma from the word go. Before long they'll find himself turning fifty and reminiscing on the best 60,000 hours of their lives spent at tasks an orangutan could have trained for.

Maybe their brainwashing will falter sooner — it happens occasionally — but the Juggernaut's shackles are too firmly fixed. They have mortgages, you see, on houses they now hate. Shared with women they haven't fucked in years. Fused to her by junior components whose antics send blood pressures soaring.

They've found a way round it, though.

They gulp a dozen Lion Red every night.

Patrolling his fief, O'Conner informs Barry and me: 'I'd better not see you two taking any toilet breaks this afternoon.' With blood-thirsty relish: 'I've got you down for urine sampling at 4:48.'

Of course, it's not really a drugs test they're imposing upon us. Not as such.

Because most drugs — alcohol included — upon entering one's system are identified as poison and immediately purged, the body embracing dehydration in its efforts to flush the stuff, hence the phenomenon of the 'hangover'.

When one's system encounters cannabis, however, the chemicals identified are judged benign, allowed to linger for months.

Word and date of the impending tests spread round the warehouse some weeks ago, giving fun-lovin' criminals plenty of warning to lay off the hard stuff a few days in advance. For many, though, abstaining from weed for the months it takes the chemicals to abandon one's body completely was a pretty major issue.

An issue not just in the deprivation of an unwind many have come to cherish, but in the very act of the Company impinging upon our autonomy through an additional sixteen hours a day.

For which we won't be paid a cent.

Why the executive decision to declare pot off-limits in the lives of under-stimulated workers? Good question. Is it simply another layer in the process of breaking us to their will? Is it a matter of the capitalist old-boy network closing ranks, defending the investments of their booze and 'bacco cousins? Are we seeing a technological step-up in their war against an acknowledged enemy of compliance? All of the above?

Of course, they say it's to maximse warehouse safety. But the tests include everyone (everyone not on a salary, that is): not just those operating machinery, but those who stand at tables and fix stickers to product all day. And the new safety policy makes no provision for those who arrive at work on half-function due to blinding hangover.

No, we of the Brotherhood number among the few who will face the truth of the matter. Unlike our contemporaries, we suffer no delusion. We see the tests for what the are: the newest layer in the banishment of intractable elements from the capitalists' vital labour pool.

Over the next two hours, then, Barry and I offer ourselves as a sacrifice to the Perfect Herd's evolution.

Because we draw the line at having faceless boards of millionaires tweak our strings beyond the workplace. But neither can we afford to be blackballed as 'drug addicts'. (And to simply resign will disqualify us from dole eligibility.)

So, by 3pm, from his forklift, Barry's contrived to drop two pallets of product.

Ever seen a full pallet of breakable stock fall from a height of two metres? Sheer beauty to treasonous eyes.

Not so to the Overseer's. All he sees is fifty grand of his budget down the fucking gurgler. Or, at least, a fifty-grand claim from his department added to company insurance premiums.

When fork-lifting, though, these things occasionally happen — though seldom twice in minutes — and O'Conner lets Barry off with a stern, 'See that it doesn't happen again.'

O'Conner then disappears for a meeting, returning an hour later to find the floor awash in smashed product from two more of a grinning Barry's 'mishaps'.

It's about now that people further down the chain begin to realise the computer is issuing faulty stock locations. Nine hundred items of X stock are supposed to be located in Aisle C, Row 67A. The said location houses something completely different, and X stock is eventually found by eye some distance away, though much too late to be of use to the clients awaiting it.

Similar discrepancies begin to show all through the system, and, livid, the Overseers soon trace the faults to the Goods In office team, who trace the 'errors' to Employee 22567, McPike, G.

Out on the shop-floor with his calculator and pen, having made, it seems, a complete hash of every pallet logged since lunchtime. Hashed them, I proudly add, in a manner manufactured to slip safety valves.

Ahhhh, the metallic tang of sabotage.

Though our estimate is by no means conservative, by the time Barry and I are escorted from site we calculate the damage inflicted in this first overt skirmish as somewhere near the $1.3 million mark.

Out in the carpark, in plain view of management, the Brotherhood debrief over a four-skin doobie.

Stressing from the news we broke pulling from the consumption centre ('Take care not to draw attention to us, Mickey, yeah? Oh, na, it's just that we kinda left an oinker for dead out the back of McDick's just now.') Mick has relinquished driving duties in search of liquid solace. We've thus gone to our back-up plan for this rare exigency: if there's driving to be done later, Barry'll take the wheel.

Barry — being Barry — has no intention of remaining sober. We're all aware of this, and in a few beers' time we'll also be comfortable with it.

The club we happen upon is a way from the crime scene and we've been able to find a crowded side-street down which to park. Short of leaving town, we've done all we can; there's no point worrying any more.

Stoned from our inauspicious session — a sealed, but present, Pandora's box magnifying the dope's inherent paranoia — walking into an unscouted ARC is the last thing I need or want. I might have sat in *The 'Dan* until straight, had it not felt so much like a neon sign.

But fortune smoothes the insertion. The 'doormen' — biker-looking white dudes — barely glance at us walking past; a smiling bird ('Hi, guys, all set for a big one?') collects our five buck cover charge and stamps a guitar on one hand. Through big swing doors. The Skinny Genius is chanting away at an early-evening level to leave conversation entirely possible. Blissfully weak, reddish light. The crowd is good but not yet claustro-phobic. My type of crowd, too — a tidyish, grungy set, plenty of hair and denim. Wooden panels and floor, the odd column stretching high. One end of the place is raised in a low balcony, accessed by stairways at each end; appears to be a band-stand/dance-floor deal. Opposite, a bar runs the length of the room, and a couple of pool tables sit in a sunken dais off to the left. The few chairs and tables are occupied, but sitting's the last thing on my mind.

There's enough space to approach the bar comfortably. Barry and Lefty head in for the first round. Steve seeks out the dunny.

Mick, to me, haggard: 'That drive was fucking terrifying, man. Every set of lights in the rear-view looked like oinkers. The flash of blue took place in my head at least forty times.'

I begin to word my reply — *How the fuck do you think I felt? I underwent the drive* stoned! — but then remember Mick didn't have a visual — *audio* — imprint of the incident acting as a sedative.

Mick, almost pleading: 'So you don't think he'll remember what ya's looked like?'

A shake of the head: 'No chance. It was dark as hell, man. He'll've noticed the races, the height, and the long hair, fuck all else. And me and Steve had Uncle Rangi split between us. Besides, with what Barry did to the cunt if he wakes up this side of Christmas I'll be surprised if he remembers his own fucking *birthday*.'

My words don't seem to allay Mick overly.

Shuddering: 'Oh, shit. That poor bastard.'

Me, snorting: '*Na*, fuck him. It's not as if normal people wake up one morning and decide they wanna spend their days strutting round with a *baton* on their hip. Just get a few brews in ya, have some laughs and chill the fuck out.'

Barry returns with a beer for us each. 'I'm gonna go get the suss of the pool table, boys.' He models a distant smile; seems at peace with creation; ambles away.

Beside us there's a half-tidy blonde orbiting the fringes of a circle. She's presently speaking to no one, seems a little uncomfortable, and Lefty's on to this like sonar. He takes the time to cadge a fag from me (I don't object: they were bought with his moolah), then strolls straight up to her.

Lefty's rolled the sleeves of his shirt up to almost shoulder level, showing off biceps he took the time to pump up out in the carpark, his heavy backpack brought along for the purpose . . . and because he pulls with such regularity he likes to keep an overnight bag within reach at all times.

Guileless smile: 'Hi, we're new to the place and we heard there was a band scheduled to play tonight. Have ya got any idea what time they're on?'

Blonde: 'I think you've got your wires crossed. It's just a DJ tonight; there was a band on last night.'

Lefty, 'disappointed': 'Really? Ahhhh, that sux. Did ya see them? What were they called?'

Blonde: 'I wasn't here.'

'Oh, 'cause we heard Axe Attack were playing, and we were pretty keen to check them out 'cause a mate of mine plays bass for them. Have ya heard of them? Me and him actually founded the band down in Vegas a couple of years back; I was the singer/songwriter, but I moved on when a better spot opened with . . .'

She turns to face him fully, sipping at a drink, and Lefty's off the mark.

The cunt.

Not that there's any shortage of wenches about. Eye-candy of various flavours dot my immediate vicinity — a nice brunette in a mini-dress, another blonde in a crop top, an Asian babe with black lipstick and eyeliner, some hot Maori chick looking set to star in a glam-rock video. But in my stoned state it's a visual dish for which I've little appetite. Only subconsciously, through habit, do I even bother sizing this talent, and then it's cursory. I'm happy just to breathe the club's ambience, suck on a gasper with the luxury only dope can offer, sip at my cold brewski, enjoy the sounz, relish our earlier good fortune. I don't even feel the need to be seen talking.

Finished already ('No thanks, bro, I'll be sweet for now'), Mick scoots back to the bar. Dude doesn't drink very often, but when he does he tends to do so with style. Barry snags Steve for a pool partner as he exits the dunnies, handing him a beer. Steve catches my eye, points to the table. I flick an acknowledging salute.

Combined, beer and fag taste of Nirvana.

'So . . . what made you quit, Tania? I mean, who in their right mind resigns as a restructuring exec' for ITS HO branch . . . to become a casual in a *library*?'

No expense account. No share-plan or staff dividend. No medical and dental scheme. No paid leave. No incentive bonus.

Peers spinsters in floral print, forty-year-old virgins, threadbare hard-covers.

Vocationally happy.

Tania seethes into her drink a full five seconds before replying. 'Which part of this answer did you not catch the last hundred times I gave it to you? I just woke up one morning', *hung over on coke and cocktails*, 'and realised I hadn't painted anything in six months. Or even *con*templated it!'

Art, the former love of her life. Part of the sacred triumvirate: art, books and good rock guitar.

Sarah waits for more. Prompting when it doesn't come: 'And . . . ?'

But Tania's had enough of the conversation. Had enough of it weeks ago. Her friends, family, paper-boy, can speak to her of nothing else. Curt: 'And I just decided to start living again, all right? Now can we drop . . . '

Sarah, snapping: '*Living*? As opposed to what? A travel allowance, jetting to conferences, an office big enough for volleyball, a company car upgraded quarterly, money most only dream of? If that's *dying*, Tan, I'm off to play on the motorway!'

Plain Janes at her beck and call; purges plotted from board-rooms; quick fucks in Daimler limousines.

Scaling the ladder on the world's oldest currency.

A harried frown: 'You obviously can't understand no matter how I break it down', *you or the rest of the human race*, 'so can we *please* just drop the bloody subject! I didn't come here to have my well being "tended".'

Sarah relents, but only grudgingly, exasperation palpable. A sharp sigh: '. . . All right, then. Have it your way. Stay with your bloody books if that's what floats your boat . . . And, by the way, I'm never coming out with you again.'

Confused, angering: 'Why the fuck not?'

Grinning: 'Because since we walked in nobody's even *looked* at *me*.'

Tania's eyes roll in boredom: another 'plaudit' she could do without.

Sarah, hardening: 'I'll tell you one thing though, Tan, I'm not letting you walk out of this place alone again. You haven't had a shag since you quit your real job, and if you're not careful, Mt Albert Library'll turn you into a com*plete* geek.'

A dismissive scoff: 'I'm here to have a few drinks and a bit of a dance, nothing more. An arsehole male's the last thing I'm after.'

'Is that right?' Sarah lifts her eyebrows. 'And you're really dressed as if that's the case, aren't you?'

Stilettos. Leather pants that might have been painted on. A white sleeveless showing more navel than cleavage . . . just.

Glad the low lighting hides her quick flush.

In all honesty, Tania herself can't put a finger on the motive for the raunchy garb. She says to Sarah it's because of the conservativeness with which she must dress for work these days: needs to OD on the 'rock moll' thing to compensate. She tells herself it's to flaunt in Man's face what he's no longer gonna fucking get.

But sometimes she worries that her former career has left her a power addict; that this is her sole remaining pusher.

And at other times she dreams of meeting a guy, while dressed just like this, who chats with her all night . . . and doesn't once stare at her tits.

Sarah: 'I'll get another round in before it gets too busy up there.' Stern: 'And while I'm gone you're gonna decide which of these ogling guys you like the most.'

Muttering: 'Yeah right.'

In truth, when she's dressed for raging, the stares of males affect Tania like gravity: ubiquitous to the point of ignorance. She's more likely to notice if one *doesn't* eye her over.

Sips at the divinity of a G&T, shifting gently with the beat.

And then she freezes; loses her sense of place completely.

Amusing itself, her eye had happened upon a guy whose level of contentment, considering he stood alone, seemed noteworthy. She lingered for a moment, shrugged inwardly, and was about to move on when his gaze found hers. He glanced down once, then looked away, apparently indifferent. All in less than a second.

What the hell?

A guy like this — young and loose, OK looking, clearly a rocker — failing to stare after noticing her happened so infrequently it called to Tania like a bugle. But a guy like this catching *her* looking at *him*, and then looking away *first*? And with such nonchalance?

This was unprecedented.

She forgets Sarah. Forgets her recent renunciation, her values reassessment, the endless flak she's copping over it; forgets general Male arseholehood.

Because she's suddenly in strange waters and can't decide how to feel about it.

Notices a small stab of consternation, as one finding an ace suddenly missing. Then she decides the uncertainty has her feeling more alive than a moment ago.

Intrigue impels her.

Socially, it's been a while since Tania's initiated a conversation with a strange guy, but from her past she knows how effortless it is; how enormously distant from humiliation such a move could ever be for her.

Still, she almost drains her drink in steeling herself.

Starts toward him.

Someone taps him from behind. 'Excuse me?'

Strange voice. Definitely feminine, but deepish, husky.

Gator turns to the startling sight of the dark stunner he noticed a minute ago, now standing not a metre from him. *Well, aren't* you *just the hottest thing since Krakatoa! The Maori Salma Hayak.* Limits his shock to a pair of raised eyebrows. Stoned, he's far too conscious of her opinion of him to check her out properly. This despite her body calling in his periphery like a magnet(s).

In fact, at present he's too self-conscious to be having *any* dealings with unknown babes.

Bluff: 'Yep?'

'I hate to do this, but I couldn't nick a fag off ya, could I?'

Why the fuck couldn't she have decided she needed a gasper in an hour or two? With more booze in him, this would have presented a nice window for an attempted witty flirtation. Probably earn little more ego boost than a smile, but from *her* this would have sent him into the fray crowing.

'Yeah, sure.'

Gator hands one over. When she mouths it, clearly has no light, he passes her his lighter without ceremony, his brusqueness born of an innate need — a need exacerbated by cannabis — to shelter behind barriers.

The cold eyebrows (*What do* you *want?*) almost abort Tania's fact-finding mission.

With the smoke in her lips, the script at this point should read: *Guy, unprompted, makes gentlemanly show of flicking and shielding a flame for her, holding station until she judges the ciga-rette on an even draw.*

But Mr Brown here just hands her the thing as if he's lending her his last twenty bucks.

She lights it herself — only smokes when she's had a few anyway — using the gesture to cover a frown.

He takes back his lighter, nods coldly, and, sipping at a beer, gives her his profile, plainly less interested in her than in looking the house over.

*Now he's dis*missing *me? Jesus Christ, this isn't happening!*

Tania's tasting an emotion old enough to be almost alien. She sets to walk away, bewildered, but a lick of anger heats her: a traditional defence to adversity.

You're not getting rid of me that *easily, cunt-face. At the least, I'm gonna know what the deal is with you.*

'So, what's ya name?'

Staring into space, willing her to leave him in peace, Gator almost splutters on his beer.

What's my name? *What the fuck do* you *care what my name is?*

He examines events further. Remembers seeing her standing

with another bird who he then saw enter the scrum developing around the bar, where Mick is somewhere. Picks this one as the type to break into hives if left without a chatter partner in a social setting.

His heart drops, his dazed serenity of a minute ago moving rapidly beyond reach. It seems she needs a body to be seen swapping air with until Tweedledee returns, and the last thing Gator needs in his state is to have to construct a conversation with a bitch like *this*.

He notices Lefty appraising him; for an instant debates attempting it for this reason alone.

Chickens out just as quickly.

Considers outright rudeness . . . hasn't the stomach for confrontation. He finally replies to her, but doesn't bother hiding completely his impatience with circumstance. 'My name's Gator.'

Uncertain smile 'What kind of a name's *that*?'

'Any kind ya like.'

Her eyes darken and he feels sudden remorse. 'It's just a nickname from childhood I got saddled with. I ran full speed into a gate and KO'd myself. They reckon everyone but me had a wicked laugh.' *Let's see if a little unbridled candour won't throw her. I'll give her the* real *G. McPike.*

'I can see why.'

'Meaning you can see how fucking hilarious such an incident might appear to bystanders, or that you can see why a group of people might take delight in laughing at a prize cunt like myself?'

Shit, this guy's a regular ball-breaker.

His profanity she takes as another setback. Tania hardly boasts a nun-like tongue herself, but she's yet to reveal that to this Gator. Men with foul mouths, as a rule, keep this to themselves until her own proclivities are laid bare.

She tries a smile. 'Meaning anyone stupid enough to run into a gate full bore deserves to be laughed at. Unless, of course, the gate didn't happen to be stationary?'

He grins half-heartedly, but it's better than nothing. 'Short of being latched, the gate was about as stationary as gates get.'

He's human at least.

'Well, Gator, it's nice to meet you.' She holds out her hand, pushing her chest forward — *only as part of the movement* — and has to blink back dizziness when he winces distaste at her painted fingers.

Dismayed, Tania's about to withdraw in disarray when he takes her hand like a snatch, smiling almost warmly.

His sudden grip is strong and sweaty; she loses half a breath.

'Nice to meet you, too . . . ?'

It's phrased as a question, but only hurriedly it seems, as though he wasn't going to ask, changed his mind for decorum's sake. She takes a quick look around, as if to reaffirm her environment. 'T–, Tania.'

He just nods, presents his profile again.

And then the answer hits her.

Please, just leave me alone.

But the handshake's pretty well sealed it. Gator's almost resigned to playing 'mouthpiece' for a spell. He sees no reason to act any other role, though.

Then, like a flash of awareness, she blurts: 'Are you here with your girlfriend?' And it's not uttered saucily either, more as the answer to a riddle.

He considers saying yes, but concludes that, should his quest to regain it succeed, pretence would cheapen the lone harmony he wants back. Instead: 'No, my girlfriend can't come out any more: she's dying of *Aids*.'

Her face collapses. '*Oh.*'

Qualifying: 'Well, she's not actually dying of *Aids*, she's dying of a brain tumour, but for over a year now she's been *telling* everyone it's Aids killing her.'

Tania, aghast: 'Why would she do that?'

'Because she doesn't want me fucking any of her mates when she's gone.'

* * *

It's a few moments before she realises he's joking. And then several elements mesh in her at once. Ease at not having revived his 'heartache'. Delight in the gag — her sense of humour was once described as 'more badly sprained than twisted'. More wonder at his aloofness toward her. Relief — *just for the sake of prolonging this bizarre encounter* — that he is in fact single.

And she's suddenly laughing uncontrollably: two high-pitched barks that draw the eyes of many, and then a long spasm into her hand, turning away, gathering control at last.

Her impetuous laughter moves him. By his book a sick, dirty, sexist joke should have elicited a diametric reaction from the typical female. *Mind you, what do I know about chicks?*

Warmed somewhat, he decides to forsake his own comfort zone, cut her some slack. *Fuck it. She seems an interesting bird, nice enough as well, and most people hate looking a Nigel No-friends in a crowded club. I know I normally do. Her mate should be back in a minute anyway.*

'So how old are ya, Tania?'

'Twenty-three. You?'

'Twenty.'

Effortless, he reels her again. Just as it looked as if he might conform to established reality after all — well, *kind* of: it would clearly have been her sense of humour that won him — he further demonstrates a lack of physical interest. Because every-one knows that women are *not* customarily turned on by the knowledge that a guy is their junior by some margin. And from this dude she would've swallowed a fresh twenty-four.

Confusion intensifies, and Tania begins to suspect that she must get to the bottom of this mystery or forever live without the revelations it surely contains. She comes close to asking him baldly (*I obviously don't do it for you. Why not?*), shies away. 'So what do you do?'

Cheery: 'If you mean what manifestation do my shackles to

the suicidal, soulless Juggernaut that is society take . . . the answer is none. In the terms of reference under which I'm guessing your question is phrased, I *do* nothing at all. In fact I'm more of an *un*doer. So what do *you* "do"?'

Tania now begins to admit that, aside from the curiosity value of Gator's detachment, the beginnings of a *little* more immediate interest in him had been stirring. She was impressed by his frankness and wit, his intelligence, by his easy composure; his free-spirited looks are presentable enough — she's a sucker for long hair anyway — and some inner spark augments these.

But at *this* extraordinary disclosure her regard for him gathers momentum.

On impulse, throwing it out like a touchstone: 'I'm a vice restructuring executive for ITS HO Branch.'

And without warning the curl of his lip, his unconscious sway from her, threaten to rupture her vague enchantment; inflate it to a craving.

Gator, flat: 'What a waste of a human.'

Her heart leaps . . . and then it remembers he's immune to her.

Quantifying: 'But I've got a huge office, a company car, expense accounts. I've got more money than I know what to do with, high-powered friends all over the Smoke. I've got a PA to do all my shit work, and I've got almost fifty people who bark "what colour?" when I say "crap".'

'And you know what else you've got?'

Snatching at the question: 'What?'

'My undying sympathy.'

Bourgeois slut! Tundra in hell before I put myself out for the comfort of the likes of you*!*

Walking away, Gator stops as she grips his arm, hard. Turning, he blinks at the raw need on her face.

'It's not true!' she yells like an appeal. 'I *used* to be that, but I chucked it in! Honestly!'

What the fuck is your story*, space cadet?*

181

'To do what?'

He senses her hesitate. Watches her plough on, daring his reaction. 'To work in a library.'

Rocked: 'You're a *librarian*?'

She misreads him, gives him her anger: 'So what about it?'

And, as if his vision has suddenly cleared, he seems to behold her for the first time, regard her with full consideration. Then he grins as if she's told him she's Freedom incognito. 'So I think that's the coolest fucking thing I've heard in shit knows how long!'

Tania blinks, scratching at her face, hiding a tear months in the making.

Gator: 'What's your favourite book?'

Her voice holds with an effort. 'Debbie Murphy: *Demons Among Us*.'

His smile twists delightedly. '"What must mortals *think* of a being like I? A creature who scares children to their beds . . ."'

Melting her completely.

Throwing back her shoulders: '". . . a being who lusts for warm flesh"', swelling her chest, '"yet stands enchanted for days by the shivering of leaves."' *Oh God, I'm sorry I took it for granted. Please let him look down. Just once. I'm not enough without it.*

Yet his eyes, though gleaming, refuse to leave her own, and all at once helplessness and loss suck the will from her spine.

But a stubborn part of her remains intact enough to insist that the 'why?' is still important.

From nowhere: 'You're not gay, are you?'

Gator's claimed by a breathless giggle.

Fuck me drunk, this is possibly the most astonishing person I've ever come across! Oh, to be juiced! I'd ask for her hand, just in case. Now I'll have to die wondering.

Still laughing: '*No*, I'm not gay! Why do you ask? Is my manner so maidenly?'

Tania, somehow melancholy: 'Not at all. It's just that . . . that . . . that when I show interest in guys I'm used to getting a response a *lot* different to the one you're giving.'

Smile withering, Gator's struck by the most appalling notion. He wants to demand of her: *Show 'interest'? Define for me please your* exact *application of the word! Soon would be good; now would be better!*

And for five long seconds he's caught in the headlights. At last, though, he finds the will to face them down or perish. *I'm no doubt wrong, but I'll suicide for sure if I don't learn one way or the other. I've not got the balls for it in* this *state but*.

Stripped of all composure, he fumbles for enough of it to keep himself in the game. Arranging his features to express regret: 'Look, I'm really sorry I seemed rude, it's just that my mates and I underwent something pretty disturbing before arriving tonight, and I just wanted time alone to reconcile myself to it. You could have been Courtney Love — or even the Beatles — trying to get me chatting, and I'd've been just as crabby . . . and that's saying something, 'cause I'm a serious Lennon fan.'

'Me too.'

She brightens markedly, and Gator's excitement renders him mute for heartbeats. Finally: 'Now that you've snapped me from my anti-social trance, you seem the most interesting sort I've come across in ages. I've gotta go to the bar and the toilet right now, but if you're still here when I get back I'd really love to hear more of your story.'

Too terrified to await a reply, he manages to fade into the crowd like a man with no questions.

'Yeah, two Exports, mate.'

Mick finally gains the bar. He's desperate to get trashed, forget about that awful fucking drive. Not to mention their impending action. From tonight's turmoil he's beginning to question how well he'll hold up on Operation Durban. From Vegas it'd sounded fraught enough, but up here, so much closer to the target, and with a taste of real stress still fresh, the prospect of the raid has begun to nauseate him.

Fuck, if the bar staff are this slow all night, I'll be diving into my powder a lot sooner than planned.

A little of Bum's nose-candy would sort things out quick smart (for a while). The night, though, is but a puppy and Mick's loath to tap his supply too early.

From the crowd behind him: 'Watch it, mate! There's a queue here, if you didn't notice.'

Gator: 'Yeah, and my bro's at the front of it. I just realised I've got all his money.'

Someone else: 'You can wait like the rest of us.'

Gator: 'Get the fuck outta my face.'

This belligerence startles Mick: socially, a sober Gator is a person Mick seldom finds reason to view as a liability.

Looking across his shoulder, he's in time to flick a questioning eyebrow as Gator wins through to his side.

Gator, wired: 'How many ya getting?'

'Two. Seeing as it's getting busier, I thought I'd get you one while I'm here.'

Handing over a twenty: 'Get three more, man.'

'*Three*? We haven't got a table to put them on.'

'Who needs a table when you've got a stomach?' As the barman places the first handle before them, Gator hoists it — 'Here's to ya!' — and downs it in four seconds flat.

Mick, twigging: 'What's her name?'

Grinning: 'Tania. She's one of us, man! And hot as Vesuvius besides. I'll never understand what the fuck just happened, but I think I fluked myself a chance.' He drops the next beer with equal alacrity, sighing deeply, muffling a belch.

Mick places the extended order, then raps his mate on the back. 'Why don't you go and snort up, dude? Get old man charlie rooting for ya.'

'Someone bring this man a chocolate Easter Bunny. See ya back out there.' Taking another handle, he heads for the toilets.

Sentenced to more queuing, the beer's half gone by the time he can enter a cubicle, lock it behind him, delve into his underpants, draw forth a small bank bag. Sprinkles a third of its contents upon the cistern and chops it fine with a piece of plastic. Divides it into two lines.

Stresses when he realises he has no notes on him; comes close to hurling curses. Regroups. Sees a crumpled flyer in the bog's far corner. Claims it. Briefly ponders its level of contamination: how much discharge from a plethora of orifices have made its acquaintance; how many billions of hazardous bacteria have colonised a home on it?

Decides he couldn't care less. *Priorities, people.* Rolls it into a tight straw. Stuffs one end into a nostril. Bends toward the powder.

Greetings, fellow slugs and weasels. Well met, I say. Again we convene in the Graveyard of Ambition.

Snorts hard, moving along the line, reducing it to crumbs, amazed as ever by the total lack of pain involved, lack of *any* real sensation, the prime cocaine numbing his sinus instantly, its cold paralysis moving down his throat in droplets.

Then the very interior of his skull seems to freeze.

He's never before encountered this, and for the barest second Gator panics, horror leaping to his mouth like cold vomit. Fighting it down, he swaps nostrils and nails the second line before he can reconsider.

For a while he dabs at the cistern with a wet finger, transferring white remnants to his tongue, and then, sniffing and snivelling, he drops his pants and sinks to the toilet seat, looking to kill time.

Negotiations ensue, and a chocolate hostage is freed without bloodshed.

He wipes up and belts up, the charlie well stashed again. Sits back down, breathing deeply. Lights a cigarette. Sips at his beer, endeavouring to forget the drugs in his system, the babe he hopes is waiting.

Three minutes later, beer and ciggie expired, Gator stands up, fast, and a wondrous beam spreads from ear to ear. For a second he laughs out loud, a breathless giggle, and he doesn't bother trying to cork his exclamation. 'Ah sayed god-*dame*!'

185

From the cubicle next door, cheekily: 'You all right in there, buddy?'

Emphatic: 'Though touched by your concern, my good man, let me assure you that I'm just as fine as red wine in the sunshine.'

Humbled by Gator's ardour: 'Fuck, what've *you* been drinking? I'm ordering some as soon as I get up the bar again!'

'Were it only so elementary.'

Strolling out, Gator's met with his own reflection in the washroom mirror. He's stuck fast for seconds, unable to get over how fucking *good* he looks! His blue shirt complements his flushed complexion with sorcerous skill, leaves it almost flawless, even under this harsh light. He doubts three hours in a salon could improve upon the untamed symmetry of his normally unruly hair, the vitality in his eyes make them seem holes in the fabric of time. He attempts to wipe the grin from his face — just to see if he can — succeeds only in expanding it.

Never mind the grin in his heart and soul, the bubbles of rapture and mirth inflating and bursting in his stomach, over and over in a ceaseless cycle.

The molten self-belief and bliss spurting through his limbs like plasma.

Washing his hands without looking, he moves toward the mirror until he stares at himself from mere inches. 'Brother, you are looking *tip*-fucking-*top*! I know what I like, and I *like* what I see!'

The mystery voice from the cubicle joins Gator at the basins — a tubby twenty-something — and to feel embarrassment at being caught in such intimacy with a mirror doesn't even occur to Gator.

Without deliberation: 'How's your night going, bro?'

Tubby: 'Yeah, decent, dude. But I'm guessing not half as good as yours. You look like you just won Lotto.'

'Yeah? Maybe I did.' And the ebullience in Gator is so over-whelming he says: 'You want a taste of it?'

Quick calculation in the eyes. 'How much?'

'On the fucking house, my son.'

Leading him into a cubicle, Gator chops up a line, passes over the 'straw', heads back to the mirror.

Minutes later and they're arm and arm, helplessly cackling over a joke they no longer remember, the fact that they can't stop laughing — and are beginning to suffer for it physically — only intensifying the paroxysm.

Gator, at last, wiping at his eyes: '*Ahhhh*, fuck me dead. You, my boy, are one *funny* motherfucker! I've gotta go, though, dude. I'll see ya later on, yeah?'

'Yeah, man. Thanks, eh? You're a fucking legend.'

'In about half an hour there's gonna be someone a hell of a lot tidier than *you* saying that.' He salutes his new friend, borne away on a conveyor-belt of confidence.

And, pondering the boast, Gator can't fault it. His innate modesty banished by the powder with more fullness than liquor could ever, he's left free to identify the many angles his earlier conversation with Tania presents. More than enough to make her worth chasing under ordinary, boozed circumstances. Under *these* terms . . . ?

Terms where he feels he would happily address the nation on topics ranging from ant-farming to the geological structure of Saturn's third-largest moon, Triton.

Terms where he feels as if his wit has been wired to the national grid, given the velocity of a super-processor.

Terms where the words reticence, self-consciousness, doubt, might as well be spelt in hieroglyphic.

Terms where he's filled with goodwill and zest to the point of needing to share it or die.

His eyes greet the sight of the now crowded club as if he owns it, all present at his invitation. Music adds a new layer to his buzz, seems to tug at his bones in small belts of AC/DC. His every movement falls into an unconscious rhythm, nodding head leading the easy dance.

He takes the time to swing by the crowded pool table and check on Barry and Steve, joined now by Mick. From the way they're both playing — sinking balls they've little right to, maintaining running banter with all and sundry, grinning like cocks in a cunt shop — Gator learns instantly that they too have been at the nose-candy. He catches their eye, brows asking a quick, *Sweet?*

They wink back fondly: *Sweet as!*

Threads toward Tania's postulated position, making good progress through the swelling throng, taking gaps he'd normally shy from, placating annoyed frowns with a grin and a jest. So impulsively does the dialogue flow, he finds himself in conversations — with blokes and girls alike — which he has no memory of initiating. Coaxes encouraging giggles from several likely ladies, dancing as he chats, bending way too close to be heard above the tunes, thrilling to some similar responses.

Moving on like a heartbreaker.

By the time he locates her Gator feels like Brad Pitt on steroids. He's set to tap her shoulder when he notices who it is she's talking to.

Lefty's slick beam brooks no imperfections, even as he makes eye contact with Gator, effects not to notice him, wordy flow running unhindered.

As if from an unseen body-shot, Gator's diaphragm collapses.

And the warm wind flees him in a rush as, for the first time ever, he experiences a foul cocktail: amphetamines and crisis.

Blood thick with scum roaring in his head, across his eyes, as the room starts revolving, music madly distorted, heard from a rollercoaster. The rushing in his limbs quickens and boils — from pleasure to pain in two easy seconds. His heart seems to falter, limping in his chest like a half-smashed rodent, sucking more vision away; Gator has to fight to keep from his knees.

And then jealousy — sick, consuming envy — curdles his marrow.

Fury follows in its wake, shooting through him in a starburst. His fists bellow for battery.

Even now, though, in this extremity, his sensitivity won't let him act; won't let him paint so glaring a picture of his perceived inadequacies.

Mortal again, Gator motions to retreat, shuffling away.

When a break in the song carries Lefty's words to him with incongruous clarity. 'Na, seriously, I'm *certain* I know you from somewhere!'

Tania, bored: 'You do . . . that's why I don't go there any more.'

A sentence like a cardiac adrenaline shot: without transition Gator's re-elevated to the role of Man Who Just Can't Lose.

Unthinkingly, he spins her to him with gentle force, leaving Lefty, for once, stranded in mid-sentence. Gator beams at her like a soulmate, points it at Lefty, as if he's included. 'You should be wary of the likes of him: when he goes to the barber he's not after a haircut . . . he's chasing an oil change.'

Her eyes holding Gator's are wide enough to seal his throat. 'I guessed as much.' She dismisses Lefty with a tiny shrug, ignoring his next line like the chorus haze it suddenly is to her. 'I didn't think you were coming back.'

Gator lets his smile fade; wills his stare to nail her own to the back of her skull. 'How could you doubt it?'

'Because you've made me doubt all sorts of things.'

'Do you hate me for that?'

'Is the Pope a pagan?'

Trademark grin fraying at the edges, smooth tones oddly ruffled, Lefty places a hand on Tania's bare arm, attempts to win back her attention. 'Listen, I'm going up to the bar. What would ya like to drink?'

Sweetly. 'I'll have a case of champagne. Get the barman to leave it with the bouncers; I'll collect it on my way out.'

Then, very deliberately, Gator moves around until his body occludes Lefty from the circle.

And then he forgets him. Completely and without effort.

To Tania, eyes twinkling: 'So, unless I'm very much mistaken, you're a vulnerable soul ripe for indoctrination.'

'Into what?'

'The Craft of Arch-Treason.'

* * *

Mick: '*Fuck*, have you seen the bird Gator's on with?'

Steve: 'Yeah, I just saw them when I went up the bar. Maori too, the sly dog: 'e's s'posed to leave those ones for *me*!'

Barry: 'What's this?'

Mick: 'Gator. He's chatting up a honey.'

Barry: 'Chatting her *up*? Fuck, when I saw them she was practically eating from his palm.'

Mick, craning his head: 'I don't think she's looked away from him once in the last twenty minutes.'

Barry: 'You're not wrong. This is the first time I've ever seen a couple masturbate each other spiritually. At this stage, it'd almost be worth betting that by the end of the evening those two will conspire to manufacture an article of Siamese genitalia.'

Mick: 'Lefty was hitting on her earlier.'

Steve, darkening: 'Where's 'e now?'

'I saw him heading for the dunnies. He's been in there a while. I'm guessing he's getting charlied up, ready for another lash at her. He'll try too: just walk straight up to the pair of them and join in on the convo'. Dude's got *no* shames.'

Steve: ''E'll be getting through me first.'

Barry: 'And me. In his time, that's cunt's diddled us out of enough fanny to start a fucking cat-house franchise. It ain't happening tonight, and that's a promise.'

Steve: 'Yeah, keep an eye out while we're playing, wool yu, Mickey. If Lefty moves in, I'm straight up there.'

Barry: 'Oh, *sweet*. Two birds from that group we've been joking with are on the table next.'

Mick: 'Could be time for you lads to throw a game. I've got dibs on the redhead.'

Steve: 'The *redhead*? She doan look a day over four*teen*! I'm guessin' she pencilled the bouncers in for hand-jobs just t' get through the fuckin' door.'

Mick: 'You must've mistaken me for a man who gives a shit. After all, in the best traditions of the Catholic Church: "once they can crawl, they're well in position".'

Barry: 'I'll drink to that. Steve? Which one you want?'

'The short-haired blonde wif the hooters.'

Barry, summarising: 'And I'll take what I can from the left-overs. Hold my cue while I nip off for another snort, yeah?'

7

Me, whispering: 'Nice house. Anyone home?'

She eases the door shut, locks it. 'Only my auntie, but she's upstairs. Once we're in my room she won't hear a thing.'

I've barely let her beyond my touch since The Moment arrived — that subliminal juncture in an encounter with a chick when you suddenly realise it's spit-swapping time. Since her demand that I take her away; the hurried conference with the lads, their hoots and jests; Lefty's sullen glare — loam to my eyes.

Down the long hallway her hand stays in mine, a finger stroking my palm, as she's done in the taxi for half an hour now: the sexual equivalent of Chinese water torture.

Into her room. She leaves me by the door to light a candle. Hunched over it, mis-striking a match or two, dim light finding purchase slowly.

A tiny frown, the sluttish clothes, leave her looking suddenly vulnerable, like a child lost to darkness on The Stairway. I shut my eyes against the pathos of the image. As if clairvoyant, she crosses to me in a vein too similar, sudden uncertainty in her step, a stare of artlessness holding mine.

So I'm taken by surprise when she shoves me hard against the wall, awaits a riposte.

Hands behind my head, effecting a ragged poise, holding her eye like a hostage with Stockholm Syndrome.

And then, enchantingly deliberate, her fingers begin to pick at the fly of her trousers.

A button at a time . . . staring me down . . .

Something inside slips its leash and I take her face in two hands. Breath arrives in a hiss; teeth clacking noisily; tongues and lips mashing together.

She pulls me to the carpet, tearing buttons from my shirt, tossing her own top into a corner, working at my belt . . .

In less than a minute we're starkers.

Then, for an instant, a sense of surreality paralyses me: a peasant pawing forbidden silk . . . guards at the door . . . 'Apologies, Your Majesty, he'll soil you no further.'

But as she pushes me flat, climbing aboard, I embrace my fate with a luscious shudder. *This woman is gorgeous . . . utterly . . . and I'm about to bonk her! Me! G. McPike, Arch-Treasonist and failed philanderer! Oh, cheer till his ears hurt, all ye sinners!*

I give extra thanks as she reveals her contempt for foreplay: taking my todger with nails alone, tugging the skin back sharply, rubbing it along her gash, three or four times, stirring those juices, heaven's own nectar . . .

I can't describe myself as the most impressive buck in the market, but neither am I the least, and with this honey straddling me, big — *exquisite* — breasts in my face, the mother of all hard-ons I've laboured beneath for a good hour now is gifted an extra inch of pure lust.

Teasing me to pants . . .

. . . impaling herself in one lithe motion.

Forgetting in a rush the inadequacies of my bean-pole physique, my soon-to-be hairy chest — factors she hasn't seemed to notice — her clenching wetness is almost too much for me — or is it the heady notch I suddenly add to that big Bedpost in the sky? — and my gasping cry drowns hers completely.

Immediately, she brings her feet forward, squatting, and

declares the bout under way: lifting high, bouncing and grinding. Faster. Wriggling like a proper lady would never.

Taking a nipple in my mouth; lips rejoicing to feel it swell; suck on it hard; bite down till she tenses. In one hand cupping a delectable arse-cheek, free thumb kneading the top of her pussy . . .

Sparing a moment of gratitude to the booze and amphetamines coursing through me. For without them I know I'd've blown my load already; would've been lucky to get it from my *pants* intact. As things are, on past form, I'm confident of putting in a good twenty minutes at 'the coal face'.

A good thing, because it isn't long before Wonder Woman's fucking like Armageddon's upon us, descending with such abandon I'm soon in delicious pain, the beginnings of bruising across my hips.

And within a minute her moans are growing in volume, her rhythms frantic. I watch her eyes roll back in her face, wildly haloed in raven hair.

Can it be this easy? Christ, let it be so! C'mon baby, come for me!

Meeting her thrusts, I pull her head down to mine, kiss her as deep as I can, hiss into her ear: 'I want you to come!'

She only nods, features twisting, and when I feel her tightening, I pull out, lifting her up, sliding down in the same motion, executing a slick muff-dive. At point-blank range, her musk affects me like another line.

Before she can comment — *You'd better pull this off, man, or you're garbage* — I slide two fingers home, twisting them frenziedly, slurping at her clit, rasping it hard, gripping a tit in one hand . . .

She sits up straight, groaning, pushing down on me, the orgasm taking her in long waves.

Some people name me the space cowboy!

She relaxes at last, easing up from me, and I pop out the back door, turning around, pushing her to all fours. Leering at the splendour of her bobbing arse, I guide myself in, ram home with authority.

194

Some name me the gangster of love.

One of her hands snakes underneath, jostles my balls, and she straightens, leans back until her head's on my shoulder, scented hair smothering me. With a palm and forearm I massage her baps; work at her snatch with the other hand; suck on her neck.

'Ah, god, you're not a woman, you're a fucking fantasy!'

She drops to her elbows, shoves against me with her hips, but I hold her still, give it to her hard and steady, kneading her cheeks, squeezing her jugs, feeling The Man and pulling faces to match.

I adopt the double-bass position: one hand tweaking a nipple, the other her clitoris — just like the musician — loins pumping merrily. Strokes weighted to perfection — withdraw *almost* clear, plunge in hard, part those sweet lips — my hips divinely cushioned, and she's soon moaning again. When I judge her close, I forsake the double bass and push her to her stomach, driving home the big ones, rooting at maximum revs.

But it seems I've made my move too early: her climax refuses to arrive; I struggle to maintain the sprint. *Wish I hadn't shoved her forward. Can't reach her clit like this. Must be what she needs.*

A minute later I'm dripping sweat and about to swallow my pride, throw in the towel, when, squealing, her back arches and I feel her flange shivering around me.

Thank fuck for that.

Seconds later, she softens like putty and I pull free, lying beside her, panting hard.

Soon, she begins to kiss my chest; moving down until she's nestled in my groin. In one hand she takes my love-truncheon, skinning it slowly, licking its length with just the tip of her tongue, tickling my balls . . .

This 'torture' protracts for minutes; I'm the first to break. 'For fuck's sake, woman, will you get to work!'

Her eyes taunt me as she strokes, maddeningly sluggish, taking me in her mouth at last, sucking hard, bobbing . . .

Wiggling my hips, bucking softly, stroking her hair, her face, reaching down to knead her hooters, praising her 'aptitude' in extravagant groans. At intervals she breaks off to — *oh,* so practically! — trap her hair behind an ear, and in horn stakes this act takes the toll of at least five strokes.

Orgasm for me is still confidently distant when she surfaces a long while later. I kiss her deep, probing her mouth, move to enter her, but she stops me, turning around, making the connection herself, riding me reverse, massaging my balls, studying the penetration.

This is not fucking happening to me!

She leans back until we're lying together, sharing sweat, my mutton-musket at right angles, though holding station gallantly. I bury my tongue in her ear, hugging her hard enough to hurt, then roll her off me, positioning her for missionary. Of her own accord she hoists her knees until they're scratching her ears, tits jutting in perfect half-orbs.

And gazing over her, in a moment of sheer reverence, I come close to blowing the whole thing, confessing my unworthiness of her sublimity, blurting the social fluke that gave me a window.

But she rescues me again, reaching down, wanking me like a woman horny beyond measure.

With no hands I enter her — *Hole-in-one, brother!* — and she hooks her ankles over my shoulders, rubbing herself while I fuck with the poise of someone who does this often. Grinding; swinging those hips.

A few minutes of this and she's up there again, begging me not to stop; I lay in the big ones. She comes again, *throwing* her pelvis at me. Her nails scrape at the carpet, at me. Head tossed one way, the other way; eyes clenched shut; breasts bouncing to her pants.

And, without warning, that *I've* reduced a girl like *her* to such a state, shocks me so bad my erection begins to wilt.

But I'll have none of it, slipping free of her growler, shifting until I'm straddling her chest, gripping her head, directing my womb-broom straight at her mouth. She takes it with gratifying haste, slurping, moving her neck like a head-banger.

Watching her clean me of her own juices turns me on close to blowing.

But, clearing my mind of her — picturing a castration by rusty guillotine — I keep the wolf from the door for a good two minutes, daydreaming merrily. When at last she stops, looks up at me, she sounds dishevelled near to breakdown. 'Jesus Christ, do you *ever* come? I feel like I'm shagging Lucifer here!'

Not sure what flatters me more, her words or her tone, and in answer I take the mouth south again, perform a five-minute workout on the old tongue-punchbag, stopping only when my fingers and mouth refuse to box on.

By now she's communicating only in whimpers, and I feel like god pouring molten gold down unfaithful throats.

Thou shalt not thrill.

Rolling her compliantly over. Enter from behind. Fucking solidly, picking my way to the summit . . .

As jaded as she is, she seems to guess when I'm near, reaching underneath to tap at my balls, sucking my finger . . .

. . . hammering home like a human jackhammer . . .

. . . unleashing several litres of baby-gravy . . .

. . . *more* . . .

. . . *and still more* . . .

. . . the orgasm stripping me of all force.

Unsaddling. Slumping to the damp carpet — record-breaking winner of the Death Valley Marathon.

Me, much later, drawing on a cigarette: 'At this point I traditionally play my cards a lot closer to the chest, but I'm prepared to go on record right now as stating that *that* was without doubt *the* finest root I've ever fucking had.'

She sounds half asleep, but in the weak light her teeth glow gently: 'Thank Christ for that.'

Saturday, 11 March, 2.09am

As loaded as Barry is, he knows that at this point in time he could be blindfolded and hog-tied and still stand a better chance of piloting *The 'Dan* to safety than Mick does. On the rare occasions Mick drinks, the dude doesn't believe in half measures; seems to follow a subconscious impulse to purge himself of the desire for another six months or so, and Barry knows that only the cocaine in his system leaves Mick still conscious; in possession of his supper; remotely coherent.

Lefty, on the other hand, throughout the night seemed to shrink further into himself the more lines he snorted. Instead of chilling him out, amping him into party mode, to Barry the cocaine looks to have sapped Lefty of his usual self-possession, perhaps twisting his thought processes through frequencies he's not used to; has few defences in place. From time to time he's patently attempted to snap himself free of this introspection, begin another of the hallmark anecdotes he never seems to finish, waffling from subject to subject, but Barry found that all he need do was bleed a little ambiguity into his grin and Lefty would falter with delightful haste.

Even better, mention how Gator might be getting on right now — a tack Mick, despite his state of near obliteration, twigged to instinctively — and Barry can almost see the amphetamines and booze corroding Lefty's smugness.

Because despite all the flak Lefty's copped in the years since teenagehood began, all the humiliation, all the mockery, all the shit he's been made to eat — a lot of it force-fed by Gator — Lefty could always take comfort in the fact that he held in his hand one almighty trump to be played at will; to be tactically thrust down the throats of his detractors until they gagged. He may have been physically weaker than all his 'friends', less able intellectually, less courageous, less trustworthy, less *liked*, but at the end of the day he could coax into bed, or steal, almost any girl he chose, and for this, in male circles, a telling riposte just doesn't exist. So long as he never pushed it *too* far, Lefty knew he would always be viewed by his 'friends' through green-tinted spectacles, and no matter how they derided him, this ultimate power was his to wallow in and his alone.

Was.

They locate *The 'Dan*; opt to kick back on the bonnet for a spell, smoking.

Barry: '*Man*, I'd love to know what lines Gator used on that bird. She's the most beddable piece of babeage I've laid eyes on in *yonks* and she practically sucked him off right where he stood.'

Mick, full length on the bonnet: 'I regon he coulda fuged her in the dunnies if he'd wan'ed to.'

Barry: 'How 'bout the *tits* on it, eh, Lefty? What's the bet he's giving those the old "famished bambino" even as we speak?'

Lefty, muttering: 'Maybe.'

Mick: 'Man, he mussa chatted her *sweeeeeet*, 'cause I saw her knog a few cats back beforehand.'

Barry, all innocence: '*You* had a yarn with her for a bit there, didn't ya, Lefty? I thought you woulda given her the come-on, a hell-babe like that?'

Lefty, laughing the suggestion away: 'Fuck off, man. I don't do darkies. Not even for practice. I've actually *got* some standards.'

Barry, helpfully: '*Oh*, na, *some*times you do, bro. Remember Natalie Winiata? Tamara Walker?'

Hastily: 'Oh, yeah, but I was off my face on both those nights.'

Mick, equally obliging: 'Well, ya weren't *really*, were ya? An' if ya were, what about Hine Te Papa? She's a lot darker than those other two — and than that thing Gator pulled — and you *drove* us all back to your joint *that* night.'

Lefty, chuckling roguishly: 'And since when did being slaughtered ever stop *me* from driving the lads around?'

Knowing what's coming, Barry resists the urge to suggest, *Since always*?

Mick, still musing: 'Wellllllll, ya *can't* of been all *that* slaughtered. Considering we drove frew two checkpoints on the way to your crib and you were breath . . .'

Lefty, hurriedly: 'I've gotta take a slash.' Shuffles away.

In their inebriation, Barry and Mick are unable to cork the mirth until Lefty's beyond earshot — or perhaps, in their states, diplomacy's just something they can no longer be arsed with — and they fall about each other, spluttering and snorting.

Mick, a minute later, sobering with the suddenness of the well-toasted: 'Where the fuck's Steve, anyway?'

Barry sighs. Mick's asked this question several times since Steve left the club with the 'short-haired blonde with hooters'. 'He bailed with that slut, bro.'

'*Ohhhh*, that's right. How come he scored and neither of us did?'

'Because you were so smashed you spilled piss all down the redhead's blouse, and I couldn't decide which one to hit on properly.'

Actually, one of the remaining two had all but asked Barry home, but with Gator gone he'd felt obliged to hang around, keep an eye out for the others.

Not for the first time Barry finds himself pondering this phenomenon: how when the chief cabalist isn't along on a mission, or disappears for some reason, or gets himself too fucked-up to function, he, Barry, can often be found doing 'the right thing' to the point of character assassination. It's not a conscious choice — Barry can see that in hindsight; just seems to happen. He wonders if his actions are inspired by concern for his mates. Or perhaps by a deep-seated need to impress Gator. But Barry once blamed this latter as the cause of a lot of the *mad* shit he pulls.

He shrugs it off. His interest was academic anyway. *We are what we are, and to fight that is to bend and spread.*

Even now, as a couple of dickheads walk by, staring just long enough, Barry swallows the impulsive *Can I help you ladies*? This despite the booze in him at last outweighing the cocaine's ebullience, fuelling the thirst in his knuckles for that intimate *smock*. For the first time since snorting, he rubs the 'sweet spot' of his knee, the part that contacted the oinker's head; relives the sensual impact that jolted him like a stun-prod, which, like pure oxygen, blew roaring life into the dark embers that smoulder inside him.

But he wouldn't feed them now. *Couldn't.* Who'd get Mick home if he, Barry, wound up in the cells, in hospital? Lefty? Like fuck.

Besides, with what they had on the boil rapidly approaching, Gator'd be even more disappointed than usual by Barry rushing the trenches alone.

Barry's next urge, a split-second behind the first, is to ask the young dudes how they're doing, how their night seems to be shaping. To shoot a bit of that socialising shit, as he loves to. Enjoy some fleeting male bonding, often the most rewarding strain, certainly the safest.

The juxtaposition of these antipodal desires is something Barry seldom examines for long enough to find puzzling.

Mick: 'I really think I should drive, man. It *is* one'a my paramount roles within the Brotherhood, after all.'

He's been at Barry to hand over the keys for near half an hour now. Whether in search of thrill, or to shoulder the gauntlet of the squealers personally, Barry can't be certain. Under different circumstances, in another mood, Barry might have acceded to the demand, if for no better reason than his instinct for chaos wishing to learn how so much potential disorder might manifest itself.

But not tonight.

Flat: 'Fucking forget it, man.'

When Lefty at last returns he seems to have more steel in his step. His eyes appear somehow graver. Barry's instinct for chaos is piqued: Lefty looks primed for friction.

Barry, licking his lips: 'All right, dragons, jump in the wagon and we'll puff right off.'

Lefty's relegated to the back seat; this goes without saying.

Pulling into the main road, Barry squeals the tyres, cuts off some pinhead in a TX5, flirts briefly with the notion of stopping when it *beeps* condemnation of him, insulted more by the horn's tinny shrillness than by its import. Just to demonstrate the sound of a *man*'s horn, he sits on that of *The 'Dan* for a good few seconds, childishly gratified by the deep *whommmp*.

Mick, mumbling: 'Yeah, get a *real* horn, ya fucking yuppie wanker.' Then, as if alerted by the incident, he suddenly rips down his window — hand slipping from the handle twice — and hollers at passers-by: 'You're all a herd of fucking sheep!'

Barry, head in the warm breeze: 'Four legs good, two legs bad!'

Mick: 'The Revolution will not be televised!'

Barry: '. . . The Revolution will be live!' A cackling whoop: '*Yeeeeeee — ha — ha — haaaa!*'

That his blood/alcohol level must be at least four times the legal limit is a statistic, a consideration — *an accolade* — that barely registers with Barry. He's watched a pissed Gator in the driver's seat before, and the dude drives as if he were a cyborg, the road-code chiselled upon his datacore; 'fighting fascism furtively'. But Barry, when younger, had read and re-read the autobiography of some captain of the fledging SAS in its WW2 infancy — he had been fond of the genre — and focused on adopting the man's mindset. Through torturous mental discipline, it became instinctive. This fellow had purported that the only way to emphatically succeed in one's chosen field, against large odds, is to carry out each and every action at full-throttle confidence, as if one has a manifest right to encounter nothing but auspicious fortune. 'In this fashion,' wrote the VC winner, 'fate Herself was cowed into batting for me.'

Fiddling with the radio, Mick tunes in some Bowie cover while Barry crosses the median line (*Yeah, they hauled us outta the oxygen tent . . .*), floors it, hoons past three leading cars (*and we rasped for the latest party*) flicking *The 'Dan* back from oncoming traffic with a good second to spare.

Stopped at lights, Lefty beckons to a couple of tarts, starts yakking with them through the window. After a minute of this they seem keen, and Barry's surprised when Lefty makes no effort to up the ante. At last they get a green light and Barry pulls away, suspicious.

It takes Lefty a minute longer to psych himself to the sortie. From the back seat, all earnestness: 'Gagging for a shag. We should've tried to get those two back there along.'

Silent, Barry listens for the incoming.

Lefty, ingenuous: 'Did that brunette remind you's of Josephine? Same kind of face, I thought.'

Peripherally, Barry watches his torched co-pilot stiffen. And at this point he almost feels sorry for Mick . . . but the anticipation felt by his instinct for chaos is by far the dominant urge.

Barry, baiting: 'I s'pose she did a bit.'

Lefty, chuckling amiably: 'I got a hard-on as soon as I looked at her, 'cause that's *exactly* the type of root I could use right now: fully submissive.'

Lighting a smoke, Mick inhales hard, his silence suddenly deafening.

A year or three back, before Josephine, Mick hadn't exactly logged an awful lot of sack-time. In fact, his fantasy had been a partner. And rumour claimed his wallet contained a condom, the instructions on which began: *Before servicing thy wench . . .*

Josephine, though, had been Mick's apprenticeship, the skirt on which his carnal teeth were cut, his first 'love affair'. And, according to the progress reports with which he'd regale the lads, she'd rogered the very arse off him, rooted him ragged, broken him to her saddle. Josephine had been around a bit, loved shagging, and loved calling the tune. To which Mick had danced happily.

Then, inevitably, trouble found paradise. Breaks in the relationship, then full splits, decreasing 'together' periods. It was outside one these that Mick — not quite tearfully — swore black and blue that he was finished with her, that she could do 'whatever she fucking well liked' with 'whomever she fucking well liked', and that the number of flying fucks he gave was significantly fewer than one.

His adamance had fooled no one — you just don't heal from such so cleanly — but all knew the rules; simulated credence well.

In retrospect, a lot of the conviction in Mick's 'apathy' toward Josephine had been lured into wordage by Lefty, who belaboured the point with skilled balance, nobody suspecting a thing.

Within three weeks, however, Lefty had bagged Josephine for himself and treated her to his patented six F's: find 'em and fondle 'em, finger and fellate 'em, fuck em and flick 'em.

Of course, after the first root he emphatically clarified — in front of witnesses — Mick's 'status' of indifference ('It just kinda *happened*, man, ya know? But I never would have *let* it happen if I'd *once* thought she still meant anything to ya! Are you sure you're sweet with it, bro? Just *say* if you're not.')

Then, for months after ditching her, Lefty treated the lads to tales of sexual dominance: how 'Jo' liked to be tied down, spanked, adorned in the pearl necklace. How she'd come around on her rags one night, but he'd simply flipped her over and 'played the back nine'. How he never once let her go on top ('Fuck *that*, man! When I shaft a bitch I like to make a decent job of it, let her know she's been *prop*erly done.') And such was the skill of his parasitism, none could voice a word of protest without 'betraying' Mick's angst.

Lefty, airily: 'I don't know why, but I'm in the mood to have some chick on her knees in front of me, begging me to come all over face. Just like Jo used to.' Chuckle: 'I'd grab a handful of her hair and twist her head right back, stick it down her throat till she spluttered.'

Despite a lot of pondering, Barry wasn't certain why Lefty had stooped so low. Perhaps he simply shat on Mick because he could; because this breed of mastery was all that allowed him to face life under the terms his 'friends' imposed. But Barry suspected Lefty's motives ran deeper. Because Mick had been the last of the crew to lose his cherry. Because, this given, to hit back at antagonism all Lefty had to do in those days was allude to the 'V' word and Mick was out of commission in a real hurry, Gator and Barry often forced to retreat for his sake.

Then — through Josephine — Mick had liberated the hostage, much to Lefty's glossed-over pique.

After Lefty's reprisal Mick had dealt with it well, too proud even to complain when Lefty wasn't around — well, not to Barry anyway; he might have confessed to Gator. That Mick seldom got shit-faced plainly helped him keep a lid on things.

Lefty, laddish drawl: 'I hope you rubbered-up when you and her were rooting, Mick, 'cause *I* certainly didn't. Screw *that*. Can't feel a *thing* with one'a those on. I'd sooner have a fucking *flog*, mate. The cunt who invented those things should be shot.'

A while later, sighing boredom: 'There's only so much of that absolute devotion shit a bloke can take, though. Well, there is for *me*, at any rate. Couldn't handle any more than a coupla weeks of the bitch. Dumped her flat. Haven't been back for another round yet, either. She might've even moved on by now; stranger things've happened . . . and ya know what they say: one man's trash is another man's treasure.'

Mick, low: 'Stop the car.'

It's all Barry can do to keep from rubbing his hands together: 'Why, man?'

Mick, with more assertiveness than he's ever addressed Barry: 'Just *stop* the fucking car! *Now!*'

Lefty, a little uneven: 'What do ya wanna *stop* for?'

But Mick ignores him, and Barry's grinning openly as he pulls down a quiet side-street.

Lefty, whining: 'What are ya's *doing*? Is this to do with *me*, Mick? I was only *chatting*. No *offence* to anyone!'

The 'Dan swings into the kerb, slows down.

Mick's out before it's stationary.

Lefty, crying: 'What's going *on*?' He slaps his door locked an instant before Mick can lift it open.

Mick, yelling: 'Open the *fucking* door, you greaseball *cunt*! It's over, now get the *fuck* out here and *stand up* for yourself!'

Lefty, shrilly wronged: 'What are you *on* about? *What's* over?'

'All your tacit *shit*, that's what!'

In a mischievous spurt, Barry's hand strikes backward, flicking the door-lock open.

Lefty: '*No!*' Snatches at it . . .

Too late.

The door is ripped almost off its hinges, and Mick thrusts in a face disfigured. He doesn't even notice the door rebounding into him, nearly upsetting him.

Is that really you under that snarl, Mickey? Barry gives a quick whoop of admiration. *Top effort, my son! Didn't realise ya had it in ya!*

Lefty, scrambling for the far door, begging: '*Stop* him, Barry! There's no *need* for this! *I* don't want any trouble!'

Barry reaches back, locks Lefty's escape route. Through smiling eyes: 'Lefty, my boy, it appears events have moved beyond you. You reap what you sow, and I'm guessing it's harvest time.'

Clinging, Lefty resists strongly when Mick grips his leg, attempts to haul him free. 'Fuck *off*, you crazy cunt!' But Mick's too far gone for nicety; simply hammers Lefty's body with a free fist until pain springs Casanova from anchorage.

Then out he's wrenched, hand over hand, like a sticky turd from a pile-ridden anus, coming to 'rest' with his arse on the kerb, his back against the car, covering up frantically.

Leaping out, Barry skips around the car, appraising events closely . . . and is quick to judge this by no means the slickest beating he's ever witnessed. The most touching, maybe, but not the slickest.

Given Mick's 'experience' of martial matters, Barry can only guess that Lefty submits to his fate with such docility through a belief that Barry will involve himself otherwise. And considering this briefly, Barry concludes Lefty dead right.

And wise.

Bent toward him, Mick unloads on Lefty with a frenzied series of windmills, apparently unfazed by half his blows striking *The 'Dan*, the other half finding only Lefty's protecting arms. Even as his glasses are whipped from his face, Mick maintains the wild tattoo.

Lefty: 'Fuck off! Fuck off! I'm *sorry,* OK!'

Mick, huffing with strain: '*Sorry*? For *six years* of the shit? Like *fuck*! This time you're gonna cease to fucking *function*!'

At last he catches Lefty a glancing left across the temple, and as Lefty's guard opens further, head sagging against the car, it has nowhere to go when the next left nails him flush. In a flurry of punches Lefty assumes the foetal position, curled in the gutter.

Straightening, bracing himself on the car, Mick begins to kick and stomp at him.

He is *gonna kill him!* Barry jolts. *Literally!* He knows he must put a stop to this . . . *now* . . . but finds he's having too much fun; can't squeeze the words from his throat, the action from his limbs.

Landing a clean boot across Lefty's nose, popping it like a plum, Mick stops abruptly, standing still, heaving breath in shudders. For long seconds he looks Lefty over, leaning down, squinting at his handiwork. Whispers at last: 'Oh, shit. What the fuck've I done?'

Barry recognises him again, knows it's over, strides past him. Kneels beside Lefty, moves his limp hands from his face, slaps him lightly, hears only groaning, frowns at the blood on his hand, wipes it on Lefty's shirt. Declaring: 'He'll live.' Then, with cold precision, Barry drives his right fist into Lefty's solar plexus. Returns his wheezing body to its side for safety reasons. Into his ear: 'That was for Becky, you sleazy piece of shit. If you feel like more, head back to Bum's joint; I'll be waiting for you. And we didn't do this. You walked away of your own accord. And the sole reason we came to Auckland was to do charlie with Bum. A word different to *any*one *ever* . . . and I'll kill you. You know me, pal: I'll do it for fun.'

From the hip pocket of Lefty's Levis Barry removes his wallet. He then opens the boot, fetches Lefty's pack, and drops it in the gutter beside him.

Mick seems shocked into autism, holding his cut hands inches from his face. Barry slides Mick's glasses back into place; bundles his limp body into the front seat.

And it's ten balmy minutes before Mick breaks Barry's after-glow. 'What the fuck are we gonna tell Gator?'

8

Bum at last reappears from the head of the alley, loping across the road toward where *The 'Dan* is parked. Maori kids playing league on an overgrown lawn stop to stare at him, as if at a circus act.

One of them, grinning, hollering: 'Cher, neat hair, mister Bawl'ead!'

Another taps at a phantom microphone, punctuating the beat with impressively accurate sound glitches, cheeks spread: 'Testing! *One*, two, three! Testing, people. *Testinggg*!'

'*Huhuhuhuhu*!'

If not for his outlandishness, Bum would've been ignored, as we have been by every darkie who's walked past the car in the time we've been parked here. This is only a ghetto of sorts; Mandela might have called it a rainbow slum.

Still, with a head full of LSD *my* choice of a two-hour loitering spot would have manifested in somewhere a little more inspiring.

But Bum had insisted on 'taking care of things' early.

I'd established contact with the lads near dawn, arranged an extraction. Couldn't bring myself to wake her; enough had been said earlier.

208

Perhaps too much.

Informing me of Lefty's withdrawal ('He pulled some bitch whose folks had a yacht, were off for a week of sailing up Russell way, invited him along. Said to count him outta the deal. Said it already scared him shitless and he wanted no more of it. Left us some pingas, though. Good of him, really.') Barry had then demanded, as lads do: 'Details, McPike. Gory ones.'

I divulged little lewd — I've learned that the unsaid impacts harder. 'We just bonked once, then chatted for hours. Y'all know what that's like — a nice-looking bird who you think is pretty cool besides; barriers gone 'cause you've already been as intimate as it physically gets, but you know nothing about each other, really; still pissed enough to say anything you like; just lying in the dark, smoking, teasing, learning, shooting the shit.'

Even Barry's eyes had misted.

For once we were free to wax sexually lyrical: Lefty wasn't there.

Barry: 'When ya gonna see her again?'

Me: 'Good question.'

With Bum along already, we'd collected Steve from a pad in Mt Eden, some short-haired blonde seeing him off the front step with a playful pat on the arse. Shirtless, tattoo resplendent, Steve had strolled across to us, catlike in his nonchalance, and even Bum had grinned fondly.

'That's one *smooooooth* brother you dudes've got your-selves.'

Barry: 'You don't know the half of it, mate.'

But as Steve slipped in beside me, the facade quickly lapsed. Sighing: 'Jesus fuckin' Christ, am I glad t'see yu cats. Roll the end credits, Mick. Get me the hell outta here. Drive t' the middla nowhere and take a wrong turn.' To me: 'I 'ope yu fared better than I did, cuz.'

Barry, puzzled: 'Why, bro? What went wrong?'

Steve, sneering: 'She's a bloody *Christian*, man! We did fuck all but lie there and *kiss* all night!'

Bum: 'Ratshit.'

Steve had smiled, though, as if the irony were worth the frustration. '*Tell* me 'bout it. Bitch wooden even *beat* me off! My prick feels like Branson tried t' fly round the fuckin' world in it.'

Barry: 'Fuck, she seemed like a goer in the club.'

Steve: 'I *noe*. The worst part was in the morning, wif all 'er God Squad flatmates kicking round. I felt 'bout as welcome as a arsonist in a arms factory.'

After killing a few hours in town, we'd motored through the city sun, up to One Tree Hill, where Bum produced his wares.

I hadn't really felt like tripping, happy and reflective enough on the natural high Tania left me with.

And acid's a commitment. Drop a tab and the high — not to mention the comedown — removes one from the race for a solid few hours, minimum. As chief cabalist, the Brotherhood in mid-mission, I saw abstinence as my sacred duty.

For about a minute or so.

Gather, all ye faithful; The Doors stand unlocked and beckoning.

Through to a fantasyland of stunned mirth; a pilgrimage to the Temple of Lateral Thought. Brains rewired in a mode to give every stimuli and notion ten connotations never before considered. Powers of insight and reasoning invested with a paranormality to render explicit so many of life's mysteries, that these solutions had hidden beneath our very noses for so long spicing the trip with bursts of utter hilarity. Under the acid all things are given talismanic symbolism, representative of, and clarifying, some vaster issue.

Answers reduced to sludge when the drug leaves your brain.

Not long after ushering us through, though, Bum decided to switch the lights out as well, surprising and alarming us all.

Because acid, like weed's bigger cousin — so far removed from booze or amphetamines — is a drug prone to mood-swings if a favourable environment isn't maintained. Paranoia and doubt of shocking force can supersede wonder in mere seconds.

When Bum ordered we bring him here our bubble didn't burst so heinously as this, but the come-down certainly kicked in a lot sooner and harsher than it might have.

Leaving us in the here, a Henderson kerbside, euphoria gone, the world still viewed through higher eyes but without its cushion of giddiness, the negativity in our insights left inexorable and glaring, like an ageing Diva in morning sun.

Bum climbs in back. Declares: 'Well, that's that sorted. As soon as ya's lay your mitts on the blow, give me a call with an estimate of how much you have, and of its quality. I'll phone the dude; he'll get the bucks around.'

Barry: 'Can your man round up that sort of cash?'

Bum: 'He's connected to all fuck, cuz. Wouldn't have tried to jack up a deal like this with your standard ghetto tinny dealer. Don't ask any more about him, please.'

'Sweet.'

Even given the introversion two hours in this neighbourhood has set to our trips, Mick's been quieter than usual recently. He speaks now, though. 'No chance of him falling through, Bum? I mean, is there a back-up if this dude doesn't happen for some reason? We don't fancy hanging on to this much pot for more than a day or so.'

Bum: 'He won't fall through. If he can only take a portion of it there's a couple of back-ups, but they're smaller scale. I'll move what I can, and I know a sweet spot to bury any surplus; it'll be shifted in weeks.'

I look to Steve; he nods tightly.

Bum: 'When are ya's leaving?'

Steve: 'Somewhere round midnight. We wanna do all our drivin' in the dark and spend the full day out there.'

Bum: 'Did ya's hear the weather report?'

Me: 'Na.'

'There's a big storm crossing the Tasman. It's forecast to reach Northland by Sunday night. Sounds like it's gonna piss down for days.'

Steve: 'Won't trouble us . . . 'less it arrives early.'

Barry: 'Where to now, then? You need to go anywhere else, Bum?'

'Na, mate, I'm a free agent. You dudes look as if you're coming down pretty hard, though; should get a few drinks in ya's, take the edge off things. I know a mellow pub nearby: low lighting, sweet jukie, dak up in the garden bar, cheap beer. '

Mick: 'Nearby, is it? Must be rough if it's near *here*.'

Bum: '*Naaa*, man. Big Maori dude runs it. Tough cunt. Ex-All Black. Good mate of mine. Tolerates no shit in his joint. Always got three or four of his cronies in the house, too. The locals know better than to rumble there.'

Everyone brightens to the suggestion — even Mick, whom I've never once known to touch a drop on consecutive days.

Saturday, 11 March, 7.12pm

That Lefty had resolved to hitch-hike home, and persevered with his thumbing for long hours — in spite of the manner with which motorists had shied from his hideousness — spoke of a depth of character none had ever credited him with.

Because even though he had found in his pack a pair of sunnies to cover his black eye; even though his missing teeth could only be seen if he grinned carelessly; even though he was able to stand tall around his bruised ribs when need be; and even though there're plenty of people sentenced to life with noses naturally larger than the size his broken beak had swollen to, Lefty believed that for such as himself to be asked to *hitch-hike* so soon after being cheated of his remarkable looks, amounted to a cheetah sent hunting with hind legs in plaster.

But he'd made it.

After a hellish night in a Smoke alley, to the Southern Motorway, to State Highway One, to the Vegas turnoff, Lefty had plugged away, stoically bearing the stares and the grins of the passers-by, even female drivers — who would customarily have burned brake-lining in their haste to collect him — stomached the horns of the heartless with no humanity to spare.

Within several rides he'd reached his city's outskirts, the achievement birthing in him pride of intense dimensions, because, stripped of one's chief assets, penniless, Lefty was all too aware of how the fate of Joe Average in his shoes would have manifested.

Back on home turf, immensely relieved for it, Lefty picks his way through the city's western suburbs, his thoughts at last free to roam.

Unprompted, they stroll immediately down the cold, stone cobbles of Retribution Drive.

We're at Bum's pub in five minutes. Mick parks along the kerb, beside a grotty little park, slide covered in birdshit and tags. The lads pile out, but I'm taken by an urge to kick back alone, suck on a gasper.

Mick: 'Here's the keys, then. See ya inside.'

'No worries.'

Feet on the seat in front of me, I rest my eyes on a group of motley kids at play in the park, perhaps eight of them, multi-hued, wrestling, the largest and oldest, a Maori girl of around eleven, throwing the others about with ease. To me these younger don't seem happy with arrangements, acceding to the sanctioned violence robotically, instinctively.

But maybe it's the acid reading too much into the scene.

Some minutes later a mangy dog slinks into the commotion, tail wagging uncertainly, hungry for playmates, for attention. Sensing a role reversal, the smallest child rounds on the mutt, baying like a Cossack. It retreats in quick order but turns back, ears flat, fawning. The boy aims a kick at it, joined by two of his contemporaries; the dog darts clear, keeping its distance, though hanging on hopefully.

Her prominence usurped, suddenly alone, Big Girl takes steps to restore things: locating a rock, hurling it at the mongrel.

It scampers away further, but turns again, confused and needy.

Her act captures her fellows' imaginations: the dog is soon beleaguered by a storm of projectiles. The fusiliers offer rowdy chase.

To dizzying impact, the scene becomes microcosmic of wider things. Under-stimulated kids, raised around violence, venting inner tempests on any victims at hand, all too happy to play aggressor for once, urges and habits to fester with 'development'.

Leaden for both parties, I leave *The 'Dan* on impulse, move into the park, toward the 'mob'.

'Hey, kids!'

As one they turn to me, reflexively defiant. 'What?'

Just a suggestion: 'Why don't y'all leave the dog alone? He means no harm to ya's. He just wants someone to play with.'

Big Girl, caustic: 'Shut up, mister! Yu can't fuckin' tell us what to do.'

Again she inspires them.

'Yeah, you ain't our parents.'

'Yu ain't even a *man*!'

A cheeky-looking seven-year-old: 'Yeah, fuck orf, bawl'ead!'

'*Hahahahaha!* '

But I have their attention. The dog goes to ground along a nearby fence, observing events with interest.

Me, 'startled': 'Do you mean to say nobody's ever *told* you guys what happens to people who're kind to animals?'

I've always had the words for kids. Of course: the Brotherhood would hardly suffer a leader unable to bait those with faith in the Easter Bunny. Also, a younger me once worked a babysitting racket — before penetrating the teenage elite — and necessity taught him the tools a child might be won with.

Oh yeah, I can play Hamlin's pipes with the best of them. Were I given to paedophilia, I'd enjoy a sex life to rival *any* man of the cloth.

Still, given their home life and mob mentality, these before me present a tough audience.

Big Girl: 'Na, we *ain't* bin told what 'appens, and we doan *wanna* be told, either!'

A second: 'Yeah, it's much better t'. . . '

The aroused youngster sets off along a tangent of nonsense I've no intention of suffering. Loud enough to slice his sentence:

'Well, if you don't *wanna* know, then I'm wasting my time with ya's.' I make eye contact with the cheeky Maori boy, judging him an agreeable medium. 'I might as well just let you carry on living *without* the secret, even if it means that one day you'll find out what it is, but it'll be too late by then, and you'll remember me standing here in front of you, and you'll say to yourselves, "Why didn't I listen for just *one* minute?"'

Shrugging, regretful and ponderous — quietly confident — I turn from their silence . . .

. . . and they let me go with zero bites.

Well, not completely.

'Yeah, *fuck* off, yu silly white cunt! Doan need no lekshas from *yu*!'

'*Hahahaha*!'

Stung by even this rejection, my cheeks redden. Shoulders shrinking, walking faster: tactical fall-back to chaotic rout. It seems my touch has deserted me.

At my back: 'I bet yu 'ad a *secret*, all right! A secret *cock* in yaw pants yu wanted us t' *touch*!'

'You fuckin' dirty *pervert*!

'*Hahahahahaha!*'

And without warning this new element douses my abashment. Taints it with a shot or two of wrath. Though I'm not sure why, exactly. Maybe it's simple umbrage at such gross disrespect from juniors. Am I merely incensed by the baseness of the category in which they seek to lump me?

Perhaps, but I don't think so.

Though I'd face firing squad before speaking this aloud, I fear my sudden aggrievement stems from the sexual spin the kids impart upon their snubbing of me. After all, without fail, my life's most agonising humiliations occur in the carnal arena.

I'm no kiddie fucker, am appalled by the notion, but deja vu needs little cover from which to spring ambush.

My feet stop. They no longer wish me elsewhere. Even as the illogic of the reaction chafes at me, I turn back to the imps, face hardening all by itself.

Their grins slip, two of them backing off a pace.

Warming me darkly.

I know this is wrong, but I'm able to ignore the voice. Iniquity offers unique thrills, and these little fucks have touched my rawest nerve.

I doubt, however, that an urge to press this vengeance further than intimidation could ever possess me — thank god. And I'm well aware of the chances even the wittiest lone mouth takes into an outnumbered squabble (*My cock's had someone a lot better looking than* you *monkeys touching it recently!*): I bite back verbal assault as well. With phantom daggers only, I move stiffly to a nearby bench, climb aboard — feet on the seat, arse on its back — looming like poised thunder.

Removing a smoke from my shirt pocket; flicking a flame; lighting up — Billy the Kid on a lazy reload.

But gradually, as physical threat fades, the alarm gripping the pipsqueaks eases.

Big Girl, belligerent: 'So yu think yu a man just 'cause yu *puff*, do yu?'

Flat stare. Flawless smoke-ring.

Then, for the barest second, I sincerely consider offering her one.

Another: 'What's wrong? Cat gotcha tongue?'

'Cat got 'is *'nads*, maw like it!'

'*Hahahaha*!'

Flat stare. Flawless smoke-ring.

So suddenly it sickens, the enmity inside me retreats — red mist lifted . . . *voila*!: a grown man harassing underprivileged children.

Way to go, tough guy.

Could've happened to anyone, though, really. That is, anyone with the arse-end of an acid-trip in their noggin.

Nausea fades obediently.

Clears a breach for more habitual impulses; awkward seconds are spent weighing options for departing the impasse with face intact.

Arriving empty-handed.

Until fate throws me a joker.

Overlooked by all, the incident's catalyst, the dog, has skulked into the scene, rounding the bench I'm on. He gazes up at me: the boundless wisdom of the mute pitying me my volatility.

With no thought for the hazards of rejection No. 2, I pat my leg and whistle. Gingerly, the dog creeps nearer, stretches his snout to my hand . . .

. . . sniffing . . .

. . . blinks at last, tension deserting him.

A tap of the bench and he springs up beside me.

Scratching his ears, just a bloke and a dog . . . we could almost be alone.

A twisted cheer: 'What're yu gonna try it wif the *mutt* now, I s'pose? Yu got sum *butter* in yaw pocket, 'ave you? Yu can rub it on yaw *knob*, get him to lick it *off*!'

'*Hahahahaha!*'

I front them with a six-gun more PC by far: guilt.

Sombre frown, bruised eyes, borrowing from the dog's benevolence shamelessly.

I offer compassion and this *is my thanks?*

A couple seem moved, compunction smothering their mirth.

Big Girl as well seems to tire with the sport. Scoffing: 'Let's *go*. Leave this weirdo alone wif his new girlfriend.'

They follow her lead. Cheeky brings up the rear, his gaze the last to leave me, sudden solemnity hollowly gratifying. Before long the group are wrestling again, the mêlée wheeling them slowly toward the park's far corner.

Stroking my new friend: 'Immaculate timing, old boy.' Gratitude outweighing the mange of its coat, the scabs beneath, the crust round its eyes.

Lefty had promised himself dire vengeance.

And they'll deserve every cold inch of it, the fucking cocksuckers.

Imagine it! Disfiguring a man for *life* for no better reason than petty jealousy. Seeking, through battery, to deprive him of his inalienable station above Joe Average; suck him into their sphere of sexual mortality.

All last night, shivering in the alley, hidden beneath a wheelie bin, fear gnawing his insides at every voice, every footstep — suffering dulled by piss and cocaine, though still sorer than a virgin at a gang-bang — Lefty had rehearsed any number of times the telephone conversation he would have with Joe, the Rabble prospect, as soon as he hit town.

Now, though, in the cold light of sobriety, Lefty slowly accepts that, without a doubt, this most baleful strain of revenge lies beyond his reach. Because given such stimulus the Rabble — or at least Hemi — would make an attempt on the lives of all four of them, perhaps even upon Bum.

And Lefty couldn't bear to have this happen . . .

. . . because what if one or some of them escaped the gang's justice? With the betrayal stemming from him so glaringly, Lefty's own life would in turn become forfeit.

He swears frustration, resolved to brainstorming, trudging wearily.

Soon, along the quiet street, a car whizzes past him. Too late, Lefty recognises it as belonging to Rachael Mills, an ex-flame. He waves an arm in her rear-view mirror, desperate for a ride (*/concern/sympathy/attention/adoration/worship/surrender*), but Rachael either fails to identify him, or chooses not to.

Most likely the latter, given that after he'd broken up with her, relegating her to his list of part-timers, Rachael had consented to 'see' Lefty on just a few more occasions, preferring instead to form a relationship with a colleague from the law firm she'd begun working for.

Snobbish bitch. He flicks a petulant finger at the car as it vanishes around a bend. *Flirts her way into a good job and thinks that makes her Queen Shit. Never mind that I could make more money than that in a heartbeat if God had given* me *a greasy hole between my legs and a couple of bags of fat on my chest.*

Lefty had lasted less than a month with Rachael for she typified what he found most nauseating in females: mawkishness. Of course, when it came to the chase this trait was a red-blooded male's dream, but after the catch was made, like so many chicks, Rachael had made a habit of clinging to Lefty and murmuring inanities like 'What are you thinking?', or 'Tell me something nice.'

Or, Lefty's personal favourite, 'What's your fantasy?' Followed by a predictable Mills & Boon excerpt, perhaps: 'Mine's riding behind you on a horse, on a wet summer day, then making love on a bed of mountain daises.'

How can any chick ask such a thing of a bloke and expect a genuine answer? Does she really wanna be told: 'Well, baby, my fantasy's to travel to America and seduce some billionaire's wife, convincing her to take him for half in the divorce courts, then slapping my own ring on its finger quick smart. I then bribe some shrink into telling my wife that rooting around's my only therapy for sexual abuse as a child; that it'll surely taper away to nothing if she shows me enough love. I'm then free to cultivate as vast and exotic a string of mistresses as can possibly be accomplished on endless money and travel; limos; Ferraris; Harleys; a super-yacht; the best drugs and piss; tailored clothes; my own nightclub . . . '

The train of thought captures him and Lefty forgets Rachael; trudges along almost merrily.

For perhaps a kilometre he then puzzles over how he might denounce his 'friends' to the police while painting himself free of all wrongdoing. It isn't long, though, before he's forced to declare this plot tantamount to the first.

And it's only a short while after this that Lefty grudgingly concedes that the only viable option he has for taking revenge will be in the manner which to him has become habitual.

Yes, following a few dentistry sessions, a bit of cosmetic surgery to straighten his nose out — *Might as well get a little extra work done while I'm there* — Lefty will simply bide his time, keep an ear to the ground, then go to work on the appropriate females.

Of course in view of the complete disintegration of his relationships with Barry and Mick — and thus Gator, who had started the whole thing by poisoning that nigger whore against him in the first place — Lefty can this time afford to do battle in fashions vastly less subtle. He'll need to ingratiate himself with a new crew beforehand, however. A tough one at that, because by the time Lefty's done, he knows Barry at least be will be hunting him high and low.

But Lefty envisages few problems in this area. Indeed, a few weeks ago he'd managed to wheedle himself an invitation to a party at the headquarters of the white bikie gang, the Devil's Disciples. For want of another date, Lefty had taken Becky along, almost bursting with pride when several of the gang hierarchy expressed lustful approval of the leggy brunette. With this leverage, Lefty had contrived to elevate himself to first-name terms with the bikies, and as he walks today he grows more and more convinced of his ability to curry favour among the Disciples by having Becky strategically sleep with at least one of them. Hell, if he can pour enough sauce down her throat, blow her enough shoties, slip a tab or two into her brandy, promise her enough undying gratitude, Lefty begins to fancy his chances of strutting through the gates of the pad with Becky on his arm, and showfully presenting her as a gift to them *all*!

Brightened, hurts fleetingly forgotten, Lefty passes an alleyway and hesitates, knowing it will lead him to a long network of fields and parks from which another exit gives direct access to his mother's place, saving him almost an hour of walking. He also knows that at this time on a Saturday he runs the risk of encountering in the park bands of homies from the ghetto, making their clandestine way toward town and the evening's operations.

He examines the sky, decides it contains another half hour of light: more than time enough to traverse the park and leave it to its traditional late wayfarers.

A while earlier, mortality close enough to choke on, Lefty

might have taken the longer, safer route. Now, with fresh visions of his 'connected' future, Lefty shrugs a 'fuck it'.

Starts down the grafittied alley.

Fag finished, the need for motion rushing me, I flick the butt clear and cross to a nearby tree. Snap a small branch from it. Shown the stick, the dog feigns disinterest. Nevertheless, when I toss it, he leaps from the bench and bounds a pursuit, enthusiastic as a creature twice as hale.

Surprise giggles from me.

He even returns at a smart trot, surrendering his quarry with the barest hint of a liberty given.

Awaits the chase with a patronising stare. I'm half tempted to throw a dummy; decency wins out.

Away again. *I know you're not food, but I'll pretend so anyway. I've these urges in me to kill things, you see — shake them to bloody pieces — but I'm pretty sure the poop'll hit the air-con should I dare to answer them.*

In the background, the mob appears to be demobilising, dribbling away in small factions.

No idea now why I bothered feeling for them, extending myself. Not a maudlin trace left of the mood that saw me bitten.

I shrug sullenly, write it off to the wonders of LSD. Emotional imbalance in one easy swallow. Shame an *entire* trip isn't like the end of one; the stuff'd be easier to quit than nightshade.

Still, as the dog shows fatigue a few casts later — pikes out of the game in favour of gnawing — as I sit on the bench and watch two of the kids toss a tennis ball; it's hard not to thaw just a little. Hard not to chuckle at their artless ardour, their frowning engrossment. Their instant joy, quicker disgust.

Those were the days, all right. No doubt that we'd grow to inherit the earth. Soles like leather. All fields Eden Park. All tries Shield-clinchers. And even when you lost, knees skinned and limping, at home there'd be ice-cream, or soup by the fire. A kiss goodnight and all ills were rights; sleeping the sleep of the just.

I wonder what Tania's and my kids'd look like?

Would a boy be like I was: all skin and bone, more energy than mass, a grass stained dynamo? What about a girl? Would she have Tania's jet hair? Her cute pixie nose? A coffee-coloured cinderella . . .

Snapping to my feet, startling the dog.

Feel my breath quicken, like a deer on the run; can't reign it in.

Even the kids feel my shock, stop to stare.

Tick followed tock, followed tick followed tock . . .

Forcing word to my feet: Let's blow this scene, boys. Now. Out of the park, away from these brats. Get me to this pub, to beer and to mates, to jugs and to sounds, to weed and to bullshit . . .

. . . And you can keep your fucking acid stashed down your undies, Bum, you treacherous bastard.

. . . Feeling better already.

Lefty emerges from the alley onto a sloping field perhaps 500 metres across, down the centre of which flows a small river. Clumps of trees dot the landscape, a fenced rugby pitch in the foreground.

Birds sing their last in the dying light, and, after a good visual scouting, Lefty starts across the park.

Minutes later, though, passing a long grove of pines, he hears a sound that rivets him in his tracks.

A laugh.

A *cackle*.

Then, not five metres from his position, a boy of perhaps thirteen clears the bushes at a trot. A Maori boy.

Whose status Lefty is immediately forced to modify to 'homie' when two comrades appear at his back.

Lefty surprises the youths almost as much as they do him, minus the apprehension.

Still, though they are three, these kids lean toward Homieism's younger and smaller denominator; present little threat to him in numbers of fewer than five.

Yet when a fourth, and larger, squad member materialises, Lefty's dread regains flickering life.

And when Dusty pops from the trees like a juvenile orc in the Mirkwood, Lefty's stomach goes into freefall, comes to rest near his heels.

At the sight of Lefty, an impudent grin splits the novice gangster's baby-face, his eyes bright like foxglove. His adolescent voice saws like a hungry buzzard's, dripping acid disdain. 'Well, well, *well*! *Whad*'ve we got *'ere* then, boys?'

Lefty, panic an inch away, backing off unconsciously: 'I don't want any trouble with you dudes!' He whips his glasses off, laying bare his black eye, hoping for mercy a part of him knows can't come. 'I'm just . . . '

One of the younger ones, aroused: ''E was in that car tha uva night! Yu noe, outside the pickshas, when those fullas sung that slave shit at us?'

The fourth, and biggest: ''E's *al*ways cruisin' in that car.'

But, as usual, Dusty's three steps ahead of his soldiers. His life is lived by fist and by boot, and his head for strife is the best in his field. Without it, given the fickleness of the circles in which he runs, Dusty would've been deposed long ago.

Crowing his delight: '*Course* 'e's always in that car! "*The 'Dan*", bawl'eads call it. "The *Holll*-Dan". Used to be Luke's car, that one. Old Redneck Luke. Yaw parta the "hitman" Barry's team. Ain't that *right*, bawl'ead? 'Im an' old Alla-Gator. The *very same* crew that jumped Tubby an' 'em up town that night, when they was all sick on the Jack's they found. Folks say this one 'ere's tha fulla 'u always *scores*. Well, yu've certainly scored *today*, beau. Scored *big* time!'

On a handful of occasions Lefty's been a member of parties that have come close to scrapping, against their will, squads led by Dusty. Once it actually happened, briefly, but Lefty had hoped, in the confusion and darkness, for Dusty's memory of him to be less than comprehensive.

Now he learns that the 'kid' has detailed files of him at instant access.

Not that it would have mattered. Given the odds, Lefty's age and colour, the emptiness of the scene, Dusty would have set upon him no matter.

Instinctively.

Dusty, smirking, stalking: 'Looks like sumone *else* 'ad a dance wif 'im not — too — long — ago. Less than a whole day, judgin' by that shiner and nose. What 'appened, *scorer*? *Ladies*' man? Did sum *hoe* slap yu silly 'cause yu wooden *fuck* 'er 'ard enuf? Maybe that's true, 'cause I 'member seeing yu dance up town one night, an' yu fight like a bitch *yawself*.'

They fan out, Dusty centring the net.

Lefty dials his whine to maximum patheticness. 'Come *ooooon*, fullas! I only hang out with those guys because of the drugs they get! I just had a *huge* scrap with them, and four of them kicked the *crap* outta me! *Don't* hurt me! *Pleeeeeeease*! Why *meeee*?'

But his abjection seems only to embolden them, and when Dusty's grin sharpens, his eyes flaring, hysteria bursts the dyke of Lefty's control. With a choked yell he turns tail, ditching his pack, sprinting for dear life . . .

. . . but the grunts run him to ground in a few drooling strides, hooting glee hyena-like; hurl him to his knees.

Dusty approaches at a pace more dignified, and through his smiling, baby-face the homie's sudden mimicry affects Lefty like satanic pantomime. 'What we've got here is . . . *failure* to communicate.' Around the streets of Vegas, Dusty's renowned for his artistry: he takes thuggery to new levels. Slapping Lefty hard with an open palm, frowning suddenly, like a wronged employer: 'Yu should know beda than t' *run*, bouy. Niggers, when they run lark that, it's on account of their crames being *tooooo* much t' bear. Lark mah pappy used to tell me, a runnin' nigger's a guilty nigger.' He thrusts his face close to Lefty's. Hushed, rueful: 'And a *guilty* nigger? . . . Why that there's a *dayed* nigger.'

Knees hugged to his chest, Lefty points his sobs at the grass.

Nevertheless, when instinct identifies a bolt-hole — the green and white scarf on Dusty's belt — Lefty's sense of self-preservation seizes it with venom. All other reason discarded — *abolished* — Lefty recalls some enemy intelligence of his own.

Dusty purports Rabble affiliation, always has; is eager to follow the lead of a patched older brother.

Lefty, babbling, purpose gushing to his eyes, through his limbs: '*Iknowsomething*! *Somethingyouneedtoknow*! *I promise*! *I swear* on my mother's *soul*! It's something about the Rabble!'

Dusty, sneering, rhetorical: '*Tssssss*. What wood *yu* noe of Rabble affairs?' He cocks his fist, grin springing back to his lips, quick as schizophrenia.

Lefty, frantic, cringing: 'It's to do with Hemi! Do you know Hemi? He'll wanna know about this *straight away*, I'm *telling* you! And he'll thank you for telling him *forever after*!'

Dusty, swapping a stare with the bigger of his subordinates: 'Just 'im noeing Hemi's *name* sa-prises *me*.'

'Me tu. Maybe it wooden 'urt t' listen to 'im.'

Lefty, as steady as ague: 'Just you, Dusty. Hemi'll do us both, otherwise.'

9

A long way north of the Smoke, State Highway 69 passes to the west of Takahera pine plantation, a sprawling exotic forest in various stages of logging and regrowth. Though smaller than the Juggernaut's beloved Kaiangaroa, Takahera Forest is of similar nature: planted on long flats, gentle undulations; broken into blocks by a labyrinth of gravel roads; bordered at its circumferences by farms and real forest — native valleys and ridges, thick and steep.

As we hit the turnoff into Takahera, I've been at the wheel for the past two hours. Steve's beside me, reading the map by torchlight. We've shared the driving since the Smoke, Barry and Mick having drunk to excess — the latter quite inexplicably — in Bum's pub and now flaked out on the back seat. Though we've smoked near a packet of fags each, Steve and I are sober and straight.

Primed for business.

At least Steve is. I'm just doing well at pretending to be. For despite the sublime opportunity almost upon us, the coming day refuses to dwell in my thoughts as anything but a rip in a surf-beach.

Moving from bitumen to the gravel of the logging roads, the

rougher ride is at first a little unsettling, but our arses soon adjust, *The 'Dan* humming across the coarse surface as only an old Holden can.

Me, attempting a thought derailment: 'So, he planted in the pine, eh? What's so sound about *this* spot? Looking at the size of the forest on the map, I'm guessing half of Northland plant in here.'

Steve: 'They probly do, but not in the north-eastern corner, where we're 'eaded.'

'Why not?'

''Cause it was logged completely in the sixties and then replanted. The seedlings they laid are now just a year or three orf maturity, so the bush up there is uniformly tall and thick. Unless yaw mad enuf to plant on the *roads*, yaw weeds ain't gonna get one *minnit* of sun all summer, let alone the few thousand hours they need. I doubt the pigs even give that parta the forest a token glance when they play cowboys in their choppers every season. The bush gangs'll move in there in force pretty soon, start logging the shit hard, but faw now they keep tha area locked up. The only cunts 'u ever go near the place are the odd pen-pushers or a thinning-to-waste crew.'

I puzzle on this for a minute, searching for my oversight. Fail. 'So if growing in that corner of the forest is so inconceivable, why the fuck did this Woodstock cunt choose to plant Hemi's seeds there?'

Steve: 'First, 'member what I told you: 'e *didin*' choose the site specifically for Hemi's seeds; 'e's been growing 'is own gear up there faw years. Second, you'll see why it's possible when we get there.'

Curiosity wants me to push for more, but a greater urge wins out. Procrastination. Like when you're off to meet someone you don't at all want to see, and the journey can't last long enough. I begin to relish every second of our dark trek through the forest; to dread each turn Steve directs me down as he counts off his map, the forest devoid of signs.

A fine day slowly dawns, sunbeams fingering us accusingly,

pilfering the false solace of night's anonymity. We pass blocks recently logged, reduced to stumps and torn earth, piles of dead waste.

Rows of infant trees.

Prime timber.

Blocks in mid-liquidation, the Juggernaut's pall-bearers hulking in condemned shadows, genocide stayed while the death squads recharge.

Swiss fairytale to mangled abattoir in one fell metre.

Deeper.

Gradually, the roads Steve chooses deteriorate, potholes and slopes eaten into them by rain erosion; our progress slows to match.

Eventually, though, as we meet a stream winding in from the south, tack up a road along its true left bank, Steve quietly informs me: 'I think we're gettin' pretty close.'

Sickly: 'To the plantation?'

'Well, as close as we'll get to it by car.'

'How close is that?'

'Not too close faw comfort.'

Smiling with effort: 'What's that s'posed to mean?'

'That yu can relax a bit longer: we've a fair amounta walking ahead of us yet.'

I decide enough's enough, pull over near where the stream gurgles in easy reach of the road. Looking in the rear-view mirror: 'Barry?'

As if he's been foxing, Barry's eyes snap instantly open. He leans forward, intent; a shake of the head and he's fully on deck.

'Oh, man, my mouth tastes like a dog slept in it. What's up, bro?'

'We're nearly there.'

His gaze takes in the forest around us, a twinkle building even now. 'Top *shit*. Great effort, guys. Sorry to doze on duty like that.'

'Wake up, Mick, will ya, man? We'll drag him down to that stream and dunk him.'

I'm yet to meet a better medium for hangovers than Mick, and as the rest of us wash and rejuvenate in the stream's waters, he cowers on the bank, dripping, shivering, holding his skull as though it's filled with nitro-glycerine. Groaning: 'Have we got any Panadol left? *Tell* me we have.'

'There's a whole packet in the glovebox.' Trying to chuckle some humour into us both: 'Two days in a row: that must be some kind of record for you, man. What's the deal? Looking to pad your CV in hopes of a move into politics?'

Not even looking up: 'Just nerves, man.'

The four painkillers Mick drops seem to be beginning to take effect as I drive past a long firebreak. Through this, to the north, a high ridgeline smothered in rough native can be seen brooding in background.

Steve, studying his map: 'That's the forest's northern border, boys. That's where we're 'eaded.'

A few minutes later and an offshoot of our road tacks east, crossing the stream via a small bridge. Unfortunately, access is formidably barred by gate, chain and padlock.

Me: 'Do we park here?'

Steve: 'Not unless yaw keen on walking an extra five k's.'

Following Steve's lead, we all jump from the car. He scans the surrounding bush with purpose. 'Can any'a yu's see a dead, forked tree, 'bout eight metres 'igh?'

Barry spots it almost immediately; leads us off to the right a little way. Without hesitation, Steve digs in moss toward three o'clock of the tree's trunk; pulls free a sealed plastic bag. It yields a key in reasonable condition. 'Eu-fuckin'-reka.'

Mick: 'How . . . ?'

'Woodstock told me where t' find it. 'Member me telling yu's 'e's a qualified 'orticulturalist?'

'Yeah.'

'Well, 'e found all 'is best spots legitimately: by taking a job wif Forest Products in the late eighties. 'E's got this place *well* sorted.'

Barry: 'This bastard sounds like the stuff legends are made

of. I can't fucking wait to meet him. How many times have you spoken with him, Steve?'

'Three or four. Where 'is camp's at, 'e can't get a signal on his mobile, but Hemi's 'ad 'im 'iking t' the top of a ridge every Wednesday at three o'clock. It was written on the map. I made contact wif 'im like that, set up my own times for rendezvous. The last one was at seven in the morning yesterday.'

We lock the gate behind us, opting to keep the key.

Within a bend or three, the rutted road swings directly north, through big thick pine, and, bouncing and jostling even at low speed, at times we're able to watch the ridge looming nearer, higher, directly in our path. Soon, topping a small rise, we limp gently downhill for perhaps a kilometre. The road then turns sharply west. By this point the steep ridge towers above us, dense with native bush, verdant in the sun, broken in patches by sheer cliff-face. We're near enough to pick out individual trees — mighty kahikatea, the tawa's spreading crown — and after our time among condemned exiles, the sight gives me fleeting release.

'Stop 'ere, bro.'

According to Steve — via Woodstock — at this point, through the pine trees that stand between us and a river at the foot of the ridge — the plantation's border — a natural corridor offers space down which one might ease a vehicle. The lads jump out to clear the path for *The 'Dan*; Woodstock and co have been at pains to disguise it.

The route is soon identified, cleared of dead foliage, and I ease *The 'Dan* from the gravel, across a shallow ditch, into green shadow, her wheels cushioned by old pine needles. Barry and Mick re-camouflage the path behind me, dusting away tyre tracks. Steve walks ahead, clearing all obstacles.

A hundred-odd metres down this passageway we find the route blocked by a thick line of native undergrowth, behind which the sun can be seen beating. Steve waves me to a halt.

On foot, pushing through the bush, we pop from shadow to the grassed banks of a lively river — the Takahera, Steve's map informs us — the ridge looming behind it, both running due east.

The bank on which we stand is a good three metres above the water, a rough path of sorts dropping steeply down.

Morning sun paints the scene so vividly idyllic that for an instant my heart leaps clear of the stress miring it.

In a thrumming of feathers, a fantail stops on a branch near my head, its cocked eye assessing me. We swap stares for seconds, but its message is far too wise. Effortless, it leaps to a perch several feet away, leaps to another, then another, stopping suddenly, more balletic than history's gold medallists combined. Then, without prelude, the 'dumb animal' throws back its head and lets rip a symphony to shame Chopin . . . just because it can.

Mick and Barry join us and the bird takes its talents elsewhere.

Against the harsh light Mick has swapped his specs for prescription sharkies, and the dude's looking pretty damn smooth, it must be said.

Barry, beaming: '*Ahhhh*, the Great Outdoors. Magnificent backdrop to a drugs swindle, don't ya's reckon? To any kind of swindle, really. Where's this draft dodger fella, then?'

Steve gathers us around the map. 'First we 'ead downstream 'bout 'alf a k, till we come to a big boulder on the lip of the far bank. Woodstock reckons we can't miss it. Then we cross the river.'

Which doesn't look to be a problem. Though brisk, the river is rocky, shingly, and at its yearly low-point; the main flow, in parts, eating channels through beds of sand. From where we stand, fords appear in excess.

Mick, scanning the clear sky: 'I wonder how quick this fucker floods in rain. Did ya's get a forecast during the night? How's that storm of Bum's looking?'

Me: 'We got a few forecasts, and yeah, it won't arrive till sometime after midnight. We'll be safely back in the Smoke by then.'

I wonder if my assurance rings as hollow to their ears as it does to mine.

Steve: 'It's a good thing, tu, 'cause Woodstock reckons the river drains the ridge faw miles t' the west; floods *real* quick in good rain. Anyway, we cross the river at the boulder, then bush-bash up the ridge faw a bit.'

Barry: 'That looks easier said than done, bro. That's pretty thick, steep terrain.'

Steve: 'Yeah, but apparently the bottom section of the ridge ain't as steep downstream as it is 'ere. And we'll only 'af t' trail-blaze a short way befaw we hit Woostock's path.'

Mick: 'There's a path up *that*?'

Steve: 'Yeah. Woodstock blazed it 'imself, wif a shovel and light chainsaw. 'E reckons it's rough, but OK. 'E wanted it t' be impossible for sumone t' find by chance, and invisible from tha air, so a lot of it's just rope hand-'olds nailed t' tree trunks.'

Me: 'Where's he growing, then? On the far side of the ridge?'

'On the far side of the *next* ridge. But 'e reckons the drop between them's only small: once we're up that fucker in front of us the hard yakka's done.'

Barry: 'There's no roads on the far side, then?'

Steve: 'According t' the map, there's no *nothin'* on the far side. Nothin' but bush and streams.'

Mick: 'So the lower part of this ridge is climbable. What about the upper? From here it looks like cliff-face, or near enough, all the way along.'

Steve, pointing: 'It is. But look along the top of the ridgeline. Yu see that low point, between the two spurs?'

'Yeah?'

'Woodstock reckons a deep, narrow cleft splits the rock in the middle there. Trees all over it, hide it from tha air tu, but he says 'is track'll take us up to it, and then through, inta the next valley.'

Barry: 'Legendary.'

For minutes no one speaks, eyes canvassing the ridge for something to do. Mick and I share a gasper in silence.

Steve, at last: 'What say we get our shit together, then, boys?'
Barry: 'Amen to that.'

Sunday, 12 March, 10.51am

If he lived to be a hundred, Wallace would remember this summer.

Vividly.

Summer is his favourite time of year. Normally. A time of long, sunny piss-ups, the lads chipping in for kegs, tapping them at ten in the morning in someone's back yard. Sluts getting pissed faster than usual in the heat, even putting out for a *prospect* if he played it right. Pissing it up through to sundown, then hitting the town. Lording it through garden bars, loitering outside when the bouncers had finally had enough — if they had the balls to do anything — or if one of the patches wouldn't remove it to conform with house rules. Perving and whistling at the ballhead chicks in their tiny outfits. Unloading on their boyfriends whenever the chance arose. Congregating round wagons in the carpark, pissing it up in public, the pigs too chicken-shit to stop them.

Out to the lake on other days, swimming and drinking by day, crashing beach parties by night, even the tough fullas backing off, because they knew who it was Wallace would phone otherwise. The bitches, especially the out-of-towners, buzzing to these shows of strength, thinking it his personal rep meriting all that instant respect.

Haha. Got maw than one fuck like that, *bro, I can tell yu.*

Out the bush at least twice a week, hunting for plantations. Ripping some good ones, too. Sometimes asked along by patches to help on planting ops. Setting up some wicked booby traps, with nails and spring and stuff, even an old rifle once.

'Ard case if a hunter, or a bush-walker, come along. Dumb fucks'd think they found a crop'a tomatoes in the middla nowhere . . . then wham! *Goodnight bawl'ead!*

233

Then this summer had neared, one that promised to be even more gratifying, given the muscles Wallace had packed onto his lanky frame through hard winter training. *Got me some choice tats t' go wif 'em, too.* The chicks were gonna be all *over* him; the guys even warier. But just as the weather began heating up, the female finery growing scantier, along came Hemi and his 'proposition'.

Wallace had nodded his usual sycophancy. 'Yeah choice, boss. Yu *noe* I'm yaw man fru thick and thin. 'Ow long yu want me ta stay up there? Pardon? *April*? Ahhhh . . . na, *course* I ain't gota problem wif that! When we leaving? Pardon? Welllll . . . it's just that . . . *nananana*, you *can* rely on me, boss!'

Four fuckin' months! Wallace's inner voice had hollered, while his head smiled and bobbed.

Four months of sleeping on a bedroll in a leaky bivouac. Near half a year of dried food from packets, tinned shit, powdered milk, stale biscuits. Twenty-odd weeks of no hot water. A hundred and twenty days of shitting in the woods like a fuckin' animal. Three thousand hours without TV, without even *seeing* a chick, let alone rooting one. Four months of the most excruciating boredom imaginable, nothing to do but get stoned and patrol the plot, shotgun in hand — the mystique of this having expired after about a minute of it — half-heartedly awaiting raiders who simply weren't going to find such a godforsaken location.

Looking back, comparatively, the few days Wallace had spent with Hemi hauling supplies and fertiliser up that hideous ridge fronting the pine forest had actually been stimulating, engrossing. Though he'd cursed beneath his breath whenever Hemi moved beyond earshot, right now Wallace would trade his left nut for a job necessitating the two-hour hike back to Takahera.

U'd've believed it? Wallace Haimona, beaten to a state where taking a journey fru the bush just faw the hell of it begins to sound like fun!

Such diversion is beyond question, though: Hemi has forbidden Wallace to stray near this approximation of civilisation. And in the chief's absence, his decrees are enforced by that fuckin', old, ugly, nerdy, four eyes, grey-beard, arsehole, cunt-face ballhead whose guts Wallace would swap his remaining nut for permission to rearrange by buckshot.

Naturally, in immediate terms, the ballhead is incapable of compelling *anything* from Wallace. But Wallace ain't no fool: he can see through the ballhead's apathy as though it were glass; see through to the mental dossier the man is in the process of amassing, detailing Wallace's wrongs, to be handed dutifully to Hemi as soon as the big man appears for harvest.

Of course, there are acres of forest all around which Hemi *hasn't* proclaimed off limits. The ballhead even purports his indifference toward Wallace spending whole days away from guard roster. But aside from the slope on which the plants grow — an area Wallace now knows like the head of his penis — the bush surrounding their campsite is just as thick as it is anywhere around this shit-hole, and picking a path through its trackless expanse soon frustrates Wallace to anger.

At first, fishing rod in hand, Wallace had entertained images of the mammoth trout he'd spend four months pulling from the stream along the centre of their low valley. The ballhead certainly manages to land them with frequency. But following a single afternoon of fishing — the arsehole ballhead taking the piss with his smart-arse advice — it became clear to Wallace that fishing in *that* stream was a waste of fuckin' time, and the only reason the ballhead enjoyed success was his long experience of the place, knowing exactly where to put his casts; sniggeringly withholding this lore from Wallace.

And to make matters worse, the bastard won't allow Wallace to entertain and feed himself by hunting either, claiming — when Wallace had first discharged his weapon hours after Hemi's final departure — the sound would carry for miles in all directions.

As if! It's only a fuckin' shotie, not a atom bomb! Jus' 'cause 'e's such a weird cunt 'e can stay entertained reading those stupid, wasta time, fuckin' booksa his.

On that day the ballhead had been some distance from Wallace, but was able to voice his censure immediately through the walkie talkies Hemi had equipped them with.

Now, as Wallace relaxes in a fern clump, shotgun at his side, constructing his third joint of the morning — *At least while I've bin out 'ere, I've 'ad free access to the best fuckin' gunga I'm eva likely to come across* — Wallace's radio crackles to aggravating life.

Curt: 'Lunch.'

Seething, Wallace shakes his head with grim promise. *I'll teach that old cunt sum manners one'a these days, just fuckin' see if I don't.*

In many ways what Wallace resents most about his exile is having no one but the ballhead to share it with.

At first Wallace had made an effort with the guy. But it soon became clear that all the blow-arse cunt ever talked about were the many countries he'd visited in his travelling days; all the 'fascinating' people he'd spent time with; the 'experiences' and 'humility' he'd gathered from 'immersing himself in alternative cultures'.

I mean, 'u gives a fuckin' shit?

And if he wasn't bullshitting about his 'adventures', the ballhead was going on like a fuckin' priest, or a social worker or something, babbling about 'our true place in the world', and 'the suffering of indigenous peoples under imperialism', and 'the methods by which man and nature could share the world harmoniously'.

''U the fuck wants t' yak 'bout crap like that *when they stoned and sittin' round a campfire?*

Yet, though he'd shut his mouth for minutes at a time, let the ballhead jabber, when it came *Wallace's* turn to speak, tell about that fuckin' *huuuuge* brawl they'd had with the Black Power down Matata that time, or joke about all the ballhead chicks Wallace spent his summers fucking out at the lake, the jealous old cunt'd just *sit* there, staring into the fire, not even asking questions!

Then there was the way the ballhead had tried to turn Wallace into the camp maid, asking him if he'd wash the breakfast dishes while he took water up to the plants, checked on their 'levels' or some bullshit, lugging his pack and tools and crap around as if he was King Shit of the whole operation.

The fuckin' cheek'a the cunt!

He'd even tried to get Wallace to do some of the *cooking*!

Whad'u I look like, a bitch or sumthing?

Wallace had said: 'In yaw fuckin' *dreams*, beau. *Yu* the maid and gardna round 'ere. That's the reason yu on board. Me, I'm just the muscle. I'm 'ere t' protect the place, not do the fuckin' chores. My job's t' kill any cunt 'u comes wifin a mile'a Hemi's plants, or die fuckin' trying. I've got that well covered: now yu just get on wif yaw job a runnin' this place.'

Now, though, things have degenerated to the level where the fuckin' disrespectful arsehole simply refuses to wash Wallace's dishes any more, letting them pile up, keeping his own locked in his pack, so that Wallace finds himself eating off dirty plates like a fuckin' bum, or a refugee, or something. And it's only Wallace's threats to raid the foodstores, break their rationing, that ensures the ballhead continues even to *cook* for him.

Not that the meals he prepares are much to write home about. *'Ardly feed a fuckin' sparrow.* With his winter spent weight training, and the chin-ups and push-ups and crunches Wallace now does every day in an effort to retain his hard-earned gains, he needs to maintain a large food intake or his muscle is going to fade away. But, just to spite him, the ballhead had imposed a strict regimen of rationing on them both, claiming their food wouldn't last the distance otherwise, utterly ignoring Wallace's demands that his meals grow in magnitude. 'If you needed extra food,' the ballhead takes pleasure in parroting, 'you should have carried it in with you when you had the chance, taken charge of your own diet.' *Oh, yeah, right, cunt, and 'ow was I t' noe I wooden be 'llowed t' shoot birds and shit out here? Or that the stream wooden 'ardly 'ave fuck all fish in it?*

Yes, things have gotten well out of hand, the ballhead never mentioning, but always, with his smiles and eyebrows, alluding to the invulnerability he enjoys as Hemi's bitch.

Lunch, eh? Wallace lumbers to his feet, opting to smoke his joint while he walks back upstream toward their campsite.

His belly grumbles cavernously.

The breakfast the ballhead had prepared for Wallace this morning had been meagre even by his standards. Over the 'meal' the ballhead had informed Wallace of his intention to march to the top of the valley's southerly ridge, spending the morning staking the plants up there. 'About four hours' work,' he had claimed. Which, by Wallace's calculations, left the man returning to camp around five minutes ago. *Bitch can't 'ave 'ad time t' prepare much of a lunch, 'less he come back early. Beda not be just biscuits an' tea again, like tha uva day.*

In fact, the ballhead had radioed Wallace twice over the morning, originally to enquire whether Wallace had heard the gunshot issuing from further down the valley — Wallace hadn't, the ballhead believing this to be because sound carried to the heights far better. He had asked Wallace to stand a watch down there. His second, later call was more in keeping with the schoolmasterishness Wallace had come to expect of the ballhead, checking that Wallace was indeed at the said location.

In any case, raiders hadn't materialised, and Wallace is looking forward immensely to taunting the ballhead with his delusions.

The foliage enclosing the valley's stream is less thick here than in adjacent areas, and through much use a path of sorts has evolved, leaving Wallace able to make reasonable progress back upstream toward base camp. Had he been willing to get his boots wet, crossing to the southern bank, Wallace might have enjoyed even swifter headway, because along a stretch of some 500 metres much of the southerly slope of the valley — rising perhaps sixty metres above the stream — is composed only of scattered manuka and flax, leaving it dotted in hundreds of tiny clearings.

It was these the ballhead had chosen as homes for the seedlings he grew from Hemi's seeds, individuals transplanted at distance, often as much as thirty metres between specimens. With solar calculations and pruning equipment, the ballhead had maximised the hours of sunlight each plant might receive, while reconciling this with the need to camouflage them from aerial observation. In addition, given that the plants are scattered across a slope sixty metres high and 500 long, the telltale storm of lush greenery overhead observers are accustomed to searching for is nowhere in evidence.

Wallace has to admit, he's seen some plantations in his time, but *this* — it's specious inaccessibility, its insidious outlay — is an operation of a slickness he could never have dreamed.

Within ten minutes Wallace reaches the space fronting their bivouac which, in good weather, serves as a kitchen/dining room/front yard. The stream burbles nearby, thick foliage close overhead, blocking the sun, providing the ballhead with the camouflage under which he insists all signs of humanity must shelter.

The bivouac itself is a stout affair — has to be, given that it doubles as a storage shed. With one wall comprising a sheer earthen bank, the shelter's rear tapers inward, toward the blockage of a wide treetrunk. The second wall is of crude posts, along the top of which a beam has been laid horizontally, providing rest to smaller roof-supports. Dark tarpaulins were then lashed across the surface of the dwelling, one descending as a door across the three-metre structure's open frontage. Drainage ditches, earthen guttering, sluice away all flooding.

Kneeling before the cook-fire, stirring at a pot, the ballhead barely glances up through his spectacles as Wallace tromps into the small clearing, shotgun absently clasped in one hand. The ballhead, Wallace fancies, is what Jesus might have looked like had he been able to stomach his flock a decade or so longer. Though Jesus would surely have taken more care over his grooming, at least removing the twigs and leaves from his beard once in a while.

Foolishly, the ballhead has left his treasured fold-up deckchair unoccupied, across the fire from him, facing the bivouac. Hurriedly fetching a plate from a nearby pile, Wallace plonks himself into the seat, sighing theatrically, placing the shotgun within easy reach beside him.

The ballhead, the distant drone of one for whom the seventies featured too much strong acid: '*Must* you, man? I've been working on my feet all morning.'

Wallace, apathetic: 'So? Do yu think I was lying down while I went on that wild goose chase'a yaws?'

The ballhead, sighing defeat, looking back to his cooking: 'More than likely. No sign of life down there, then?'

Wallace, delightedly mordant: '*Welllllll*, there was a few *taniwhas* . . . and a few *elfs* . . . *oh*, and sum *dwarfs* as *well*! But *noooooo*, there weren't any . . . ' Wallace's sentence, his train of thought, explodes cleaner than a seed in a joint as he watches the ballhead glance upwards, face draining like a plug's been pulled . . .

. . . horrified eyes resting on a spot above Wallace's head . . .

. . . mouth working at nothing.

The fork with which he's been stirring falls to the dirt as the ballhead rocks to his backside reflexively, hands reaching for the air.

Wallace, alarmed: 'What the . . . '

Something hard enough to stun jabs the rear of his skull, but before Wallace can leap to his feet, or even turn around, a low growl stills him. 'This is a gun, muvafucker. A big one. One move from yu and it goes orf.'

Pathetically united of a sudden, Wallace's eyes ask the ballhead a question, to which the man nods dumbly. Then, of its own accord, Wallace's right hand eases toward the shotgun at his feet . . .

'*Yes*. That wooda bin my next move too! Doan think it, just *do* it . . . and let me watch yaw boyfriend spend the next five minnits scraping yaw brains orf his face.'

As if burned, Wallace's hand *leaps* into his lap.

Disappointed: '*Oh*, man, yaw no fun at *all*. That's yaw last chance, by the way. Now stand up . . . *Slooooowly* . . . Good boy. Hands in tha air . . . *Higher*. Now turn round, just as slow.'

Wallace, choked: 'I doan wanna see yaw face, bro. *Please* doan make me look . . . '

This time the blow's hard enough to drop him yelping to one knee. A strong hand drags him back up by the hair and something hard and cold is thrust into his ear, tilting his head.

Macabrely level: '*Now* look what yu made me do: break my word. I doan much like cunts 'u make me break my word. Yu gonna disrespect me again, boy?'

Snivelling: 'N–, *no*, sir.'

'Turn round.'

If anything the sight of the 'man' only aggravates Wallace's horror. Tall and strong, old jeans and brush-cotton shirt, sleeves rolled down. Dark sack-cloth hooding him to shoulder level, headsman-style, the lenses of black shades lining the hood's eye slits.

This complete lack of identity lends the being an inhuman air, scaring Wallace as atavistically as a five-year-old's closet demon. Though Wallace hasn't the composure to articulate as much, only the figure's accent and hand colour attest to its Maoriness.

Its chilling weapon Wallace acknowledges obliquely: a rifle, perhaps a 30.06 calibre, bolt-action, the barrel sawn to eight inches, stock shaped into a pistol-grip.

It, calm: 'On yaw knees.'

Though — according to Wallace's favoured execution fantasy — this development is dire, defying the creature is an option he doesn't consider, slumping to the ground without thought, gulping.

'Get up 'ere an' join 'im, bawl'ead.'

Wallace barely senses the ballhead crawl into position beside him.

'I want yaw 'ands 'igher.'

Any higher now and they'll both strain ligaments.

241

'All right, Maori boy.' The sudden warmth in the thing's gravelly voice is so discordant with the setting that for a desperate instant Wallace wonders if he isn't dreaming. 'I want yu t' watch sumthing *real* close.' Easing three inches of barrel between Wallace's teeth, with its left hand it takes a big hunting knife from it's waistband. The ballhead whimpers softly as its tip is used to indicate a spot on his throat. 'Yu watching, Maori boy?'

Wallace, turning his head, gagging around the metal: 'Uh-huh.'

Breezy: 'This 'ere's the carotid artery. This *'ere*, is the jug-ya-la vein.' The ballhead's eyes close tight to block X rays. 'Shood I choose to shave one'a them, 'e'll lose enuf blood t' kill 'im in about . . . *mmmmmm* . . . fawdy-odd seconds, I s'pose. An' yu an' *me*, Maori boy . . . *haha* . . . well, our clothes'll be in need of a *real* good wash!'

Without warning the knife slides across two inches of skin, blood welling in its tracks, falling in a steady curtain.

Panting like a natal exercise, the ballhead's efforts to remain still attain a pulse of their own.

Continuing the lesson: 'Now that'*s* just a scratch. But if I were t' cut 'im *one inch furva* . . . '

Smoothly, it shifts the knife to Wallace's throat, the ballhead sagging like a popped sex-doll, chin ground into his collarbone, attempting to staunch the flow without hands, gun-barrel kissing his cheek unerringly.

At the steel's wet touch the ice-water in Wallace threatens to swamp him. Breath enters his lungs in low grunts.

Low, tender: 'I wanna noe where the resta yaw friends are, Maori boy. An' I wanna noe eg-*zakly* what they armed wif. Faw every wrong arn-sa I'll open yu anuva inch. At a guess yu'll be allowed, sayyyyy, *three* fuck-ups. And 'member: there's two'a yu's, and that's one cunt maw than I need.'

Wallace, instantly: 'Theres*nooneelse*!'

A pain so sharp Wallace barely feels it.

'*I fuckin' promise, bro! Just us!*'

Far more insistent is the sudden sensation of wetness,

flowing down his neck, trickling inside his shirt, tickling his nipple, his stomach.

Hissing: '*Doan. Please* stop, bro. *Ah fuck*, I doan wanna *die* like this! It's just us two, I swear to fuckin' *god*!'

The rushing in Wallace's ears builds until, with a dull *thud*, he finds himself staring at the forest canopy above him, arms still outstretched.

It, apparently peeved: '*Shit*, nigga. Why didin' yu jus' say so?' Louder: 'Yeah, it's jus' this pair'a pussies, chief. No maw muscle.'

Again, it hauls Wallace up by his hair, steps back a few paces. 'Botha yu's use yaw right 'and t' stop that bleeding . . . befaw we got a accident on our 'ands.'

Clapping palms over wounds, for a moment Wallace's gaze finds the ballhead's; they cling like orphans in a holocaust.

Another figure appears at the edge of the clearing, speaks quietly: 'Yu *shaw* it's jus' them?'

Similarly dressed, head disguised likewise, this second apparition is much taller than its accomplice: were he free to rationalise, Wallace may have put its height at six foot seven. Lean, its shirt nevertheless juts around a neat pot stomach, and underneath its shirt cuff a big, square dressing can be seen taped across a wound on the back of its brown hand.

Gunman: 'As shore as can be wifout bleeding one'a them prop'ly. If that's what yu *want* . . . ?'

A few seconds later: 'Not yet.' — Wallace groans loud relief — 'Get 'em in the shelter.'

Gunman: 'Yu 'eard the man. Get in yaw fuckin' kennel.'

With Gunman following hard, they scramble to obey, slumping to cringing positions near the pile of supplies at the bivouac's rear. Even with its flapping door thrown across the roof, the bivouac remains shadowy.

Shorter folk might stand erect in the high shelter, but these reavers, especially when the second enters, a small army pack in its hands, are forced to stoop. Awkwardness, though, divests them of no authority whatsoever.

Number Two, crouched like a spring, looks both captives over for long seconds. At last, sneering darkly: 'So yaw Hemi's pet bawl'ead, are yu?'

The ballhead, stammering, avoiding eye contact tangibly: 'Uhhhh . . . it . . . I guess you *could* phrase it that way.'

Wallace can't cork a yelp as Number Two explodes, snatching the ballhead in two hands, hurling him to his back in a far corner. Yelling: 'Yu think yu in a piz-i-shin t' be a *smart* cunt?' He drops a vicious knee at the ballhead's midsection — '*Uuuuugggggghhhhh!*' — holds him still by the hair, and hits him hard in the face with a short right.

Hits him again, smashing his glasses free.

Again.

Shrieking; gulping.

Again.

Smearing blood from the ballhead's nose, from a cut eye, across his face in a grisly stain.

Again.

Gunman, crooning, picking Wallace's nostril with the barrel of his weapon: 'Make a move, beau. *Just* faw me.'

Manhandling him back to Wallace's side, Number Two rams the ballhead's face into the ground, one, two, three times . . .

. . . stops as suddenly as he started.

The ballhead, huddling into himself: '*Oh fuck, oh fuck, oh fuck, oh fuck . . .* '

Looming over him, for a second Number Two's right arm dangles inches from Wallace's face, and the prospect sees that his exertions have dislodged part of the tape holding the dressing across the rear of his hand, letting it flap almost free . . .

And Wallace learns that the hand isn't wounded at all; rather that the function of the dressing was to cover a four-inch tattoo — a scorpion, sting held high, done in green, black and red.

Realisation dehydrates Wallace like a blow-torch. He snaps his face away from the hand, screwing his eyes shut.

Number Two, panting, seeming not to notice his tattoo's conspicuousness, rapping Gunman on the shoulder: 'Let's get it done befaw I kill this smart cunt.' From the backpack he hands Gunman a roll of industrial-strength duct tape. Louder: 'Let's go gard'ning, bawl'ead. Yu first.'

A brutalised puppy, the ballhead crawls from the shelter on all fours, whimpering, blood soiling the groundsheet beneath him in a steady patter.

When Scorp trails after him, Wallace almost faints from gratitude, utterly tractable as Gunman spins him about, using the tape to reduce his fingers to mere flippers, binding his wrists behind his back, his feet at the ankles, linking both appendages in a hog-tie. Cutting smaller strips to act as blindfold, gag, a cover for the neck wound.

Departs without word.

10

When Steve and Barry arrive at our position in thick bush along the plantation's westerly reach, their prisoner's not in the best of spirits.

Ron, rounding on Barry as Barry unmasks, laying down a strange shotgun: 'You fucking, psycho sonofa*bitch*! When I said make it look genuine that wasn't a licence to beat me to a bloody *pulp*! You *complete cunt*!' His voice saws through damaged sinus; adds weight to his epitome of victimhood. 'My nose feels *broken*, I almost choked on a god-damn *tooth*, and when I told you I had a spare pair of glasses out here, I guessed you might trash the ones I was wearing, but not while they were *still on my fucking face*!' Turning to Steve: 'And *you*! You sick, black *mother*fucker! You didn't say *shit* about *using* the fucking *knife*! I swear to *Christ* I thought I was deader than disco!'

Barry, smiling disbelief: 'Can you believe this old fuck? We go to the trouble of putting his beatnik arse in a nice safe place and he kicks up a song and *dance* about it! What did ya want us to do? Paddle ya bottie and send ya to bed with no play-lunch?'

Steve, placing his hood in one of four hiking packs: 'Look, Ron, perhaps we went a little furva than yu were expecting, and

246

we might've bin able to simulate the violence wif less force, but yaw *fear*? Man, unless yu moonlight as De Niro, that 'ad t' be au*thentic*. And it *was*. Yaw reactions to us did maw to convince Wallace of yaw surprise than a hundred mock punches could *ever*'ve done.'

Me, though shocked at the comparative condition of the poised hippie who had furtively met us this morning, guided us in: 'Ron, dude, we're sorry it had to go down like that, but you'll thank us in a day or two.'

Barry: 'You're not fucking wrong. When that piece of shit rings Hemi with the bad news, the first thing Hemi asks him'll be how *you* reacted to the raid. He'll be hoping it was buddies of yours who pulled it 'cause that'll present his best chance of recovering the gear. And when the prospect cunt tells him how both of ya's had your throats partially slit in a hunt for info you would have passed on anyway, and then you got the living shit bashed out of ya, Hemi'll exonerate you instantly. Reluctantly, but instantly.'

Ron, morose, but calming slowly: 'Yeah, well, I fucking hope so, man. Like I said this morning, I phoned my missus, got her and the young fella to piss right off out of it for a while, but if that black fuck suspects me for one second, the three of us'll be living outta suitcases till the next Hendrix gig.'

Steve: 'Just make sure, when yu pretend to work yaw way outta the bonds sometime tomorrow morning, that Wallace is the one to phone Hemi. Cause if it's yu, 'e woan believe a *word* that comes outta yaw mouth; yu've got too much to gain from double-crossing 'im. That prospect, 'e's got *nothing* to gain from it. 'E was chosen faw 'is greenness. Vegas is 'is universe, and Hemi its centre. Wif the shit in the fan, 'is only 'ope is to convince Hemi of the truth as 'e sees it, and Hemi knows this. 'E'll yell like a motherfucker, and cut up ugly as, but 'e'll swallow everything Wallace tells 'im.'

Ron, nodding eventually: 'Yeah, that's true. That's why Wallace'll *insist* on being the one to break Hemi the news. He's failed; he's got no choice but to start atoning ASAP.'

Mick: 'How did the tattoo gambit go? Don't tell me Steve's artwork was for nothing.'

Barry, grinning: 'It worked *sweet* as. The tape was barely touching the skin anyway, and I managed to pull the dressing half off while I was fucking Ron over — sorry, man. Then I waved the fucker in Wallace's face. I looked at him from the corner of my shades and *fuck*, you should have seen the pussy *crumple*. I thought he'd been scared *before* that! This Scorp must be one hard hombre.'

Steve: ''E is. That's why 'e's a nationwide Rabble legend when 'e's never been outta Wellington. 'E's certifiable, suspected in the shootings of two pigs, and *fuck* noes 'ow many real people. Even 'is chapter leader, Donk, 'ardly tells Scorp what t' do. There's a photo of 'im up on the wall round the Vegas pad, that's 'ow I knew 'bout the tat, 'ow I knew *Wallace*'d know. 'E'll be sitting in there right now shittin' kidneys wondering what Scorp might do when 'e realises the cover's 'alf orf.'

Barry unbuttons his shirt, slips out of it, removes the bundled T-shirt we'd taped to his stomach. The heavy caking of dirt and dark foundation with which we'd layered his hands from forearm down, is beginning to show sweat streaks. Starting on his boot-laces: 'I'm glad Scorp's beer gut's no bigger than it is: I felt I should be playing Santa Claus, not some Maori hitman.' He takes the wooden blocks from inside his boots. 'And if he'd been any taller I'd've needed fucking stitches in my heels right now. *Ouch*.'

Me: 'Bloody nice touch, I must say. The biggest variable *now* is what Hemi'll do when he hears it was Scorp who ripped him.'

Steve: 'There's a few directions 'e might jump, and all of them take 'im furva from any of us. At first glance, yu'd guess 'e'd phone Donk and check if Scorp's alibied or not. But t' do that he's gonna 'af t' tell Donk what's 'appened to 'is gear, and 'e's still got a few weeks to play wif otherwise. 'E'll even have t' consider the possibility that Donk *sent* Scorp on the mission. If somehow 'e *can* quietly verify that Scorp can't've bin 'ere, 'e'll start t' suspect every cunt around 'im, and the paranoia'll 'ave 'im loose-cannoning all *ova* the fuckin' shop.'

Ron, to Steve: 'You're *positive* there's no chance of Hemi persuading this Donk that the best option for them both is to pool resources and try to lay hands on the culprits?'

Steve: 'Snap out of it, man. I told yu on the phone a hundred times, the type of arrangement Donk 'ad wif Hemi includes no clauses. To Donk, the statement 'e'll issue by topping Hemi'll be worth as much as the pot anyway. If yu didin' believe me when I reassured yu of this, yu wouldn't've thrown in wif us. Yaw in the clear, bro. Chill the fuck out.'

Ron, almost to himself: 'So the worst-case scenario from here is that Hemi concludes it *was* me who fucked him, starts hunting me, while the entire Rabble hunt *him*, and I have to lie low till they find the fucker and deal to him; maybe even head across to Aussie and hop on the treadmill awhile.'

Me: 'That's about the sum of it. What'll you do after you "bust" free tomorrow?'

'Well, the "bust" itself shouldn't be a problem. I keep my scaling knife under a corner of the groundsheet in the bivvy, so as long as I'm not hog-tied — something Wallace'll never know — you can do to me what you did to him and I'll escape it authentically.'

Mick: 'Yeah, on that, wouldn't this Scorp dude just ice them? Hemi might smell a rat there.'

Steve, waving this off: 'Na, no way. Scorp's got nothing against them personally. As far as "he" noes, they can't ID 'im t' no cunt. And 'e got what 'e came faw. From what I've 'eard, 'e may be a psycho, but 'e's a cold one: he doan go racking up life sentences just faw the hell of it.'

Ron, beginning to mellow to the flavours of freedom and revenge: 'Yeah, it all seems groovy enough. So I'll seal and bury my share of the reefer somewhere out here today, then "break" free tomorrow morning, giving you cats plenty of time to split the scene. While fuckhead's up on the ridge breaking it gently to the endangered papa bear, I'll assemble my vitals in my pack. Lately I've been conscious of erasing what evidence might point back to me should the fuzz wind up out here, so I know exactly what I need to pack out, and I can have it ready to go in three minutes flat. Last, in case Hemi orders Wallace to detain me, I'll fetch Possumbane — my .22 rifle — from where I keep it beyond Wallace's reach. You lot, of course, will have taken his weapon with you. Then it's a simple matter of awaiting my "sidekick's" return and bidding the little cunt *adios*.'

Me, surprised: 'Are you gonna *hitch* out? It'll take you at least a day to walk to the highway: you might meet Hemi coming the other way.'

Mick: 'If I were you, I'd hole up in Takahera a few days.'

Ron: 'No stress, chaps. There's another way out.'

Me, intrigued: 'Where?'

He waves a hand vaguely eastward. 'Down the valley. It's slow going, thick and trackless, but you can wade in the stream a lot of the way. At a certain bend, if you bush-bash across the northerly ridge, you hit farmland. Then it's a matter of working your quiet way around the fringes and back to civilisation. I trialled the route years ago. Takes about six days. You don't think I'd plant enough weed to flood the market and leave myself in a cul-de-sac, do you?'

Mick: 'How did ya find this place, anyway? Studying the map, I doubt any other humans have ever set foot in here.'

'A mate of mine used to hunt deer from choppers.'

Barry: 'How about heading back to the pine? Is that track of yours the only way up the ridge?'

'Yep. I tried to scout another — just in case — but the first one alone took me a good two months to build, and the next most likely location wasn't half as good. Just wasn't worth the hours, man. There's a second route down, though. That was a piece of piss.'

Me, half-hearted: 'Where is it?'

'The valley behind this one, between here and the ridge down to Takahera. Walk upstream for about a k. Again, it's tough going, but possible. When you hit the first streamlet joining it from the south, follow it. A lot of it's waterfalls, but you can scramble up beside them. At the top of the ridge, past a little cave where the water sources, you'll be at the top of a series of three cliffs that drop almost vertically into the Takahera River. In a sealed plastic bag, you'll find a rock-climbing rope with hand-knots in it. There's also a bolt to fix it to. That'll take you to a shelf thirty metres below; you'll find another rope on that. Then another. Then you'll be in the river almost.'

Mick, checking his watch: 'Hate to be the whip-cracker, gents, but I suggest it's high time we got picking and packing.'

Ron: 'Yeah, we'll be hours stripping the buds, and even given the solidity of these babies, I reckon you dudes'll be lucky to fit five pounds in each of those packs. Maybe you'll be able to carry another five each in your rubbish bags. After my cut, you'll be left with eighty-odd pounds between ya's. Whatever, you'll be making two trips, and I hope you've got torches because the second trip'll be a dark one.'

Barry, basking: 'Fear not, Ron, my man. The situation's well in hand.'

Me: 'Let's do this thing.'

Sunday, 12 March, 5.57pm

Like a beast chained inside him, frustrated fury twitches and pulls at the muscles of Hemi's face. Though he's insisted on silence since arriving, the forest around them seems cowed all the same, as though it can smell the crackling fuse.

Livid but hushed: 'Whadayu fuckin' *mean* it ain't got no juice? What did I *say* t' yu back in Vegas?'

A hulking, bearded Maori eases closed the boot of a Commodore that's seen better days. It's parked behind *The 'Dan*, bumper to bumper. Over bare skin the giant wears a patched leather vest, his torso latticed in tattooing. In one hand he holds a torch. Defensive: 'Yu said t' bring my torch and t' make shaw it 'ad good batrees. Well, it fuckin' *did*. But it ain't *now*, and I aint sa'*prised*, consid'reen tha *bashing* everyfing back 'ere got from yaw form-ya-la one driving. The switch musta got knocked on while yu flew roun' sum corner. We just lucky the

251

fuckin' *shoties* weren't loaded, else they wooda gone orf *too*.'

Hemi, incredulous: 'Well, yu *packed* it all, Johnson! Why the *fuck* didin' yu *say* something?

Johnson gives this thought. Shrugging at last: 'Didin' think of it. What's the problem, anyway? It's only six a'clock. Yu said it only took 'bout two an a bit hours t' get t' the weeds. Doan get *dark* till afta eight. Wool make it *easy*. We can walk fast *as* an' get there wif *heaps*'a time t' spare.'

Hemi, scathing: 'Oh, yeah, an' *then* what? What if we walking fast along that shit track, making a huge racket, and come across 'em on their way *back*? They'll get a *sweet* jump on us. Anyway, unda the bush it'll be dark as by 'bout seven-thirdy! And what if we *doan* meet 'em? What if we get there just bafaw dark an' can't lay our 'ands on 'em strade away? Yu bet *they*'ll 'ave torches. We'll be fuckin' blind!'

Johnson, scoffing: 'So? Steve's tha only one we gotta sort out quick. The ovas are *only* a buncha bawl'ead kids.'

Head back, chest puffed, Hemi's tirade is little short of a haka: 'So *what*, yu fuckin' *meat'ead*! We *noe* they got *one* shooter! I noe that dead Ron cunt's got a .22! By now they probly got Wallace's shotie as well! And yu can bet yaw fat arse they all got torches! Wifout torches, in a forest at night, they could be *Smurfs* an' they'll still fuck us easy as!' He punches the fender of his car hard enough to lose skin. 'If yu 'adn't bin out fucking that ugly hore yu said yu'd stopped rooting, I coulda found yu before morning and got 'ere *early*!'

Johnson, indignant: ''Ow was *I* t' noe yu'd need me? Yu neva *told* meda stay close. I ain't a fuckin' psychic.'

Waving a fist in disgust Hemi storms away from him, towards the older Holden, from the inside of which comes the sound of industrious foraging. With the heel of his workboot, he kicks a dent in a door then demands: 'What've yu found, Dusty? Any battrees or torches?'

With typical zest, Dusty thrusts his head from a back window. 'Found sum good stuff so far, chief. A bottla piss. Heapsa smokes. Tapes an' shit. Bita food. Condoms. No torches, though. Found a coupla *small* battrees, but they look fucked as.'

Since relaying the news to Hemi and being 'pressed' into service, Dusty's been in seventh heaven, bouncing like a speed freak, grinning and snickering, chanting gangsta rap tunes. And once they found Johnson, completing the trio, watching him load three shotguns into the Commodore, Dusty's animation had doubled. His antics soon exhausted the goodwill he was owed by a surly Hemi, however, and, told as much, Dusty slackened his ebullience studiously. Extremes aside, though, Hemi's powerless to tarnish the glint in Dusty's wide gaze.

Hemi: '*Fuck* it all!' Elbows on *The 'Dan*'s roof, he holds his face in his hands for close to a minute, breathing long and hard.

Straightens at last, returning to Johnson with firming purpose. 'All right. We got noe choice but t' take 'em here. It should stool be a clean hit. They'll climb the bank here, exactly where they left from, 'cause it's tha only way up it for fuckin' ages. We can 'ide in the long grass overlooking it. If they come back soon, we'll see 'em from miles away, and if they come back afta dark, we'll see their *torches* from miles away. And the thieving liddle cunts woan see *us* till it's *way* too late. Get those shoties loaded and show Dusty 'ow they work; we outta time: they cood show up any second.'

Had a person once insisted that future events would conspire some day to leave me jaded with the sight of enormous, seedless, *Cannabis sativa* buds, I'd've advised them never to shit before an exam. Yet, on reflection, it would have been my own IQ in risk of depreciation by bowel movement.

I once grew a ten-inch dope plant on my window-sill that failed to flower and left me feeling the Maggie Barry of druggiedom. At the moment I've the beginnings of a callous on my palm from the grip of the secateurs I've wielded all day on my campaign to liberate Bud from Stem.

The lads and I once scored a $20 tinny from a seller in the ghetto, opened it, learned it was composed of a single bud, and were so impressed with the thing we rushed back to Mick's and took photos of it. About two hours ago I lost count of the number of buds felled that were longer than my leg.

When breaking up resinous dope to be rolled, I used to be in the habit of afterwards wiping my fingers with the tobacco paper in order that no stoning potential be lost. Earlier, I scrubbed my hands and forearms in the stream and grimaced when, after three minutes' effort, they continued to pong like a Dutch coffee shop.

I once stole from a friend's car a two-ounce bag of leaf, made a hundred bucks off it in a schoolyard deal, and strutted like Marcellus Wallace for the next three days. At present I've enough gear on my back, in the rubbish bag cradled in my arms, to lay a down-payment on a fucking house.

But for the spectre of the botanically cuckolded Hemi, our day would surely have been one of fanfare and horseplay. Instead, once rhythm was established, we toiled like priests at an orgy — heads down, near silence reigning, manning an armed lookout in shifts.

Now, in keeping with this, we four bandidos find ourselves strung along Ron's 'path' like VC along the Mekong. Steve has point, twenty metres in front of the rest of us. His hands alone are free of green encumbrance, cradling instead Wallace's former shotgun. Barry has reclaimed his 'pistol' and seems to have more faith in its safety catch than I: thrust down his waist-band, the bolt is home on a chambered round.

Traversing the long, low valley between Ron's domain and Takahera ridge, the 'path' is in evidence only where the thick bush is inconceivably navigable: a chainsawed branch here, the odd ditch spanned by small log. For the most part, travel consists of squeezing between tree trunks, closing eyes and blundering through thickets, scrambling over giants toppled by time, sometimes under, sometimes just swearing at those placed to thwart either tactic.

Barely burdened, the contemplation of strife distracting, the *inward* journey had been arduous enough. *Now*, arms otherwise occupied, the need for haste pressing, my barked shins, torn hands, scratched face, ragged lungs and I would sooner be elsewhere.

But my companions voice little complaint, and though, as we cross the stream at the valley's centre, begin the trudge uphill, I feel the Demon Asthma building in my chest, pride has me reluctant to call rest even long enough to fetch the Angel Ventolin from my pack's interior. That I've recently filled my pack from near empty to eruption point, and can't recall the position of thine Holy Inhaler — or even its presence, for that matter — further discourages me from the potentially messy attempt. Perhaps more forbidding, though, is the knowledge that were I to launch the arduous search and taste no success, my fickle mind would make a sudden and large contribution to the Demon's campaign-fund.

So I labour on, half shielded by half ignorance, ruing the 10,000 cigarettes I've consumed in the last few days, wincing at each fresh, breath-sapping obstacle.

But by the time we enter the shadow of the cliffs topping Takahera ridge, approaching the deep split by which we'll cheat them, the inhalations my chest manages to heave seem sufficient to slake oxygen needs for only an eighth of the time it takes to exhale and breath again.

My ego endures a death by suffocation: I inform the others of my predicament. Barry calls Steve back — I certainly can't spare breath for it.

Distressingly, a hurried search of the pack's side pockets unearths no chemicals that might be of use. I sigh, unzipping the motherlode.

And five long minutes later, I'm forced to concede that the then dispensable Saint Atomiser was overlooked in the morning's commotion, remaining in *The 'Dan*'s glovebox.

I play little part in the quick discussion which concludes with myself lying prostrate a ways from the path, encircled and pillowed by contraband, with Barry and Mick bound again for Ronland and further packhorse duty, with Steve on a medical mercy dash, into the murk of the bisecting cleft.

I choose preserving wind over the calling of farewells.

As sometimes happens — as seems inconceivable while pining for pharmaceuticals — relaxed breathing time soon makes inroads on the hunger in my chest. Indeed, within an hour I'm weighing the pros and cons of breaking out the Winnie Reds. In the end only shame at capitulation stays my hand.

An hour and a *half* later, as Steve becomes officially overdue and my level of incapacitation starts to seem a little laughable, I begin to assess my options as far as returning to action goes. Steve had been convinced of his ability to return to the car and back within ninety minutes, and though by my reckoning the journey is more like an hour each way, my familiarity with Steve's athleticism leaves me in no doubt of his claim. Reasoning that leads to the postulation that something unforeseen has befallen him. Something like a twisted ankle.

Or . . .

I choose not to delve the 'or'.

Neither do I choose to follow Steve through the cleft, though I'm growing surer of my ability to ward off the asthma at least long enough to make the car, albeit in a possible stagger. I'm worried what Barry and Mick might do if they return to find me missing. I guess I'm a little conscious of the 'or' as well: my vulnerability in picking my way down the ridge without a gun, or even the breath for a sprint in a given direction.

And even if — worst-case scenario — Steve's delay *is* due to some breed of human intervention, my reverence in his competence, in his strengths and talents, is so unequivocal I just *know* he's rolling with the punches.

Yet *two* hours after watching him leave, with the punctual return of Barry and Mick, Steve's deific status of imperishability has sappers well beneath its walls.

Learning of his no-show, in the gathering gloom of the forest the pair exchange a look that lays keen claws to my insides.

Mick, rueful: 'There's something you gotta know, man.'

When he's done my asthma is forgotten, insides no longer scratched . . . rather lacerated.

Mick, distressed: 'Look, Gator, I weighed it up, and I'm *certain*

Lefty's fear of Barry would've been too strong for him to grass us to Hemi *or* to the oinkers.'

I'm dazed not so much by their actions, as by their leaving me in ignorance. But recriminations are quashed by factors far weightier.

Barry, for once unsettled: 'I reckon, too.'

I'm able to swallow my fright long enough to draw a similar conclusion. But . . .

'But that doesn't change the fact that Steve's late enough for us to be sure *something*'s gone and fucked with his mission. It might be minor . . . and it might not be. Either way, he needs our help.'

Mick: 'Yeah. I say we get down there pronto. We've got all night to lug the hooch; let's find out what we're up against.'

Me: 'And let's allow for the worst.'

Heading down the riverbed, keeping to the shallows and shoals, Steve makes good time, moving at a trot despite the pack on his back, the shotgun in his arms. This is hardly the first mercy dash Steve's ever made for Gator's inhaler, but it *is* the first in years.

As schoolkids, breaks invariably spent at sport or high-jinks, Gator would, on average of twice a week, reduce himself to a state of such breath deprivation the journey back to class was beyond him. In those days, owing to Gator's 'proclivity toward misplacement', his mum forbade the removal of his inhaler from his schoolbag, and so it would fall to a friend to fetch, and return with, the stuff of life.

More often than not, Steve would invest himself with the grave charge, delighted at the chance to do his friend a service. Because, as much as he never would have verbalised it, Steve had had a large dependency on Gator in those days; almost deferred to him in fact. Gator it was who conceived the most rewarding fantasies for their rowdy bunch to enact. It was Gator who insisted on choosing even teams for sporting sagas, ensuring greater drama and gratification for all. It was Gator's flair for schoolwork, for tales and history, for special projects and culture class, that manifested infectiously in Steve and others, leaving their days rewarding both in and away from class. And — of this Steve is convinced — helping equip him with a level of intelligence he may otherwise have found elusive.

Even though Gator had seldom presumed to give overt orders — to Steve or to any — it was understood that his dynamism and competency left him something of a leader. Steve had thus derived satisfaction from performing indispensabilities for his friend: helping patch Gator's few vulnerabilities, finding methods by which to level the perceived debt between them.

Today, seeing Gator again at the mercy of his health, Steve had been quite thrilled by the reawakening within him of old instincts. Because, given the amount of water to have passed beneath the bridge since those days — much of it murky — the unambiguous purity of such principles is something Steve had given up for lost.

Though he can't repress a grin at his mawkishness, as he crosses the river and struggles up the bank fronting the 'carpark', Steve begins to enjoy the nostalgic glow of a grave service half completed.

Throwing the shotgun up the bank's final leg, hauling himself up after it, this and all else drowns in vertigo as he's warmly greeted by a lazing Hemi.

'*Cherrrrrr*, cuz! Ain't seen yu in *ages*! What brings *yu* t' these parts?'

Less cordial is the stare of the barrel of Hemi's sawn-off.

Steve's shock fades in a split-second; resolution hardens in his gut. But before he can act — throw himself to ground, snatch for Wallace's shotgun — Johnson materialises from under-growth a pace away, claims the weapon for himself.

Impressed: 'Nice shotie, Steve. Looks just like tha one I lent t' Wallace. Doan 'e need it no maw or nufing?'

Eyes leaping from one to the other . . .

Checkmate.

A situation from which no mortal could triumph . . .

. . . but Steve knows he's not mortal.

Not in Gator's eyes.

11

From head to toe I'm drenched in the Takahera's waters, and in the heavy gloom of the pine forest the bed of dead needles on which I lie offers little warmth.

This hoarfrost in my bones, though, this ice in my lungs, owes nothing to physics.

Visibility-wise, we couldn't have timed our arrival better, stealing through the forest shadow without the use of torches, approaching the 'carpark' in the last of the light.

At which point all my nebulous dreads sprang to hellish life.

Side by side on the ground, the dying light in which we've lain paralysed for minutes fades at last to near zero, protecting our eyes at least from the chariot Satan chose to ride to this particular workshop.

The Fiendish Beast has tracked us . . . and this time I'm guessing it has more in mind than urination.

No movement or noise from the Commodore, or anywhere beyond, has me in the grip of an indecision so complete I might be quadriplegic.

Instinct is loud. It hollers: *RUN! Run till exhaustion drops you, then get up and run some more! Get the fuck out of here, while you still can! Deal with the ramifications later!* Much *later!*

259

And, oh *God*, how I want nothing more than to listen. To ignore it is to cling to an electric fence. At a stroke the realities of our venture have been laid hideously bare, and the terror I'm feeling seems rooted in my very genes; lies on my back like a chunk of tundra. In my life I've cracked under fear microbes the size of this.

I offer a silent prayer for something to *happen*. Anything to limit the endless array of possibilities and actions lying before us, crevasse-like. Something to provide a hint of focus.

But the carpark just waits, patient as an insect in ambush.

Almost as crippling are my feelings of sheer foolishness. Because but for *one* rational decision of a hundred, we simply wouldn't be here. My biggest 'problems' in life would remain budgeting my dole money to smoke weed every day and leave enough over for a night out here and there, lamenting a world that sought to kill me spiritually, over decades. Instead I've walked into *this*! Walked into it *willingly*; eyes wide open.

What the hell were we thinking?

I feel like a hedgehog who convinced itself the country lane in front of it actually *wasn't* the Southern Motorway.

Barry, whispering: 'What are we gonna do?' For once he sounds worried, but 'worry' is a state I would currently host as bliss.

On my other hand, I can feel horror rolling from Mick in waves. He's swapped his glasses over again, and I wish he hadn't — his eyes are flakes of pure dread. Even whispering, Mick's words sound strangled from him. 'What *can* we fucking do?'

Barry: 'We've gotta do *some*thing. Soon we won't be able to move in here without torches . . . and then we're in a *lot* more shit.'

Mick, pleading: 'They could be *anywhere*, though. They could be watching us from the rear window of the Commodore.'

Me: 'What do you suggest then?'

I find myself hoping he says it. I'm not sure why. Perhaps I believe there's strength to be drawn from the revelation that someone in this world is currently more terrified than I am. Perhaps I just want to hear it vocalised, thrown on the table for regard. Maybe I'm hoping if Mick says it first, my shame will be able to hide behind his for long enough.

But he doesn't say it. He says nothing, and, listening to the frantic wheels in his head, I soon realise he's not going to.

Perversely, his silence steels me some. The wonders of peer dynamics. *He ain't gonna say it, which means I can't say it, which means Barry most* surely *ain't gonna say it.*

Which means we're staying.

Barry, flat: 'We can't abandon him.'

The bottom line.

Me, shuddering on the words: 'How do we do it?'

Barry: 'You're the ideas man. How would a SWAT team do it?'

Mick: 'A SWAT team'd have a fuck of a lot more *muscle*. We've got a knife and club each, and a mutilated rifle inaccurate over more than a few feet . . . Do ya reckon *they*'ll be tooled?'

Barry, harsh: 'If you still need to mull on something that's been at the fore of our fucking minds long enough to sprout moss, then you just lie here and deliberate.'

Me, still mired, trying to envision myself rising, moving: 'They'll be tooled, all right. And they'll be along the riverbank waiting to spring us, just like we agreed on the way here. They must've arrived too late, opted not to come after us in darkness. We can't second-guess that now; it'd be fear talking.'

Mick: 'Given our lack of firepower, how is this "knowledge" gonna help us?'

Me: 'Fuck knows . . . but it'll have to do.'

Mick, waspish: 'And what if it *doesn't* "do"?'

Me, vehement: 'Will you *shut the fuck up*? Your overlooking of logic helped bring us to this, and now you won't go in without a plan proofread by Mossad? At least we've got surprise on our side. Let's go and help a mate.'

Mick, barely audible: 'He's far more your mate than ours.'

He's dead right, and with what's at stake I shouldn't hold this against him. I choose to anyway. 'And he wouldn't fucking *be* in this mess if you hadn't let green eyes override your much-vaunted reason. And worse: you then wimped out of fessing up. If I'd known you'd actually *beaten* Lefty off the team, I might've done things differently.'

I feel something on my hand, realise it's Barry's own hand, give him mine. He squeezes until it hurts. Relents. Squeezes again, as if pumping me with the fire I need; the fire he has to spare.

I can feel it wanting to work.

Mick, choked: 'What if we all die for nothing? What if Steve's already dead? And what if he told them about the second route before they were done with him? What if this "element of surprise" of yours is a crock of shit?'

Barry, grim: 'Steve wouldn't've told the cunts a fucking thing.'

Click.

The angle I needed.

Because I know in my heart that, even under torture, Steve would have found a way to lie — or die — without betraying us.

Without betraying *me*.

And were it *my* fate in question, Steve would've come for me as soon as he saw the car, if only for revenge.

Yet chance chose to reverse the roles . . . and I've lain here for five whole minutes.

Barry, in my ear, crushing my hand: 'No choice, bro.'

None whatsoever.

No parachutist in history struggled more to leave the plane than I do to simply stand up. But once there, I'm free to move again.

Just.

To Barry, who snaps to his feet as if he wants to, pistol held low, cocked: 'Let's just get to the car and take a look from there.'

There's enough light to creep from tree to tree, the club in my hand heavy as a rattle. Each step feels like my last. As the black car looms into view, I make the final few metres on my belly, convinced my hammering heart will any second denounce me.

Barry joins me at the tow-bar . . . and together we notice the dark mass between the car's axles.

Panicked, I roll away, inserting a wheel into its line of fire. Barry, though, holds his ground some seconds, reacting at last to the shape's utter stillness by reaching out. I see him tugging on something without success. Watch him lay down his pistol and tug with both hands. In the gloom I can't see what Barry's dragging until it's directly beside me.

Until it's far too late.

Steve's recognisable only by his hair, though chunks of it are missing, patches of scalp gleaming like phosphorescence. He's been hit in the face so many times he scarcely has one any more. But for an eye glaring with hideous fixation, rusted blood masks him flawlessly. Half his right ear is bitten clean through. Finger marks mar the blood at his throat. His ripped T-shirt clings around only one shoulder, his torso so uniformly bruised it could almost pass for Negroid.

But my only reaction is disbelief. That such a fate could befall Steve, the most vital human force my life has ever known, is as believable as hearing my mother pokes herself to snuff films.

This lifeless slab of meat is not Steve. Not my Steve!

Croaking: 'No way. No way in the fucking world.' I roll him over . . .

. . . and the yin-yang tattoo on his shoulder cackles at me.

But I still don't accept it. As well a rat accepts *pi* radius squared.

It hits me a second later.

My best and strongest friend is dead. Murdered. Punched and kicked and bitten and choked and butted and kneed and elbowed and Christ knows what else, until he stopped moving.

It hits me as if delivered anally, by firehose, iced filth filling me to bursting in a heartbeat.

I flee it, moaning thickly, my heels and fingers scuffling the forest floor, pushing me from this lump of cold tissue, this collection of inanimate cells, this *thing* that a few hours earlier was a walking, dreaming, hair-mussing miracle.

263

I barely notice Barry scramble around behind me, stopping my retreat, clamping one arm across my mouth, holding me tight with the other.

Adrift in purgatory. Drowning on frozen scum.

The intensity of Barry's whisper finally wins notice.

'His *hands,* man! Look at his *fucking* hands! He never gave up! Not once! *Don't* you pussy out on him now!'

Steve's knuckles are bloodied and skinned, and I know instinctively that he fought until they had no choice but to kill him, then and there.

In time the sewage clogging my organs eases so that I can breathe again. It floats to the surface in an endoskeleton, freezing over completely.

Raw grief spurts into the vacuum.

I crawl back to my friend, lie with my cheek on his chest, feeling the flood but an inch away, a sob that's going to bend me double . . .

Rage arrives first, scaring all else clear.

Crowds my head with snarling; scorches my veins like battery acid; directs me like a puppet.

Relieved of pain and duty, surrendering to it utterly, imprisoned in a crazed dislocation. Rise, claim the pistol from Barry. Walk. Toward the river. No hurry, sisters and brothers. Bless me, father, for I love sin.

Check that the bolt on the pistol is closed, safety off. Hoist it once for balance; let it dangle from one hand.

Demonically calm.

I cross the space from which I'd earlier cowered as though it's my own living room. Stopping at the line of undergrowth, but not through fear, or even caution. Only efficiency. And in my state, that Barry and Mick are standing to my right, clubs at the ready, is something I accept blankly. Mick points: once, twice, three times.

I show him a palm — *any more?* — but he can only shrug, shying from something in my eye.

I shrug myself, mentally; rush through the brush without a

care, tense only in the hand that holds the pistol before me.

Reclining on the grass near my feet, Hemi moves in slow motion, rolling to his back, hand scrabbling for the shotgun by his side, and, deliberately, I'm able to insert the barrel of the pistol into his mouth with what seems like seconds to spare.

I've time enough to examine the emotions chasing across his face: shock, purpose, alarm. And then ire, the habitual arrogance of the sovereign above challenge, his hand even moving an inch toward swatting the barrel clear.

And then I watch him absorb the realisation that a friend of someone he just murdered is one reflex from unleashing the physics of gunnery *inside his mouth*.

A dead stranger deep in my breast: 'Any of you cunts shift a finger and I use this prick's skull to water the grass.' I know there's two more of them, lying to Hemi's left. I know also that they've weapons; my periphery noted it earlier. It notes now Barry standing above them, Mick arriving belatedly, cudgels at the high point.

Then, for an instant, like a glimpse of Steve's ghost, his mark on the faces of his killers — cut lips, bruised eyes — stops the breath in my throat.

Barry, a record on slow speed: '*Dusty! Mate!* Fancy bumping into *you* out here! Un-*fucking*-real! Did ya catch up with Steve? You remember him from Vegas, eh?'

The homie panics, scrambles for his gun, raises it an inch . . .

Barry clubs his shoulder with a gleeful grunt.

Crrrunch.

A prolonged scream splits the twilight, sets birds to the wing, but my red trance dials it down with ease.

The giant in the centre seems barely put out by events, lying on his stomach, chin rested on a fist, shotgun untouched beside him, presumably awaiting orders. The Rat on his back snarls a grin and a dare at me.

I watch as Hemi adjusts to his plight, crushed to see him recover from fear so quickly. Or perhaps he's just learned to hide it well. He moves to ease back from the barrel, raised hands

265

and face stating I've no choice but to grant the concession. I do, transferring the barrel to the gap in his collarbone, needing to hear him speak.

Hemi, imperious: 'Let's work sumthing out 'ere. I'm willin' t' cut yu kids sum slack, even though yu got fuck all t' bargain wif.'

Mick: 'What do ya call that shooter set to drill you a new windpipe?'

Hemi, sneering lightly: 'Yu's noe what 'appens if that goes orf. Y'all get t' spend the next thirdy years of yaw lives gettin' bashed up, slashed up and bum-fucked by cunts like us. In the Joint dudes like yu's've only got one name: *bitch*.' He shakes his head, grins a cocky dismissal of me. 'As much as yu wan'u, yu ain't gonna pull that trigga . . . 'cause you doan wanna choke on cum an' wear lipstick faw the rest of yaw life.'

I need to contradict him. To spite him. To refute this arch-bully from whose sovereignty the world has for years cowered, who ekes his fortune among us through terror and extortion, whose very word is a law of sorts, who knows this full well, gloats on it, thrives on it, *feeds* on it. I'm taken by the pure and spontaneous urge to prove him wrong, to be the first in years to deny his authority.

For this reason — and at that instant, for *only* this reason — I step back from Hemi, train the pistol to the back of his fat friend . . . and squeeze the trigger.

The *thud* is atrociously intimate: a clap of thunder in my skull. The weapon leaps in my hand, bucking my arm like the world's finest orgasm.

The gangster *bounces*, as if the ground beneath him's become a trampoline. Blood, black in the gloom, sprays from under him, spattering Hemi and Dusty, flecking our boots and legs.

He begins to spasm, jerking and twitching like an eighties breakdancer.

In half a second I've ejected the spent cartridge, chambered a freshie from the six shot magazine, fixed the barrel again on Hemi.

Barry bends to the dying killer for a closer inspection, unconsciously dabbing blood from the neat entry wound, tasting it. Watching the lagging fit with rapt intensity. Giggles breathlessly: 'How fucking wild is *this*, lads? *Fuuuuck meeee!*' He looks from my face, to Mick's, to Dusty's. 'Did you guys know they *flopped* like that?'

The actuality of the deed — my reaction to it — is held at bay by both the trance and my need to scrutinise Hemi. Twisted at the trunk, the Rabble boss glares at his dead pal — the Ghost of Christmas Future — his eyes wider than any I've ever seen, whites huge in the gloom. Hissing: '*Holy fuckin' shit!*' He shifts his glare to me and I watch it fade a degree, dulled by denial, then wonder . . . and then respect.

Fear comes last. The curdling awareness that his life is to end falls across Hemi's face like a membrane, festering at the eyes.

I stare back at him blankly, knowing I'm the first white person to intimidate him in god knows how many years — perhaps the first person to terrify him *ever*.

The knowledge fills me with sick pride.

Me, crooning: 'Your own fucking cousin, Hemi. Your own flesh and blood. You punched him till he stopped moving.'

But even in extremity, Hemi's nature rescues him from weakness — to my huge disappointment — banishing the terror as if it hadn't been there, leaving only hostility and bitter acceptance. Blurting: 'Yeah, Steve was my cuzin, but *so what*? 'E plotted t' *rip — me — orf*! 'E plotted t' do sumfin' t' me, *unprovoked*, that 'e *knew*'d result in 'is death if I found out! 'E *knew* the price, an' 'e tried t' shit on me anyway! By acting 'ow Steve did, what I did t' im became my *right*! *More*, it became a *fuckin' necessity!*'

I find myself giving this thought . . . and accepting the logic.

Hemi reacted to Steve's action in the exact manner we knew he would. In a sense, Hemi's behaviour was as fathomable, and justified, as a lion swatting vultures at a kill-site. This whole situation is *our* fault.

Hemi didn't murder Steve.

I did.

What in god's name were we thinking?

The murderous tide ebbs away, leaving only a shell.

A husk named Gator. A kid with lead chunks in his heart. A kid deep in the brown stuff. A kid in need of months to weigh things in and around him.

A kid with only seconds.

I drop Hemi's glare at last, nodding, grimacing. 'You're right. By that logic, you're no more guilty than a knee tapped in the jerk-spot.'

His sigh is stentorian. He scrubs a hand across his face, bearing stealing back into him.

Me, in time: 'You remember what Steve did for me outside your pad the other night, though?'

Hemi, wary: 'Yeah?'

'Then, by your logic, you'll understand why I still have to kill you.'

Steeled only by an image of Steve at his feet, drenched in gore, striking feebly at nothing . . .

Panicking, Hemi shapes to move . . . but his sand ran out minutes ago.

Sucked into the time within time, I'm braced for the kick . . . but not for the passion: I'm all alone now . . . and white-hot rapture rips me to ribbons, lifting me high, hurls me down the face of a breaker in a black sea . . .

. . . a ride of such insanity, thrill and horror are soul-mates . . .

. . . glory and ruin divided by inches.

The bridge of Hemi's nose sprouts a third eye and he's thrown to his back as if kicked by a stallion, inertia snapping him around in a neat backward roll. He comes to rest face first, twitching limbs splayed diabolically . . .

. . . the back of his head a dark cavity.

Blinking, I wipe at an eye, my finger coming away wet with blood and *something* . . .

. . . then, gently, I'm wafted back to the banks of the Takahera River . . .

. . . scene today of triple homicide.

For an instant the sense of loss is devastating, and I consider moving toward Dusty . . .

. . . until I realise I'm on my knees, head in hands, wanting to vomit or faint, to giggle or scream.

Knowing there's no refuge in any of it.

Sunday, 12 March, 8.33pm

Back against a tree trunk, GATOR *stares into space, out across the river, gore from the head shot spread across his face in obscene streaks: the product of oblivious hands. In his lap he holds the pistol still, finger hooked around the trigger, but he is yet to reload; has barely shifted in half an hour. The corpses of his victims lie as his bullets left them, with* DUSTY *huddled alongside.*

The youth weeps steadily, trembling in the dark, but after a 'request' from BARRY, DUSTY *dares not speak. From his relaxed position on the grass near the undergrowth,* BARRY *keeps a shotgun loosely trained on his captive. A Jack Daniel's bottle is clasped in* BARRY's *hand; he takes long pulls at it, eyes reddening steadily.*

Nearby, MICK's *squatting posture is far tenser, a pile of cigarette butts growing around him.*

MICK [*frazzled*]: I wish he'd *say* something!

BARRY: He'll be back on the job soon enough. Just let him mellow right the fuck out.

MICK: I'm not sure if 'mellowing' is what he's doing.

BARRY: Well, that's a strong possibility considering he just hugged the corpse of his oldest friend goodbye, and then made himself up in the brains of one of the fuckers who killed him.'

MICK [*exhaling smoke in a hiss*]: Will you stop *saying* shit like that! As much as we've got the props for it, this isn't a fucking Tarantino movie! [*He breaks off long enough to haul more smoke into his lungs. Fidgeting, demanding*] What the fuck are we gonna do? *Eh*? We are in *sooo* much shit and I've got *no* idea what to do next! *None* at all! We've got two . . . *three*

269

fucking *corpses* on our hands, a prospect who knows too much, a pothead old hippie cunt who'll nark on us to save his own arse, and a homie piece of shit who eye-witnessed the *whole transaction*!

BARRY [*unruffled*]: 'Let's just wait for Gator to snap out of it a bit. Then we'll assess our options.

MICK [*shrill*]: *Options*? What fucking options? Our options were cut to zero as soon as Gator *killed* that fat fucker!

BARRY [*sharp*]: And what would you've suggested he do?

MICK: From this angle one or two other possibilities do spring to mind!

BARRY: Yeah, well, that dose of retribution's obviously wiped your memory then, mate. Our options became one as soon as we saw that fucking Commodore. For now just be glad we pulled it off, that it's them not us. Because that's all it boiled down to: them or us . . . and we kicked their black arses. And as to your eye-witness, pretty soon he's gonna be telling tales to no prick other than the Fallen fucking Angel Himself.

MICK [*caustic*]: What are you talking about?

BARRY [*downs a slug of bourbon before answering*]: What do you fucking *think* I'm talking about?

[MICK *loses several appalled seconds.*]

MICK [*high with incredulity*]: We're already in more shit than a hundred cunts encounter in their whole lives . . . and you're *actually* gonna sit there and suggest we *add* to the body count?

BARRY [*matter-of-fact, the drink hoarse in his voice*]: You can phrase or look at it any which way you like, but I'm *telling* you, one way or another, I'm gonna kill this little wanker before the evening's out.

[*Looking up,* DUSTY *whimpers the beginnings of a plea.*]

BARRY [*snarling*]: Get your fucking head *down*, you poisonous little prick!

[*He's rapidly obeyed.*]

BARRY [*level once more*]: In fact, if Gator doesn't feel like talking soon I'm either gonna take Dusty into the woods and give him a practical on karma, or I'm gonna lock him in the boot of *The*

'Dan*, climb that ridge, and haul down a load of blow. The night is a'wasting.

MICK [*marvelling*]: Jesus Christ, how can you even *think* of the dope any more? I'd forgotten it completely!

BARRY: How can I *not* think of it? It's the whole reason we're in this mess. We can't just leave it here.

MICK [*to a dyslexic*]: Yes it *is* the whole reason we're in this mess, that's why it no longer fucking *matters*! Don't you *see*? Our Quenchless Cores proved just as hungry and fatal as *any* capitalist's! We've got about one chance in ten thousand of getting out of this; we certainly can't give priority to getting out of it at a fucking *profit*!

BARRY [*unconvinced*]: Let's just wait and see what Gator reckons.

MICK: . . . If he ever reckons anything again. When I shone the torch on him before, tried to clean a bit of that shit off his face, I got a good look at his eyes, man, and I'm not convinced Gator's still with us. He looked like an old soul that's been here before; been here too often.'

GATOR [*A dead croak*]: If either of ya's have a fag handy, I could really murder one right now.

[*Though he's on his feet,* GATOR's *limbs seem too heavy. He slumps to ground between his friends, accepting a lit smoke. He drags on it greedily, three or four times. Its illuminance on his tainted face is demonic and* MICK *looks away every time* GATOR *puffs.*]

BARRY [*at length*]: Any ideas on what our next play should be, boss?

GATOR [*no concern in his voice, no sentiment, nothing at all*]: I've been thinking on it for a while now.

MICK [*eventually*]: And?

GATOR: I've got one or two thoughts on the matter.

[*As if they're already home and dry,* BARRY *breathes a luxurious sigh, a grin threatening to sever his face.*]

BARRY: You *fucking* champion! First things first, though: I'm gonna take care of Dusty. [*But he waits for* GATOR's *nod. As* MICK *waits for his 'no'.*]

GATOR: Don't be too long.

MICK: [*aghast*]: You *can't*!

GATOR: Why not?

MICK: You just *can't*, man! We've seen enough brutality today to last us all *lifetimes*! Maybe what you did just now was merited, but any more and it's murder, plain and simple. Real men don't *do* things like this!

GATOR: Then you'd better book me a *Cosmo* subscription.

BARRY [*climbing to his feet, swigging at the bottle before capping and dropping it*]: And I'll take *The Sheila's Weekly*. Block your ears too, lads: he's gonna be singing.

GATOR: No noise, man, for fuck's sake.

[*Plastered in tears and snot,* DUSTY *screeches for mercy. He's hysterical beyond words; wails like a toddler.*]

MICK [*distraught*]: *Look* at him, Gator! Take a *good long look* at him before you decide to play *god* again!

GATOR [*miles away*]: If I look at him any longer I'm gonna do the little cunt myself.

BARRY [*brightly*]: Like fuck. You've ridden the Big One *twice* tonight. This ticket's got *my* name written all *over* it.

GATOR [*offhand*]: Bludgeon him or something, will ya? I can't have any of your blood or prints on him.

BARRY: Sorted. [*Looming over a cringing* DUSTY, *he croons*] The last song's about to start, precious, and you've been promising me a dance all evening.

MICK [*to* GATOR, *frantic*]: If you won't stop him for the sake of his humanity — and *yours* — do it for practical reasons: a few years less on our sentences!

[*Moving as though his neck's rusted,* GATOR *at last faces him, eyes vibrant as oil stains.*]

GATOR: Can you think of any way out of this?

MICK: No, but . . .

GATOR [*Pancake flat*]: Shut up, then. I've got something that might work — with a bit of luck — and it makes no provision for Dusty's survival.

[*With one hand* BARRY *hoists* DUSTY *by the belt, torch gripped in the other.*]

BARRY: Say goodbye to the nice men, sweetheart. [*Whistling, he lumbers into the forest like a Bram Stoker patent, deeper, and soon* DUSTY's *wracking sobs have faded completely.*]

MICK [*desperate*]: At least have him do it quickly, then, for Christ's sake!

[MICK *starts as* GATOR *works the bolt of the pistol suddenly; sends the empty shell-case spinning into the night; chambers a live round.*]

GATOR [*offering* MICK *the weapon*]: Be my guest.

[MICK *turns away almost immediately, and at last* GATOR *shows some emotion: a shade of weary pity.*]

GATOR: Forget him, man. He's fifteen-odd years and an evil piece of slime already. Look upon this as altruism.

MICK [*sickened*]: That's not the point and you know it.

GATOR [*uninterested*]: Do enlighten.

MICK [*Pleading*]: Can't you see? You're acting on behalf of a force you're supposed to despise!

GATOR [*a dull scoff*]: Get over it, bro. You're about as capable of doing hard time as I am; it's a case of him or us. You wanna probe souls when this is over, I'm there with the fucking endo-scope, and so long as it's not in Club Fed I'm pretty sure I'll be able to live with what I have to live with. [*Eyeing the forest around them*] Right now we need dead wood and you're gonna help me gather it.

MICK [*thrown*]: Dead *wood*? What the fuck for?

GATOR: Steve's going to Valhalla.

[*When* BARRY *returns some ten minutes later the pair have amassed a substantial pile. Eyes glazed,* BARRY *lays* DUSTY *with expired associates.*]

BARRY [*through a crooked smile, drinking again*]: Now that's what I call a mind-fuck. You dudes should've been there. I just ripped off his shirt, wrapped it round his neck, then choked the living shit out of him. I held the torch in my mouth, so I could watch his face, and eased off the pressure when he neared the threshold. Did this about six times. *Fuck*, he was in a state by the time I flatlined him! Pissed himself, shat himself, bit clean through his own lip. Oh, yeah, mate, all the trimmings. I know a fair few cats down Vegas who'd've shelled out top dollar to see that but instead it was just me, an audience of one. I watched the lights go out, man. I watched the *exact* moment when his little soul moved on. Must see TV folks, I assure you of that.

[*In the darkness* MICK *can be heard choking on something.*]

BARRY [*wistful*]: Where do you think he's gone, Gator? His essence, that is.

GATOR [*dead*]: Fucked if I know. Or care. But I tell you what, if we get nicked for this, I'll be finding out first hand.

BARRY [*almost eager*]: Yeah, me too, dude. We'll all do it together, eh? Convene the Brotherhood and climb the Stairway in full dress uniform.

MICK [*coughing*]: You cunts have lost the fucking plot.

BARRY: You just go on rationalising then, bro. Perhaps you had a right to be a sanctimonious cunt out *there*, but in case you haven't noticed, we're in the woods now. *Deep* in the fuckers. Your domain was left behind some time ago. Just keep on with your candy-arse reasoning and see how far it gets you.

[*But he stops abruptly, standing stock-still for several seconds, clearly losing himself. Then something shifts beneath his face, throws ripples without surfacing. A little too quickly,* BARRY *spins from his friends, suddenly interested in the darkness beyond the river.*]

BARRY [*turning back at last, voice gruff*]: W–, what's with the wood, anyway?

MICK [*sarky*]: Steve's going to Valhalla.

BARRY: In English?

MICK: As if he hasn't had a rough enough time of things lately, Gator wants to *mutilate* his best friend, and *burn* the guy!

BARRY [*taken aback*]: You wanna *burn* him?

GATOR: Cremate him.

BARRY [*frowning*]: Won't that leave a bigger mess than burying him?

GATOR: Not if we do it down on one of those sand-bars in the river.

BARRY: How will that help?

GATOR: Because if we choose our site well, within a few hours it'll be under water.

[*For a long moment* BARRY *remains blank. Then his eyes light up.*]

BARRY: *Fuck*, yeah! We can get rid of *all* of them like that!

GATOR: I don't think so. I've never given it a lotta thought, but, by my reckoning, with two of us working hard we can reduce Steve to ash in a couple of hours. But I don't think we can rely on the rain holding off long enough to let us properly torch these other fuckheads as well.

BARRY: What then? Do you wanna bury them?

GATOR: I thought of that, but we ain't got much in the way of tools, and it'll still leave us with the car to dispose of.

BARRY [*nodding sage agreement*]: The shallow grave method's a mug's game, anyway.

MICK [*ragged*]: Will you two *listen* to yourselves! All you're doing is digging the hole *deeper* and *deeper*!

GATOR [*quickening*]: Give us an alternative, Mick. *Please*. I'm all ears.

MICK [*low, turning away*]: You know what we have to do.

GATOR [*harsh*]: Spell it out.

MICK [*a hopeless grimace*]: It's over, man. We've gone too far. People just don't get away with murder . . . let alone *multiple* murder. If we go to the police right now, explain everything, we've got a chance of getting our lives back one day.

GATOR [*bitter as bile*]: You fucking gutless wonder. First sign of strife and you wanna hoist the white flag, run and suck on the Juggernaut's bell-end.

MICK [*incredulous*]: *Listen* to yourself! This isn't a couple of kids, smoking pot and fantasising anymore! This is *actually* happening! We are *actually* at the centre of a crime that's gonna occupy headlines for *weeks*! And you're still playing fucking *brotherhoods*? No one's got any irony in their voice any more, Gator.

GATOR [*in time*]: Yeah, well, maybe I just don't give a fuck. Maybe I've decided the game's worth playing *without* the irony. Maybe I *wasn't* planning on pussying out when things got real.

[*Exasperation leaves* MICK *speechless for some while. Twice he seems set to reply, turns away in offended disbelief, and when at last he speaks it's as one reasoning with a compulsive liar.*]

MICK: Well, if you won't admit that our 'pact' was nothing but a stoned diversion, how about showing some sense for your *friend's* sake? Does Steve deserve some anonymous cremation? Don't his mum and family deserve to know what's become of him? Does he deserve to be *dismembered*? I thought you fucking *cared* for him, man.

[GATOR *erupts without warning, snatching* MICK *by the shirtfront, wrenching him to ground.*]

GATOR [*screaming into* MICK's *face*]: *Do you think this is easy for me?!* Do you think I *wanna* send my hero and guardian into oblivion without a *single — fucking — obituary*?

[*For seconds* GATOR *seems certain to strike at the friend slumped beneath him. But eventually his snarl fades to grimace and he lurches to his feet.*]

GATOR [*croaking*]: Don't you *dare* use Steve's image for your own ends. At least have the sack to do what you've gotta do candidly. I'm not gonna coerce you into anything: if you think it's the right thing to do, go jump in *The 'Dan* and drive to the nearest pork-pen. Next to us, you're guilty of fuck all; I'm sure you've considered that. Testify, and you'll probably walk free.

BARRY: Just remember what you said, though, Mick, and 'reason' a little further. As a story this thing is huge. Once the media get hold of it names are gonna fly . . . and the Rabble sure as fuck ain't gonna take this lying down.

MICK: [*head bowed, vanquished*]: We're fucked. It's over. For all of us.

GATOR [*implacable*]: So sit there and cry about it. Some of us have work to do. Barry?

BARRY: Yo?

GATOR: I need you to mission back to Ronland.

BARRY [*gently*]: And?

GATOR [*fighting for a business-like manner*]: Talk to Ron. Tell him what we did. Had no choice. Tell him to fuck off home ASAP. Tell him we're taking the stiffs back to Vegas for disposal, and that, so long as his end's clean, there's nothing *at all* linking him to things. Convince him we're the only ones who stand to go down. It's true, anyway. Unless we give him up for cultivating on a plea bargain, he's home free — and what kind of deal can mass-murder felons cut with *that* to offer? Ron's a sharp man: I'm pretty sure he'll see things our way. Remind him that none of the Rabble except Hemi know him from a bar of soap. Say what you've got to, man — just make sure he won't squeal. Threaten him if you have to, but only afterwards.

BARRY: And?

GATOR: Take Steve's map. Ask Ron to point out a spot in the forest, as far from here as poss', where we can get a car off the road and where no one's likely to come across it for ages. If no such place exists, find the next best thing, even if it means hitting the highway for a while.

BARRY: And?

GATOR: And bring Wallace back with you.

BARRY: Dead or alive?

GATOR: Alive.

[BARRY *flinches, frowning incomprehension.*]

BARRY: *Alive?*

GATOR: Yeah. Work him over in front of Ron, but leave him in a state to 'accompany' you back. Use a club or something; don't touch him with your own skin, whatever happens. Give him a torch and make him lead the way with the shooter up his arse. Put a load of pot on his back; the two of you should be able to bring the rest piece of piss — that'll leave all of it at least at the cleft. And *hurry*.

BARRY: Done like a kipper, Skipper.

GATOR: You'll have to change your clothes before you leave:

we've gotta burn everything with their blood on it. We'll wash our boots in the river and ditch them down the highway somewhere, when we bury those shotguns.

BARRY: Sweet.

[GATOR *then shuts his eyes for a long moment. When they open he lets them rest on Barry only fleetingly.*]

GATOR [*awkward*]: And . . . ahhh . . . and I need to ask you a . . . another favour.

BARRY: Name it.

GATOR: Can . . . ah . . . can you do . . . can you do the . . . the work on Steve?

BARRY [*frowning*]: Cremate him? You guys have got that covered, haven't ya's?

GATOR [*low*]: Not that. The . . . the other job.

BARRY [*hesitant*]: What is it?

GATOR: Ah . . . [*He tries to assemble the words, a parched man mustering saliva.*] We . . . ummm . . . we have to . . . [*In a grimacing rush*] Some of him has to come with us. Come for a walk and I'll show you. Bring your knife.

[BARRY *waits until* GATOR *faces him squarely. Holds his eye captive while a clear transaction takes place.*]

BARRY [*grudging*]: All right.

[*Rocking himself, head in hands, over the minutes he's left alone it's difficult to judge whether* MICK *giggles or weeps.*]

[BARRY *and* GATOR *return some minutes later and, necessaries assembled,* BARRY *starts down the bank, toward the riverbed.*]

BARRY [*strangely subdued, over his shoulder*]: See ya's when I see ya's. I'll do a raindance around midnight.

[*For a while* GATOR *and* MICK *absently watch his torchlight bobbing downstream.*]

GATOR [*out of nowhere*]: Eleventh hour, Mick. Make your decision and make it now. Are you committed or just involved?

[MICK *leaps to his feet too quickly; almost stumbles, catches his glasses an inch before they tumble.*]

MICK [*wild-eyed, defiant*]: And what if I choose *not* to make a

278

fucking decision? *Eh*? What *then*?

GATOR [*unimpressed*]: So you can sit there sulking? Absorbing events like an overheated engine? Then you're an even bigger dickhead than you've so far acted, because with three of us co-operating, with you doing your *job*, my idea stands a far greater chance of saving our arses. And you will've burned your other bridge, anyway, 'cause if your next sentence isn't, 'I'm leaving. See you in court,' I'm revoking the option. You don't have to stand tall, Mick . . . but you gotta stand up.

[*For a long moment it appears as though* MICK *will throw the challenge back at* GATOR, *perhaps just for its own sake. At last, though, the tension leaves him.*]

MICK [*hoarsely mordant*]: Let me see. Decisions, decisions. Do I go to the oinkers, take the stand against my two best mates, with the world watching, condemning me for a turncoat, later to suffer abduction and agonising death at Rabble hands? Or do I throw my lot behind a plan of maniacal audacity, conceived by a dude who's plainly thrown a rod or three sometime within the last hour? [*He spreads his arms in bitter supplication*] Pray direct me, oh, murderous one.

GATOR [*stooping for an armload of wood*]: Logic at last.

Sunday, 12 March, 10.40pm

The fire does Steve justice. Encapsulates his life. Or perhaps I'm just being maudlin. How could I possibly know any more?

With petrol from the Commodore's boot, we've increased the pyre's volatility as much as we dare, and in seconds of being lit the flames have forced us back, roaring a more stirring dirge than mortal throats have ever, returning to Steve's body a dignity the Fiend had robbed him of.

He's soon in my nostrils; I sniff him deeply.

Mick also seems moved, silent alongside me, and for minutes I'm free to feel as one with my dead brother. Indeed, the flames leap with such height and vigour, reflected on both sides by rushing water mere feet away, glistening off the sheer banks, off the trees nearby; with such benevolence does the spangled sky accept the palls of smoke; with such force does the fire heat me, for a time my heart thrills in my chest, convinced such a goodbye can never be final, wishing almost to share the flames with Steve. Even when his skull explodes it feels more zenith than termination, and for a while the icework around my soul, the hole at the core of my gut, grants me sweet release.

But before long, as the flames ease, thunder mocking me in background, they become reflective of other things.

And soon they're simply a tool for disposing of a dead friend I'm never going to see again.

This time the coldness has greater purpose; the apathy more calculating.

'Let's go get a load of blow.'

12

Barry — locking his battered 'companion' in the Commodore's boot — returns from his mission about forty minutes after Mick and I do from ours. By this time the storm's begun in earnest. For once Jim Hickey got it right, and if this front behaves itself the heavy rain and gusting winds should last days.

More than long enough to expunge from Takahera's gravel roads all traces of a '74 HQ Holden.

More than long enough to wash the crime scene of forensic evidence.

Though no one will ever visit it in that capacity, anyway.

I hope.

Me to Barry, loud above the wind: 'How did ya go?'

Barry: 'Not bad. Ron freaked out, but there's no way he's gonna grass us unless the oinkers show up on his doorstep. I'm pretty sure of that. 'Specially after he watched me give Wallace the full facial. And, yeah, on the map Ron pointed out a disused single-laner in the forest's south-east. He reckons there's plenty of places to squeeze a car from the road a decent distance, and as far as he knows no cunt has any business there right now.'

'Good shit.' Relief blooms in me, but it's queerly subordinate to the listlessness: a sprinkle of sugar on ice cubes.

Me: 'How many trips do ya reckon for two of us to lug the rest of the pot down from the cleft?'

Barry: 'That goat track up the ridge was getting slippery when I came down. It'll be lethal by now. But if me and you go we might just get it all in one hit.'

Even with what Barry and Wallace brought down, the load Mick and I recently returned with, the pack-load of Steve's we found in the Commodore's boot, a good twenty pounds remain on the ridge-top.

'Yeah, it has to be us two: Mick's busy in the Commodore right now. There's a load of our stuff in there. Someone fancied petty theft as a warm-up. It's *all* gotta come out, and you and I aren't allowed in the car. At all.'

I find myself thankful the roster fell in this fashion. There's something about a forest at night, when alone. Something even more, with wind howling along tree-tops, old growth thudding to ground around you . . .

. . . fresh corpses nearby, a spirit newly unshackled . . .

. . . an inmate on death row.

I learn that my bleak indifference to the world extends no further than the tangible.

Barry: 'How's Numbnuts taking it?'

Me: 'Well, he's not trying for a Nobel Prize any more, and he's doing everything I ask of him. I doubt he'll enjoy staying here alone, but he'll have no choice. We'll leave him the pistol for a bit of moral support.'

'He's the one allowed in the car because of his hair, right? But there's no *way* he'll be able to do the second job alone.'

'I know.'

'So before we go you and me should drag the cunts over, give the rain more time to wash the grass under them.'

'Sweet. We'll do it on bin-liners to try and keep as much blood from the carpark as poss, just in case the rain lets up before it can drip through the canopy properly.'

Barry: 'Mick's gonna have to pilot the meat wagon as well, isn't he?'

'Correct.'

'Has he realised?'

'He hasn't put two and two together yet, no.'

'What are the chances of him jumping ship in our absence?'

'Not good . . . considering I've got both sets of keys in my pocket.'

Lashed by squalling rain that has never refreshed me more, embracing shrieking gusts, we pass the charred site of Steve's departure and learn that the river level has barely risen an inch. Apprehension attempts a tantrum in the mud of my stomach; manages a sluggish kick or two.

Even the strain and pain of the slog up the ridge seem somehow cathartic. As siblings I welcome each banged shin, each scratched cheek, every complaint from climbing thighs.

Awkwardly laden, arms of barest use, the slope growing slicker, the down-climb is more perilous and I rouse to the danger, courting it as a desperate man might a jury of his peers.

We're deemed innocent, arriving at the bottom to a sentence no greater than muddied bruises.

Only to face another trial. As augured, the Takahera River has risen to the occasion, The Mother freeing Steve with more finality than we ever could have. However, her growing tempest is such that fording presents her an opportunity to add to the passenger list.

At our point of crossing Barry and I hoist hand-held gunja to one shoulder, link arms, and step into the water with what might approximate curiosity.

Midstream, waters charging at thigh level, I slip on a rock, a stumble gleefully seized upon by the current. But Barry stands tall, as if in foundations, swinging me to verticality.

Another minute and we're free, Barry expressing a desire to repeat the feat.

I find myself genuinely tempted.

Once, during Mick's hour-long ostrich patrol, he made the mistake of shining his torch into the Commodore's interior. Jammed with bloody bodies and limbs, sightless eyes and twisted faces, neat entry wounds, *explosive* exits, the car struck him as something from a Holocaust reel.

Or a Stephen King novel.

Of course with Gator appointing him head valet, Mick had himself interned the car with its awful cargo, cleansed the deceased of potential evidence, Barry and Gator helping only with the hoisting of the massive Johnson. But throughout the deed, shock at the actuality of what he was doing had cushioned Mick with surreality. At times he had even found himself giggling, though this is almost all he can recall of the labour.

Oddly, it seems to Mick that completing the grisly task — his first authentic implication in the killings — has fortified him with a measure of the dislocation and acceptance Barry and Gator so clearly wallow in. He now finds himself unable to empathise with the logic that had earlier impelled him against their tide. With such *shamelessness*. He finds himself chagrined by the attempts he made to manipulate events in his then desired direction. Indeed, he finds himself chagrined of even *possessing* that desired direction.

Strangely enough, though, that he can feel shame at his near capitulation actually *eases* this selfsame burden somewhat. Because the consequences have not lessened, and at this point in time, to Mick, his inner mortification seems the more pressing issue.

And this surely amounts to a bravery of sorts.

Doesn't it?

So Mick, doffing the head-scarf and gloves he wore while working in the car, hurled himself into his next task with all the aptitude his innate pragmatism had to offer: searching and cleansing of human trace every inch of turf his band or their foes may have had reason to tread. In the wind and wet of the storm, Mick found cigarette butts, matches, a beer bottle, a chip wrapper, shell cartridges, tissues, coins, old batteries. He even located the site of Dusty's strangulation, consigning the murder weapon to the boot of *The 'Dan*, alongside Rabble shotguns. All smaller flotsam he offered to the swiftening Takahera.

In his industriousness, his belated commitment to the undertaking, Mick was able to all but shelve the fears that had earlier crippled and warped him; able to forsake any analytical evaluation of the coming aftermath.

As he worked, though, fear of a different nature began to lurk near Mick's shoulder, like a being of shadow — something cold and punctured, patched and tattooed, its thick fingers stealing for his neck . . .

Like many folk of intelligence, Mick's imagination at times got the better of him. Illogical impulses had refused to forsake him as he grew older — as he expected they would — many of them reverberations from grim literature, books with which he had thrilled himself late at night, the covers warm, light switch handy.

But the mind can prove an erratic companion; treacherous. Can throw into being notions and characters, scenarios and forces, that should, on certain occasions, be left in the vaults.

On certain occasions when in forests after dusk, as good as alone — *apparently* — the wailing wind laden with souls, silhouettes cavorting in the fringes of one's torchlight, all else black as the grave.

And with *the car* nearby.

No matter where his search for rubbish took him, Mick was acutely certain of *the car*'s position, as if it beat malign rays. On several occasions, as the wind rocked it on its springs, as debris from above dislodged, as Wallace shifted in the boot, Mick grew illogically convinced of hearing a door eased stealthily open, a heavy tread crackling twigs, the rasp of leather on pine needle . . .

. . . the thud of sudden rush.

Swinging the torch wildly, Mick half expected to encounter something bloodied and smirking.

When searching near the car-park his eye and torch began to avoid *the car*, working studiously at denial. Yet despite himself he remained electrically aware of its presence, as though it had a sentience, an enormous and feral intelligence. Its very stillness began to seem a tactic, a stratagem; its colour a hellish boast. And when torchlight caught its windows, glimpsed peripherally, there seemed no doubt that *something* inside it was stirring.

As the storm blows on, his companions failing to return, Mick begins to exhaust all areas in need of searching. Everywhere, that is, except around and beneath *the car*. He finds he can force himself no closer to it than four metres. Yet, like a tongue with a sore tooth, the treacherous urge to peer in its windows becomes inexorable.

A part of him knows he mustn't. Knows that what he will find — *two* corpses, not three — will unhinge him so badly the broken, grinning gangster at the verge of the clearing will hunt him to ground with ease. *Scuttle* across to him, and . . .

'Ya all done, bro?'

Choking on a roar, whirling to find Gator and Barry tramping toward him. He's seldom been so overjoyed to lay eyes on people. Seeks to hide this almost instantly.

Barry walks straight past him, toward *the car*, as if it won't sound its stentorian horn, impale him in headlights, throw open its doors, unleash its vile servants . . .

Which it doesn't.

Gator: 'You all right, man? Who did ya think we were? The Rabble or something?'

'In a sense.'

Gator joins Barry at the boot of *The 'Dan*, where they add their contraband to the rest, cursing the cannabis as if it's hay when the lid won't close on its bulk.

Barry: '*Fuck* all this shit! We'll have to load more in the back, on the seat.'

Gator: 'No can do. Steady me, I'll bounce on it, compact it some more . . . That's it. Reckon that'll do us?'

Barry: 'Jump down, I'll give it a whirl.'

Thunk.

'Sorted.'

Gator, as he crosses to the Commodore: 'Did you do an evidence sweep, Mick?' He shines his light into the black car's windscreen, recoils a little, turns away, face soured.

Mick: 'Yeah, we've just gotta do right here, but we might as well wait until we've backed the cars out a bit. I've searched everywhere else top to bottom.'

Gator takes in the mad dance of the trees around them. Grimacing: 'Rather you than me, pal.'

Like a man reunited with his mind, Mick enjoys an inane rush of gratitude.

Then Gator stomps on it, twisting the heel. Handing one set of keys to Barry, another, unfamiliar, set to Mick: 'You dudes back the cars out a bit and give it death on the headlights, light this joint right up. I'll do a final check along the riverbank.'

For a moment Mick glares at the keys as though he holds a hand-grenade. Blurting: 'I'm not *driving* that thing. I *can't*.'

Gator, matter-of-factly: 'Yeah, you can. There's no other option.'

Shrill: '*Why* isn't there?'

'For the same reason you had to be the one who cleaned and loaded it: your hair. I don't know how often human hair falls out, but if you drop one of yours in there they'll need a microscope to find it. One of *ours*? Stevie fucking Wonder'd see the bastard.'

His logic is unimpeachable. Sickeningly so. And the level of additional risk it lays at Mick's feet is negligible.

But Mick's abhorrence has nothing to do with logic; has its roots in a force vastly more imposing.

Mick, pleading: 'I can't do it, bro. *Please* don't make me.'

Barry, frowning: 'Hang on a tick. Just let me clarify something here. Through some clear thinking, we've got a chance of being awarded Crime of the Year, and you, Mick — Mr Logical, Mr Reason, Mr Prudence, Mr Caution, Mr Methodical, Mr Pragmatic, Mr *Pedantic* — you wanna throw a key component of our plan out the fucking window for no other reason than that you're too *superstitious* to drive the hearse for a while? Have I summed that up about right?'

For good or ill something in Mick breaks.

Leaving him the will to contemplate opening the door of *the car,* sliding behind its wheel; *sealing himself inside it.*

Shuddering: 'Just let me fetch the Jacks, then.'

Barry, contradictory: '*Oh,* na, ya can't drink and drive.'

Mick's so preoccupied he doesn't realise Barry's joking; aborts his walk toward *The 'Dan,* dropping his head.

Barry, grinning: 'What if there's an oinker out there pulling breath-tests?'

Ron's suggested road seems sufficiently disused for our needs. Indeed, pot-holes and channels soon slow progress to a crawl, and after a few minutes of this my patience expires.

From the passenger seat I lean from the window, probing my side of the forest with torchlight, as Barry does his. Mick follows close in the Commodore.

Back at the scene Mick's grim determination for his role had suffered a palpable setback when he learned that, for reasons of navigation, he would need to bring up the rear of our motor-cade. But though it cost him, he didn't complain audibly, perhaps feeling too foolish to voice the misgivings.

But what if . . . and there's nobody to see?

I sympathised entirely . . . but declined mentioning this.

Me, to Barry: 'Yeah, next decent spot'll have to do us. We need to be motoring real shortly: we wanna be well clear of the junction of 69 and 1 before it gets light enough to start IDing *The 'Dan* properly.'

Barry, a long minute later: 'Oh, *yeah,* that's our baby *right* there. We'll get the cunt in about a hundred-odd metres.'

He brakes to a halt and I spring from the car, head to the trees on my right. A natural causeway has developed over a ditch flanking the road, and the forest beyond appears commodious enough.

Dazzled by high beams, as I beckon to Mick I can see nothing near the hearse but wind-driven rain. He motors toward me, turning early, easing over the ditch, hitting the gap in the treeline square. Barry follows hard.

Worried mostly of bog-holes, I lead the way in, clearing the odd branch, but the pine bed is solid enough.

By my reckoning we're able to pick our way some eighty metres from the road before the trees bar passage. I signal the halt with a thumbs up.

At the Commodore driver's window, its interior lit by *The 'Dan*'s headlights, my eye is jarred by the surreallity of the scene. *Mickey Goldstein, chauffeur to the rich and lifeless. Dial 0800 666.* He's pale and jaded; seems too spent to open the door. Perhaps he's just too pissed: the Jacks bottle in his gloved hand is significantly scrawnier. I open the door for him. In the passenger seat I notice that Dusty has his seat-belt on, baby-face lolling on a shoulder, and I surmise that Mick was forced to buckle him in when the pace Barry set keep throwing the homie toward the driver on left-hand corners.

Helping him out: 'I'm sorry you had to do that, man.'

Dull: 'Not as sorry as me.' He backs away from the car as though it's the Overlook Hotel, face suggesting his soul remains a guest. Pushing the Jacks into my hand, shuffling clear.

On impulse I nail a long slug. It drops like water.

Barry begins a rapid hunt of the area, selecting a wide tree trunk offering a chair-like space between thick roots.

I sanction his choice immediately. 'That'll do us. A throne fit for a king.'

Moving to prompt Mick back to work, I find him at it already; leave him be and fetch what remains of Steve; begin my own chores.

Before long our tableau is nearing completion and we stand together, casting critical eyes, more united in purpose as a trio than perhaps ever before.

Me: 'Have we missed anything?'

In time: 'Not that I can think of.'

My conscience orders the final brush-strokes with barely a shrug.

Later: 'Let's get the fuck outta Dodge.'

13

Around the Smoke Detective Constable Troy Wilkinson is renowned as a man in the know. And to those in the know the skinheads are moving up in the world. The recent amalgamation of the Smoke's three internecine factions is proving, for the moment, a fruitful matrimony, and around town evidence is accumulating to argue that a neo-fascist extra-legal empire is on the ascendancy.

It's said that the Skins have significant holdings in an Onehunga chop-shop. Not to mention a legion of skilled jackers contributing to it daily.

It's rumoured that the drug trade among the follically absent is currently enjoying a period of sustained growth. With growing links to the Smoke's high schools, and puzzling relations with more affluent demographic sectors, the Skins are apparently in the market for everything and anything.

For those with the passwords, it's alleged that house-calling 'leisure therapists' can be ordered through the Skin's delightful website. Indeed, more hearsay suggests the Skins are involved in the current purchase of several K Road 'establishments', the recent escalation of property crime in this area having neatly driven prices down.

As a fence, the variety of goods on offer through the Skins is second to none: Nike trainers to Sony Playstations; designer jewellery to Harley Davidsons. For the right price, a .357 Magnum Snubnose.

Their facilities for illicit gaming are said to be on the rise. For example, if you've a dog you fancy, the Skins provide the forum for you to demonstrate and profit from its prowess. (Losers, of course, have invariably fetched their final sticks.)

And — perhaps most disturbingly — conjecture whispers that, through younger members, the Skins are establishing covert recruiting offices in the Smoke's high schools, offering cash and drug incentives to those who show interest. Indirectly, they also offer protection and fellowship, and, given the virulence of the Smoke's colossal homie population, white trash youth are flocking to these banners in unparalleled numbers.

Not that the city's established federations are prepared to stand by and watch this usurping of their markets. Polynesian gangs — Black Power, Mongrel Mob and the Rabble — are said to have several destabilising actions in the pipeline. And it's also been muttered that a list of the Skins' *Reichstag* members is under assembly, something brown triggermen will soon attempt to shorten.

As pugnacious as they are, this intelligence gives the Skins reason for pause. Because for all their burgeoning might, they will be several years yet in matching the power base of the Polynesian gangs. Also, members of the Skins seem to hold the prospect of prison in greater regard than do their adversaries — perhaps because these adversaries have had a three-decade head-start in the 'manning' of the nation's penitentiaries. Whatever, this tentativeness leaves the Skins handicapped in the extremism with which they might campaign. Even the connections the Skins maintain with New Zealand's more moderate white supremacist gangs are of little avail: on the maps of these, the Smoke has long been daubed an impregnable shade of black.

Which, in a manner of speaking, accounts for Detective

Wilkinson's evening vigil outside the Skins' three-storey head-quarters in deepest darkest Penrose.

The plainclothes policeman remains uncertain whether or not the Skins yet associate his big, beige Falcon sedan with the long arm of the law. In case they do, though, he's parked some fifty metres from the entrance to the urban fortress — a swinging section in the corrugated iron, barbed-wire fence.

Though tonight is exceptional — he's scouting the ground for an upcoming raid — that Troy's reduced to spending his evening thus disposed, when he might have been at home soaking footy-training aches in the spa pool with Gale, is a source of vexation to the big redhead. Because, as much as his business here is, in truth, of an extra-vocational nature, until today it's been child's play for a veteran like Troy to arrange for underlings to carry out the bulk of his round-the-clock surveillance. Their observations and photos are handed directly to him and then either added to official records, or to Troy's personal dossiers.

Dossiers he refers to as 'The Excrement Files'.

For though Troy is remunerated handsomely in his after-hours role as 'chaperone' to the Skins' enterprise, experience tells him that when working both sides of the ball paddock one can never have too much talent on the bench, available for subbing.

On top of this, Troy is coming to suspect that the party bankrolling the Skins is vastly more solvent than he'd first been led to believe, and as soon as his homework helps him put a name to this shadowy face, Troy will be in a position to negotiate an improvement of his fee.

How the Skins had known to approach him, of all the coppers at City CIB, had been a strong clue in itself.

The risk to Troy, of course, had been significant — as much as the Police Complaints Authority is a departmental rubber stamp, lefty libertarians are not above the use of *agents provocateurs*. Troy's need of the capital, however, had been dire. What with the hammering Denise had given him in the family court, the amount any self-respecting detective is obliged to spend on wardrobe; the payments on the houses and boat; Gale's modelling courses; the cocaine that work pressure forces him to use (a substance not always readily available in the evidence room) . . .

Of course, given the opportunity Troy would far rather earn this money legitimately. But years of watching inferior cops making promotion ahead of him through no merit but colour — beneficiaries of furtive equal rights covenants, shady quotas from Wellington — has Troy convinced his career is at its peak. And, sadly, the lifestyle to which he's become accustomed — the privileges earned by a cop who clears the streets of so many pieces of shit — simply exceeds the salary he presently commands.

He once considered transferring from the Smoke and its hordes of kaffirs to a place where a good white copper might get a fair go at advancement. But any servant of the public who gives as much to the job as Troy does needs a regular source of release — aside from rugby, golf, and boating — and Troy knows that elsewhere in the country the amphetamine scene is lamentably lacking.

So for a few years now, occasionally, Troy's been balancing his books with a little 'personal policing', performing good deeds for society usually forbidden by the pedantry of due process . . . and meeting a few bills at the same time. Because what type of banana republic are they trying to make of his wonderful country when a businessman who creates thousands of jobs, who earns his country billions of dollars, can't phone for a couple of call-girls now and then and blow off some steam? Where's the harm in stressed executives snorting a little coke with their cognac after a hard week at the office? And should they find themselves needing to drive home, surely the torrent of water they draw for the community merits them a little partiality?

But are your *average* coppers — those making detective sergeant ahead of Troy — willing to apply the law with such innovation? Is your *standard* dipshit bobby capable of withholding the common-criminal tag from some understimulated corporate leader who, bored with the constant sex his position wins him, needs occasionally to dip below the age of consent? Of course not! Troy, though, for one, is utilitarian enough to act on the fact that a minor loss of childish purity is outweighed greatly by this self-same CEO effectively feeding, housing and educating *thousands* of kids.

Nonetheless, many of Troy's more sanctimonious superiors would take a less upbeat view of his 'moonlighting' should they ever learn of it. A fact that had weighed on him heavily when the infamous Jim Singleton had bought him a beer in a club one night, taken him aside.

Jim was distinguished throughout the Smoke for his work with delinquent youth. More specifically, delinquent *white* youth.

When this minor detail of Jim's selfless toils had emerged a few years back, the press has taken Singleton to the cleaners, and it wasn't long before Jim's ideology was unmasked. A member of white supremacist groups since his youth, when the scandal-crested Jim had made appearances on current affairs programmes, defending his principles, naming himself reformed, an advocate now only of 'non-violent National Socialism'.

An oxymoron few chose to take him to task over. The episode was allowed to blow over; Jim to return to his work, although the true nature of his labours was more ominous by far than anything the media had unearthed.

Warily accepting Jim's offer, Troy had proceeded to find reason to arrest and incarcerate several prominent figures from the Smoke's principal skinhead packs. With inside assistance this had not proved difficult, and the removal of these reactionaries smoothed the way for the amalgamation Jim had been conspiring toward for some time.

When the actions of this new super-gang grew noteworthy enough, Troy had gone to his superior with a mountain of dire tidings, and, through the credit of his earlier busts, contrived to have himself placed in charge of a small taskforce trusted with

monitoring skinhead developments. A position from which Troy
— on top of fulfilling the 'assignments' Jim issued him with —
was able to create for himself all manner of freelance work, regularly tapping the flow of ready cash that the Skins seemed in
sudden possession of.

A level of solvency Troy's investigations were unable to
attach solely to the Skins' unsubtle shift into the world of organ-
ised crime.

Jim remained unforthcoming about benefactors, but as Troy
featured from time to time on the payroll of several of the
Smoke's prominent business circles, he had to assume that an
element of the corporate quarter had found reason to take an
interest in the Smoke's fastest-growing gang: Jim hadn't pulled
Troy's name from a hat.

The quality and quantity of a lot of the narcotics Troy had
discovered the Skins to be moving also pointed to this. Because
for those with the international contacts, and with the courage
— or the proxies — New Zealand was all but an A-class virgin.

Awaiting penetration.

About fucking time, too.

And so long as Troy's 'Excrement Files' could be made extensive enough, soon enough, Troy had visions of carving for
himself a prime slice of this very large platter.

For now, though, it was business of a less lucrative nature.

His recent preoccupation had left one or two of Troy's superiors disgruntled with his work rate. There was even talk of
demoting him from the taskforce.

What he needed was a good high-profile bust. Something like
a bank robbery. Or a juicy murder. Fat chance of that under
present circumstances.

For the keeping of appearances then, at around eleven
o'clock on Tuesday night, Troy — along with two carloads of
uniforms — plans to smash in the gate to the Skins' headquarters and conduct a raid with, ostensibly, the enthusiasm for
which he is notorious.

The Skins know the bust is coming. Of course. Down to the

precise minute. They may well have a little business on the cards at around ten o'clock — their customary time for drug deals — but they've assured Troy the place will be cleared and sanitised by 10.45.

It's been arranged that Troy's search team will locate little of a lawless nature inside. A gram or two of speed in the possession of one member; perhaps a switch-blade on another. He does, though, have clearance to prosecute these with maximum vehemence, and might even record an incarceration in his task-force's credit ledger.

The Skins, it seems, are at last reconciling themselves to the tactic of 'strategic imprisonment'.

Monday, 13 March, 10.30pm, The Smoke

— Jesus fucking Christ, Gator! I still can't get over this. This house has been no stranger to weed since I moved in, but this . . . this is like something off a Cheech and Chong flick! I'm not sure how much more drying duty the microwave's gonna stand, and, for the first time ever, I'm about to run out of pound baggies!

— Barry and Sally should be back with more soon.

— Yeah, so long as Rick's car don't shit itself on them. Fucker's been running rough as guts for weeks. What's our grand total getting up to, Mick?

— That's the majority of it bagged and weighed, Bum. That bag you're fine-tuning now will be pound sixty-four . . . I've gotta go take a slash.

— Yeah, well just remember not to touch any of the baggies until you get your dish-gloves back on: the last thing we want is prints on the plastic. Those hessian sacks I dug out are sweet, though. They'll take ten pounds each.

— No worries.

— OK, that's more than enough for my man in Henderson. Mind you, when he sees the *quality* of these fucking things, I wouldn't be surprised if he scrapes together some extra laros and ups his order. Pass us another bud to top this one off, will ya, Gator? Too big. Yeah, that'll do it. Fuck, there's gonna be some *mighty* disappointed Rabble members in a coupla three weeks. Are ya's *sure* you got away clean? . . . I know, I know, it's just that you two look like conscripts back from the Eastern Front, and I've never seen Barry so keen to rack up sack miles — ya's have only been back a few hours and he must've banged Sally in the dunnie there at least five times already. I bet that's what's keeping them now. *Promise* me ya's walked away sweet as!

— Promise, man. The secret is known to us and the grave. Like I said, though, Bum, we passed a heap of oinkers on the way back. That's why we're keen to keep *The 'Dan* off the road for a few days.

— Like *I* said, if ya's need an alibi just ask: you blokes were round here drinking my piss all weekend . . . and there were four of my mates enjoying your company also. Wouldn't be the first time we've entertained people in just such an official capacity. Just make fucking sure I get a bit of notice before any pork trots round here poking its snout in the door.

— Cheers, man, but there'll be no need for that. Unless I tell you different, just play it like none of us have ever met you, let alone visited.

— Never?

— Ever.

— Sweet. Shame Steve had to hitch home for work so soon, though. I dig that dude, eh. Fucking top cunt. Make sure ya bring him when you're next up. Gator . . . ? Gator!

— Ahhhh, yeah. Sure thing.

— Sounds like Barry and Sally back now.

— Just shift the curtain and make sure of that, will ya, Mick?

— It's them.

— Cool. Where's *The 'Dan*'s keys? I'll shift it out of the garage for a sec and back Rick's wagon in while me and Barry load 'er up. I suggest you two get some kip before your eyes drop out.

By the time we hear Bum return, pulling into the garage soon after 3am, I've barely slept.

Neither have I shed Steve a tear, an inability that has me trying to brand myself a total bastard.

Not that I'm in danger of breaking into a Brit pop number either.

I can feel the grief gathering, behind the leaden dyke, but its weight is yet contained with ease.

As if I've been spiritually napalmed.

Indeed, the bleak stoicism that has been with me so long shows so few signs of taking leave, it's beginning to scare me.

Is such a thing possible? I guess anything's possible in the fantasy world we've been building these past two days.

The urge to phone Tania — *I owe her a goodbye* — is overwhelming; her image the only thing eating at this coffin round my chest. But I'm scared the mere sound of her voice, my name on her lips, will split the dyke wide open.

And that can't happen.

Not here. Not now.

One thing I *do* know, one thing the three of us have agreed upon: as soon as we've unloaded enough gear, as soon as we can throw together a paint-job for *The 'Dan*, we'll be stopping at Vegas only long enough to collect passports.

Mick's thinking Darwin.

Barry's thinking Tahiti.

I'm thinking (*Mt Albert Public Library*) the Northern Urals.

Mick, Barry and Sally have been sampling the merchandise all night. For me this isn't an option. The ramifications of ushering paranoia and introspection into my wasteland could prove incalculable.

Bum, striding through the door like a man who just buggered a supermodel, kicking it shut behind him: 'Where's Barry?'

Mick: 'In the dunny shafting Sally again. Can't ya hear them?'

Bum, louder: 'Barry! Your presence is required.'

He's out in ten seconds, legs a little wobbly, zipping up on the move. Behind him come the sounds of the shower starting.

Mick, casual: 'How did ya go?'

In answer Bum swings out of the bag on his shoulder, clicks

it open . . . and dumps enough wads of used notes on the table to keep Lefty in Brylcream for several centuries.

In my breast the sight elicits barely a flicker.

As one expecting answers, Barry hefts a wad, frowns at it.

Mick: 'How much?'

Bum, intoning: 'Forty thousand dollars, ladies and gentlemen. God bless the world's fifth-oldest profession.'

Mick: 'He took the lot, then?'

'Indeed.'

A pound of good buds retails at around two grand. A pound of 'our' buds, closer to three. Bum's man had placed an order for twenty pounds, negotiating a bulk price of forty grand.

Leaving us the simple task of moving another sixty pounds.

Me: 'Does he want any more?'

'As impressed as he is with the stuff, he's got no use for any more till he's shifted the first batch. Given the uniqueness of the blow, and that I told him it *might* be a little hot, he's planning on boiling most of it down to oil. Which means he'll need to lay his hands on a shitload of isopropyl. Once he's cooked it, though, it'll sell like hotcakes, so, at a guess, he'll be ready for the same amount again in about . . . six weeks.'

Mick, summing up: 'Fuck.'

Barry: 'Did you take some samples around to those others, like you said?'

'Yeah, but mostly no joy. They *love* the stuff, make no mistake, and they all want a pound or so — mostly for personal use — but most of them'll have their own plants up within a month or so, and rounding up the readies for a big score off us is a little out of the budget.'

Me: 'Is that across the board, is it?'

Bum, darkening: 'Not completely. There's one . . . *consortium* who reckon they'll take as much as we can bring them.'

Barry, sceptical: 'All sixty pounds? Who the fuck is it? The Tony Soprano crew?'

Bum: 'If only. They're skinheads.'

The house grimaces collectively.

Me, dismissive: 'We couldn't let sixty pounds go for much less than a hundred gs, man. As if a pack of cocksucker skinheads could lay claws on *that* type of dosh. Widowed grandmothers don't tend to have more than loose change in their handbags.'

Bum: 'Strangely enough, I reckon these clowns *could* rake the capital together. Don't ask me what the fuck went on, but a few skinhead factions united a while back and ever since they've had cash and *good* drugs coming out their fucking arseholes. The amount of psycho kids they've got running around jacking cars and doing houses might account for a fair bit of it, but it still don't seem to fit. A mate of mine got a speed lab cooking in his garage a while back. He worked his arse off and stockpiled for a year, waiting for a shortage in the market. Then he started moving the shit in ounces. Me and him've gotta mate in the Skins — reasonable guy, as far as those cunts go — and when they heard how much whizz he had, they offered to relieve him of it in one hit. Three days later the deal's done, and he's fifty gs the richer.'

Barry, puzzled: 'So what's the problem?'

Bum: 'The "problem" is simple: these guys are skinheads.'

I know where he's coming from. It's a well-recorded fact that your standard skinhead is as much in need of a silver bullet as J. Edgar Hoover ever was.

Barry, disdainful: 'Na, fuck the cunts. So long as they've got the laros, it'll be sweet as. They give us any grief, we'll sort them out quick smart.'

Barry doesn't rate skinheads. ('The fucking pansies are only tough in packs of ten or more. They all *talk* a good beating, though.') Then again, Barry doesn't rate graduates of the Bangkok Kick Boxing Association.

Me: 'You don't trust 'em, Bum?'

'As well trust a gut-shot puff adder, mate. Sure, they're doing a fair bit of business around town, and they can no longer afford to be seen as a pack of loose cannons who'd stomp their mother for her milk money if she turned her back. But in my book a skinhead's a skinhead. Those arseholes are just as destructive as their role-models, and anyone with half a brain'll tell you that if Uncle Adolf and his mirthful monks had known a bit more restraint, we'd be eating blue whale sushi right now.'

Mick: 'You reckon they'll jump us?'

'All I'm saying is if you put a milky-bar in front of a five-year-old kid and leave him be, the odds of him eating only half on the promise of a visit to McDick's in a month's time are pretty fucking slim.'

Mick: 'What about your mate? Isn't he a guarantor?'

'He would be, but he's in the Joint at the moment. The oinkers raided his house and found a knife with blood on it from a stabbing the week before. That Jamie had never laid eyes on the thing didn't seem to trouble the judge overly.'

Me: 'You must know more of them. Didn't you just go and see them?'

'I went and saw Jamie's little brother round at his mum's place. He prospects for them. But that was only in the hope of moving a pound or three. One of the big shots happened to call round while I was there; he had a sample as well. That's the only reason I know for sure that they'd take more. "As much as you've got," he said. I never would have gone to their *pad* to sound them out, not without Jamie. I'd feel safer in the hyena enclosure down the zoo. And they won't consent to doing a deal of any significance away from the fucking place. Their cars are too well known to the oinkers for that kind of risk. That's their excuse, anyway.'

Me: 'How much notice would they need to get the hundred grand together?'

Bum, vexed: 'Probably not much, but I don't see why you's are even *considering* using them. You've each got about eight gs to "tide you over", and if we use a bit of patience, I'll be able to shift the rest under far less dodgy circumstances.'

Me: 'Can ya give us an estimate on that?'

'Before it's *all* sold? Well . . . with the harvest coming up, it'll be a buyer's market for about two months . . . with the quality of *this* gear, though, pound sales should stay regular even then ... so ... let's say ... three months, tops. Why the rush?'

From where Bum's standing that's a fair question. And to bring him into frame fully would require an answer along the lines of: *Because five people got killed over this weed, Bum. That's right:* killed. *Whacked, iced, capped, rubbed out, or any other euphemism an actor might practise before bed. And though we've made what might just unfold to be a decent salvage, we're pretty keen to put a few thousand miles between here and us ... oh, and we won't be back for a year or three.*

But that's not the whole story, is it? No, a fuller account would delve into blurry abstract; might sound a little something like: *Well, Bum, in the last two days we've gone and plunged ourselves into a dimension where the usual parameters no longer cut a lot of ice. A place where chaos runs the table. So far us three have surfed the rough stuff, and milked the sweet, but as stupid as we were to leave the real world in the first place, we're not halfwits: our luck's going to expire at any second, and we'd quite like to see the arse-end of this thing sometime before then.*

But, of course, Bum's not going to hear a syllable of that. For were he to learn the real details of our swindle of the Rabble, we'd be minus a massively haired accomplice as quick as you could say 'accessory to murder'.

Granted, retaining Bum's services under false pretences is a pretty low act. But next to some of the sins we've executed in recent times, when we're finally capable of sane recollection I'm guessing this one will sit pretty comfortably.

Naturally, if news of the slayings breaks, there's a chance of Bum putting five and five together. If this occurs he could cut up rough.

But after Takahera Forest, I'm suddenly in as much fear of this prospect as I am of contracting Creutzfeldt-Jakob disease.

Whatever; with Bum's stare demanding answers, I discover that my instinct for disinformation has survived apathetic dementia. A contrite wince: 'Look, Bum, we should've said something about this earlier, but there was no way we could accommodate another partner and we didn't wanna look like pricks if you asked for in.'

Hard: '. . . I'm listening.'

Blending in a sheepishness I wouldn't normally have to feign: 'Well . . . you remember that "Final Solution" of mine I told you about?' The best deceptions, of course, stray least from the truth.

Bum, irately taken aback: 'What? Selling online story sessions to kids?' Sarky: '"Truth for our youth"? "Impeaching the preaching"? What the *fuck* has that shit got to do with anything?'

Seamless: 'We're gonna take a crack at it.'

Bum squints at me for a good five seconds . . .

Then rocks back on his heels, declaring darkly: '*Bollocks*. You were as serious about that as Lefty was of joining the seminary.'

Me, 'insulted': 'Oh, wow, thanks a lot, man. Remind me never to share any goals with *you* again.'

But my 'resentment' isn't challenged. Mick sees to that, backing me up with the currency he deals in so well. Flat: 'It's true, Bum. We only settled on it the other night, after Gator met that chick. She's worked in IT for years, and she reckons the market's got a yawning chasm in it for something like this.' A wry little shrug, a touch of shame: 'She says if we act now, get the money and the plans to her, we could all be millionaires by springtime.'

This stuff's more Bum's language by far. Still, the dude's not a *total* moron.

'But why the fuck would you need so much dosh to get started?'

Mick's wise enough to step aside smartly, letting me weave. Chuckling at Bum's 'naivety': 'Are you kidding me? For a start we'll be buying at least five computers, new ones at that, not to mention all sorts of hardware plug-ins; the software alone's gonna set us back fifteen gs, *if* we shop around, then there's the patents we'll be taking out, the market research . . .' — His eyes holding mine are still in no-man's-land, but the new me stares

303

back at him with ease — '. . . the advertising, the line rental and ISP bills, the copyright fees, the rent on a property, insurance for the whole kit and kaboodle, the hiring of a networking firm . . .'

At last Bum breaks the gaze, and I can see my hook wedged firmly in his gullet.

Thank you and good night.

He's far from happy, though. 'What ya's are telling me . . . is that you're willing to risk dealing with the Skins?'

Me, to my associates: 'Is that what we're saying, boys?'

Barry, automatically: 'Too fucking right it is.'

Mick's answer's a little longer in coming. His eyes look nauseous; have done since he entered the Commodore. Finally, in a dribble: 'Might as well, I guess. What choice is there?'

Dismayed, searching for reason, Bum gives each of our faces another inspection . . . finds only vacuum.

Flabbergasted: 'I want *fuck all* to do with this! Understand? *Sweet* fuck all! I'll jack up the deal if ya's are desperate enough to risk these pricks — it's your pot, after all — but with sixty pounds in the offing, you ain't got a hope in *hell* of getting me anywhere *near* those cunts!'

Waits again for a backtrack . . .

. . . which will never arrive.

And at last shakes his head. Sighs coerced complicity: 'But if it's important to keep *The 'Dan* off the road, for the right price, *maybe* Tony'll drop ya's off, wait down the street, and then pick ya's up again. He's running round in a hot Torana at the moment with good clean plates on it. As for *me* . . . I'll take my cut from the deal *now*, thanks . . . in poundage.'

Me: 'Done.'

14

There are many seams along which a society might be ripped. In 'progressive' society these fissures are well highlighted. And seldom in our history has humanity spawned a shortage of those with the ruthlessness to engineer convulsions.

Less naturally occurring are the catalysts from which these demagogues might refine their combustion.

The bad news is that our expand-or-die societies disseminate one such mineral in abundance, its fabrication a growth industry, flourishing in correlation with a nation's economy.

The substance is spiritual TNT: *disillusionment.*

Because as the world's wealth polarisation intensifies — responding to the 'free' market's evolutionary laws — we're able to witness the inequalities of our multicultural communities dispossessing souls by the very hour.

Brown souls resenting White the theft of 'hereditary wealth'; the imposition of a way of life in which White drive Rovers to work, dressed in suits, while they, Brown, wear hard-hats and dust masks . . . if they're fortunate. In the evenings, on ancient TV sets, Brown broods over White's newsreaders — who earn in a week what an average Brown family will in a year — enthusing on the fortunes won and lost daily by White at their playground, the stock exchange.

Brown resenting Migrant Yellow the sale of their labour at basement costs, 'cheating' so many Brown of work, lowering the wages and work conditions of others.

Migrant Yellow resenting Brown for racial abuse on the streets; for the amount of their tax dollar spent feeding 'Brown bludgers'. Migrant Yellow resenting White for more implicit prejudice; for bureaucratic safeguards halting Yellow's entry into upper spheres.

Migrant Brown just resenting.

And what of White itself? What of the thriving corporate class with its hands on the cosh?

As such this class doesn't exist. In defiance of the rhetoric of Brown firebrands, only a percentage of White in fact rules, and this faction wallowing at the crest of consumerism, erecting ladders for its children to climb, greasing the routes of others, embraces but a slither of its racial brothers.

Leaving impoverished White resenting Brown its constant handouts, its privileges of colour, its rampant crime rate. Impoverished White resenting Yellow its growing 'hordes' and money-grubbing. Impoverished White resenting 'professional' White its beach homes and vacations abroad, its carpeted offices, its luxuriating in impoverished White's wage-slavery.

To my more open-eyed compatriots, the theory of this is sound, worthy of grimaces over the Sunday breakfast and papers. Worthy of loud lamentation around a boozy barbecue, of pensiveness though the ad break in *Friends*. But — for the moment — practical manifestations of the problem ebb into their living rooms with no frequency, sanctioning inner utterance of the institutionalised 'she'll be right'.

A phrase which to me, at this point in time, begins to sound worse than hollow.

Because without this deepening status quo, I doubt I'd currently be watching Tony back 'his' Torana beyond a shrinking gap of iron and barbed wire. I doubt Mick would be starting at the clash of metal as the gate is rammed home, made secure. I doubt Barry would be standing straight-backed beneath the bristling scrutiny of five apprentice Nazis.

Five young men conditioned to daydream of genocide and megadeath, of torture and pillage.

I doubt we'd be standing in the courtyard of an urban fortress, home to an organisation for whom brutality is an opiate, six bulging sacks arranged at our feet.

In intimidation stakes these white gangsters may lag second to the Rabble, but the margin isn't a large one. Denims are worn and ragged, adorned in fascist insignia — the *Wehrmacht* eagle, the Iron Cross, enough swastikas to decorate a Munich beerhall. Uniform jackboots black enough to kick a man to his casket and further, buffed to a high gloss, coloured laces indicative of a secret code, perhaps rank.

Like roosters in the wings of a cock-fight, their every motion suggests aggression held poorly at bay, eyes *shining* with it.

Then there's the hair. Or rather the lack thereof.

There's something primally alarming in a human head shaven bare. No matter the truth, a shears job adds illusory layers of toughness to anyone's demeanour — just ask Mick. The shorter the shave, the higher the staunch points.

Done with a fresh razor, the look has become universally symbolic of viciousness.

There exists in sociology the theory that long hair grew synonymous with the peace movement of the sixties through its members seeking to distance themselves from the murderous antics of the US establishment and military.

One wonders what sociologists make of current bristly trends.

If not for the extremes of the past few days, for the lines of speed I snorted a few minutes ago, I'm sure the prolonged glares of these skinheads would be edging me close to a bowel movement.

Already I've the impression that coming here was a mistake.

But I find myself barely able to care. Perhaps disaster is what I subconsciously need.

We've come to this party incognito — Mick's wearing Uncle Rangi's moustache, a cap pulled down, prescription sunnies; Barry and I, hair beneath beanies, shades across the windows — and as the face-off protracts, these latter let me take part with ease.

We decided earlier that to treat with these guys meekly would be a mistake. Unlike a lot of hard cunts — who believe the picking of unfair fights shows them only in poor light — skinheads seem to find arousal in shows of weakness.

Me, at last: 'You guys wanna play I spy all night, or shall we get this show on the road?'

One of them steps forward. He's bigger than the rest, wears a goatee, and his bare arms are well muscled under a coating of vile tattooing. On both sides of his neck, where the collar of an officer might have rested, he sports the twin slashes of the SS.

He fits Bum's description of a piece of work known as Helmut, a member of their *Reichstag*. I'm not sure what he's Minister of: perhaps Incompetent Body Art. Bum claimed Helmut was well down the chain of command but that tonight, due to a 'briefing' elsewhere, Helmut had been left in charge and would supervise the deal.

Helmut, chin high: 'Who are you ladies s'posed to be: the fucking Blues Brothers or something?'

Me: 'Yep. How 'bout I phone my people in Wardrobe and book you lot in for an upgrade?'

He bites his words off like *Spandau* fire. 'Let's get a few things straight, Jake: you or your boyfriends lip off once more and it'll be the last thing you ever fucking say. Savvy? Second: on this property you're out-numbered and out-gunned; if you're planning on fucking around on this deal in any way or shape, you'll be sucking *Zyklon* B before you've even smelt it. Am I understood?'

Me: 'Abundantly.'

Helmut, squinting: 'You taking the piss?'

'*Nein*.'

'Nine what, arsehole?'

'*Nein, Standartenfuhrer?*'

'What the *fuck* are you on about, bitch?'

Mick: 'He said no, he's not taking the piss. Can we get on with things?'

A second skinhead, glancing at his watch: 'Yeah, we don't got a lot of time, Helmut. Kaiser ordered us to have this gear cleared no later than 23.15.'

Helmut, scoffing lightly: 'All right, Bunter. If you're intent on earning nursemaid stripes. *Again.*' He levels an ominous finger at me: 'But if this fuck here doesn't re-examine his attitude, I'm gonna do it for him.'

I'm taken by the crazed urge to challenge our Helmut, in front of his boys, to a one-on-one punch-up. I find his simply speaking in the same accent as me mortally offensive.

Instead, with strategic emphasis: 'You won't get any hassle outta me, Helmet.'

Helmut: 'You'd better believe it, fuck-face. Now pick up your shit and fall in.'

Hoisting sacks, we're led through a front door that could hold a rabid sabre-tooth. Up a staircase, single file.

Their three-storey pad appears to be a former office-block or something: long, thin-walled.

Barry: 'You know what, Helmet?'

'What?'

'If this is how ya's treat a party with whom you're seeking to do mutually satisfying business, I'd hate to see ya's down the main drag of a Friday, staunching up for the ladies.'

Helmut turns, halting the procession on the stairway. Sneering: 'Try not to cry about it, Elwood. It just fucks me off to let a bunch of outta-town poofters into our pad like this. Who knows *who* you're liable to go squealing to. You wouldn't believe the amount of hostiles around at the moment who'd pay top dollar for inside info about our base.'

Mick: 'It was your choice to do business here. Another location could've been jacked up piece of piss. Still could, really.'

Helmut, squinting: 'Yeah, you'd *love* that, wouldn't ya, Half-pint? That way you fucks could've lined up the Rabble or someone and run a double-cross.' Hackles rising: 'Is *that* what's going on here? You arseholes collaborating with the Rabble?'

Me, chuckling darkly: 'Whatever, bro. If you only knew how fucking funny that is.'

Helmut, swelling further: 'You fucking *bet* whatever, *bitch*! In here I'm the *man*, and what I say goes! And don't "bro" me either: do I look like a nigger to you?'

From further down the stairs: 'Are they outta-towners?'

Helmut: 'Affirmative. Where're you pink triangles from?'

Mick: 'Somewhere near Taupo.'

Helmut: 'Yeah? Well, you just make fucking certain no cunt from "somewhere near Taupo" hears a *word* about any of this. *Ever*. Cause if they do . . . '

Me: 'Yeah, yeah, we heard ya the first time, Helmet: you'll string us up like a pack of baby-thieving gypsies.'

Helmut, glaring: '*One* more word, tough guy. *Please*. Just *one* more. I'll . . . '

Bunter: 'C'*mon*, Helmut! Kaiser said it was *vital* we transferred the hooch on time. We've still gotta weigh and check it all.'

Helmut, lordly: 'I'm not rushing this for any cunt. I'm commandant here tonight, and these cocksuckers . . . '

Bunter: 'That's what I'll report to Kaiser when he asks the reason we ended up late, then: because you wouldn't rush for *any* cunt.'

Flinching, Helmut ends the exchange, leading on.

Down a hallway. I take in the place with a cursory eye. It's been done up recently, that much is apparent: new carpet, wallpaper, curtains, light fittings. But rats'll soil a mansion as soon they will a cage: the carpet appears yet to have seen a vacuum; rubbish piled along the walls; dirty washing scattered in heaps; the sickly smell of spilled hot stuff and vomit; holes in the walls, from slam dancing or other recreational violence.

The other Skins in residence seem under orders to keep a low profile: they're nothing but voices behind walls. We pass several open doors, though: a room full of top-notch gym equipment; a giant TV Nasa would be proud of; stereo systems to have the deaf phoning noise control; a full-size snooker table; computer equipment; waterbeds; even a spa pool, for fuck's sake!

It seems that, like their mentors, the Skins are finding fascism profitable.

Though I find it difficult to attribute all of this opulence to crime. They can't be *that* good. Perhaps someone's already financing the Skins for their own ends. Probably the same bastards who mapped their unification.

These are the ones in *direst* need of wooden stakes. Of burial beneath cross-roads. Nationalist politicians. At least — for now — *would-be* politicians. Though current climes leave white extremists posing a lesser danger than those multitudes stirring the brown cauldron, the 'patriotism' of each is but a mask on the same creature: powerlust. A lust fully intent on exacerbating minor differences until, to enough lost minds, these distinctions appear the root of all evil.

Let the claret then flow.

In a progressive climate, if left to preach and recruit unchecked, racial extremists will in time weave a fate for a country to make asphyxiation at the hands of mad capitalists seem like good sex. No, we must hear the lectures of history and take the active approach: lop heads from the nationalist hydra wherever they should surface.

Activists must be hauled from their beds by masked gunmen, driven to places 'where the wolves fuck', and handed shovels.

Apartheid in Aotearoa? You should *be* so lucky, you shit-stirring pricks. Try '*Einsatzgruppen*, Kiwi-style'. For your ilk at least.

At the head of the passage a hefty ladder leads into a loft.

Helmut, starting up it: 'Fall in, bitches.'

Barry: 'You dudes gonna give us a hand with these sacks, or what?'

Bunter: 'What do we look like to you? Forced labour?'

Barry, muttering to be heard streets away: 'Can you believe these pieces of shit?' Dropping his sacks, he climbs to near the peak of the ladder. I follow him aways, and, with Mick at the bottom, we human-chain our wares into the loft.

The loft turns out to be more of a hall, occupying the entire third storey. A long table runs the length of its centre, benches flanking it. Windows perforate the walls.

And as we enter, the Brotherhood have all words knocked from us, the remainder of our escort surfacing unnoticed to our rear. For upwards of a minute we simply stand and stare, incredulity prising jaws wide.

Horror crawling like skin-worm.

The Skins have adorned their hall in Third Reich memorabilia. Enormous swastika flags of several designs. Banners of individual SS divisions — the leering Death's Head of the *Totenkopf*; the eagle of the *Waffen*. Recruitment and propaganda posters — Nordic angels slaying red monsters, a smiling Blackshirt kneeling to blond children. Portraits of the mirthful monks themselves: the Austrian house-painter; the Bavarian chicken-farmer; several other pen-pushing demons. Inflated photos of *blitzkrieg* in action; of teeming rallies; of pits crammed with bodies; of firing squads; of smoking chimneys; of towns in flame; orchards of 'bizarre fruit' . . .

At the head of the table an enormous brass throne takes pride of place, the eagle spreading wings at its back. In a case behind it, I notice Lugers — *replicas?* — and ceremonial daggers.

As surreal as recent times have seemed, at this latest twist in the dream I begin to feel as if I should really like to wake about now.

The portrait on the rear of my eyelids is suddenly made more garish: a pair of almond brown eyes, wild black hair, a cute pixie's nose . . .

Barry, blithe: 'Wow, you dudes are regular history buffs, aren't ya's?'

I wish I could muster the will to flee this place; nothing good can ever happen for me here. But I'm too exhausted to fight the current.

Mick appears in a state of near vertigo; I empathise only too well.

We follow an ambling Barry toward the head of the table, along its rightward side, where Helmut stands beside the throne. Only now do I perceive the presence of a sixth skinhead in the hall. Slouched on the throne, he's bigger than Helmut even, tall and solid, well padded in fat, head like a cannon-ball. Across one knee he cradles a pump-action shotgun. I imagine he believes the cold cigar in his mouth adds a rakish twist to the look.

Helmut: 'This here's Larcho. He's my security, so if you've got any tools in those sacks of yours, now's the time to declare them.'

Larcho hauls himself up from the throne, fronts us from across the table, alongside his brethren. A bass rumble: 'Did you frisk them, Helmut?'

Helmut: 'I was gonna do it up here. Bunter? Frisk . . . '

Me, digging deeply for energy, feigning vexation well: 'Hang on a minute, Wolfgang. You cunts have got the numbers, we're on your turf, you's have already brought *one* shooter to the party, and now you propose to give *us* a search? We came here to do a drug deal, man. Nothing else. We knew we were handing ya's every advantage, and we decided "fuck it, let's throw all our cards on the table, let good faith win the day". So far you boys have repaid us with nothing but hostility. And now you wanna fucking *pat us down*?'

My only true objection to this development is the thought of being fondled by these serpents. In this shrine to unreserved hate, avoiding the touch of the priests seems suddenly crucial.

Helmut, sarky: 'Yeah, that sums it up nicely. Search them, Bunter.'

Larcho: 'Second thoughts, Helmut, we really ain't got the time to fuck around any more.' To us: 'Lift up ya shirts for me and we'll call it quits.'

Testily, we do as he says, showcasing empty hem-lines.

Helmut: 'Now turn out ya pockets.'

Larcho: 'No time, Helmut. I've got 'em covered. Just get on with it.'

For a moment Helmut bridles at the insubordination. At last, though: 'All right, bitches. Let's do it. Show us what you've got.'

Me: 'It don't work like that, *Fraulein*.'

Mick: 'Yeah, where's ya *Deutschmarks*.'

Helmut: '*Fuck* you, Half-pint. If you don't . . . '

Bunter interjects by lifting a duffel bag from the floor near his feet. He bangs it to the table, unzips it, gestures.

It's full of cash. New notes and old. Large and largish.

Larcho, to us: 'One of you boys get counting, one of you start emptying them sacks. Now.'

Mick sits at the bag without prompt, as diligent a treasurer as ever.

Barry hoists a sack, lecturing: 'Six sacks. Ten-single pound bags per sack. Nothing in 'em but pristine seedless. But don't take my word for it.' He upends it across the table, pillow-size bags cascading around the skinheads, dropping at their feet.

I follow suit. Reach for another sack, careful to touch none of the smaller bags inside.

Mesmerised, Larcho hands the shotgun to Helmut and opens a bag, withdrawing a bud as thick as his forearm. He sniffs at it. Whistles long and low. Sceptical: 'It's *all* like this?'

Barry: 'Every last fibre.'

Helmut, to underlings: 'Check it *thoroughly*. *All* of it.'

Wielding hand-held scales, Bunter begins weighing individual bags, handing them off to a colleague who quickly checks their contents; re-sacks them. They've done this before, hurtling through the task with efficiency.

Unneeded, I wander into a near corner, with windows at each side. Frontwards, I've a view of the courtyard, the fortified fence, the dark wasteland beyond. Sidewards fronts the bare side of a windowless warehouse, some twenty-odd metres away. An alley of sorts runs between the fences of both properties, beginning at the road and giving onto what appears to be a derelict building site, a pair of hulking workshops at its far border. I know from Bum that another road can be accessed from between these.

Looking down I notice the roof of the house's high garage some three metres below me. From there I wonder how possible it might be to leap the barbed wire.

Larcho, at my shoulder, dwarfing me: 'What are ya looking at?'

'. . . Anything to keep my eyes from this filth on the walls.'

Growling: 'Filth, ya reckon?'

Distant: 'Given the suffering behind it, suffering for the Krauts as much as anyone in the end, I don't see what else you *could* call it. You guys could turn this place into a symposium on misguided youth, charge ten bucks at the door.'

His stained teeth leer at me: 'Misguided? We're the only cunts with *any* guide. It's traitors like *you* who let down our race. If more of you peaceniks'd open your eyes and see the siege our people are under, we could finally lift it, bring some decency to our shit-house world.'

Weary: 'In case you haven't noticed, mate, our shit-house world is ruled and maintained by Aryan businessmen, and I don't see them doing you or me too many favours. With those cunts tweaking the strings for profit, and stitching up *all* the common Joes, I fail to see how racism's gonna pull us from the hole.'

Larcho: 'Don't go branding *us* racist, pal. Don't you fucking *dare*. We're not racist. How can we be? We draw no distinctions at *all* between yids, coons, dagos, sandniggers, wops, kikes, spiks, kaffirs, spades, *or* nig-nogs . . . We see them all as equally worthless. Now, get back over here with your girlfriends where I can cover your arse.'

Bored, Detective Constable Troy Wilkinson sits in his car, half-heartedly debating the merits of a third flick through the sports pages. He's worried his interior light might attract undue attention. But then again, it's fast approaching time when he'll have good reason for being here no matter *who* happens to notice.

He checks his watch again; it's moved perhaps a minute since he last looked.

Uniforms'll be here soon.

He hopes they won't be early. Remembers they're *never* early. Yet one couldn't be too careful, and the Skins are still entertaining whomever exited that car.

This is obviously the business the Skin hierarchy had promised him would be concluded and cleared by zero hour. Judging from the car that had pulled through the gates, and then exited just as quickly, apparently discharging most of its crew — *and freight?* — the deal involved low-life druggies, or some other form of pond scum. Small fry. Troy hadn't even bothered noting the Torana's licence plate.

But if the Skins dallied for whatever reason, and their guests left in view of the uniforms, or if a Skin car departed too late bearing contraband, Troy might find himself unable to retard his search-crew's instincts. This could interfere with the script dangerously; cost him a payday.

Or worse.

He tries to relax. After all, the uniforms aren't due for ten more minutes.

Mick's a born coward. The uncertainty of entering into physical altercations with strangers frightens him witless. The very idea of placing himself at the whim of so much potential chaos is something Mick simply cannot countenance. And he's the first to admit as much. Indeed, he sometimes takes a certain pride in the fact.

Sure, there are times when he's wished he had it in him to fly boldly into brawls, take some stupid prick right the fuck out, sup on the glory and camaraderie of later. But when he thinks of all the shit he's avoided through a strong sense of self-preservation, Mick finds it hard to mourn his innate proclivities.

But now he's beginning to find them a little difficult to locate.

Ironically, this scares him some.

He knows where he last saw them. Takahera's wooded 'carpark'. But some of them had fractured when he faced down superstitious dread and entered the hearse. The rest had snapped over the course of the drive.

Only they had done more than snap, hadn't they?

For the drive had been prolonged enough to scoop together the splintered pieces and bake them to powder. Because for thirty-odd minutes Mick had had thrust in his face the extremes of violence, and the extremes of terror. *Corpses* riding in his taxi, alone with him, had screamed in his ear the fact that there are fates in this world far worse than copping a hiding.

And his passengers had simultaneously hollered an allusion to a second fate, this equally appalling, not least because it had dangled above Mick's head, suspended by a rope millimetres thick.

Life imprisonment.

The sheer vehemence of the realities at the core of his night-marish assignment had for the duration of the drive acted on Mick like a drowning; had left his former dreads looking positively frivolous, a notion that endured.

How else had he found the will to agree to come here? Jesus, *agree* to it? If Gator hadn't, Mick would've *suggested* it.

Nazism occupies an especially black pedestal in the corridors of Mick's dread. Though he's Jewish by little more than surname — has more foreskin than Dirk Diggler; has trouble *spelling* 'synogogue' — this link with the persecuted past has always been enough to fuel his treacherous subconscious.

But as for the Skins themselves — their bluster, their ideology, their dead eyes — the terror Mick once felt for their like is eclipsed now by contempt.

Arranging the cash into thousand-dollar bundles, he wonders if there isn't an element of self-destructiveness in this new-found daring: the stoicism of the Tommy at the trench-lip, his 'superior's' whistle but seconds away.

Though this act of counting the money — this tangible remuneration of their losses — serves now to melt Mick's guts somewhat, banish a little of his leaden expectation — his pragmatist's belief that, no matter what they do, he, Barry and Gator will soon be serenaded by the fat lady.

Mick has worked part time from an early age — delivering papers, serving burgers, pumping gas — and he knows the value of a dollar. Indeed, some claim that if coal were inserted in his ring he'd shit diamonds in a matter of minutes. He prefers it couched in terms less vulgar: economical; provident.

He's pretty sure his old man's going to leave the house to him before long, and added to the few grand he already has squirrelled, his slice of the cake in front of him right now should see Mick set for life.

He can't help but smile, this physical intimacy with his nest egg buoying him considerably.

Soon though, as his count reaches twenty-five thousand, Mick dips into the duffel bag in search of more notes and feels his finger scrape along its bottom.

Sudden alarm jolts him, and Mick skips to his feet. Peers into the bag.

Gutted: 'What the fuck game are you trying to pull here, Helmut?'

Helmut, defensive: 'What are you on about, Half-pint?'

Mick, meeting his glare: 'The deal was for a hundred big ones. So far I've counted twenty-five, and we'd be lucky if there's five more left in the bag.'

Barry, standing along a wall, shows his teeth, stiffening. Beside him, Gator quickly notes the progress of the dope counters — they're almost finished — and then appears almost . . . *relieved*.

Helmut, mocking: 'Don't panic, ladies. There's a safe up here and the rest of the money's in that. Unlike you retards, I wasn't about to hand over all my trumps until I was certain no covert ops were taking place.'

Mick: 'That question's been well and truly answered, Fritz. Now break out the rest of the moolah.'

Then, over slow seconds, a certain furtiveness slinks across

Helmut's eye. Commanding: 'Toby. Voss. You're no longer needed. Stand down. You're dismissed. Get back downstairs.'

With silent grievance, the pair depart.

And then there were four.

Helmut, lightly: 'Ya know, I reckon Kaiser fucked up on the negotiation of this one, Larch. There's no way this shit's worth a hundred large. What do you reckon?'

Larcho: 'I reckon that's beyond your mandate.'

Bunter: 'Me too. If we . . . '

Helmut, hushed: 'Five grand in each of ya satchels change any minds?'

Silence.

Across the table from them, the Skins seem to all but forget the existence of their visitors.

Bunter: 'How do you propose we engineer *that*?'

Helmut, bluff: 'Simple. These cunts had a hidden agenda. Tried to renege on the deal. Then they tried to blindside us. For fucking us around we slapped them up a little then gave them the bum's rush with just the fifty we left on the table. Their fucking fault.'

Mick, incensed: '*Hang* on . . . !'

Helmut, raging, flourishing the shotgun: 'No, *you* fucking hang on! Another word and I unload in your face!'

Larcho: 'You know how pissed off the Brass'll be if it finds out. The days of us *blitzkrieging* on deals are over. We can't afford clients doubting us no more.'

Bunter, pondering: 'They *are* outta-towners, though.'

Helmut, intent: '*Exactly*! We let them keep the thirty already out, and split another twenty between us. Once they've settled down they'll realise they came out of it OK and stand to gain nothing by telling tales to Kaiser. Even if Kaiser believed them, they're only outta-towners and he's fifty gs up. No matter what they say to him he won't give them any more money, or any pot back, and they'll know they're dead meat from us four.'

Gaping, Mick looks to his friends for a play, but Barry seems in shock almost, muttering to himself: 'Lousy skinhead fucks,' eyes only for the shotgun. And Gator just gazes slackly, like a man in a whole other place.

Skinhead Four: 'What about this Bum? He might blow the whistle.'

Helmut: 'With Jamie in the brig, Bum's got no angle round here. He'll know better than to get on the wrong side of *any* Skins. Why do you think he isn't here now? He wants no part of us.'

Larcho, musing: 'And even if Kaiser *did* find out the truth, our only crime is shafting some outta-town kids and saving the firm fifty big ones. We won't exactly get gassed for it.'

Bunter, brightening: 'Yeah, that's right. *Fuck* it. We've put a lota hard work in lately that's gone unnoticed. Let's take some plunder.'

Larcho: 'Seconded.'

Helmut, grinning fiercely, steps away from his confederates and rounds the table, toward the swindle's casualties. 'Hear that, bitches? The deal's about to undergo one or two minor alterations.'

But the way to Mick's spirit has always been through his pocket.

He stands slowly, like a man resolved to Hades. Faces Helmut from several feet. Low, trembling: 'You've got no i-*dea* what we went through to get that shit to this room, Helmut. There's no *way* we can walk from this with a *quarter* of its fucking worth!'

Helmut, caustic: 'If you don't *wanna* walk, then you don't *have* to. You can be carried.' Levelling the shotgun: 'In a body-bag.'

For long seconds Mick peers into the barrel.

He reddens, breath arriving in small snorts. Then his face twists with harsh resolve and he gulps visibly, as if swallowing the dregs of his doubt.

Then, without menace, palms spread, he shuffles forward until the weapon stares at him from inches. Torn from him in fits: 'G–, g–, *go* on then! I p–, promise you'll have to *kill* me before . . . b–, b–, before I leave under your terms!' He sniffs back snot, panting though his teeth, features rung like a dish-rag. '*Do* it, you *cunt*! There's n, *no* other way!' His head cringes from the shotgun unconsciously, leaving his chin thrust forward . . . like a boxer paid to dive in the fifth. Behind his dark glasses, Mick's eyes are surely closed in dreadful anticipation. 'C'*mon*, Helmut! Kill me or get our m–, money! Those are your *only* choices!'

Scoffing lightly, mockingly impressed, Helmut shifts his grip on the weapon — 'Is that right, hard-man?' — and swings the butt at Mick's jaw: the Hollywood staple.

But almost before Helmut moves, Mick drops to a knee, armed with forethought . . .

. . . and hurls a left like a *Stuka* at the skinhead's crotch.

'*Huuuughhhhhh*!'

Helmut doubles at the waist as if snapped, eyes bulging, and as Mick rises he takes the weapon as easily as from a child.

Mick's face feels hot, swollen and throbbing. He hears himself drawl: 'You dopey Nazi bum. Learned *fuck* all in fifty-odd years, have ya's?'

While Helmut's three colleagues gape disbelief, Mick lifts the weapon high . . . and smashes the butt over Helmut's skull.

A flaccid pile; an empty receptacle.

Mick, distant: 'Now *that* was fucking . . . *orgasmic*.' He trains the barrel on the Skins across the table. 'I won't bother saying it, chaps.'

Two sets of hands go up. Larcho, though, starts round the table smartly. Brash: 'It's not loaded. You're fucked. Chuck it down and you'll walk away.'

Mick, to a stirring Barry and Gator: 'You dudes know how to work this thing?'

Barry: 'See if you can cock it.'

Shunk-shik. 'Now what?'

Larcho, nearer: 'Now nothing. There's no shells in it.'

Ever the pragmatist, Mick draws deliberate aim at a portrait of Hitler . . . and reduces the fucker to confetti.

In the turmoil of gunsmoke and Fuhrer flakes, stunned ears and stunned minds, all four Skins are suddenly face down on the floor.

Mick, a crisp order: 'Gator, would you mind closing that trapdoor?' He cranks home a fresh shell. *Shunk-shik.*

Sprinting, Gator's at the hall's opposite end in seconds. He slams the lid of the trapdoor; flicks home a large bolt. 'Sorted!' He bounces back, leaping, tearing at flags and banners, a manic redecorator.

Like a soccer star with a shot on goal, Barry dances toward Larcho . . . and kicks him in the head with all he can muster.

Clunk.

Larcho finishes on his back, gargling inhumanly.

Gator, wired: 'What's the plan, fellas?'

Barry, drooling: 'Hold the gun on these bastards, Mick; I'll slap the safe's whereabouts outta one of them.'

Mick: 'I'm not so sure we should do that.'

'Why the fuck *not*?'

'I just think we should cut our losses and bail, while we still can. We'll take the thirty gs on the table and leave them a third of the dope, as if the deal went sweet, only smaller. That way they might not feel the need to come after us. If we start torturing them, dicking round in their safe, I think it's given that we'll acquire a new set of enemies.'

Barry pauses to absorb this. At length: 'Na, let's go for broke.'

Gator: 'I reckon Mick might be spot on with this, Baz. This thirty and the other lot'll do us well enough. The rest'll be pinga in the bank.'

But Barry's got the taste on his tongue. His eyes *roil* with it.

A frantic hammering from the underside of the trapdoor.

Barry, seizing on this: 'How the fuck are we gonna scrap our way outta this joint holding four big sacks? If we can find the rest of the bucks, one of us can carry all of it *and* a couple of sacks, with two others freed up for action.'

Gator: 'If that's your only issue we ain't got one. We're taking the fire exit.' He beckons Barry to the windows facing the neighbouring warehouse. Reluctantly, Barry follows.

Gator, pointing: 'Out the window, over the fence and clean away.' He raps Barry's shoulder with finality, producing from his pocket a mobile phone. Pushing a button, he hands it to Barry. 'Tell Tony we'll be leaving via the tradesmen's exit.'

Without a glitch, Gator strides back to the table, but Mick watches him blink relief as Barry begins speaking.

Sullenly: 'Tony? Where are ya? . . . How far away's that? . . . All right. Go to Plan B, man . . . In a minute or so . . . Tell ya then. Later.'

Hoisting a sack, Gator asks Mick: 'You all right, man?'

Mick weighs this for a moment. '*Yeah*. Yeah, I'm happy as a nigger with a watermelon.'

Gator: 'Grab the money, will ya, Baz?'

Barry, still miffed: 'Here, Mick, pass me the shotie. Let's revert to type: you play accountant, I'll play bombardier.'

Mick, showing teeth: 'Not tonight, buddy.'

Barry seems set to make an issue of it when a loud crash from the front yard freezes them all. It's followed instantly by the screech of metal in agony.

Running to a front window, Mick yelps, recoiling in pure revulsion.

Gator: 'What the fuck *is* it?'

'*Oinkers*, man! *Carloads* of the cunts! They just rammed the front gate with a fucking meat-wagon!'

As if on cue the unhurt skinheads leap to their feet, sprinting for the trapdoor.

As helpless as a predator, Barry moves to give chase.

Gator, roaring: 'Barry, *no*! *No* time, man! We're *gone*! *Right* now!'

A few strides into it, Barry pulls short with a grunt, a face like Eve's in a greengrocer's. Spins instead to the table, bagging cash in thousand-dollar handfuls.

The skinheads rip open the trapdoor; disappear. Sounds of pandemonium filter upwards.

With the weed forgotten, Gator claps Mick's back and leads him at a run down the hall, to a window near the halfway point. '*Smash* this fucker! If we stay at the edge of the garage maybe no cunt'll see us from the courtyard or road!'

Breaking the glass with the gun-butt; sweeping shards from the frame.

Gator, over his shoulder: '*Fuck* the bucks, Baz! We gotta go *now*!'

Barry, discordantly calm: 'It's done.'

He turns from the table and hurls the bag at Gator in a long halfback's pass. Gator promptly tosses it through the broken window. He's about to take hold of the window frame when he catches himself. 'Prints, fellas! No prints on the aluminium!'

He has his shirt off in a second; spreads it across the foot of the window frame. Mick offers him an arm, helps him ease out and down, stretching to arm's length, dropping to the roof, knees bent.

He straightens immediately, catches the shotgun Mick lowers, places it beside the money.

In seconds Mick's beside him in the night, regathering the weapon. From the head of the building comes the crunching of sledgehammers on wood.

And then wild hollering: 'Get the fuck down, *all* you bald cunts!'

'Get your face on the floor or you'll fucking lose it, I swear to god!'

Gator, hissing as Barry swings from the window: 'The *shirt*! Don't leave my shirt behind!'

Heavy boots eating stairs.

From behind a dark window Mick hadn't noticed, a few feet from his face, a door is kicked off its hinges and a torch beam flickers about . . . crosses the wall . . . impales them.

'*Out on the garage*, Sarge! Three of the fuckers! Getting away!'

Fleeing the light, the Brotherhood pelt across the roof . . . and freeze. Between them and rolls of barbed wire lies a black abyss. But it's the drop into the alley, beyond the fence, that gives them pause. Two or three metres? More? Who can tell in this light?

Shirted again, Gator throws the bag across and they watch it fall, get a feel for the height. The shotgun goes next, clattering on rocky dirt.

Still they hesitate.

From the front door: '*Joe*! Take team C into the alley! Get into the alley! They're escaping over the wire!'

Mick leaps through pure panic, clears the barbs by inches, strikes the wire fence of the alley's far border, bounces off, lands on his back. Springs to his feet uninjured.

He locates the shotgun as Gator hits the far fence, sliding to his feet cleanly.

Barry follows . . . and snags a foot on the wire. It's torn free almost immediately, but his equilibrium's gone . . .

. . . and he lands in the alley on a single, straight leg.

Mick, wailing: '*Noooo*!'

Slumped on his side, Barry says nothing for several seconds. At last: 'Fuck.'

Frantic feet thudding on bitumen . . .

. . . nearer.

Gator: 'How bad is it, Barry?'

'Help me up and I'll tell ya.'

They do and Barry takes one step, snorts back a howl. Panting: 'It's gone. The knee. Completely.'

Gator to Mick: 'Half each?'

'Yep.'

Shotgun and money-bag in free hands, supporting Barry between them, down the alley in a five-legged race.

Reaching the square building site and veering left, crossing it diagonally, aiming for the narrow gap between the hulking work-shops.

Barry, puffing: 'We *can* get out down here, right?'

Mick, panting: 'Bum reckons there's a culvert between those buildings. It gives good access to the road.'

To their right, on the wall of a workshop, lights begin to dance as their pursuers make the alley, torches bobbing.

Mick: 'Can we go any faster?'

They try but the site is littered in debris, lit only by stars.

Pounding steps to their rear. Louder and louder.

Almost at the byway . . .

The ground at their feet lights up.

'*Oi*! Fucking *freeze*, you arseholes!'

Ducking between the workshops, dropping into the dry culvert, Mick's heart implodes. There's a road at the narrow passageway's end, all right. In fact, they can see Tony's Torana at idle by a streetlight. Unfortunately, the workshops are much longer than they looked, 'safety' remains eighty metres away.

Gator, raging: 'Sonofa*fucking*bitch!'

Mick: 'We'll never make it!'

Barry: 'Squeeze a shot off at the cunts. They'll go to ground for the next three hours.'

Mick: 'Search team, man! They'll be Glocked-up. We fire at them they'll think Santa's here early!'

From around the corner, closing: 'Get *back* here, you pricks!'

Barry, a moment later, shrugging: 'You dudes break for it. I'll make a stand. One cunt could hold a thousand here . . . if he's hard enough.'

Desperation makes a brutal prioritiser: the moment is worth less than seconds.

Gator: 'Cheers, man.'

Mick: 'You'll go down in history, Baz.'

Barry, speaking fast: 'I'll tell them I met you dudes at an Otara tinny house; don't even 'member ya names. Phone Amy and tell her I was home till two hours ago, have been for the last week; she knows that anyway . . . And leave me the shotie, Mick: I'm ordering the smoked pork.'

Yeah, *right*. Mick backs away. *So you can make Valhalla — through a weapon with my prints — while a manhunt tears the Smoke up on a cop-killer payback.*

Gator seems to agree. 'Sorry, bro. Your true role is yet to be played.'

Hobbling, Barry snatches at the weapon as his cohorts desert him, pelting clear.

At their backs: 'Ya fucking killjoy bastards!'

Several seconds later: 'Don't *hurt* me! *Please*! I *surrender*!'

Sprinting hard at Gator's heels, Mick risks a backward glance.

In the beams of several torches he sees Barry, hands aloft. The first policeman, intent on the chase, attempts to pass him at pace . . . and runs flush into a merciless clothesline.

Mick: '*Give 'em hell, Bazza*!'

Barry claims his victim's long torch, clasps it like a club, holds his ground. '*I — smell — bacon!*'

Hurling themselves at the Torana's back seat: '*Go*, bro! *Go, go, gooooooo!*'

15

Windowless. Cramped brick walls. Linoleum floor. Undressed wooden table and chairs. Bare lightbulb dangling from a cord. Half-full ashtray.

Minus only the black drapes, B-grade movie buffs.

Especially when the iron door swings open, a burly detective easing in, clipboard in hand.

Shutting the door behind him, he smiles at the sight of Barry, feet on the table, chair on two legs, braced against the wall, cigarette in handcuffed fingers. As if to spite his black eyes, his split lip, the cut along his jaw, Barry brandishes a mocking grin.

Copper: 'How're you doing, mate. Not too sore?'

'I've had sex that left me sorer.'

The redhead offers a laddish chuckle. 'That's the spirit. I was at the bust and I heard about what happened. I can't condone your actions, but I'd be the first to admit that you've got plenty of ticker. Now that the heat's off they tell me you seem like a clued-up fella. Let's you and me have a wee chat and I've got a feeling things for you are gonna be *juuuust* fine.'

'Yeah, why not? I've gotta window in my diary right about now.'

'Good man.' The cop draws back a chair and seats himself.

328

Reading from his clipboard, he flips a couple of sheets, absently removing a pack of cigarettes.

Head down: 'Barry, is it?'

'If you say so.'

'Well, that's what the driver's licence in the wallet found at the crime scene says.' Quick grin. 'Nice move trying to ditch it before the shit hit. That could have set the pen-pushers back days. Cigarette, Barry?'

'Just put one out, pal.'

He flips the packet on the table. 'Help yourself whenever. Yeah, let's see here: Barry Reginald Trotter. Builder's labourer. Got a record, Barry?'

'You tell me, mate.'

'According to the database, Vegas have a pretty extensive sheet on you, but your age got you out of anything concrete for a long time. Since turning eighteen you've had several assault charges filed against you, but the plaintiffs later withdrew the charges.' Shrugging: 'It barely seems worth keeping a note of to me; boys will be boys, after all.'

'Since when was it legal to keep unofficial files on people?'

'How long ya been in the Smoke, Barry?'

'Year or four.'

'What did ya come up for?'

'Work.'

The cop nods neutrally, consulting his clipboard. He eventually draws a weighty breath and leans forward, suddenly intent. 'OK, my name's Detective Constable Troy Wilkinson.'

Barry, dire advice for a phantom third party: 'See what I mean? Turn your back for a *second* and they sneak in with the humans.'

'Now, that's not the attitude, Barry. What you've gotta understand here is that right now you're in a *world* of shit . . . and I'm the best friend you've got.'

'Got a glass'a water to go with that? I'm having trouble swallowing.'

Earnest: 'It's true, Barry. You see, the Skins are my pet

project. That raid was mine, and you're proving a real fly in my ointment. Those coppers you hurt, Barry, they got wounded under my command, and my chief wants the book thrown at you. I'm keen to avoid that, because the last thing I need is an official logging of the belief that I can't look after guys under my leadership. And the fact that you aren't a Skin means I've nothing to gain *at all* in seeing you take a rap for this.'

'Lucky me.'

'You don't know *how* lucky, Barry. You need all the support you can get, because right now, in addition to the pot, the chief wants to see you charged with resisting arrest, assaulting officers of the law with the intention of causing grievous bodily harm, and perhaps an attempted murder rap on the bloke you bludgeoned with the torch.'

Barry, frowning: 'Back up a sec, there, Sarge. What pot are you talking about?'

Troy, stern: 'Let's not play silly buggers, Barry. I don't have the time, and you *certainly* don't: the chief wants the charges against you filed by noon.'

'Tell me what you're on about, then.'

Troy, ignoring: 'What's gonna happen if you don't co-operate is you get charged with everything I just listed, it comes to court, you plead not guilty without a leg to stand on, and the judge bangs you up for near on two decades. Do things my way, plead guilty to *just* the reefer, and I'll personally see all the violence charges go down the self-defence gurgler. This way I don't get painted an incompetent leader, the Sarge stays happy because you'll still do a little time, and my Skins project gets saved a mountain of needless paperwork.'

' . . . I've only got one problem with that scenario, Troy.'

Troy, eager: 'What?'

'I've no idea what the fuck you're on about.'

Sighing: 'C'mon, Barry. Jerk me around and I won't be able to help you.'

Barry, an artless laugh: 'Jerk you round *how*? What the fuck are you *talking* about?'

Disappointed: 'All right, Barry. If you insist. I'm talking about the cannabis. The hoochie-coochie. The sixty pounds of marijuana you and your mates took to the Skins to try and move.'

Startled: 'That's the first I've heard of any *cannabis* . . . *or* any mates. I went there to try and pick up some whizz.'

'Lying to me's only gonna cost you in the long run, Barry. We had surveillance on the place and we saw you and four friends arrive in the Torana and unload six ten-pound sacks of marijuana, before the car pulled away.'

A flash of remembrance: 'Oh, *those* guys. Na, they were just some fullas I met round at a tinny house about a week ago. They said they could help me score some speed so I gave them my number and they phoned me yesterday, said they'd pick me up on the way to the dealer's. I never even caught their names. I know they didn't have no six sacks of *cannabis* in the car, though.' A startling thought: 'Hey, *shit*! That might've been what those sacks I saw up in the Nazi den were! Were they greyish?'

Troy, smiling sadly: '*Come* on, Barry. We've got fingerprints tying you to the dope, and we've got photographs *showing* you all unloading it. As well as the written accounts of five-odd eye-witnesses.'

'Yeah, five skinheads. They've hardly a vested interest in lying, have they, Troy? As for fingerprints: I'm not denying being in the house . . . ' Pauses suddenly. Then, quietly: 'Are the prints off the actual sacks, are they?'

Troy waits a beat . . . grimaces sympathetically: 'Of course they are, Barry. They'd be of no use to us otherwise.'

Barry, impressed: 'That's a fucking *top* effort on the part of forensics then, isn't it? Not only were they able to beam themselves into a dimension where I actually *touched* the sacks, they were also able to advance technology to the state where prints can be lifted from *hessian*. Fuck *me*, that's first-rate oinkering. Congratulate them for me, will ya, Troy? While you're at it, bring those pictures in here. I'm interested to see how photogenic I am under a long lens that can see through corrugated iron.'

Troy's eyes narrow, upper lip lifting a little. He shifts his stare from Barry's raised eyebrows. Takes the time to light a cigarette, settling himself.

Barry, brightly: 'You mind if I grab one of those, friend?'

Leaden: 'Help yourself.'

Barry does, contriving to make the proximity of his cuffed hands appear part of long routine. Exhaling smoke with a sigh: '*Ahhh*, B&H. That's a man's fag, isn't it, Troyo?'

Troy, scratching inside his jacket absently: 'Ya know, I wish you'd begin to appreciate the trouble you're in, Barry. Constable Nightingale — the young guy whose head you smashed in with the torch — he's lying in intensive care right now, fighting for his life.'

Barry: 'And I'm rooting for him every step of the way.'

'That's why everyone round here is keen to see you locked up for a *very* long time.'

Smiling: 'But not if you get your way, eh?'

Troy, shrugging: 'I've been around the block enough times to see past the emotion. He was a copper on a chase. He knew the dangers. I can't be there to hold the hands of *everyone* under my command, and I'm not willing to see my career damaged because some rookie was negligent enough to leave a desperate man with no options. For that reason, when you own up to the pot, I'll see the chief placated and I'll make the self-defence angle stick.' He stands slowly. 'In the meantime, Barry, if you're gonna treat me like an arsehole, I've got other work to do. There'll be an officer to escort you back to your cell soon. Keep the durries; I reckon you'll be needing them more than me.'

He starts toward the door slowly, stopping to examine his clipboard.

Knock, knock.

The door's opened to an anxious policewoman. She hands Troy a mobile phone. 'It's for you, Troy. Greenlane Hospital.' Exits quietly.

Troy, holding Barry's eye: 'Yes? . . . Hello, doctor . . . I know.

How is . . .' His face crumples. A deep sigh: 'I'm sorry to hear that . . . I'm sure you did all you could. OK. I'll pass that on. Bye.'

He ends the connection, hanging his head for some seconds. Takes two deliberate steps toward the table, flopping down again. Distracted, he pockets the phone.

Meets Barry's eye at last. Grimly: 'That was Dr Wu from the Greenlane IC unit.'

'Wrong number, was it?'

'No, Barry.' Weighty pause. 'I'm afraid the doctor phoned to inform me that Constable Marcus Nightingale lost his battle for life at 9:25 this morning.'

Barry's silent for a long time, cockiness ebbing from him visibly. His eyes roam everywhere, seeing nothing. Eventually he slumps forward, elbows to the table, face in hands. '*Shit*. Oh, for *fuck's* sake. That leaves me on a cop-killer rap. Yeah?'

Troy, leaning toward Barry with sudden intensity: 'Not if we act *now*. If I can take your confession to the chief *right* now, I give myself a seventy per cent chance of getting you exonerated on a self-defence plea. Come *on*, Barry! *Work* with me here! Our nuts are on the line, and I can get them off it . . . but only if you *work* with me!'

Barry, gazing at him, haunted: 'What am I looking at now?'

'*Barry*, it's a *cop-killer* rap. You'll *never* see daylight again, mate! Max security without parole. You'll never hold another woman. You'll never share another beer with your pals. You'll spend every day for the *rest of your life* rumbling tooth and nail to keep your anal virginity intact.'

Barry, vanquished, tears very near: 'Fuck. Oh, *fuck*!' His eyes plead with Troy's. 'Can you *really* help me?'

Adamant: '*Yes*. I can and I *will*.' Hurriedly, Troy takes a statement sheet from his clipboard. 'I took the time to smooth things earlier.' Placing the page before Barry, he points to a middle paragraph.

```
      . . . with the intention of offering it to
  the  Skins  for  sale.  Rumour  told  us  they
```

                    might   be   interested.   Around   10.30pm,
                    _____
                    and I removed about sixty pounds of
                    cannabis from the interior and boot of the
                    car. The car was then driven away by
                    _____ .
                    The three of us were led through the front
                    doors of the Skins' house and up to the
                    hall on the top floor. I began negotiating
                    a price, but the Skins were yet to express
                    interest when the police raid began . . .

Barry, voice catching on a sob: 'Will I have to nark on my mates?'

Troy, gentle: 'Not for the moment mate, but the more you give me the more likely the chief's gonna let the violence charges slip.'

Barry, nodding, swallowing: 'I'll think on that part for a while. Have you got a pen, please?'

Troy, handing one over: 'You're a smart young man, Barry.'

Taking the sheet from the table to his lap, Barry begins scribbling.

Troy eases back in his chair.

Barry, returning the confession, sniffing: 'Here you go, mate.'

          The preceding statement is true and
          authentic to the best of my knowledge.
          Name (Printed):
          Name (Signed):
          Keep ya day job, pig. Tell ya floozy not to hold her breath
          4 an Oscar either. I've seen possums run after nailing
                   them with X4 of what your faggot pal got.
          Date:

Snarling, Troy lunges across the table, snatching Barry by the shirtfront. Drags him to the floor, furniture tumbling. A clenched yell: 'You fucking little piece of *shit*! You think you can *fuck* with me! You're *pond scum*! You're just white fucking *trash*! I'll nail your balls to the wall over this!'

Barry, ostensibly stunned: 'What are you *saying*, friend? Are you and I no longer?'

Troy, holding Barry's head against the cold floor, cocking his fist: 'You little *cunt*! What makes you think I won't just *bash* you into signing it?'

Barry, chuckling: 'Hate to spoil your ego trip, Troyo, but it wouldn't be the first time I've copped extra-legal punishment at the hands of the Thin Blue Line. I'm no fool: I know every nick in this country's got a slippery staircase in it. But you're no fool either — this isn't Russia: confessions obtained under duress don't tend to stick in these parts.'

Huffing deeply, Troy finally climbs to his feet. A menacing mutter: 'Let me tell you this, you mouthy fuck: that pot was *yours* . . . and you're going down for it. That's a promise.' He walks from the room stiffly, slamming the door behind him.

16

'Look, Barry, you're obviously a man of staunch principle, and I respect that totally. But this has gone beyond loyalty. This is madness.'

As opposed to Troy seated beside him at the interview table, Detective Inspector Duncan Fletcher — compact and dapper, moustached and methodical — waves two fingers at the stereotype of a plainclothes copper. To Barry, his appearance and bearing seem more to befit an accountant.

Or an Inland Revenue auditor.

Barry first met Duncan thirty minutes ago, when the three of them began their 'chat'. Duncan had handled most of the talking, smooth and obliging, Troy confining himself to black stares and veiled threats which Duncan seems to find quietly unpalatable.

He continues: 'Because, Barry, how can you expect me to help you if you won't co-operate even *marginally*?'

'You'll have to refresh my memory here, Duncan: when exactly was it that I asked you for help?'

Duncan: 'Well, Barry, you really should give that some serious thought, because if you decide you want to let your mates walk away scot-free, not only are you going down for the resisting arrest we charged you with on Thursday, but you'll also be done for GBH on an officer, attempted murder — charges worth fifteen years, should we prosecute with full vehemence — *and* you'll be taking the rap for possession with intent to supply *sixty pounds* of cannabis. You'll be lucky to see a sunrise before your fiftieth, mate.'

Troy, gloating: 'Just think of *alllllll* the pussy that'll slip through the fingers of a young stud like you over a period like that, Barry. When did ya last spread a nice bird wide and slip into the honey? I hope it was a good root, mate, because, let's face it, an old man and out of the loop for thirty years . . . Even when you get *out* you'll be lucky to find somewhere to stick it. Of course, by then you'll be so conditioned to doughnut-punching you probably won't *want* any fanny.'

Duncan, tutting, edging from Troy minutely: 'Just one name, Barry. It's only fair that one of your friends share the weight of your misfortune. Just give us one name and we'll go easy on both of you. The prison time'll be split between you both, and with good behaviour you'll be lucky to serve a year each on a wilderness hobby farm. Assuming they're half as loyal as you, Barry, were they sitting here right now, given the choice between two of you doing a year each, or just yourself doing *thirty*-odd mandatory, they'd jump on my offer in a shot . . . and you *know* they would. If you won't forsake this idiocy for your own sake, Barry, do it for *theirs*. Because how do you think they're going to face themselves in the mirror knowing they cost a mate the best thirty years of his life?'

Troy, crooning: 'Ever seen the inside of Paremoremo, Barry? The cells are about as big as this room, and you'll be sharing it with eight *sick* pieces of shit. The food? Think of the worst meal you ever ate, douse it in dog spoof, and that's *all* you'll be eating for *three decades*. But that'll seem a minor inconvenience when the lights go down. You see, that's when the big men on campus — psycho Maoris and bongas to a number — that's when they choose which white boy they wanna make wear a dress for them and park their cock inside of for the night. And don't count on any help from the screws: they know better than to fuck with those who *really* run the nick.'

Barry, yawning: 'You know what I reckon? I reckon you ladies should switch roles for a while, just as a change of routine for us all. You play good cop for a spell, Troyo. God knows your acting could use the practice.'

Jaw bunching, Troy forces himself to shift attention to the papers in front of him.

Duncan: 'The thing is, Barry, without one of your friends . . . '

Barry, irritated: '*No*, Duncan, the thing is, I've told you guys ten thousand times and I'll tell you just *once* more: I met those clowns at a tinny house in Otara about a week before the bust. We got talking, and they reckoned they could score nose-candy round at the Skins' pad. So I gave them my number. We went to the Skins' to score speed. I couldn't name or identify any one of them if you offered to make me the new Commissioner of Oinkers. The sacks of whatever was in them were in the *Reichstag* when we arrived. Is that quite clear? Now that's my final word on the matter. So if you pricks can't think of anything different you'd like to shoot the shit about, I'm not gonna be saying another word, as is my right, and as advised by my lawyer.'

He leans back in his chair, hands behind head, eyes closing.

A mobile phone rings.

Duncan: 'Yes? OK, chief, we'll be right along.'

Standing: 'There's been a new development. We have to leave I'm afraid.'

Troy: 'Don't go anywhere, Barry.'

'And miss another of your performances? You've *gotta* be kidding.'

Slam.

Barry folds his arms on the table, rests his head on them, handcuffs cold on his cheek.

He wonders how much longer before the Ds lay more cards on the table.

Down the corridor from the interview room, the policemen lag momentarily.

Duncan: 'That's that, as far as I'm concerned. The kid's no fool. Despite our best efforts, he knows that with what we've got on him so far he'll be unlucky if he serves more than a year or two. His lawyer's assured him of that. He's not gonna rat on anyone . . . for the moment. It was worth a try, though, because there's no telling which way he's going to jump when the ante ups. You might as well add the dope to the charge sheet you've got on the Skins. I've no doubt that'll please you.'

Troy, unconvinced: 'Well, let's not be *too* hasty on that. The Skins are adamant it *wasn't* their gear.'

Duncan, smiling: 'Can you blame them? What do you care if it wasn't, anyway? You've got enough to pin it to them. Be a good feather in the cap of your taskforce.'

'It wouldn't be justice, mate.'

Duncan, laughing: 'Troy Wilkinson, passing up a bust in the name of *justice*? Whatever next?'

'Well, maybe at this stage I'm eager to forsake a little credit for the sake of getting a cop-basher banged up good and proper.'

'I hear that. Anyway, go get something to eat and I'll meet you back here in twenty minutes. And let me do the talking. Remember, you're mostly in this for the love/hate thing you've got going with him. Maybe his bolshiness'll cause a slip-up.'

'Wakey, wakey!'

Troy slaps the door closed.

Barry, head down, muffled: 'What, are they letting *any* prick into these places now?'

Duncan, firm: 'Sit up please, Barry.'

They make a fuss of removing jackets, placing folders, positioning chairs. Barry eases back in his own, legs fully stretched.

Duncan, at last: 'OK, Barry, it's beginning to seem as if we've got no choice but to accept your version of events.'

'Ye-fucking-ha.'

Duncan: 'We just need you to clarify one or two things.

Firstly, where exactly were you when you met the gentlemen with the Torana?'

Barry, sighing at someone backstage: 'Start the broken record, Wolfman.' Eyes back on Duncan, a theatrical monotone: 'I was at a tinny house in Otara. I'm not giving you an exact address 'cause if I were to nark on these cats my life'd be worth sweet fuck all. Feel free to add withholding information to my "extensive" sin-list.'

Troy: 'And where did they collect you from on the day of the Skins bust?'

'From the place I share with one of my bitches. The place I'd been inside of with the flu for the last few days. Ask her. '

Duncan: 'We have.'

'And?'

Troy: 'And we don't believe her.'

'Tell someone who gives a fuck.'

Duncan: 'Did you give the lads any money for petrol after they collected you?'

'No.'

'Did they pick up anyone else?'

'No.'

'What time did they arrive at your place?'

'About nine-thirty.'

'Did they have any drugs already on them?'

'No idea.'

'How many in the car?'

'Don't rightly remember. Maybe four.'

'On the day you met them, around at the "tinny house", how many then?'

'The same.'

'So the darkie wasn't with them at that stage?

' . . . What darkie?'

A part of him had hoped she wouldn't come. Even though this would've left him high and dry.

Four in the morning, it had been. Rendezvous arranged just a few hours earlier: a phone call from nowhere, a cold voice in the dark. No explanation, no translation, just orders. The briefest of briefings.

Don't speed near any cameras. Don't pass through traffic lights within a mile of the park. Don't turn into the park if there's a cop in view . . .

He hadn't even said thank you.

But it didn't matter now. She'd come. She'd passed.

Cruising the dark lanes of Cornwall Park, right on time.

For better or for worse.

Crouched in bushes, he'd let her glide by: she was never to see him in that form. Trust is one thing; blind faith quite another.

The wig, beard and sunglasses had vanished already, stowed in his back-pack, alongside the gloves. From out of his mouth he'd pulled wads of cotton wool, wedged in the gumline. Fished more from his nostrils, mindful not to drop a shred of it. Scrubbed makeup from his face with wet-wipes. Stripped, quickly, relieved to be rid of the layers beneath the jersey, the sweat-soaked trackpants under his jeans.

Back from the grave.

I was never here. Only Steve was. Steve the fingerless.

Oh, bro, even in death you pull me from the shit. I know you don't hate me for what I've done; I know you'd've wanted it so . . .

She'd passed him again, in the opposite direction, head swivelling like a searchlight.

And the simile had had him shuddering. He'd knelt in the dirt, letting her drive. Stared at nothing, sucked in warm air.

A man at a murky crossroads.

Troy, crisp: 'Why the hesitation, Barry?'

Easing back further, pulse thumping: 'Just pondering an odd question, Troyo.'

Duncan, conspiratorial smile: 'He didn't say much to you, then?'

'Who?'

Duncan, reading: 'So the Torana arrived at your place at eight-thirty?'

'Ye . . . nine-thirty.'

'Did you invite them in at all?'

Barry: 'Na.'

'They didn't ask to come in?'

'Na.'

'Was there booze in the car?'

'Not that I noticed.'

'They weren't drinking, then?'

'Not to my knowledge.'

'Not even the darkie?'

'. . . *What* fucking darkie?'

'The bloke who helped you put Constable Ryan Miller in hospital.' Bright-eyed: 'Remember? The rear of McDick's? Greenlane? Friday before last?'

Barry, mopping sweat from an inner brow: 'What the fuck are you *on* about, Duncan?'

Troy, scoffing: 'Come on, Barry. When Ryan woke from his coma on Friday night he helped us construct identikit pictures of his assailants. One of them bears a *striking* resemblance to yourself. Uncanny, really. Check it out.' Slides a sheet across the table.

Barry stares into his own eyes. Near enough, at least.

Too near, in fact. He hopes. What with the poor light that night; the haze a decent concussion puts on one's memory.

He shrugs, flicking the picture away. 'I'm not gonna argue with you dickheads. Why should I? You're oinkers: I can't believe a word that leaves ya snouts. If you think I'm guilty of this, chalk it to the slate and we'll discuss your evidence in court.'

Duncan, 'surprised': 'You don't know the Polynesian bloke then?'

Quickening: '*What* fucking Polynesian bloke?'

'The one who helped you do the constable. The one whose prints we found on the truncheon taken from Ryan and used to shatter his arm.'

Barry, exasperated: 'How *could* I know the cunt? I wasn't fucking *there*.'

Troy, 'helpful': 'This jog your memory at all, Barry?' Hands him a photograph.

A telescreen still, black and white, focus far from sharp, date and time blacked out with felt pen. The wide face centring the shot could well belong to Steve; it's difficult to tell with the beard and sunglasses, the dreads around his face, the grainy picture quality, the poor light on the subject.

Barry, desperately trying to place the scene of the photo, shrugging disinterest well: 'Na, I think I'd remember having anything to do with someone like him. Besides, I was never one to hang with the sooties.'

Duncan retrieves the photo smartly, before Barry can place it.

Troy, smiling: 'Don't like sooties, Barry?'

'Well . . . ' Shrugs a concession: 'S'pose their kids are quite cute when they're little.'

Duncan, abruptly: 'OK, so you say you don't know him?'

'Who?'

'The chap in the photo.'

'Never met him in my life.'

'And you claim not to have played a part in the Greenlane bashing?'

'Correct.'

'You were nowhere near Greenlane Friday before last then?'

'No.'

'Can anyone back that up?'

'My missus can.'

'And you've *never* seen your friends with the Torana in the company of this Polynesian bloke?'

'Nope.'

'Were there *any* Polynesians in the car when they picked you up on Tuesday?'

'Na.'

'Was the car still muddy from Takahera?'

' . . . Taka-*what*?'

* * *

He'd seen the headlights returning, heard the note of the engine. He'd stood with a grunt, perhaps a clenched yelp. Cleared the bushes at a rush.

He hadn't even waved; knew she'd see him; knew she'd stop, throw open the door.

They'd pulled away without a word.

And she looking at him with quick glances only, noticed in his periphery. He could feel how much this had cost her: it was in the set of her shoulders, her movements through the gears.

The silence had held for five short minutes.

Tania, at last, accusatory: 'What the hell've you been *doing*?'

'. . . How do you mean?'

'Well . . . since I last saw you you've . . . you've developed a thousand-year stare.'

'. . . Don't worry, I can feel it fading . . . finally.' A sharp sniff at something. 'Don't be surprised if some day I tell you all about it.'

She'd frowned worry at him, but turned back to the road, no words to fit.

A little later: 'Where're we going, by the way?'

'Would I be asking too much to come back to your place?'

A quick grin: '*Course* ya wouldn't, ya dickhead. You know you're welcome there. Stay as long as ya want.'

'A friend's gonna meet me there in the morning. He'll have a bag of mine I might leave with you for a while . . . if that's OK?'

A pause: 'What's in it?'

One last test: '. . . Is that important?'

A few seconds later: 'No, it isn't. Not at all.'

'Good. It's got money in it.'

She'd just shrugged, but not until her eyes aborted on a double-take.

'Money I don't need to be found with.' A weak laugh. 'Don't leave town, will ya?'

She'd barely bothered scoffing at that, driving on in silence.

Later, trying to sound airy: 'What about your mate? Will he be staying a while too?'

'Me and him've got business down south. We'll be leaving as soon as he arrives.'

She'd hid the wince well.

But he hadn't hesitated; his faltering had already been done.

'Let's get something straight: at the moment there's only one thing in my head worth looking at and it's got your name all over it. As long as you're stupid enough to have any interest in me, I couldn't fob you off if a nutcase held a shooter in my mouth and ordered me to.'

She'd turned to smile at him. 'Good. I was starting to think I'd dreamed the other night.'

But he couldn't bear the sight of her; shut his eyes hard. Sighed: 'It was a dream, all right.' He held his face to the wind from the window: 'One of the few worth repeating.'

17

Up to this point, through the hours of interrogation he's under-gone, Barry believes he's worn his poker-face convincingly. The belief that the police could in fact prove little against him had fortified him well. And even now, as he takes a second proffered photograph on instinct alone, a detached part of Barry tells him of his poker-face holding true.

Unfortunately, he's powerless to contain the colour he feels fleeing him like a bleeding.

Duncan, casually: 'I'd be bloody surprised if you aren't acquainted with *this* sooty, though Barry. He is one of your former townsfolk, after all. Unless it's just a *big* coincidence. Looks like someone didn't like *him* very much either, though, doesn't it?'

In sharp technicolor, Wallace seems almost comfortable, propped between pine roots, head lolling on a shoulder, finger hooked through the trigger guard. The wound on his forehead looks little more than a big pimple, carelessly squeezed, allowed to bleed. His expression seems more baffled than lifeless.

Until one sees the smear on the tree behind him. The wide stain of dried blood and hair.

Of skin and brain tissue.

346

It's been several years since Barry experienced true, physical dread. The bravado he began effecting at teenagehood eventually grew to consume him.

Now, though, his heart begins to pump ice-water, freezing him so badly his penis looses a spurt of urine before he finds the will to close it.

Barry, praying his voice is less cracked than it sounds: 'Looks like the bloke wasn't too enchanted with existence. What do you guys attribute that to? Lack of a father figure?'

He flips the photo to the table, but the cops make no move to take it from his view. In the corner of his eye, it yells at him like fluoro.

Duncan, smiling easily: 'Well, it does *seem* that way, doesn't it? But why do you think he went so deep into Takahera to do it?'

Mystified: 'Taka-what?'

Troy: 'Doesn't it seem strange that a guy with *two* families would wanna top himself?'

'I don't . . . What do ya mean two families?'

Duncan: 'How do you think they're going to feel when they discover what's happened?'

'Who the fuck are you talking about . . . and why are you asking *me*?'

Duncan: 'I doubt they'll be too happy about it. How would you feel if *your* car was used like that?'

Blind in a cell of snakes, Barry searches desperately for some anger; gives it slack. 'Can you guys give the loaded questions a fucking rest and tell me why you're showing me this black fuck-up?'

The policemen exchange a knowing glance.

Duncan: 'Well, he's not as big a fuck-up as that picture suggests. Though we *did* at first draw a similar conclusion. But with the car nearby our judgement was perhaps a little clouded.'

Barry, vexed: 'All right, I'll play your game. *What* car?'

Troy: 'This car.'

This time Barry's ready for it. Gaping at the picture: '*Fucking hell*! Have you guys been raiding the FBI website for jack-off material again?'

Troy: 'When the deer hunter phoned us with his story we were pretty dubious at first. I mean how many people've got the balls to whack even *one* Black Power member?'

Barry, 'incredulous': 'These cunts are Black Power? Are you saying this happened *here*? In *New Zealand*?'

Duncan, informative: 'I was one of the first detectives on the crime scene. On the face of it, it all seemed pretty cut and dried: gang business gone wrong, one of them turns on the others, decides afterwards his own life's as good as over. From a detective's viewpoint, it hardly seemed worth the drive up there.'

Barry, meeting Duncan's eye suddenly, willing dark revelation to poison his glare. 'Hang on a second. What the fuck's going on here? You guys think *I* had something to do with this? Don't ya's?' Louder: 'What the fuck's going *on* here? Why are you *asking* me this shit?'

Duncan: 'Because, Barry, after the evidence had been collected, forensics discovered a few things that established the fact that there was actually a *lot* more to the crime than first impressions suggested.'

Weighty silence is allowed to protract; Barry's heart hammers in his ears like a bass line. His hand moves an inch toward mopping the bead of sweat he feels descending his temple; he reigns in the impulse, instead turning the offending profile from the policemen a little.

Barry, at last, 'baffled': 'Feel free to fill in the blanks sometime before Easter.'

Troy, smirking a hard line: 'What's your rush, Barry? A little warm in here for you of a sudden? Why don't you take a sip of water: your mouth's making that dry, sticking sound mouths tend to make when they're terrified and lying.'

Duncan, suddenly: 'You'll agree that there wasn't an awful lot of room on the rifle to dust for fingerprints, won't you, Barry?'

Fresh hope spurts in him.

Frowning: 'That thing is his hand? Too small to be a rifle, isn't it?'

'Nevertheless, Forensics obtained some good sets from it, prints consistent with our first impressions of the crime scene: Wallace's mark was all over it.'

Barry, shaking his head: 'This is getting *way* too bizarre for me, sorry, Duncan. I'm not saying another word till you reach the part where I'm supposedly involved.'

Duncan, continuing: 'Wallace, however, had left a few bullets in the magazine. Prints from these were also lifted. And guess what, Barry?'

Silence.

Troy, helpful: 'Can't guess?'

Barry shows his palms.

Duncan: 'This second set of prints belonged to somebody *completely* different.'

High on relief, Barry sends demented panic into the whites of his eyes, leaping to his feet, manacled hands pounding the table. Throwing his glare from one cop to the other. 'You motherfuckers! You're gonna stitch me *up* for this, aren't ya's! You cunts have doctored it so it looks like *I* touched your bullets! You fucking . . . !'

Duncan, grimacing: 'Calm down, Barry. We've done no such thing. We haven't set up anything. The prints belong to your Polynesian buddy.'

Barry, sitting down warily, 'perplexed': 'What the . . . ? This mystery spade of yours did it?' Dumbfounded. 'Why are you telling me this?'

Duncan: 'Because, Barry, we know that *you* know exactly who our Mr X is. We've got an eye-witness tying you, him, and one other to the McDick's bashing. A day or so later, your Mr X — perhaps with Wallace's aid — found a need to kill two patched Black Power members and one associate, all hailing from your home town of sunny Roto-Vegas. Mr X, with Wallace, then drove the gang car deep into Takahera Forest, dumped it, *executed* his accessory, and fled the scene unnoticed. What *we* find hard to believe, Barry, is that Mr X — with or without help from Wallace — commited these quite remarkable feats with *no* other accomplices.'

Barry, 'delighted': '*Aha*! At last! Why didn't ya say that in the first fucking place? You think I helped your Mr X make the world a better place *four times over*! Aside from your "eye-witness" account "linking" me and Mr X, from what else do you draw this conclusion?'

Troy, smug: 'Well, forensics *have* made one or two other breakthroughs.'

Barry: 'Namely?'

Duncan: 'Let's just say those DNA samples we took from you earlier could prove . . . interesting.'

Scoffing: 'If they link me to any of this they'll be more than interesting, mate: they'll be fucking sorcerous, 'cause I don't know a thing about it. You know what I reckon? I reckon you clowns've been spending too much time in the evidence room.'

Duncan: 'What you need to think about, Barry, is what happens to you when Mr X gets nicked. With those prints, you see, we've got him on multiple murder, no questions asked. At that stage we'll want to know the full story, and — with the Rabble so eager to learn the murderer's identity — we'll offer him name suppression in exchange for more names. Your life for your story, kind of thing. I doubt Mr X'll find it a difficult choice. And if *your* name happens to crop up somewhere in his tale, Barry, why that'll leave you with a rather juicy addition to your charge sheet, won't it, old son?'

Barry: 'I thought they were Black Power? Anyway, if you're so confident of catching this Mr X, and of the forensic "evidence" you've got, why are you wasting time playing your little games with me?'

Troy: 'Let's just call it hedging our bets.'

Duncan: 'The incident was released to the media yesterday, and we're coming under big pressure to solve it quickly. For this reason we're willing to solve all of *your* problems for *you*, Barry.'

'. . . Meaning?'

'Meaning we're prepared to wipe all current charges pending against you, and give you immunity from prosecution, in return for your help with the murder investigation.'

'What kind of help?'

'Just names, Barry.'

Barry, mordant: 'Oh, I get it. In your hoggy little minds the game hasn't changed at all, has it? You just think the stakes have been upped. Through nothing more than my "link" with "Mr X", you're hoping me and my "friends", who escaped your clutches at the Skins' place, hold the key to solving these murders. Is that about right?'

Duncan, standing, shrugging into his jacket: 'We're going to leave you to examine your position for a wee while, Barry. Just think: four little words from your mouth — perhaps only two — and you walk out the door of this station free to do *whatever — you — like*. The only other hope you've got is to wait for Mr X to fall into our hands, pray he's willing to die for you, and hope the charges we've all ready got on you don't see you go down for too long.'

Troy, assembling his particulars: 'Pretty slim hope really, eh, Barry? Face it, mate: talk to us or kiss your arse goodbye.'

Barry, sneering: 'If I actually *had* helped Mr X, then maybe I'd have to give your generous offer some serious thought. Though having briefly glimpsed the "capability" of the Smoke's police force, I'd be surprised if you tossers even *catch* the black cunt.'

Duncan, airily: 'Really, Barry? I guess you're unaware of how much of a loose cannon your dusky mate actually *is*, then. You see, while you sit here suffering for your friends, at least one of them is out there right now, free as a bird, shitting on your sacrifice, nutting out and throwing wee tantrums all over town.' He conjures another photo from an inside pocket. 'Yesterday your Mr X made a big mistake, Barry. Rampaging down the Greenlane shop-front? Security cameras everywhere? That wasn't too smart either, but given the time of night he probably would've got away with it. Only he forgot to take his weapon home with him. Got a little carried away, he did, finished with a flourish, smashed his last window from thirty metres away.' Impressed: 'Good throwing arm on him.'

The picture Duncan waggles for Barry is of a cricket bat, sealed in an evidence bag.

He continues. Chummy: 'Finger-prints, Barry. Absolutely *chocker* with 'em. A perfect match to the Takahera bullets and to the McDicks bashing.' A weary sigh: 'The bloke you're sheltering's leaving a trail a mile wide, Barry. We'll have our hands on him inside a day or two. You've got till then. Think on it, mate.'

As the door closes Barry manages to count slowly to ten . . .
. . . before sweet glee shoots from his nostrils.

Uncle Rangi, my man, I'd have your fucking babies! This, McPike, surely confirms you as The Chosen One. Were you only before me so I could kiss your scrawny arse!

Troy, tight: 'Do you reckon he knows?'

Duncan: 'Oh, he *knows*, all right. He dealt with most of the traps quite deftly, and he's a pretty smooth customer, but he's not made of stone. At a guess, I'd say that he's definitely the bloke from the Greenlane bashing, and that he at least has information on the Takahera job.'

Troy, salivating: 'How long do we let him stew?'

Duncan, shrugging: 'For now, I can't really see the point in pressing him further.'

Sharply. 'Why the fuck not? You said yourself, all we need is one name from him. Even if he doesn't rat on Mr X himself, it's unlikely his other two buddies are as tough as he is, and I'd have money on all of them being involved, or at least having info.'

Duncan: 'That's true — one name and we'd be away. The way things stand, though, he knows the only thing linking him to Mr X is the word of a cop hammered comatose in near darkness. I think he guessed the identikit picture we showed him was phoney. You've seen the real picture, Troy: it barely looks like him. If I hadn't been in the station when your lot brought him in on cop-bashing, and if I hadn't have happened to hear the description Ryan gave when he woke up, I wouldn't have made the connection. The height, the hair and the charges were all I went on. Any decent lawyer'll laugh that out of court . . . and Barry's got enough balls to take that chance. His alibi for the time in question is flimsy — just the word of his girlfriend — and with more investigation we might be able quash it, but for now, unless forensics *do* find something tying him to Takahera, we're as good as helpless.'

'What else *have* they got?'

'On the fists and clothes of the gangsters and the homie they found a lot of blood, some of it matching Wallace, but most that doesn't match anyone — they're guessing it's Mr X's. The picture they're drawing at the moment is this: the gangsters and the homie had a beef with Mr X and Wallace. They took them somewhere to fuck them up. At some point in the beating Mr X managed to capture the sawn-off from one of his assailants. He drills Rabble One in the face. Rabble Two tries to run, gets it in the back. Mr X or Wallace then strangle the kid with something. Where all this took place is so far a mystery. We're working on the assumption that Mr X — his prints were on the wheel — wouldn't have wanted to drive the corpses too far, so there's a good chance it all went down in Takahera itself. We're running dogs over the place right now, but it's far too big an area to cover meticulously, and with the amount of rain the storm laid down last week it's almost certain the place has been washed clean regardless. Anyway, they drive round till they find a place they can get the car well off the road. Then, for whatever reason, Mr X turns on Wallace. Wallace tries to fight his way clear: X's skin and blood was found under Wallace's nails. In time X subdues Wallace, sits him down, and tops him. Mr X then cleans his prints from the shooter, rubs Wallace's fingers all over it, and places it in his hand. But he forgets about his own mark on the bullets. He then pisses off, either in a car Wallace drove out there, or by phoning for a pick-up.'

Troy: 'Which is where my boys come into it.'

'Based on Barry's reaction, quite possibly. With what we know of gang culture, it's pretty safe to assume no white faces were present while the Rabble went about its business, but who knows *who* X might've called on *after* doing the deed . . . If only Barry'd give us a name. The descriptions your Skins gave us of the other two were too bloody sketchy to be of much use.'

'That's not surprising. They were practically incognito. On top of that, those cabbage-brain Skins couldn't remember their middle names, and trying to get any two of the argumentative fucks to agree on something is an act of futility. They fingered the bloke who set up the deal, though. There's no doubt about this "Bum" character.'

'If you choose to believe the Skins, there isn't. But we'll need evidence a *lot* more concrete than that before Bum can even be *brought in*, let alone charged in relation to any of this. If nothing else turns up we'll keep talking with Bum, but unless he makes a huge foot-in-mouth he'll be no use at all. If he knows his rights, he'll just tell us to piss right off . . . and by what the lads reckon, Bum knows his rights well.'

Troy: 'So, as far as the search for the two who slipped us at the Skins raid go, all we've got to go on is that they're possible acquaintances of Barry's?'

'That's right. From the identikit pictures Ryan made, Barry's reaction just now, and the stills from the shopping centre rampage, we can unofficially finger Barry as an accessory of X's at the Greenlane bashing. But pictures of the third bloke from the alley don't look anything like either of the descriptions the Skins gave us.' A terse shrug. 'Anyway, as soon as I linked Barry to Mr X yesterday morning, and spoke with you about it, I phoned the homicide team down canvassing Vegas, gave them Barry's details.'

'And?'

'Well, I spoke with Dick again just a couple of hours ago, and he reckons they're getting nowhere fast down there. Everyone involved in the case is either a druggie, a delinquent, or a gangster, castes not renowned for their collaboration with the Force. The Rabble of course refuse to say a word about anything. Every civilian acquaintance of Hemi and Johnson asked who might want them dead, laughs out loud and tells the boys to pick names from the phonebook. Mates of the prospect and homie can't even be browbeaten into making a peep: they know better than to interfere with Rabble business. Wallace's family hadn't seen him in a while, but that's apparently nothing new: judging by the state of them, Dick doubts they've seen him since he turned five. The team managed to get a list together of Barry's old chums, but they're all alibied, and not a one of them is talking beyond "Fuck off, Flatfoot".'

Troy: 'So Barry and the pair who fled the bust are proving a dead end. What about the vandalism? What are the chances of tracing Mr X through that?'

Duncan, scoffing: 'Forget about it. Half three in the morning? A few neighbours heard the smashes, but no one even bothered opening the curtains. Security footage suggests he fled toward Cornwall Park. Uniforms gave the area a fly-by when they showed up an hour later, but he could've been anywhere by then. We can't mourn that, though. I mean, being able to get *pictures* of Mr X through something so petty was a *huge* slice of luck.'

Troy, sighing: 'Yeah, you're not wrong there.' But his mollifi-cation lasts only seconds. Growling, summarising: 'Just the one solid lead on the murders, then, we're certain that arrogant little druggie fuck has crucial clues in his head . . . and we're *help*less. If ever a better example was needed of how the sandal and tofu brigade have fucked up our justice system . . . !'

Duncan, gently: 'It's not your concern any more, Troy.'

'But . . . '

'But nothing. We had our crack at him. I know how badly you need a high-profile bust at the moment — and I could sure've used the other half of the credit — but it's out of our hands now. The only reason you were kept involved was because I made the link between Mr X and Barry and hoped your prior experience of him might come in handy. But we're getting nowhere fast and the chief only gave me till eight o'clock tonight on this. I'll phone him in a minute and pass the torch on. As of now, Troy, Mr Barry

Reginald Trotter is your prisoner no longer. Homicide'll start drilling him before the night's out. This'll go on for as long as we can hold him, while we hope for a development to give us some authentic leverage on the kid.'

Troy turns away abruptly, kicking the wall. '*Fuck* it all! This was exactly what I needed! Fate *gave* this to me! *Fuck* that little cunt! Ten minutes alone with him and my life's sorted for ever!' He faces Duncan, appeal gushing from him. 'Just give me *one* last shot at him, Duncan. *Please*, mate. I'll share anything I get with you, that's a promise! Just *ten* minutes, that's all I ask!'

Duncan, rueful and hushed: 'Would that I could, Troy. But your "ten-minute chats" are a little too infamous, I'm afraid. You know as well as I do: his old man's a big wheel in land development and Barry's getting his arse wiped by the best lawyer money can buy. You go damaging the goods on *this* occasion and you and I are in serious strife.'

Troy, through desperate teeth, low: 'No marks, Duncan. That's a promise. C'*mon*, this'll make *both* of us!'

Eventually: '. . . Well, I guess *someone* has to escort him to the cells.'

Barry: 'Well, here comes Jenny, but what's she gone and done with Burton? What gives, Troyo? Did ya leave him incapable of walking this time?'

Troy shuts the door behind him. He removes his jacket, rolling back shirt-cuffs. Unstraps his watch, slow and brooding.

'I must insist the pants stay on, Troy. You know I stipulated a longer courtship than this.'

Fists braced on the table, Troy at last meets Barry's eye. Rumbling: 'Now, you listen to me, you little of piece of shit. In about three minutes from now you're gonna be *begging* me to let you talk . . . and if it's your lucky day I might just oblige.'

Barry, frowning, musing: 'Hang on a sec. It'll come to me. *Heat*, right? Was it *Heat*? It was either *Heat* or *Serpico*. He can't'a said it in *Scarface*, 'cause he played the robber in that, didn't he?'

Troy, an ominous mutter: 'You know what I'm going do if you don't give me a name, Barry?'

'Strap on a riot helmet and turn rolly-pollies in the smoko room?'

Leaning forward, grinning: 'Not quite. I'm gonna leak it to the Rabble that you were involved in the murders. I'll tell them where you're doing your time and everything. I'll give them your fucking *cell* number. You won't last *two* minutes . . . pal.'

Barry, scoffing: 'You're a regular paragon, aren't ya, Troyo? Well, ya know what? If that's the game you wanna play, I've got a couple of shots to fire myself. Ya see, my lawyer filled me in on the reputation you've got around town. And what she found even more interesting than I did was the way you were so frantic to prosecute *me* for the sixty pounds of dope, when it can so easily be stuck to the Skins, an organisation you've supposedly been invested the job of taking down. I gave her a detailed account of our "conversations" on the matter, and when I next see her I'll also tell her about the threat you just made — make affidavits detailing the lot. I'll then tell her to sit on what she knows till I leave the Joint in a body-bag. At that point she's to forward the information to every journalist and politician in the country. There may not be any proof as such, but when the story "Troy Wilkinson: Rotten Cop?" hits nationwide headlines, given that it wouldn't be the first time you've been mentioned in such a light, I'm guessing your career could be in for a bit of a nose-dive. What do *you* reckon, Troyo?'

Troy's teeth snap closed. He starts around the table. A low rumble: 'Insist on doing *every*thing the hard way, don't ya, Barry?' He takes Barry's ear in one hand, twisting viciously. Purring: 'How does *that* feel, Barry? Still cocky? I might just rip the fucker right *off.*'

Barry, thickly, face set: 'I guess it's lucky I've got two of them, then.'

With his other hand, Troy snatches a handful of Barry's long hair, wrenching it in the opposite direction. 'You think you're *sooooo* fucking tough, don't you?' The pressure mounts, the cords of Troy's forearms bunching. 'You and I've got *alllllll* day and night in here, pal. You just sing out when you've had enough, OK?'

Eyes wide, teeth grinding, Barry pants: 'You couldn't break a virgin's hymen, cunt. I've got *fuck* all to say to you!'

Troy releases his hold suddenly, hauling Barry up by the underarms. Hammers his ribs with an upper-cut, does it again, all the torque of his shoulders in the blows.

Throws him to the floor. Rolls him to his back with one foot. Crouching, pinning a knee across Barry's chest and cuffed hands, holding him still.

Draws careful aim, high back-lift . . .

. . . drives the heel of his palm against Barry's sprained knee.

Barry convulses like a shock-shop patient . . .

. . . mewling like a lamb in the slaughterhouse . . .

. . . one foot trying pathetically to push him free of the big cop.

Troy, neighbourly: 'Ya ready to continue, Barry . . . or perhaps you've thought of something I might like to hear?'

At last Barry nods, face red and wrung; Troy suppresses a long sigh. When he speaks, though, Barry's whisper is too thin.

Troy, leaning to him: 'Again, please, Barry. I didn't quite catch that.'

Barry, strengthless: 'Hope ya brought thumbscrews along, bitch, 'cause you hit like a fucking fairy.'

18

— G'day, mate. So you're the new bloke, right?

— Ah, yeah. Name's Travis.

— No worries. I'm Danny. Close the door behind ya and take a seat; you'll be working aboard C here.

— Cheers, Danny.

— Tell ya what, Travis, you look pretty bloody familiar, mate. You a Steak and Kidney local, or what?

— Certainly am. Cabramatta born and bred.

— Dead set? Me too! Cabramatta High?

— Yep.

— That'd make you Travis Georgalis then, eh? Steven's younger brother?

— Spot on, cobber. Do you know Steven?

— Not overly well, but I was in his year and played a bit of footy with him at Wests. How long ya been out of the neighbourhood then, mate?

— Oh, a couple of years now, I guess. Head back in for the footy and the family bit quite often, though.

— Yeah, me too. Don't miss the joint at all, but. Things ain't getting any rosier in there.

— You're not bloody wrong. About a hundred *more* families in the shit as of last week.

— Oh, *yeah*: the West Rail restructure. My brother-in-law looks set to get chopped through that. Poor prick. He'd just found his feet again after the Telstra lay-off. He'll probably have to go back to selling knick-knacks out of his boot, just to keep the kids in school . . . even though the coppers busted him through security footage a coupla years ago.

— Yeah? Well, I know lads in there doing worse than that for bread and butter right now. What choice've they got with all the factories being shipped off to Slopeville, and the suits in Canberra selling out us fair dinkum trying to stop the flow?

— Privatisation, mate: the worst thing to happen to Cabramatta.

— Except for the Wests–Balmain merger, that is.

— *Haha*. Too bloody right.

— Anyway, you'll find yourself with a fair crack of the whip now, Trav. The Cabra lad made good!

— *Ha*. Yeah, well, I'm planning on making the most of it, I assure you of that. Tell ya what, I've been looking forward to learning *this* side of things, though.

— I bet ya bloody have! All right, I'll talk ya through your duties as we work. See this screen here?

— 4E?

— Yeah. It's currently showing the arrivals off Flight QA07, Auckland to Sydney, entering the baggage carousel area. Full consignment deplaning from a 747: about 400 punters.

— Fuck me drunk, *more* of the bastards. You can't move in Sydney for Kiwis these days. Everywhere you listen, 'fush and bloody chups'. What's the attraction here?

. . . — I reckon they're just looking for something they used to have; something we're losing more of by the day.

— Yeah, I s'pose. And I'd sooner live next to ten Kiwis than two Coons. This is where most of our surveillance happens, then, is it? The baggage carousel?

— No, only part of it. You can learn a fair bit watching

someone here, but passport control's the best place for it. Do you remember how to use the cameras from training school?

— Certainly do.

— Good on ya. You'll wanna skill yourself *right* up on the system here: it's state of the art and with CCTV spreading as fast as it is, a good operator can write his own pay cheque. No more food-stamp dinners for you, my son. OK, fire ya board up.

— Done.

— Good man. Now, New Zealand's not a high-risk country, so without special orders our quota is five people in a hundred. From a flight like this, then, it'll be your job to select about twenty-five passengers. Around the carousel, because they've got something to focus on, it's much easier for a felon to disguise their body language, so what we're mostly looking for here are those arrivals who avoid the roving dog-handlers. You'll see we've got two beagle teams on the floor at the moment, and if someone's got something illicit in their luggage or on their person they'll steer clear of wee Snoopy as if he's Cujo on a crash diet. Look for that. Once you've a little experience it'll stick out like 'roo balls.

— OK. So where are *most* of our selections made, then? In the queue before passport control?

— That's right. That way we get a real good look at them while they've got nothing to do. We then pass descriptions and queue positions down to the shift co-ordinator and he takes it from there, interacting with us when necessary.

— This is the zoom key here, right?

— That's the one. *Strewth*, you've found a likely piece of crumpet there, digger! *Haha*. You're a quick learner. She'd inspire soggy-biscuit in an old-folks' home! Go in on that cleavage a little, will ya . . . just for the practice. That's the beauty of these cameras: on full zoom ya can sit here and watch a sheila blowing fanny-farts through work overalls.

— Actually, I was more interested in her behaviour. I noticed her leaving the dunnies just as I sat down, and now she's heading back in again.

— Well, that's that, then. A double dunny user goes on the list automatically. She's sweating like a pig besides.

— Excuse me, ma'am. Could I see ya passport, please?

— Sure. Here you go. Why, though? The bloke back there just stamped it.

— Just routine, ma'am. No need for alarm. You've nothing to declare then?

— That's right. Nothing at all. Green aisle all the way.

— Good for you. I'll just need ya to accompany me for a short while. If ya'd like to head through that door?

— . . . Why?

— Just a routine search, ma'am. Nothing at all to worry about.

— . . . Oh. . . *Must* I?

— Fraid so. Pack ya own bags, did ya . . . Tania?

— Bugger *me*! You must have missed the signs!

— . . . Signs?

— At Auckland airport? Telling you it's illegal to take more than ten grand cash from the country? . . . *Tania*?

— . . . Yeah, I guess I missed them.

— *Obviously*! It'll have to be counted, of course — as soon as the federal police arrive — but, at a guess, I'd say there's a *heap* more than ten gs here! Quite remarkable, really. It isn't every day you meet a girl carrying readies like *this* in her luggage! You seem to've done out*stand*ingly well for yourself in your . . . twenty-three years. Over-achiever, are you: the ambitious type?

Or just plain greedy?

19

The loons are away eating breakfast when the hack brings Vicki to the dayroom. Neither of them sees me at first. Sprawled on the couch's rubber upholstery (*resistant, ma'am, to Mars Bars, vomit* and *arterial spurting; a steal at twice the price*). Surrounded by books. Though not my books. I don't read any more; the prose won't stop grinning. These days walls make a far better read.

Walls and doors.

No windows, though. They can keep their fucking windows.

The hack smells me and points. Vicki sees me and starts across, uncertainty tangible.

Me, rehearsing my Parole Board grin: 'It's OK, Vick; this ain't a *real* prison . . . and I still don't know how to bite.'

A smile tickles her lips; her steps firm up: firm with the resolution of one who has done this before.

More than once.

'Almost didn't recognise ya there, girl. By Christ, if *you* don't look a million big ones!'

It's true too. What's happened to the gangly girl I read Roald Dahl with? The Form One Dux with her mouth too busted for acceptance speeches? The Rabble moll in jeans so tight they winked?

Frowning shy pleasure: 'Oh, these are just my work clothes.'

'Yeah? Where are ya working? Diva, Boutique and Beauty?'

A tight giggle; a warm blush: 'Shut up, man. I'm just doing secretarial stuff for a mortgage broker.'

Hearty: 'Oh, that's really awesome, eh.' *Were you wanting a large noose or a tighter one, Miss Smith?*

And I'm set to blow more air at her when the sentence's real words soak through.

'I'm just doing secretarial stuff . . .'

'. . . just doing secretarial stuff . . .'

. . . JUST . . .

. . . For fuck's sake, Vicki, when I last saw you, you were just about to screw a whole pride of urban poison!

Again, meaning it, surprised I still can: 'Seriously, Vicki, that's the best news I've had in yonks. When did all this happen?'

She takes a chair and sits across from me. 'I moved out to an auntie's place 'bout a year ago.' She can't meet my gaze. 'Done a few courses up at Tech to help get started. Been at the job for six weeks now.' Mystified. 'They all think I'm wonderful.' The hue of her skin completes the sentence: *If only they knew.*

Me, reflexive: 'That's because you *are* wonderful.' Tentative, fishing: 'Did Hemi give you any problems?'

She looks at me *now*, eyes wide, spellbound. 'Didn't you hear? Hemi's *dead*, man! Him and some others got hit on a drug deal.'

'No *shit*?' (*With this finger I free thee.*) 'Fucking hell! That's the *second* best news I've had in yonks!'

Then her gaze finds the floor again. A dull mutter: 'Yeah, I bet it is.'

I test her will with a long silence. Find it lacking.

Swallowing boredom: 'Look, Vick . . . I hope you don't think you owe me anything.'

A scoff to strip paint: '*Owe* you?' With a single glare she takes in the dayroom: its picture books, its meshed windows, rubber lounge suite. 'Jesus *Christ*, Gator . . .' *I owe you your sanity.*

But I gloss the debt with a headshake. 'If anything, it's me who owes you. Let's just put it behind us, eh? Besides, like I keep telling all the shrinks round this place, I'm as sane as any prisoner in the country. *Saner*, in fact . . . I've found a way to do *easy* time.'

This surprises her. '*Honestly*? What about . . . what about what your mum told me?'

Feigning ignorance. Making her spell it.

'*You* know?' Clearing her throat: '. . . The breakdown? The suicide attempt?' A dawning beam: 'Was that all bullshit?'

Me, winking: 'You know me, Vicki: I'm insulted you even have to ask.'

Sitting back in her chair, rocked: 'Jesus! Rumour round Vegas has you in straight-jackets, dribbling and crapping yourself!' Her release is so sweet I can taste it from here. 'Way to go, Gator!'

Grinning to herself, she says nothing for a while, wallowing in the sight of clear conscience. Eventually: 'What did you get done for, anyway? Your mum was pretty vague.'

'Trust.'

'. . . *Trust*? How do you mean?

Trust, lust and a C-cup bust.

. . . The Juggernaut's snares are glossy and legion.

'My crime was trusting the wrong person, Vick.' *The wrong gender. The wrong* species.

'Who?'

Slut! Slapper! Harlot! Jezebel . . . !

'No one special. Thanks a heap for visiting, anyway. How's everyone out in the real world?'

'Ammm . . . ' Grimacing: 'Lefty's not doing too well. Did you hear what happened to him? Some chick — Rebecca Thomson, the papers called her — she ammm . . . ahhhh . . . she . . . *damaged* him with some wire-cutters.'

I merit an Oscar for throttling peals of laughter. Instead, sombre: 'I heard about it, all right. He lost the plot when he got out of hospital; ended up in *here* for a while.' *In the cell down from mine . . . the padded one.* 'He told me all about it himself.' *Along with the rest of the joint, every night, in a wail like Kiri Te Kanawa on steroids.*

Me, changing the subject before my mask can crack: 'What about Mick? I haven't heard from him in a while. Any news on that front?'

Vicki, delighted: 'Oh, *yeah*. I ran into him at a cafe the other day. He's working as a clerk for Sullivan & Sullivan, doing accountancy papers at night school. He reckons he'll be fully qualified and creaming it within a year or two. Yeah, he's doing *really* well!'

'. . . Pardon?'

I hear not a single shot as the bitch re-fires her salvo. It's suddenly colder in here than I can ever remember.

Onya, Mickey. So glad I spat their deal back at them.

Vicki's still gushing. 'He seems *really* well suited to it, eh?'

Hearty: 'Oh, he's well suited to it, all right.' *A kike with balls like a bitch.*

Slag! Cunt! Judas!

Vicki: 'As for your mate Barry: I heard he's doing two to four in Paremoremo.'

Speaking without hearing: 'And having the time of his life, no doubt.'

A hesitant giggle: 'Yeah, maybe.' Then, like an eclipse, a sudden dread comes over her. It's cold enough to scare me through the frost she's already lain.

I know what's coming. Can think of no words to stall it.

Vicki, bleeding: 'Steve's still missing. No one's got a clue where he is.'

That's not entirely true, my girl.

Hiding in my hands. 'Yeah, I heard he hadn't been seen yet.' Wooden, muffled: 'Don't worry, I'm sure he'll turn up soon.'

Cracked: 'Oh, god, I *hope* so. He's one of the best guys I've ever known!'

Two whole days without thinking of Steve . . . she shows up and flings him from a catapult at me.

'The amount of times, back in the . . . the bad days . . . the amount of times he went *right* out of his way for me.'

Really? Steve? Out of his way?

Vicki, a haggard sigh: 'He's the best guy in the world. He doesn't de*serve* this.'

Oh, will someone shut this little whore the FUCK UP!

Feel a hand on my knee.

Anxious: 'Gator? Are you OK?'

Oh, yeah, baby. Tickety boo.

Gently: 'You're not crying, are you? They told me you did that . . . sometimes.'

Crying? Crying? Me? G. McPike? Jailed Treasonist and butcher of blood-brothers?

She tugs my hands from my face. 'Oh, shit, you *are* crying!'

But the look of sympathy she paws me with dries my eyes like wind.

Bitch! Slag!

I'm going to tell her to fuck off. To get up and take her gang-moll arse, the Warehouse power-suit I can see straight through, right the hell away from me . . .

When one of the flawed cogs crosses the dayroom. I knew his name once. Tongan. Scraggly beard. Indian ink oozing down his forearms. Down his *weedy* forearms. Too weedy to trouble me, anyway. These days. I'll sort the cunt *right* out. *Brother, you've got* no *idea what you're fucking with!*

Especially if he doesn't stop leering at Vicki like that.

Throwback! Cast-off! Reject!

He's got three more seconds — *drink her in, buddy, top up the wank-bank, could be months before another passes through* — two more seconds before I leap up and yell: *Take your* fucking *eyes off my Vicki!*

But I look to her first. I want her permission; ever the gentleman, me. Or do I want to ask her why she's letting the loon ogle her like this? Is she staring back *at* him? Is that what's going on here?

But Vicki's doing no such thing. In fact, she has her back as squarely to the nutter as it could possibly be. Brow knitted. Shoulders hunched as though his gaze is a layer of leeches.

Unknotting like clairvoyance as he silently leaves the room.

She hands me a weak smile, draws a breath, groping for words to hide behind.

So that I'm looking right at her when the slipped-disc slams a door down the hallway . . . as she flinches on cursed cue — a war-baby near a building site.

Then swallows the start quicker than it happened.

And this stings me like the flinch itself — like the old terror in her that can never die — her instant recovery stings me like these did not.

She doesn't even realise she did it.

I know then that I should take her to me (*no sudden movements*), sit with her close, stroke her hair, teach her a mantra: *It's not my fault: god's just a cunt sometimes.*

A year ago I might have done exactly that . . .

. . . but that was before I learned.

I know better now. *Oh*, yes. No more fooling *this* former cuckold! All hollow horses to be torched at the walls. Nice try, though.

Slut! Whore! Delilah!

. . . angel, dove, Madonna . . .

. . . Vicki.

Just Vicki, man.

She balks for only a second as I take her by the wrists, guide her to my side. Wrap an arm round her shoulder.

Her cheek against my chest.

Me, softly: 'It's not your fault, you know. God's just a cunt sometimes.'

I feel her tears through my shirt, but she makes not a sound: years of practice. My own eyes start to bleed, but I don't realise until I'm wetting her hair. It's not crying for me. I don't cry any more. I shed sap like a tired pine.

Hardly hearing her. 'It's not your fault either, Gator.'

Yeah. Whatever.

Later, in dim background, the loons file across the dayroom en masse, off to appointments at the dispensary (*feeding in earnest; fog and haze in a capsule; out of Eye out of Mind*) but we pay them no heed. Even the catcalls aren't important. No, It won't find us if we stay still, stay close . . . like when we were nine.

How I wish we still were.

She looks up at last, spares me a damp smile. 'I feel like I'm nine again.'

I'll see you canonised, girl, if it's with my dying breath.

Vicki, firming: 'You can do it, you know, Gator. You can get out of here and get your life back on track.' Wiping at her eyes: 'God, *I'm* doing it — a step at a time — and if I can do it, *any*body can! You can still go as far as you like, man. You've got gifts. Don't waste them. Don't waste your talents another day, *please*.'

Well, that's right. I've got more talent in my trigger-finger than the rest of me has in my whole body.

But I believe what she's telling me. I *have* to believe it. *Everyone* used to say this to me once: teachers; relatives; friends; coaches; milkmen. I heard versions of this speech so often I stopped hearing it.

But no one says it to me now. No one has in years.

No one except Vicki.

Kissing her forehead reverently: 'I'll give it a shot, then, Vick. Just for you.'

'OK, Mr McPike. Well, you've certainly given me — and my colleagues — a hectic week: Parole Board hearings, health reviews, etc, etc. I'm in a position now, though, to report to you that the conclusions we've drawn to this point have been . . . ' a shuffle of papers, the crossing of a 't', '. . . favourable.'

Of course they've been. I'm ready for You.

Gator has his arms on his knees, leaning toward the desk: eager obsequity personified.

Ready for Your needs. And Your wants.

Even Your expectations.

'I can't tell you how pleased I am to hear that, Ruth.'

She looks up sharply. 'Dr Saunders, thank you.'

Cringing: 'Of course, Dr Saunders. Excuse my impropriety.' A

369

sheepish chuckle: 'Good news has that effect on me.'

'Well, let's not get carried away at this stage, Mr McPike.' Stern: 'It's been left to me to assess final reckoning.'

Ducking to her pre-eminence.

Shuffling through papers, fixing him a hard stare: 'Right. Let's get on with it then, shall we?'

'By all means, Dr Saunders.'

She consults a list, peering through spectacles, a finger flicking at her stylish, greying fringe. Wrinkling her nose: 'It's not my field, but I've been asked to address it, so let's first deal with the . . . *felonious* side of things.'

Grimacing his shame: 'That's a good idea, Dr Saunders. I'm as eager as you to conclude those matters.' Weary smile: 'And, I'd just like to stress, never again will it be *my* field, either.'

She fixes him an arched eyebrow, holding it . . . until he looks away.

Until he looks *down*.

He'd learned the trick within a minute of meeting her.

A declaration: 'Your crime.' Suffixing it with silence, watching his posture deflate with the seconds. 'It was never resolved, was it? In spite of the best efforts of Our law enforcement services, the . . . *cash* you were tied to was never accounted for, due largely to your intransigence on the matter.'

Shifting in his seat like a lice-host, brow knitted to file steel.

'What say you on the matter, *now*, Mr McPike?'

He takes his time. Torn. Scrubbing a hand across his face. At last, appeal raw in his throat. 'Getting out of here, Doctor, my re-acceptance into Society, means so, *so* much to me.' A slight hardening: '. . . But it means less to me than survival itself.'

Light, dubious, jotting at a pad: 'You've no intention of changing your story, then?'

Through frustration near to anger: 'For god's sake, I *can't*! Like I told the Police, the Judge, the lawyers, the Parole Board, I was holding the money on behalf of an acquaintance. For my services I was to receive a little of it. I'm not sure where it came from . . . I didn't like to ask. Because of his reputation, I felt too scared to turn him down . . . and I *certainly* felt too scared to name him to the Authorities when they took me in.' A rueful sigh: 'That situation hasn't changed, Dr Saunders, and, short of the man's death or ordination, I'm afraid it never shall.'

'*Hmmm*. Well, I'm told the young lady who denounced you seemed to find this story somewhat unlikely.'

Jeza . . .

She waits for Gator to begin his retort before speaking over him, waving a hand grudgingly: 'It's not vital, anyway. The Judge convicted you of the crime you confessed to, and you've served your minimum sentence with adequate behaviour.'

What the fuck did you bring it up for, then? Looking to jump payscales?

Gushingly grateful: 'I'm glad to hear that, Dr Saunders.'

'Hmm.' The ambiguous eyebrow. 'Yes, I imagine you are. Let's now deal with the *real* issues then, shall we? . . . Your mental state . . . ' Another measured wait. Coolly: 'You claim to have faked the breakdown in order to serve your sentence in more . . . *relaxed* confines.'

'That's correct.' *Relaxed: freedom to shower without fear of rape.*

Tutting: 'In *other* words, you believed it proper to manipulate the Authorities in accordance with your own wants. I take it you don't approve of Our system of incarceration then, Mr McPike?'

What kind of knee-jerk liberal do you take me for? Twenty-stone Moses Alofi molests a great-granny in her rest-home bed: he gets five to ten in a themepark. Donald from PR gets pinched with a bag of coke: he gets five to ten in hell itself.

Hastily reassuring: 'Oh, *no*, Dr Saunders, you wrong me *totally*. I view our justice system as a model of perfection, an example to the uncultured world. . . I simply offended the wrong person early in my stay at Mt Eden and was left in fear of my life.' Regretful: 'Again, Dr Saunders, as much as it pained me, survival preceded ethics.'

'Really?' She spends a minute leafing through her file, reading, jotting. Announcing: 'The thing is, Mr McPike . . . ',

observing him closely, 'in spite of the findings of every psychol-
ogist to examine you in the last six months . . . *I'm* not altogether
certain your breakdown and suicide attempt *were* faked.'

Bitc . . .

Reeling in his seat, hurt: 'What makes you say that?

Examining a paper from under her glasses, head tilted back,
as if it reeks of decay: 'Your first few weeks here were spent
ranting to all who would listen — and plenty who wouldn't —
ranting of some *creature*. Some *mechanis infernalis* you felt was
hunting you.' Quoting distinctly: '"Hunting every fucking one of
us; every man, woman and child of the Noble Pillage".' Eyeing
him flatly: 'How do feel about that now, Mr McPike?'

Gator laughs for her. Straight into her face. 'I feel my origi-
nality wasn't all it could've been. And I feel bloody lucky none of
the doctors who first examined me were young enough to have
grown up on Playstation. If they had I'd've been back in Mt Eden
quicker than you could say "Tomb Raider".'

Ruffled by his cheer: 'Really?' More jotting. 'Well, most of the
specialists who dealt with you in recent months *did* come to
concur with this assertion.' A long pause, a resettling of the
plumage. 'All, that is, except Dr Ralston. Dr Tony Ralston,'
leaning back in her seat, 'who took the time to observe you in
your sleep some weeks ago.' Reading like garnish: 'On the night
of 7 October in fact, from 3.25am to 4.05.'

Cocksuck . . .

Still reading: 'Dr Ralston writes that he distinctly heard you
moaning in your sleep . . . moaning and sweating in fear of this
"Juggernaut" of yours.' Looking up, arching the eyebrow.

Flinching at Gator's loud scoff.

'Yeah, and Dr Ralston was also suspended from practice a
week later for filching laudanum from the dispensary.'

She takes a long time over this and Gator holds her eye for
every second of it.

At last, nodding slightly: 'That's correct. And on the strength
of that dismissal, my colleagues resolved to ignore his findings
on the matter.'

Gator, eyebrows high: 'But not you, huh?'

Composing something on her pad, head down: 'Well . . . it's not within my licence to authenticate the invalidated.' Tight smile: 'I was more interested in your reaction to the *illusion* of my doing so.'

This time she's the first to break their gaze.

Gator, a sad laugh: 'Chicanery, it would see, is alive and well in the mental assessment process. A comforting thought. Care to enlighten me on your reaction to my reaction to your false reaction to Dr Ralston's opiated reaction?'

A light cough: 'Well your behaviour does appear to conform with our requisites.'

Hard smile: 'We would seem to be getting somewhere.'

She begins flicking through her papers, too swiftly. In time, authoritative: 'Right, then. We will consider concluded the issues of your criminality: you've served your time quite quietly and demonstrate significant remorse. I'm also as comfortable as I'll ever be with your degree of mental health: if indeed you *were* ill, you seem acceptably cured.' Clearing her throat loudly, straightening her shoulders: a reach for the high ground. Grave: 'There remains then, only the matter of your ability to assimilate back into Society.'

Again, Gator meets her stare squarely, matches her silence.

'What have *you* to say on the issue? . . . You certainly have intelligence on your side.'

And heaven forbid the dumb be equated with productive units.

A stately nod: 'Thank you, Dr Saunders. Yes, in all modesty, my head does contain a brain or two . . . ' *unlike some I've seen* '. . . and I'm certain I can use this to fast-track myself back to the right path in life.' Swallowing stale bitterness: 'Believe me, Doctor, you see before you a man ready and willing to fill a niche in Society.'

Reading from another sheet: 'By that I take it you refer to the business idea you shared in a group therapy encounter chaired by Dr Halloway.' Reluctantly bright: 'He seemed most impressed by the concept itself — its integrity *and* viability — and more so by your enthusiasm for it. I can tell you now, this has weighed heavily in our assessment of your suitability for release.'

A winded silence.

. . . soul-patrol, mine young minds, spread the dread, fiction conscription . . .

'Mr McPike?'

Gator finally finds voice; blurting: 'I don't wanna do that now.'

Puzzled: 'Pardon?'

Too loud: 'I said I'm not interested in that any more!'

'Oh . . . I *see*.' Behind her mascara, a dangerous frown slowly forms. 'Well . . .' Brandishing her pen like a gavel: 'If this is the *case* . . . you leave me no choice but to return to my colleagues a significantly less upbeat conclusion than the one We'd almost arrived at.'

Colour drains from Gator as he stares at a place the doctor can't see.

And for a while he sits perfectly still, perched on his seat like a bird near flight.

Nothing shifting but a pulse on his neck.

A beat so small it might've gone unheard.

Eyes snapping to focus with no warning; something lifting the corners of his mouth. 'You know what? I'll bloody well *do* it, then!'

She shrinks a little from the sudden cast of his features: the grinning eyes, the twisted lips. 'You will, will you?' Pausing. Grim: '. . . If this is an attempt to *con* me, Mr McPike, it won't go unnoticed, I assure you. You see, for releasees like yourself — the employably challenged with sound business notions — grants are available. Indeed, there's been talk of arranging one of these for you.' Levelling a finger: 'But *if* you were to be released and failed to pursue the venture with adequate ardour . . . you'd be forcing me to reassess any decisions made at this point.'

Rich irony wreathes itself around Gator's grin; his whole body seems to ripple with it. 'Trust me, Dr Saunders. My time here had created something of an . . . "ambition-dearth". But you've just lit the wick again. I believe you'll find my "ardour" frightfully adequate.'

Sucking at her teeth, she feigns indecision . . .

. . . by degrees allowing mollification to creep over her.

A proclamation: 'Let us put the onus on *you* then, shall we, Mr McPike?'

But as she bends her head to the desk, writing hand skimming across the pad, Gator's expression clears with awful suddenness . . . and his stare at her crown is as blank as a Gatling cannon's.

Reading as she writes: '"Inmate exhibits sufficient empathy for the requirements of Society."'

Impossible that the verve in his words could leave such a visage: 'Oh, I think I know what Society requires, all right, Ruth.'

'Good.' A companionable smile. 'I'll be seeing you, then.'

Beaming back at her: 'You can count on it.'